QUEEN HENRY

LINDA FAUSNET

Published by Wannabe Pride 2014

Editing by BZ Hercules and Lisa Winders

Cover Design by Evan Lerman

FIRST EDITION.

Library of Congress Control Number: 2014907584

❀ Created with Vellum

For Harvey, Matthew, Tyler, and all the other LGBT brothers and sisters we've lost along the way. Your beautiful rainbow colors were too bright for Earth, but they shine now in Heaven.

HARVEY MILK FOUNDATION

100% of the proceeds net of taxes from the book, Queen Henry, will go to the Harvey Milk Foundation.

·

1

"**B**ig news in the sports world today. According to Page Six in the *New York Post*, a major league baseball player was spotted kissing another man on a recent road trip to New York," the local radio DJ informed me as I drove to batting practice.

"Oh, dude. Don't tell me that. Gross!" I said aloud, grimacing. I took a big swig of my Diet Coke as if to wash the bad taste of that idea out of my mouth.

"The source's photograph of the incident was too blurry to allow a positive ID, but the player was rumored to be a member of the Baltimore Orioles."

My eyes bulged out of their sockets, and I barely managed to swallow the mouthful of Diet Coke without doing a spit-take all over the interior of my red Corvette. The Baltimore Orioles. That was my team. There was no way one of my guys was gay.

Was there?

The idea was too horrifying to contemplate, yet that's all I could think about. Was it really possible that one of my teammates was gay and I never noticed? We showered together, for fuck's sake. I just couldn't picture one of my teammates with another guy. Well, I could picture it. But I tried not to. Ick. I didn't have a problem with gay people. They could do whatever the hell they wanted. I just didn't want to know about it.

As soon as I suited up in my uniform and headed onto the field for practice, I cornered Charles "Tuna" Manero. He was my best friend on the team.

"Tuna! Did you hear about-" I stopped and lowered my voice. "Did you hear there might be a gay guy on our team?"

Tuna's eyes opened wide. "What?" He looked as horrified as I felt. "Where did you hear that?"

"They just said it on the radio! They don't know who it is, but they said it's an Oriole.""Oh. That's kinda weird," Tuna said. He grimaced a bit but shrugged. He glanced over at some of the other players on the field, no doubt wondering who it could possibly be. "I guess it's not that big of a deal." He didn't look entirely convinced.

"Yeah. I mean, yeah. I guess not." Maybe I was being a little overly dramatic. At least that's what I thought until Kyle McCracken, our first baseman, came charging onto the field.

"You guys hear this shit about there being some faggot on our team?" Unlike me, Kyle didn't use his indoor voice when discussing this rather sensitive topic. I winced. Sure, I understood where Kyle was coming from and I was glad I wasn't the only one freaking out, but I felt kinda bad about him calling the guy a faggot. I mean, sure, I used that word all the time, but only when I was joking around with my friends. Shit, I'd never call a real gay guy a fag.

Word spread pretty quickly throughout the team and people were fairly divided. Some guys claimed they didn't really care if we had a gay player while others were all

worked up about it. One thing was for sure, it was on everyone's mind.

As I stood in the on-deck circle during the first inning, all I
could think about was the homo player. Was it possible that
he had checked me out without me knowing it? That idea
made me feel a little queasy. I tried to shrug off the thought.
I needed to focus. I practiced my swing and eyed the pitcher.
I'd gotten six career homers off this guy. If I just concentrated, maybe I could make it seven. I had to stop thinking
about this alleged gay player. Besides, I had more pressing
things to worry about.

For one thing, I couldn't breathe.

I needed my asthma inhaler bad. Like, really bad. Before
the game, I'd tried to reach the inhaler hidden on the shelf
in the clubhouse, but Tuna walked in before I could grab it.
I couldn't use the one in my locker either, because Kyle
came in to ask me about the Oakland A's reliever just as I
pulled it out.

My chest locked up tight. I had an appointment at Johns
Hopkins tomorrow to take part in a clinical drug trial for my
asthma. If all went well, I could just take a pill instead of
relying on that geeky-ass asthma inhaler, but right now, I
was stuck with it. No way was I gonna take it in front of the
guys.

"Right fielder...Henry! Vaughn! Jr.!" the announcer
yelled. I glanced up at the scoreboard at my jumbo-sized
picture. My official MLB photo was quite flattering, showing
off my muscles, my light brown hair, and my blue-green
eyes. My name was met with wild applause and lots of
female screams. I loved it.

"We love you, Henry!"

"Go Henry, go! Go Henry, go!" A group of preteen girls chanted my name. I loved that. I really did. Loved those cute little twelve-year-old girls who probably had posters of me in their bedrooms.

Okay, wait. That sounded pervy. I didn't mean it like *that*. I just meant that they were really sweet. I loved signing autographs for girls that age. They got so excited when they saw me coming over. When I signed for them, I knew I was giving them something to tell all their friends at school. Their little faces lit up like I was some movie star or something. They were so adorable. It totally made my day.

I wanted to hurry up and finish my turn at bat so I could somehow sneak off and grab my inhaler. I swear other people took breathing for granted. My chest ached so bad.

The first pitch was a breaking ball, way outside. I didn't chase it. Second pitch was more like it. I had a good feeling I was gonna nail the next one.

BWHAP!

I prayed the ball would leave the park so I could simply jog the bases and be done with it. Unfortunately, it was just a single. I knew it was awful, but a little part of me hoped the next guy would hit into a double play.

No. I had to do what I had to do. It wasn't my team's fault I was too stubborn to take my medicine in front of them and it wasn't fair to the fans for me to just give up because I couldn't breathe.

I stepped off first base and got a good lead toward second. I was pretty good at stealing bases because I was a master at psyching out pitchers with my antics. The A's pitcher turned around, and I hopped back on first base. As I waved innocently at him, I heard laughter from the crowd. I loved it because I was a total attention whore. No doubt about it. As soon as the pitcher turned back to face the batter, I took a few cartoonishly long strides toward second. The crowd laughed again. The pitcher whirled around and I darted back to first. The first base coach watched me warily. I made him nervous, but I was successful more times than not, so he usually waved me on if he thought I had a good shot. On my next try, I damn near stole second base, but it didn't matter because Tuna hit it out of the park. I jogged the bases and hoped I wouldn't collapse before I got back to home plate.

When we got back to the dugout, Tuna and I enjoyed the requisite fist bumps. I let the crowd die down for a moment, then I popped my head out of the clubhouse and waved to the fans as they went nuts all over again. Sid Welliver, our shortstop, shook his head at me, but I saw his grin nearly hidden under his cap.

I seriously felt like I was gonna pass out. There was barely enough oxygen getting to my lungs to keep me standing. I felt like I was breathing through a straw.

I casually sauntered up to the Gatorade cooler. With my back to my teammates, I pretended to drop the paper cup. I bent over and groped blindly for the inhaler that I'd taped to the back of the Gatorade stand. As I poured a drink with one hand, I grabbed the inhaler with the other and took a deep hit. Ahhhh. I breathed out the medicine and took a few gulps of delicious, nearly flavorful air. I turned back around and was relieved to see that my teammates were far too invested in the game to worry about what I was up to.

Now that I could breathe, I could enjoy my favorite part of the game: the seventh-inning stretch when they played "Take Me Out to the Ballgame." I also loved when they played "Y.M.C.A." When we were at home, I always jumped up on top of our dugout and led the fans in singing along, waving my cap and my hands. They absolutely loved it. Fans didn't usually get much personal attention from the players, which was a shame because it really meant a lot to them. If I had time, I jumped down from the dugout and went all the way over to the bleachers to sing with those guys.

Bleacher fans were the best. They weren't business men and women sitting in corporate seats that they bought just for show and to give away to clients. These were fans who didn't have a lot of money, but they loved the game. They totally flipped out when I headed over there. I was the right fielder, so I even waved to them during the game.

I also loved the upper deck fans for the same reason. I'd visit those folks up there if I could, but security wouldn't let me. Sometimes, I blew kisses at them from down here, though, especially if there was a troop of Girl Scouts or other groups waving their banners. One time, there was a group of breast cancer survivors up there. I'm still pissed that security wouldn't let me go up there to visit with those ladies. Instead, I had somebody go up there and get their posters and hats and stuff for me to sign. Better than nothing, I guess.

Tonight, the mascot, a giant Oriole bird, joined me on top of the dugout and we really got the fans going. It was awesome. It helped that we were winning 10-2, so everybody was in a great mood. I finished the song with the fans, took my usual bow, and then swung back down into the dugout.

None of the guys looked up. It was our usual ritual. I jumped around, played with the fans, and in general acted like an idiot, and my teammates ignored me. They played like they were too cool to care. Fine. It just meant more attention for me.

After the game, there were a bunch of reporters in the clubhouse. I loved talking to the reporters after a win.

"Another great game for the Orioles and for fan favorite, Henry Vaughn, Jr.," said Lucinda Mackleroy, reporter for *Channel 13 News*. That was why I loved reporters. Especially Lucinda. Fine, luscious Lucinda. I didn't know if those things were real or not, but they were a work of somebody's art. Either God's or Dr. Silicone, M.D. I didn't care who was responsible. I was just grateful. I gave her my best, exaggerated Baltimore accent.

"Well, you know hon, we're just out dere giving it the best we got an' tryin' to win dem ball games." In Baltimore, "hon" is a term of endearment. But you had to say it right. It's pronounced *hawn*. Lucinda laughed. "But seriously, we've got a great team this year, and it feels great to be in first place right now," I told her.

"So, Henry, are you aware you're featured in the gossip column once again?" Lucinda asked.

"No, I hadn't noticed," I said. I yawned nonchalantly and stretched my arms out wide, revealing the gossip column taped to the inside of my jacket. Some of my teammates chuckled.

The headline from *Around Town* read *Henry Vaughn, Jr. and Alexis Darlen Dance the Night Away*. That was from our recent road trip for a series against the Yankees. I loved New York. I really, really did. Most of us guys were able to pick up girls everywhere we went on the road, but New York? In New York, we could get celebrities.

Speaking of girls, I was ready to go out. I tried to be polite to the reporters, but I seriously didn't want to be stuck talking to them all night. I needed a shower, a beer, and a lady. Lucinda looked like she was about to ask me another question, so I just blew her a kiss and winked at the camera. She took the hint, and turned around to find somebody else to talk to.

I went over to my locker to grab my stuff. I heard the reporter nab Sid for an interview.

"Sid Welliver! Great game today," said Lucinda.

"Yeah, I'm proud of what we did out there. We got a great bunch of guys this year," Sid said.

"What would you say if one of those great guys was gay?" another reporter asked out of nowhere. It was Michael Perry from *Around Town*. *Around Town* was a so-called "local entertainment and arts" newspaper, but it was mostly just a gossip rag.

Shit. I'd really hoped nobody in the media was going to come right out and ask us about that. It was just a stupid rumor and nobody seemed to have proof of anything. The *Baltimore Sun* and *Channel 13* were reputable enough news outlets not to jump on the gossip bandwagon, but there were no limits when it came to *Around Town*. I usually didn't mind that, though, because I loved being featured in the magazine with my arm around some hot girl.

"*Around Town* has it on good authority that one of the Baltimore Orioles is a homosexual," said Michael. I looked around to see him holding up an article entitled *Possible Gay Baltimore Oriole?*

"Your thoughts on this?" continued Michael.

Don't answer that, Sid. Don't do it. Seriously, there was no good way out of it.

"Uh, at this time, I'd have to say no comment," said Sid. And he walked away. *Good boy.* I looked around at the other guys, who all waved off the reporter.

I wished I could figure out who it was. Could be Sid. Nah, he just got married. Unless that was just a front. Tuna's married, too. Brady Clayton's way too much of a jock. Jackson and Paul are single. But then so am I...

All right. This was stupid. It was just a rumor. It was

probably not even true. It was time to get out of there and get my drink on already. Where the hell was my inhaler? I felt my lungs tightening up again; I needed one more hit before I left. Sure, I had an inhaler hidden in my car, but I'd rather not wait until then to get some relief. I rooted around in my locker. Seriously, where the hell was- aha! I finally hit on the precious, cool metal of my inhaler. It was truly a love-hate relationship with this thing. Life-giving, sweet air packaged in this embarrassing nerd container.

I found it all right, but my hands were sweaty. I yanked it out from the back of my locker and the damn thing went flying across the clubhouse. It made a horrifying clattering sound as it skittered across the floor.

I slowly looked up to see if anyone had noticed.

The inhaler had hit Tuna in the foot. He bent down to investigate. He grinned as he grabbed it and stood up.

"Well, what have we got here?" He held it up to the light and inspected it like it was some ancient artifact to be studied. I ran over and tried to snatch it out of his hand.

"Nothing. Give it back."

Tuna pulled it back just before I could get to it. Damn Tuna and his quick reflexes! Came in handy playing second base, but it sucked right about now.

"Calm down, Henry. It ain't steroids," Tuna said.

"I'd rather you caught me with steroids!"

"The great Henry Vaughn, Jr.'s got asthma? Say it ain't so." Tuna wheezed and pushed up imaginary glasses on his nose. "Henry's got the geek disease. How did I not know that?"

"*Nobody* knows that," I said in a hoarse whisper. Except for my dad, which was bad enough. You'd have thought I had herpes, the way he denied it. I was only eight years old and wheezed like an old man with emphysema. It was my mom who took me to the hospital, and just in time, too. You don't mess around when it came to breathing. My dad's not a bad guy. He's really not. He's just got a thing about what makes a man a man, and I don't think wheezing like a high school chess club member fit into that image. Henry Vaughn, Sr., better known as Hank, was certainly aware that his only son suffered with asthma. I still never used my inhaler around him. He never said so, but I knew it annoyed him to think that I needed to use it.

Tuna waved the inhaler around like a bully playing keep-away. He wasn't really a bully. He was just being a dick. Still holding the inhaler up in the air, he made a motion toward the TV reporter who was packing up her stuff, like he was about to out me as an asthmatic on local television.

"Tuna..."

He chuckled and handed the inhaler back. "Take it easy. I'm just screwin' with ya. Who cares if you have asthma anyway?" I cared and he knew it. Tuna probably wouldn't give a shit if he had asthma, but I found it completely humiliating. Kyle walked in and I hid the inhaler just in time. I didn't know how much longer I could keep hiding it from people. I couldn't believe I'd kept it up this long. I guess it wasn't a big deal, but it wasn't exactly a macho condition. It made me feel so weak and helpless. I couldn't stand it. My only hope was this clinical drug trial thing. I hoped it would work.

"You guys comin'?" Kyle asked.

"Hell, yeah," I said.

"Tuna. Let's go," came an icy, female voice that could make a man's balls crawl all the way up to his esophagus. Look out. It was Mrs. Tuna. Emily Manero kept Tuna on a very tight leash and I felt sorry for the guy. That was Exhibit A in the case of Why Henry Vaughn, Jr. Wouldn't Get

Married Ever, Ever, Ever. Emily got mad if Tuna did anything without her, so understandably, Tuna preferred just to stay home, rather than start a big argument. She'd been out with us a couple of times and it was excruciating. It was horrible enough to have a bitch wife like her call the shots for you, but it was downright emasculating when it was in front of the guys. Tuna cut loose a little when we were on the road, but he still refused to cheat on her, unlike some of the other guys whose wives weren't half as bad. I admired that about him. I really did.

I shot Tuna a look that was a mixture of both *sorry your life sucks* and *that's what you get for stealing my inhaler.*

As I headed out to go drinking with the guys, I couldn't help but think about the other thing the guys didn't know about me. Something a hell of a lot more embarrassing than asthma.

Sid, Kyle, Jackson, Brady, and I went to Max's bar to have a few drinks and to see if we couldn't find some female friends for the night. Well, not Sid. He just got married, so he was no fun anymore. Max's was the perfect bar because it was far enough away from the ballpark that there weren't a lot of rowdy, drunk fans. There were enough of them to stroke your ego, but not so many that they ruined your evening when you were just trying to unwind after the game.

I was drinking my usual: beer and shots of Peach Schnapps. Peach Schnapps was really supposed to be used in mixed drinks like Fuzzy Navels or whatever, but I liked it straight. I much preferred the sugary, delicious tasting Schnapps to the more bitter shots people usually swig. I know a shot of Schnapps is kind of a queer drink; I might as well be drinking friggin' Appletinis. I used to only chug Schnapps at home because I knew the guys would rag on me about it, but I finally figured that if I was gonna go out drinking several nights a week, I might as well drink what I liked. The first time I ordered it, Kyle asked me if that's what I usually drank at the Hippo. Club Hippo is Baltimore's most famous gay bar and club. It was also the butt of never-ending jokes among me and my teammates. We joked constantly about which one of us was going there tonight, who knew the bartenders intimately, etc. "How was the Hippo last night?" Wink, wink, nudge, nudge. The guys ran out of Peach Schnapps fag jokes years ago to the point where it was old news now. Besides, people were used to my, shall we say, eccentricities. They probably figured I just drank Peach Schnapps shots as another way to draw attention to myself. Which might be partly true.

"So, how's the new wife, Sid?" I asked. I loved to hear about married life because it reminded me why I was single. I had no desire to become a cautionary tale like Tuna.

"Fine. Except..." Sid began.

"Except what?"

"Guess where she's making me go after the game on Saturday?" asked Sid. He picked up *Around Town* from the table and rifled through it until he found the page he was looking for. "There." He pointed to a half-page advertisement for the musical *Oklahoma* that would be showing at a local theater for the next week. I hated like poison that my first reaction was *that would be fun.* I squashed that thought back down to hell where it came from and joined in with the other guys' normal reactions.

"Isn't that the one about the gay cowboys? *Brokeback: The Musical!*" I said, doing jazz hands in the air. That got a big, satisfying laugh from the other guys. Sid looked down at the ad, which featured a goofy, smiling cowboy.

"Man, nobody told me I'd have to do this crap once I got married," Sid complained.

"Holy shit, speaking of fags..." Kyle grabbed the newspaper out of Sid's hands. He tossed aside the gossip article about me and Alexis Darlen.

"Hey!" I protested as I rescued the paper from the floor and hugged it to my chest. Kyle found the page he was looking for and held it up. The one that read, *Possible Gay Baltimore Oriole?*

"What are we gonna do about this?" Kyle demanded. "We got some queer running around our clubhouse!"

I glanced around at some of the fans at the bar who were listening to our conversation. I hated the idea of them knowing there was a gay dude on our team. I felt like it made us look so weak. And I just couldn't wrap my head around the fact that there might be a guy on the team who was attracted to us.

"Ugh. The whole idea is just creepy," I said, physically shuddering at the idea.

Jackson leaned over and touched my shoulder. "Oh, you know you would love it, honey." I punched his arm away. Harder than I meant to. I think. Not really. He deserved it. "You know you'd love a nice, big, strapping gay man watching you in the shower."

"Quit it!" I said too loudly, even for a bar. A bunch of people turned around to look at us.

"This isn't funny, you guys. This is serious," said Kyle.

"It is?" Sid laughed, clearly the only one undisturbed by the notion of a gay guy on the team. What was wrong with him?

"Yeah. You want to be known as the queerest team in

baseball?" Kyle growled.

"I mean, would you seriously want some guy checking you out in the clubhouse? Ugh. I mean, shit. We walk around naked all the time in there," Jackson said.

"Exactly! I wonder who the hell it is," Kyle said as he shot an accusatory look at us.

"Oh, come on. You think it's one of us?" I asked.

"Well, it's gotta be somebody," Jackson said, sporting the same suspicious look as Kyle.

"Unless it's not. Look, it's just a rumor. You're all freaking out over nothing," Sid said. He sipped his beer calmly. Wow. He really didn't give a crap. Weird. Maybe it was him. He just got married, but that didn't necessarily mean anything. I glanced over at Brady. He was awfully quiet....I don't know. I guess we were probably making a big deal out of nothing.

"Yeah, it could be just a stupid rumor. Chill the hell out already," I said.

"Well, maybe it's you, Peach Schnapps," Kyle said. I jumped up, sending several empty beer bottles rattling into each other. The bar suddenly got quiet. The sports fans had been watching us anyway, and now they stared at us to see if there was going to be a brawl in the middle of the bar.

"Dammit, Kyle!" I roared. "You leave Peach Schnapps out of this. Come along, darling." I kissed my empty glass and headed up to the bar for a refill. Laughter filled the room and the tension was broken. I turned back briefly and said, "When I get back, you guys had better be talking about something else. Blawwwww..." I shuddered, trying to rid my mind of the queer images our discussion had forced into my unwilling brain.

As I headed up to the bar, I checked out the scene. There were some fine-looking ladies here this evening. Fine-looking ladies. Who was I kidding? These girls were *skanks*.

I knew it and they knew it. Not that that's necessarily a bad thing. I like a good skank as much as the next guy. Sure, it was exciting to bring home a different girl every night, but after we hooked up, I usually felt lonelier than if I hadn't brought someone home at all. Drunken sex was fun, but sober reality was depressing as hell. As gorgeous as some of these girls were, it actually did get boring after a while. Of course, I'd never tell the guys that. Then they really would suspect me of being the fag.

I didn't have to tell the bartender, Alice Beckford, what I wanted to drink. She knew. I loved when Alice was working. She was a sweet little pixie of a girl and I think she had a crush on me. It was cute. She was about my age, maybe a little younger. She was rather ordinary looking, especially compared to the girls I usually liked to bang, but she was nice.

I scanned the room while I waited for my drinks. I spotted a woman who barely fit into her tube top. She had definite potential to be a nighttime companion.

"Here you go, Henry. Peach it up," Alice said. I didn't register her voice at first. "Hey, Peaches!" I turned around. "Sorry, did you want to finish undressing her with your eyes? Looks like you were almost done." Her tone was dry and she smiled at me, but I could see a hint of hurt in her eyes. Here I was clearly checking out this hot woman when the least I could do was spend thirty seconds talking to her while she fixed my drink, especially when I knew she had a thing for me. I felt like such an asshole.

"Thanks, Alice," I said, winking at her. "You're the best, darling girl." She smiled at me again. I headed back to my table.

As I walked away, I heard her say to the other bartender, "Should I warn him that he won't get far with her? You know

Lynette. She's already had her four drinks. She'll pass out before they get to the car." It was sweet, if a bit warped, that Alice was concerned about my one-night-stand prospects.

"Sure, throw him a bone," I heard someone at the bar answer.

"I'm sure he's already got one," Alice said. I laughed at that. She was funny, that girl.

By the time I sat down with my drink, Kyle had snagged himself a lady for the evening. He pinched her ass.

"You got one, Henry?" he whispered.

"I thought I did," I said as I watched Tube Top wobble precariously across the room. I was afraid Alice might have been right. I didn't think she was gonna make it.

I managed to find another girl after my first choice indeed passed out before she could make it out of the bar. This one I picked up in the parking lot. Classy, I know. But it worked.

Parking Lot Girl was a terrific lay, but as usual, I felt lonely afterward. She was still there in the morning, which made it worse. It was so much easier when they just left after we'd had our fun. I made some extra coffee for her and settled down to read the news on the internet while I waited for her to get up.

Dammit. My lungs felt tight again. I hated being so dependent on that stupid inhaler. I got up and pulled one out of my utensil drawer and took a mighty hit. I sat back down at the table and just stared at the device. There it sat. Mocking me and my inability to breathe without it. I was supposed to be this invincible athlete, but without that stupid thing, I'd probably collapse in the middle of a game.

That was my biggest nightmare. Oh no! Henry Vaughn, Jr. just collapsed on the field. People yelling. My female fans crying in the stands. Everybody thinking it was something heroic, like a heart attack. Nope! Little Henry's just had an asthma attack. Then the trainer comes running out onto the field with my inhaler and shoots it into my mouth and the whole thing is captured on television.

I shuddered just thinking about it.

Jeez, was this woman ever going to wake up? I had places to go, mainly Johns Hopkins hospital. I was excited about the drug trial, but I guess it was stupid to get my hopes up about it. What were the odds that the drug would be some miracle pill that would let me throw out my inhaler? Still, it was worth a shot.

I was getting really restless. I got up and walked over to the ridiculously expensive oil painting of Mickey Mantle that I had on my wall. I lifted up the painting to get to the safe that I had hidden underneath it. I put in the number combination and was about to open it when I heard the girl finally come downstairs.

I quickly shut the safe and put Mickey Mantle back over it. It wasn't that I had money or anything valuable in there. If you were gonna steal from me, you might as well steal the painting. It was worth a lot more than anything I had in that safe.

Besides, I'd rather be robbed than have anybody find out what I had hidden in there.

I got Parking Lot Girl some coffee and politely shooed her out, telling her I had a doctor's appointment to go to. It was time to go play guinea pig for a bunch of drug researchers.

Dear God, please let this drug work....

2

I sat in the examining room waiting for the doctor. I hoped nobody recognized me when I came in, but I knew it was stupid to worry about that. There were a million reasons why I could be at the hospital. Nobody would ever guess it was for asthma.

I couldn't help but be excited about what this drug might do for me. I figured it couldn't hurt, and it was better than trying some weird, untested alternative remedies on my own. Instead, I would be trying a weird, untested remedy under medical supervision. Who knew? This could be the miracle asthma cure I had been waiting for.

And if it didn't work, well, what's the worst that could happen?

The whole process sure started off on the right foot. The doctor turned out to be this gorgeous woman with shoulder-length black hair, ice-blue eyes, big boobs, and a perky little ass. Seriously, it was like the beginning of a porno. Oh, yeah. I was ready to play doctor.

I had to stop thinking like that. I had to be cool, especially while she was examining me, or things could get embarrassing real quick. Still, she was a sexy lady doctor, and I'm sure she was used to male patients getting hard-ons while her hands were all over them.

"I'm Dr. Lucy Gallon. It's a pleasure to meet you," she said, extending a slender hand to shake mine. A pleasure indeed. "It's very exciting to have a celebrity participate in our study."

My heart sank, and I felt like my guts were about to spill out all over the floor.

"Uh, yeah. About that..." I began.

"Don't worry. Everything here is strictly confidential. We never release the name of anyone participating in the study. It's against the law," she said, smiling at me reassuringly. She was so hot I couldn't seem to get the whole porno scene out of my head. I imagined the two of us on this reclining patient bed. *Oh, baby.* "Thanks again for helping us out with the trial. The research assistant, Sam, will be here in just a minute to examine you."

Crushing disappointment didn't even begin to describe it.

"Sam....mantha?" I said hopefully, but Dr. Gallon didn't hear me. She just shut the door, taking all her hotness with her. Damn. I should have known it was too good to be true.

The door opened and in walked a young guy about my age. I had expected someone older, like some friendly old guy in scrubs who'd been here for fifty years. Not some guy who looked more like one of my teammates.

This was the guy who was gonna examine me? I hoped I wouldn't have to take off my clothes. He'd probably just listen to my heart and my lungs. I mean, what else was there to do?

"I'm Sam Aubrey." I shook his hand with far less enthusiasm than I had with sexy Dr. Gallon. "Very nice to meet you, Mr. Vaughn."

"You can call me Henry."

"Henry it is," Sam said, smiling. He seemed like a nice enough guy. I was just a little worried about how well we were about to get to know each other. "Okay, let's see here," Sam said as he flipped through my file. "Got your question-naire, your consent form..."

"All that stuff in my file is confidential, right? Nobody knows that I have, you know..."

"Not to worry. This is completely confidential. Though I assure you, you're not the only famous athlete with asthma. Jackie Joyner-Kersee has it. Jerome Bettis from the Pittsburgh Steelers, Greg Louganis-"

"Hah!" I snorted at that one. Wow, talk about a double whammy. That guy was gay *and* had asthma. Hard to believe he was a successful athlete. "Greg Louganis. That's exactly why I'm here. Using my inhaler makes me look like a fairy boy, you know?" I laughed, waiting for Sam to join in.

He didn't.

There was only one explanation for that look on his face. Oh, shit. *Shit, shit, shit!* Sam must be gay. I felt horrible. Sure, I talked shit about gays sometimes, but damn, I'd never do it in front of them. Sam was a nice guy and I hadn't meant to insult him. To his credit, I never would have guessed he was gay in a million years. He didn't have that rainbow vibe. He walked normal. He talked normal. How was I supposed to know?

"Shall we continue?" Sam asked coldly. His whole demeanor had changed. He hated me. That much was clear.

A horrifying thought suddenly dawned on me. In a matter of seconds, I was going to have a gay man's hands all over me. I tensed up and Sam noticed. This was not helping my case. *Shit.* He'd probably submerge all the metal instruments in ice water before he used them on me. He'd draw blood and take twenty minutes to find the vein. He took a step toward me.

I flinched.

Sam sighed deeply. "You can't catch it, you know," he said.

"Catch what?"

"Gay. It's not contagious. I do have a stack of pamphlets, though, if you're interested in joining up. That's what we homos do, you know. We try to convert people to our alternative lifestyle."

I laughed nervously. He shook his head. He was seriously pissed. He looked like a different person than the friendly Research Assistant who had walked in the door just a few moments ago. Nice to see I had that effect on people. Great.

"Moving on," Sam said. He didn't look like he had moved on. "When was your last asthma attack?"

"Uh, this morning. Lungs were real tight," I said. Sam picked up a stethoscope and I steeled myself, determined not to flinch this time. Instead, I tensed up tighter than a virgin on prom night.

Sam sighed heavily again. He put the stethoscope in his ears, and he lifted up my shirt. *He lifted up my shirt.* Damn, I needed to chill out. How the hell else was he going to listen to my heart?

"Heart sounds good. Let's have a listen to your lungs." Sam walked around behind me.

There was a gay man standing right behind me.

He lifted up the back of my shirt. I swear, he was breathing on my neck on purpose! There was no reason to get that close to me just to listen to my lungs. His soft

chuckle confirmed that, for once, I wasn't just being paranoid. He *was* screwing with me.

"A bit of a wheeze. Not too bad," he said. "Take another
deep breath. In and out. In and out. In and out." He was
talking like that on purpose. I knew how to breathe, for
God's sake. That obnoxious smirk on his face proved he was
doing everything he could to make me as uncomfortable as
humanly possible. A great healer, this guy.

Sam finally put my shirt back down. He walked over to a
drawer and pulled out a peak-flow meter, which is a little
plastic device used to measure how much breath you can
blow out. I had one at home. Hidden somewhere. I'd put it
away once when I had some of the guys over, and I hadn't
seen it since.

"I'm sure you know how this works," Sam said, holding
up the peak flow meter. I nodded miserably. Were we
done yet?

Sam leaned in toward me and held the device in front of
my face. He still wore that infuriating smirk.

"Now, put your mouth around it and blow," he said.
"Come on. Blow it for me. Blow, blow, blow, blow, blow...." I
exhaled as deeply and forcefully as I could, like I was
blowing all my fury at Sam into that stupid meter. I probably got the best reading of my life. Even Sam looked
impressed as he read the number on the side.

"Excellent. Best blow I've had in weeks." Now he was just
being mean. "Okay, blow for me one more time." I tried to
argue, but he plugged the damn thing in my mouth. I blew
into it, faster and angrier than the first time. I practically
spat the thing out when I finished.

"Are we done yet?" I practically yelled.

"Almost." Sam looked weary. Even he seemed tired of

this charade and wanted to get rid of me. "Next, we need to do the EKG. Won't this be fun," he muttered.

"I doubt it."

Sam left the room for a moment and I exhaled deeply. Immense relief coursed through my body once he was gone. When he came back, I tensed up all over again. He wheeled the EKG machine over to me.

"Take off your shirt and lie down."

"Are you kidding me?"

"Dude, just let me do my job," Sam said. He didn't look any more excited about this part of the exam than I did. I actually felt a little disappointed. What, he didn't find me attractive? Didn't he know how many baseball fans would give anything for the chance to be in a room with me with my shirt off? *Did I really just complain that a gay guy didn't seem interested in me?*

I quickly pulled my shirt over my head and then clutched it to my chest. Sam held out his hand, and I reluctantly handed him my shirt. He draped it across the chair. My shirt looked so far away. I never realized how much I took my clothes for granted.

"All right. Just lie back," Sam said, as he pulled out the little drawer for my legs to rest on. I hesitated a bit, which was a mistake. Sam put his hand on my chest and gently pushed me down on the table. After that, I vowed to do everything he said so as not to give him another excuse to touch me.

"Just relax, Henry. It takes longer to set up the EKG than it does to actually run the test. We'll be all done soon." Was it my imagination, or was he actually being nice? He had that soothing voice medical people use to keep you calm. He put the electrodes all over my legs and chest. I tried to relax but it was really hard. He was right that it only took seconds to actually run the EKG. Before I knew it, he was taking the electrodes off and we were done. I glanced anxiously at my shirt, which looked very lonely over there on the chair. Sam rolled his eyes. He grabbed my shirt and tossed it over to me. I put it on in record time.

"Well, everything checks out. You're a fine specimen of a healthy man," Sam said. I wanted to punch the smirk right off his smarmy face. He washed his hands at the little sink and then walked over to the cabinet and took out a bottle of pills. He filled up a small paper cup with water.

I suddenly felt a little apprehensive about taking the pill, though that was what I had gone through all this trouble for. It would be a dream come true if I could just take a pill every day and throw out that humiliating inhaler for good. But still, this was an untested drug. And that's what I was doing. Testing it for them. I could drop dead for all they knew. I eyed the pill nervously.

"There's no way this can be dangerous, right?"

"I assure you, it's perfectly safe. We do animal testing first." He spoke in his gentle, medical voice again. "Right now, we're just trying to determine if the pill is effective. We test it on a control group of people who still have their inhalers nearby in case they need them." I made a face at the word inhaler. Sam actually smiled sympathetically. "We know the drug won't hurt you. We just need to make sure that it works."

I nodded and opened my mouth to take the pill. I stopped.

"Do you really think this will help me get rid of my inhaler?"

Sam sighed. He was losing patience. Can't say I really blamed him.

"I don't know, Henry. The research looks promising. The

pill is designed to stay in your bloodstream for a month, controlling the inflammation of your lungs. We'll just have to see."

"So I only take it once a month?"

Sam nodded. Good. That meant I wouldn't have to come back to see him for another month. I eagerly opened my mouth to swallow the pill. I stopped again when another scary thought occurred to me.

"Wait! This won't mess up any random drug tests, will it? I mean, some asthma drugs use steroids."

"Not this one, Henry. This one doesn't use steroids."

I had to admit, he was way more patient with me than I would have been. I would have smacked me upside the head by now or used one of those plastic pill-shooter deals you use on cats to force the pill down my throat. Maybe he wasn't such a bad guy after all. I finally took the pill. He handed me a paper cup of water.

"Bottoms up!" he said, smirking again.

I hated him.

3

I stood, cap over my heart, with the other players while some opera dude sang the National Anthem. He was actually pretty good. I always felt a little jealous of the people who got to sing the Star Spangled Banner at ball-games. I always thought it would be really cool to get up there and perform in front of all those people. I've actually got a pretty decent singing voice. It would be fun as hell to get up there and just belt it out in front of all the fans and shock everybody. Show 'em that I wasn't just a jock who could hit a ball.

When the song ended, none of the players moved. Every head on my team, plus a few from the Mariners, turned toward me.

"Let's play ball, hon!" I shouted. The crowd roared their approval. Now the players started walking. They might not let me sing the Anthem, but I got attention in other ways.

My dad was in the stands today, about three rows behind home plate. He loved coming to games and he especially loved telling everyone around him that he was Henry Vaughn, Sr. I always made sure I waved to him from the on-deck circle. That might not seem like such a big deal, but in professional sports you never see guys waving at Daddy. Sure, you get the occasional player holding up a sign saying "I love you, Mom" or whatever. But waving like a kid in a school play? It just wasn't done. Which was why I did it.

The fans loved it. So did my dad. I also waved to him to prove to the fans that he was who he said he was. I'd seen him pull out his driver's license to prove it too. Made me feel good that he was proud to have the same name as me.

If he only knew how I really felt about playing baseball.

Having a son as a major league baseball player was a dream come true for any father. That was all that mattered to me. My mom died when I was ten and he took really good care of me, so I owed him a lot. It couldn't have been easy for him, and I knew he was proud of how I had turned out. He had the ultimate bragging rights among his bowling buddies. Oh, your son's an accountant? That's great. Mine plays for the Baltimore Orioles. Game over, bitch.

It was a pretty good game, I guess. I'd been hoping to hit one out for my dad. When I hit a homer, I always pointed at him as I rounded home, as if I'd hit it out just for him. I couldn't get it done today, but I did go two for four with a run batted in.

I signed autographs after the game in the parking lot. It always amazed me to see how many people hung out in the back lot, waiting for the players to come out and sign. There was a big fence surrounding our cars, so fans couldn't get to us or to our vehicles, but the fence was low enough so that we could pass back signed baseballs, programs, and in some cases (like mine), signed, shirtless photos of ourselves. If you got lucky, there were some nice hotties waiting there for autographs.

I got lucky.

My dad often came out to the players' lot to watch me sign autographs. I liked to take him out for a beer afterwards, but if he saw me chatting up a Debbie Double-Ds, he would wave me off and made sure I took her home instead. I think he was just as proud of my batting average with the ladies as he was for my success in baseball.

What a dad.

THE NEXT MORNING, I woke up with Debbie Double-Ds in my bed. I *had* to stop calling them that. More than once, I'd accidentally called a woman "Debbie." One girl let me know in no uncertain terms (a slap across the face) that Debbie was *not* her name. Funny how some woman I had met seven hours earlier for what we both knew would be a one-night stand could get so upset about me not recalling her name, especially when there was alcohol involved.

Right now, I desperately needed to remember the real name of the woman with the rockin' body who was currently stretching out in my bed. Lindsey? No. That was that other one. The brunette. Shit. This one began with an S. Or was it a J? Yes, it was definitely a J. Jane! Jane was definitely it. I remembered because last night we had played Tarzan and...never mind.

It was funny. I mean, she looked great, but somehow I remembered her being hotter last night. Beer goggles, maybe. I don't know. She was pretty smokin', I guess. She had this lacy black bra, black thong, and she looked amazing. Somehow, she just seemed more amazing last night. She leaned back in bed and spread her legs a little. It was clearly an invitation for an encore performance of last night.

"Come on, Henry. Come back to bed," Jane said seductively.

"Sorry, I wanna get in a run and some lifting before batting practice," I said and I wasn't really sure why. I could have gone again. No question about that. Jane looked disappointed and I was kinda disappointed in myself. I just wasn't feeling it.

I went for a run through the neighborhood. It was a nice area. There were lots of trees and it was fairly quiet with the huge houses spread pretty far apart.

Another jogger, wearing unnecessarily tight athletic pants, ran by me. I nodded at him and he nodded back as he passed by me. Then I turned around and checked out his ass.

I turned around and checked out his ass.

Okay, that was a little weird. I really didn't know what possessed me to do that. Sometimes you couldn't help looking, I guess. If a guy wore tight shorts like that, he couldn't expect people not to look.

What?

Never mind. I kept jogging and tried to put the guy out of my mind. Except I couldn't. I had a really odd feeling in my stomach. I hoped I wasn't getting sick. That was all I needed. The Orioles were on a pretty hot streak lately and I didn't want anything to screw that up.

I felt a little better as I ran. A guy on a bicycle rode by me. He had really strong, muscular legs. Wow, not bad.

What?

That uneasy feeling in my stomach started to spread through the rest of my body. Something felt very, very strange. I couldn't put my finger on it at first. Suddenly, I had the sharp realization that I was noticing those guys the way I usually noticed big-breasted women or ones with long legs.

It was attraction that I felt.

I stumbled while running and it took me a good ten paces to catch myself. I probably looked like something out of a Jim Carrey film. I was grateful for the distraction, but it didn't last long. I tried to deny it to myself, but there was really no mistaking it. For the briefest of moments, I had felt attracted to not one, but two men.

Okay, okay don't panic. This was stupid. I'd never experienced anything like this before. I don't think. I mean, I'm sure I'd noticed guys sometimes when they looked good, but that was normal, right? *Right?*

A test. I needed a test. I needed to go find some more men to look at. Gah! What a thought. I jogged faster, looking all around to find some guys to look at to see if I felt anything. I couldn't find any at first. All I saw was a girl in her twenties or so bent over, weeding in her garden. I jogged past her.

I jogged right past her.

A sexy girl in her twenties, bent over with her thong visible in the back and I jogged right past her without turning around for a second look. I had to check out Tight-pants Jogging Guy, but I ignored Thong Lady?

I was totally psyching myself out here. I saw a blond guy walking to his car. I hoped he was hot. Just so I could test to be sure, not because...anyway. I nodded politely as I ran near him. He waved and smiled warmly. I knew that smile. It was an *I know you. You're Henry Vaughn, Jr.!* smile. I concentrated. I searched my whole being for any sign of attraction. I knew objectively that he was a good-looking guy, but I didn't feel anything.

Relief flooded through me. I was just being paranoid but I really couldn't help it. I was raised to avoid anything even remotely faggoty. My dad wouldn't even hug me. Ever. Not as a kid and certainly not now. My pointing at him from the field and him giving me a manly handshake after a good game was about the extent of our physical relationship. No unnecessary touching. Gays were about the lowest form of life for him. Sissies. He still called them "sissies" sometimes and he and his friends used the word "fag" as a mock term of endearment. As in "Hey, fag, what's up?" and "Nice to see you, homo. What's going on?"

I headed back home, ready to put this whole weird experience behind me. I couldn't help thinking about Linds- Debb- no, no, it was *Jane* who was in my bed. Jane, who I could've had sex with again this morning, but I didn't. I turned her down.

But what about last night? Last night was pretty impressive, right? Right. Damn right. Just ask Jane. I needed to see her again. If she was still there when I got home, I was gonna rock her world. She'd tell her grandkids about the things Henry Vaughn, Jr. did to her. Well, maybe not her grandkids. But her friends. She'd definitely tell her friends.

I ran toward home as fast as I could. On the way, I passed a shirtless guy riding on a lawnmower. Damn, there sure were a lot of hot guys in this neighborhood.

Uh-oh.

4

Jane was gone by the time I got back. It figured. When I didn't want a girl to hang around, she wouldn't leave. Now that I needed her to prove to myself that I hadn't completely lost my mind, she'd disappeared.

I headed to the ballpark, grateful for the distraction. I had some time to kill before the 3:05 start, so I got in a work-out. I got on the stationary bike and pedaled as fast as I possibly could. I wished it were a real bike so I could be halfway to Mexico by now.

"Henry!"

"Ah! What?"

Tuna scared the hell out of me. I hadn't even noticed him on the bike right next to me.

"You okay? You don't look so hot," he said. I looked at over at him and was grateful that *he* didn't look so hot. It was just Tuna, one of my best buddies on the team. What was I expecting?

"Not really. I don't feel so good." That was an understatement. The room was getting more crowded as more of the guys showed up to work out. I avoided looking at anyone if I could possibly help it, but it wasn't easy since there were mirrors all over the damn place. I accidentally caught a glimpse of Kyle lifting weights. He was a good-looking guy, but I didn't feel any kind of attraction toward him, either.

I exhaled heavily with relief. I chuckled a little to myself and shook my head. I didn't know what I was worried about. Noticing that a guy was hot didn't make me queer. It was just a stupid observation, for God's sake.

I started to relax and slowed my pedaling a bit. I looked up to see Brady Clayton walk in, wearing a tight T-shirt and gym shorts. Brady was a young guy, just sent up from the minors. In his early twenties, the guy was *ripped*. His biceps bulged out of his shirt and those shorts he wore showed off his muscular calves.

I felt everything in my body stiffen and *I do mean everything.*

I felt sick. Sick and completely out of control. It was so involuntary. I just couldn't help it. No matter how desperate I was to believe otherwise, I could not deny the fact that I had just gotten a boner from looking at one of my teammates. Sure, it wasn't a *raging* boner, but it was there. Liquid fear pooled in my stomach. What in the hell was wrong with me? I'd never felt attracted to a guy in my life before today.

Had I?

No. No way. Never. What was happening to me? You couldn't just wake up gay one morning and-

There was only one humanly possible explanation for what was happening to me.

The pill.

I'd been straight as an arrow my whole life, then I take some strange pill with God knows what in it and I wake up gay the next morning. It had to be the pill. It was the only thing that made sense.

Right?

I mean I *had* been straight my whole life. Of course I had. With my dad around, I couldn't even have entertained the notion of being gay even if I was. Oh God, I hadn't been suppressing this my whole life, had I? No way. That was insane. How could I not be straight? Look at all the women I'd been with. It was a wonder my dick hadn't fallen off yet. You couldn't fake sexual attraction like that for all those years. How else could I have performed so many, many, *many* times?

But still, what I was feeling was so intense. It was hard to imagine that some drug could make me feel like this. I was as turned on by Brady's muscles as I ever had been by a woman's tits.

"Henry!" Tuna managed to startle the hell out of me again even though neither one of us had moved from our spots. Tuna looked at me with total bewilderment. I suddenly realized why.

Oh, shit.

The entire time I had been sitting there, pondering my sexuality, *I had been staring at Brady Clayton working out.*

"Ah...ah..." I said, covering brilliantly. "S-sorry. I must have zoned out there for a second." Much to my relief, Tuna looked more worried than accusatory. With my track record with the ladies, it would take more than just an occasional slip-up like staring at a hot rookie to make people question my manhood.

"Are you okay? Seriously, you look awful."

I'm sure I did look awful. I felt like hell. I swallowed hard. I couldn't help but look around the room. It was like a morbid fascination. It was just so weird looking at these guys that I'd worked with, played with, gotten drunk with and now I was seeing them so differently. There's really no way to describe what it feels like to suddenly be sexually attracted to your friends. I couldn't help being curious to see which ones would actually turn me on.

Oh, God, was I actually enjoying this? Of course not. No way. It was just an experiment. So far, Tuna and Kyle did nothing for me. Brady the Hot Rookie (I *had* to stop calling him that) was undeniably gorgeous. To be fair, I remember thinking that even before...

Oh man, did I really think that before I took the pill? That didn't exactly help my case. I was making myself crazy. I looked around and found another sexy guy. Jackson Peters. He was a little older than Hot Rookie, but not bad. Not bad at all. He had abs of steel, I liked the definition in his shoulders and--

"What the hell you lookin' at?" Jackson asked loudly enough for others to look up. My legs got tangled in my stationary bike and I nearly fell off the damn thing.

"I-I uh..." I don't think I'd ever been so panic-stricken in my life. Everyone was looking at me. They knew. I just knew they knew. This was worse than the inhaler on the field nightmare. And it was really happening.

"Back off, Jackson. Give him a break! He's got the flu or something. Seriously, Henry. You need to go lie down. You look awful," Tuna said. I wanted to hug him for standing up for me. I nearly laughed at the absurdity of that thought. If I hugged him now, my life would be over. They'd all burn me at a rainbow-colored stake.

"Whatsa matter, Henry? You got a little head cold? Want me to call your mommy?" A loud voice filled the room. I closed my eyes and breathed out. I was so terrorized at the thought of my teammates finding out about my sudden foray into gay territory, I had forgotten about the most fear-some creature of all. The manager, Eddie "Boomer" Wilkens.

Boomer had the reputation of being the toughest manager in baseball. Because he was. Sometimes this was a good thing. It made our whole team seem more intimidat-ing, which was pretty cool. Other times, like now, it kinda sucked having him as a manager. Sure, he won ball games, but he was a tough old bastard. You pretty much needed an x-ray showing a bone broken in half before he would believe you were really hurt.

"No. I'm fine," I said. Boomer eyed me studiously, then nodded. I glanced around at the other guys, who now looked at me with sympathy. They could tell I wasn't feeling well and they knew I wasn't going to get a pass from Boomer. They'd all been there.

I wiped the sweat off my face and reminded myself that I wasn't actually sick. Physically, I felt fine. There was no reason I couldn't play today. As soon as the game was over, I would go pay Sam Aubrey a visit. Obviously, I was gonna drop out of the trial, but I had to go see him to make sure I would be okay. Not that I was gonna let him examine me again. I shuddered. It made me happy that I still reacted that way to the thought of Sam, even in my current state. That would be the perfect ending to my living nightmare, being attracted to that smarmy, smirking son-of-a-bitch.

"Good thing. Not that we even need our best bats for tonight. Playin' the goddamn Kansas City Royals, for Chris-sake." He walked off muttering as he often did.

I exhaled slowly and felt some of my tension walk away with him. If nothing else, I knew I had to keep my horrible secret from him. Boomer was worse than my dad when it came to gays. Like many coaches and managers, he had zero tolerance for weakness and being a fag was about as weak as

it got. He'd sooner put a girl on our team than a gay guy. I
really believe that. Besides the whole "sissy" thing, Boomer
Wilkens was also a pretty heavy duty Christian. And not the
regular kind of Christian, either. He was one of those Evan-
gelical nuts. Between his Southern Virginia upbringing and
his religion, I had no doubt he would get me traded if he
knew I was gay. I mean, if he thought I was gay! There was
nothing to know, because I wasn't. Still, Boomer was hard-
core. It would kill him for other teams to think there was a
fag on the Baltimore Orioles. He wouldn't stand for it.

I thought about that article in *Around Town* about the
gay player. At first, I'd been thinking *how did they know?* But
then I remembered the story broke before I took the pill. I
might be losing my mind, but I was very sure I hadn't made
out with a man while I was in New York and then forgotten
about it. There was obviously another gay guy on the team. I
wondered if he felt as terrorized as I did.

I started sweating and feeling sick again. I was absolutely terrified at the idea of being found out. Dear God,
what would happen if people knew? The fans, the players,
Boomer... my dad?

For the first time in my life, I found myself feeling sorry
for gay people. So this was what it felt like to realize you
were gay and be utterly horrified thinking what would
happen if you came out of the closet. I was lucky; my curse
was temporary.

Wasn't it?

Real gay people had to live with it forever. I couldn't help
but imagine what it must feel like to be fifteen or sixteen
years old and have the awful realization suddenly dawn on
you: *Oh my God, I think I might be gay.* It was hard enough
being a teenager when you were straight.

Yeah. That was sad and all, but I had bigger problems.

Like how I couldn't seem to stop staring at Hot Rookie. Brady Clayton was benching an impressive amount of weight and I just couldn't look away. I had spent years ogling women, which was socially acceptable. I found I couldn't break the habit now that I'd switched teams, albeit temporarily.

But what if it wasn't temporary? What if the pill had messed up my body chemistry and the effects were permanent? What if I was stuck this way forever? And even more terrifying, *what if it wasn't the pill that was doing this to me?*

I wiped my forehead with the towel again, if for no other reason than to stop staring at Brady. I realized it was safer just to get out of there. By tomorrow, maybe the pill would have worn off and I'd be back to normal. But if any of the guys suspected, even for a moment, that the rumored gay guy was me, I might never get my reputation back. I grabbed a clean towel and headed for the shower.

Bad, bad, bad idea...

What the hell was I thinking heading, to the shower? There I was, surrounded by naked men.

Good-looking naked men. And not just your average, handsome guys like the dude mowing his lawn or the bicyclist in my neighborhood. These were professional athletes. I wasn't the only player whose shirtless picture was hanging up in bedrooms all across America. Why did these guys have to be so damn hot?

I was trapped. There I was, completely naked in the shower room when it happened.

In walked a completely naked Brady Clayton.

Within seconds, I was sporting the biggest boner I'd had since the 8th grade when Amy Carlson let me put my hand up her shirt.

I awkwardly ambled across the room to put a towel around my waist.

My heart pounded and my lungs tightened. I knew I was only seconds away from a full-blown panic attack.

Boomer Wilkens be damned. I had to get the hell out of there.

I knew I couldn't just sit around waiting for the effects of this pill to wear off. It was just too risky. I was terrible at hiding this gay thing from other people. At least real gay people had their whole lives to figure out how to hide. I'd had less than 24 hours to get used to it. Scratch that. I didn't plan on getting used to it. I needed to get rid of it. Now. Maybe Sam had some kind of antidote. A shot. Electroshock therapy. A frontal lobotomy. Anything to counteract the pill's effect.

Two things I knew for sure. Sam was gonna cure me, and then I was gonna kick his ass.

5

I dashed into the Johns Hopkins waiting area, startling the receptionist half to death. Poor girl. Here comes this giant athlete running at her full speed with a wild look in his eye. I had to calm down. I took a deep breath.

"I need to see Sam. The assistant guy," I said.

"Do you have an appointment?" she asked. I shook my head. She smiled apologetically. "Well, I'm sorry. If it's not your appointed time for the trial-"

"I know, but it's really important. Like, *really* important," I said. I looked around at the crowded waiting room and started to panic all over again. What if they wouldn't let me in to see Sam? I couldn't stay like this for another minute. I felt my heart seize and my lungs tighten just the way they had at the ballpark.

Which gave me an idea.

"It's just that...I'm having a hard time...breathing..." I gasped and wheezed. I grabbed onto the counter to steady myself. A nice touch, I thought.

"Oh, my God! Here, come this way!" She jumped up out of her little receptionist box and grabbed my arm, dragging me toward the exam room. I gasped and clutched my way down the hall. I was getting pretty good at this. I had given the same kind of performance for Boomer Wilkens just a short while ago. Of course, that time I blamed it on my heart. Gets 'em every time. You can call a guy a pussy if he wants to sit out a game 'cause he's got the flu, but you can't screw around with chest pains. I promised Boomer I'd go right to the hospital to get checked out. And I did go to the hospital. Just not to the ER like he had in mind.

The receptionist led me to an examining room and sat me down on the crinkly paper on the exam table.

"Stay right there and try to relax," she said, looking a little panicked. She ran out and shouted down the hall. "Sam! Sam, this asthma patient can't breathe!" A few seconds later, Sam hurried into the room. A momentary flash of distaste crossed his face when he saw who the patient was. I was still wheezing heavily.

"Okay," Sam said in a calm but concerned voice. "Sit tight for just a second. You might need a shot of adrenaline. I'm gonna go get Dr. Gallon." A bolt of fear shot through me. No way in hell could I face sexy Dr. Gallon in my state and I sure as hell wasn't going to confess to her what my real symptoms were. I miraculously stopped wheezing.

"No, don't! I'm fine. I only said I had trouble breathing so they would let me in," I said, trying to look apologetic. I needed to get on Sam's good side. Much as I hated it, I desperately needed his help.

Sam looked at me, slowly processing what I just said. His expression rapidly changed from worry to confusion to anger.

"You did what? Why? What do you want? Shit!" Sam said, exhaling with relief that I wasn't dying after all. I jumped up so suddenly that Sam actually backed away, as if he thought I was going to hurt him. I shut the door and walked slowly back to the examining table and sat down. I was dreading this whole conversation. How the hell was I going to explain this?

"I'm...umm, having some unusual side effects that I needed to talk to you about," I said. Sam studied me curiously.

"But you're breathing okay?"

"Yes."

"You're sure? No tightness in the lungs, no chest pain?" Sam said, all business as he jotted down some notes.

"Yes. Fine. Breathing is fine. It's not that. It's just..." I didn't know where to begin.

"So what's going on?" he asked, clearly getting a little irritated.

"Uh, well..." I was at a complete loss for words. Sam looked at me for a moment, then nodded his head. He put the notebook down.

"Ohh...I think I see what's going on here."

"Really, really, really I doubt it," I said.

"You're having man trouble." My head snapped up at that. "What is it? Trouble urinating?"

"No."

"A rash on your genitals?"

"No, nothing like that."

"Trouble obtaining and maintaining an erection?"

"No!" I practically shouted. Trouble getting an erection would be a useful problem to have right about now. Hell, even a rash on my genitals sounded fun compared to what I was going through.

"Then what's the problem?" Sam asked, growing more impatient by the second. I closed my eyes and just blurted it out.

"Your stupid drug made me gay!" I said finally. Wow, that came out *way* louder than I intended. I hoped Dr. Gallon hadn't heard it. I still wanted a shot at her once I was cured of my gayness. When I opened my eyes, Sam was staring at me.

It was not a happy stare. It was not a curious stare. It was an *I'm gonna kill you in your sleep* stare. He grabbed his notebook and got up.

"Wow. You're really a piece of work, you know that? Look, if you've got a problem with me being gay-"

I grabbed his arm to keep him from leaving, but I quickly let go and jumped back. I couldn't help it. Old habits die hard. I'd gone my whole life avoiding any kind of physical contact with men and I couldn't change that overnight.

"No! I'm serious! E-e-ever since you gave me that pill, I've had sexual- I mean, I've been attracted to m..." I couldn't say it. I couldn't. I wouldn't. "And now, when I look at hot women, it's like *nothing*." Sam looked like he wasn't sure what to think of me. Who could blame him? I must have looked as terrified as I felt, though, because he seemed to get that whatever was going on with me, I wasn't making it up.

"You're sitting here telling me that you're suddenly finding yourself sexually attracted to men." He said it as calmly as if I had said the pill had given me a headache, nausea, or any of those 500 possible side effects on pill bottles. I could imagine the warning label on this one. May cause you to faint, vomit, or spontaneously burst into show-tunes and wear a rainbow hat.

He looked at me studiously and, for a second, I thought he believed me.

"So you took the pill I gave you and now you're gay!" he nearly shouted.

"Shhhhhhhhhh!"

"That's really what you breeders think, isn't it? Gay people are all out to recruit you." I guess I should have expected that. After the way I'd treated him when we first met, I guess I couldn't blame him. What surprised me was the pain in his eyes. He wasn't just mad. He was hurt. His expression was just like that of a dog that'd been mistreated. You could still see the sadness and fear in the dog's eyes long after he'd been taken in by a nice owner. He still jumped when you went to pet him because somebody used to beat him. I wondered who had beaten Sam.

Probably guys like me.

"You think I gave you some kind of gay pill? Are you insane? Are you really that homophobic and paranoid?"

"No. I mean yes! Kind of! I mean, not really. I don't know," I said. I struggled to explain what I meant. "No, I don't think it was a gay pill. I mean, I don't think you guys...I mean you research guys, not you, like, you know gay guys..." Sam sighed wearily. I knew I was losing him. He'd never help me now. I took a deep breath and tried to get the words straight in my head. "I just mean, I'm not saying you research guys did this on purpose. I'm not some right-wing jerk that thinks gay people have an agenda and they're out to convert people, okay? I'm just saying this particular pill has a bizarro effect and it made me gay." I forced myself to say those last four words without grimacing, for fear of offending Sam even worse. It wasn't easy. I hoped I never, ever had to say that aloud again.

Sam sank down on the stool near me. He shook his head, still having no idea of what to make of me.

"You're sure you've never had these kinds of feelings before? Be totally honest with me and with yourself here. A lot of guys are in denial for years and years before they-"

"No! Never. I swear," I said. I was still holding out hope that he would tell me there was a simple medical explanation for this whole thing. That I wasn't the first person in the trial to complain of these crazy symptoms. That everything was going to be okay.

"Henry, there is just no way that this drug made you gay. It just isn't possible. You're either gay or you're not."

"Well, I'm not!" I said, more forcefully than I should have. I wanted to jump up and scream at Sam, telling him that suddenly becoming gay was the worst thing that had ever happened to me.

"Don't be so sure. I'm telling you, denial is a stronger force than you think. I know you hide your asthma from your teammates because you think it makes you less of a man. I'm sure you hide a lot more from yourself to protect your male ego." Sam squinted, scrutinizing me further. He reminded me of *The Mentalist*, that show on TV where the guy can pretty much tell your whole life story and all your secrets just by looking at you. "You're the type that would tell your friends you listen to heavy metal music when you really listen to easy listening. Am I right?"

He was frighteningly close on that particular analysis. I mean, I hated easy listening music, but he wasn't far off. If he could figure out my musical tastes just by looking at me, how on earth was I going to keep my being gay, however temporarily, from my teammates and everyone else?

Sam smirked. He knew he had hit on something. I wanted to hit *him*.

"And I'll bet you have an overbearing father who would disown you if he thought you were gay." And, with that, he cut to the core of my most terrifying fear of all. Hank really would disown me. He was the only family I had left in the world and he would leave me if I was gay.

"Henry," Sam said, shaking his head. "There are a hundred reasons why it makes sense that you've been in deep denial about being gay and no reason at all why it even remotely makes sense that it was the drug that made you homosexual. Face it. Baby, you were born this way."

"I WAS-" I started to shout, then lowered my voice to a fierce whisper. "I was *not*." I jumped up off the exam table and got right in his face. The little prick didn't even have the decency to act afraid of me at all anymore. He just shook his head and smiled. He had the upper hand now and he knew it.

"Look, I know you think being gay is the most horrible thing that could possibly happen to you, but you'll get used to it. Maybe someday you'll even learn to be proud of it," Sam told me with more gentleness than I probably deserved. But I was way too upset to be placated right now.

"Oh, yeah. I can just see me wearing a dress and marching in a gay pride parade. Look at me. Aren't I just faaaaaabulous!"

Sam glared at me menacingly. "That's really what you think we do, isn't it?"

"I don't want to know what you do. I don't care. I don't want any part of it." I sank back down on the exam table and put my head in my hands.

"You make me sick, you know that?" Sam said. I looked up at him. I'd never seen anyone look so disgusted by me. "I can't believe how childish you are. I've seen doctors give patients a cancer diagnosis – a terminal cancer diagnosis – and the patients didn't carry on like you."

"I'd rather I had a cancer diagnosis!" For a second, I really thought Sam was going to hit me. Instead, he grabbed his notebook and headed for the door.

"Yeah. We're done here."

He wasn't going to help me. I was gonna be stuck like this. My teammates would find out and lynch me. Boomer Wilkens would bench me. My dad would desert me. I was about to lose everything.

"Wait. Please. Please! I'm begging you. I really need your help," I pleaded. Sam paused and turned around.

"You need help, all right. But not from me. Look, what you need is a counselor. A psychiatrist, a therapist. Somebody to help you through this. There is absolutely nothing medically wrong with you. Which means I'm done here."

"Why can't you even consider that it's the drug?" I asked him.

"Why can't you just admit for just one second that maybe it's not?"

"Because I don't want to!" I shouted. Sam looked at me calmly. He walked back to his stool and sat down. He just looked at me. I tried hard to read his face. I couldn't tell if he felt sorry for me or if he was about to punch my lights out.

"Look, just take it easy. Okay, Henry, just for fun, let's say it's the drug. Then the effects will wear off, right?"

"Yeah. Yeah, they'd have to, right?"

He nodded. "Okay then. Give it some time. Then, if you're still experiencing symptoms, give me a call. Okay?" So he wasn't going to help me. Great.

"But it's been more than 24 hours since I took the pill. How long would any side effects last?"

His smirk was back. "The pill's designed to stay in your system for a month, remember?" Dread washed over me. I felt like someone had just handed me a huge boulder and told me that I had to hold it for a solid month.

"So, I'm gonna be stuck like this for a month?"

"That's right, Henrietta," he said in a high-pitched voice.

"Don't call me that. It's not funny."

"Oh, it's a little funny. Don't be such a drama queen, Charlotte."

"I mean it. Stop it," I said. I stood up and got in his face again. He really wasn't intimidated by me anymore and it was starting to seriously piss me off. In fact, he jumped up and got right in my face.

"But that's what we queers do, right? We call each other girl names and say 'hey girlfriend'!" He snapped his fingers effeminately and lisped on the word "girlfriend."

"I never said that!" I did think that was what they did. I mean, some of them were like that, right? "I don't think that at all." I could tell he didn't believe me. Jerk. "I don't know. Maybe this whole thing is some kind of punishment from God to teach me a lesson."

"Punishment? Are you kidding me with this?" Sam said, more disgusted with me than ever.

"No, really. I mean, what if this is God's way of teaching me to be nicer to fa-hah-hah....I-I mean, gays?"

"First you blame the drug, then you blame God. You really are in denial."

"Look, can't you just take a closer look at what's in the pill? Just look into it real quick and see if there's anything that could have caused this. What have you got to lose? If you still think it's not the pill, then you can say I told you so and move on with your life," I said.

"Fine. I will look into it. I will explore the nearly nonexistent possibility that Johns Hopkins researchers have accidentally invented a pill that makes people gay instead of curing their asthma." He rolled his eyes and shook his head.

"Wasn't Viagra originally supposed to treat heart disease?" I asked. Hah! Score one for me. I could tell by the look on his face that he knew I had a point on that one.

"Let me finish. I will explore the possibility that it's the pill if you explore the possibility that you might actually be gay," Sam said.

"Yeah, sure. Fine. I hereby announce that there is a possibility that I just might have been gay all along." I managed to say it with a straight face and without squirming. More points for me. But Sam shook his head.

"No, no, no. No way. You can't just say that. You have to do something...*gay*." I must have looked utterly horrified because Sam laughed out loud. Wow, I didn't realize the guy had a sense of humor. Even if it was at my expense. Jerk. "Look, you can't just say you might actually be gay to shut me up. You expect me to do something to help you, then you gotta meet me halfway. I will do some research on the drug if you do something to prove that you will seriously consider the possibility that you've been in denial your whole life." Sam looked at me for a moment and said, more gently, "It's for your own good, Henry. You can't hide forever. Sooner or later, you're gonna have to figure out the truth."

"Well, what exactly is it that you want me to do?" I asked, afraid of what he was going to say.

"I will help you on one condition." Sam folded his arms and grinned. "I want you to meet my boyfriend." I grimaced, which seemed to delight him rather than piss him off. He loved watching me squirm.

"Come on, Sam. What good is that going to do?" I asked him.

"Because, contrary to your belief, it won't actually kill you to spend some time with gay people. Part of the reason you're in denial –" I was about to argue, but he put a hand up. "The reason I think you *may* be in denial is because you're just really uncomfortable with gay people. It's not even all your fault. I'm sure part of it is your upbringing. What you need is exposure to gay people."

I made a face. "You guys aren't gonna, like, make out in front of me, are you?"

Sam raised an eyebrow and smirked. He'd french his boyfriend right in front of me just to spite me. Of all the research assistants in the world, why did I end up with this guy? Sure, it would have been really embarrassing to admit my problem to Dr. Gallon, but I bet she'd have been a lot nicer about it.

"Either you come by my place, let's say Friday night after the game, and meet Jeremy or you stay gay for a month. I'm sure your teammates will love that! You won't be able to hide it. You're not that good of an actor." Showed what he knew. I actually was a pretty good actor. Better than you would think. "If it were me, I wouldn't be able to keep it a secret for long," Sam continued. "Especially with that Brady Clayton strutting around. Mmmmmm." I felt an unexpected stab of jealousy when Sam mentioned his attraction to Brady. Brady was *my* crush.

What the hell was wrong with me?

I knew he was right. I couldn't believe how on the money Sam was, considering the close call I'd already had with Brady. I knew I could hide my conflicted emotions if I worked hard enough, but my body would betray my arousal. Women had no idea how lucky they were in that department. I sighed.

"Fine. What choice do I have?"

Sam grinned.

6

I took my dad to lunch because I felt guilty that I hadn't seen him in a while, but it was the last thing I wanted to do right now. Strike that. Going to Sam's house of gay love was the last thing I wanted to do, but that was tomorrow night. My stomach felt queasy every time I thought about it, so I tried to put it out of my mind. I met up with my dad at the deli downtown near the stadium.

"You guys are slippin' a bit, ain't ya?" asked my dad as soon as we sat down to eat. He was referring to the Orioles' recent losing streak. Hank was not a guy to pull any punches. He always said exactly what was on his mind.

He was right. The team was hitting the skids lately. I was distracted over the whole turning gay overnight thing and it was affecting my performance. It wasn't just me. The gay rumor was affecting the whole team. Some guys were flipping out over the idea of a fag on the team and others didn't give a damn, but everybody was on edge about it. It was screwing up the team dynamic; that was for sure. Hell yeah, we were losing again but I sure couldn't tell my dad what the real problem was.

"Sure ain't helpin' that there might be some queer on the team," Hank said. Then again, maybe he already knew. He was retired. He had plenty of time to sit around all day, reading the paper and complaining about what was in the news. "What the hell is that crap all about? You got any idea who the faggot might be?"

"No-no. Not really. I haven't thought that much about it," I lied.

"Well, watch your back," Hank said, stabbing a fork into his coleslaw. "You don't want that creep watching you in the shower." He shuddered. I knew that shudder. That was my shudder. Now I knew where I got it from. I had to admit, it was rather ugly. Kinda made you look like a jerk. And, for some reason, I felt offended by his comment. I guess it was because, however temporarily, *I* was the creep in the shower. It wasn't my fault. I really wasn't trying to check out Brady or any of the other guys. Ever since that first day, I was able to control myself easily. I was a professional, for shit's sake. It's not like as soon as I was gay I couldn't help but check out every guy in sight, okay? People could be so paranoid!

I changed the subject quickly and steered Hank toward safer topics. We had a nice talk after that. It was good being with my dad.

I found myself imagining what my life would be without him. I knew he loved me even though he never said it. I also knew he would drop me in a heartbeat if he thought I was gay. I felt an awful ache in my chest so I tried not to think about it. It wasn't easy.

THE REPORTERS WASTED no time trying to stir up trouble with the team before the next game. We were already on edge and their pushy questions were not helping matters. I sat in the dugout and helplessly watched Lucinda Mackleroy grill Kyle on the field about everybody's favorite topic lately.

"There seems to be a lot of tension in the clubhouse lately and the possibility of a gay player on the team seems to be taking a toll. Would you care to comment?" Lucinda asked.

"Hell, yeah, it's causing tension. Look, I know it ain't exactly politically correct to say this, but having a queer guy on the team is already fu...I mean, screwing up the team. It just don't feel right. The idea that there's some guy in there in the clubhouse with us, that, you know...I mean, gross," Kyle said, sounding seriously pissed. He never did know how to keep his mouth shut. I could hear him getting madder and madder the more he prattled on. "Sorry, but the idea of having a fag on the team sucks and it's dragging the whole team down."

What an idiot. He was gonna pay for that remark. Sure, he had only said what we were all thinking and I was sure Boomer would be proud, but there was gonna be one hell of an uproar over this. Shades of John Rocker, the baseball player who had ranted something about queers with AIDS a few years back. He'd caught hell for it.

I was relieved when it was finally game time and the reporters got shooed off the field. My relief was short-lived, however, as I remembered that the sooner the game started, the sooner it would end, and then I had to go see Sam and his boyfriend. My stomach felt sick every time I thought about it, but I had to do it. It was the only way Sam would even consider helping me.

Tonight, they had a former Miss Maryland singing the National Anthem. She wasn't horrible, but she clearly hadn't clinched the title with her voice. I stood there, cap over my heart, staring at her instead of the American flag. I was sure I wasn't the only one doing that, but my reaction to her was different than most.

Nothing. Just nothing. I stared at her tight ass, her huge, probably fake but still awesome boobs, sexy long hair. I sighed deeply. I hated being gay.

I had a flash of sheer panic as I realized that everyone was staring at me.

Dear God, I hadn't said "I hate being gay" out loud, had I?

After another few seconds of blind terror, I realized I had simply missed my cue.

"Let's play ball, hon!" I shouted. The crowd cheered and all was right again. For now.

I SAT STIFFLY on the bench in the dugout, sandwiched uncomfortably between my teammates as I awaited my turn at bat. I tried to relax, but I just couldn't. I was afraid to look at anybody.

"I think it might be Carlos," said Kyle, watching Carlos Montez as he took practice swings on the on-deck circle.

"I been thinking that, too!" Jackson said. "I always thought he had kind of an effeminate swing." I sat there debating whether or not I should agree with Kyle and Jackson or just keep my mouth shut and not draw attention to myself. Trouble was, I was *always* drawing attention to myself. I was notorious for it. Would my silence be more obvious?

"Then again, it could be Brady," Kyle said. My heart flipped a bit. I couldn't help it. Was it really possible that Hot

Rookie was gay? The idea appealed to me way more than I wanted to admit. I glanced at Brady, who was currently on first base. I couldn't help but think of all the bases I'd like to get to with him.

"Will you guys shut up? You sound like a bunch of schoolgirls. Who the hell cares who it is?" Tuna said.

"Exactly. I don't give a shit. If he's a good ballplayer, what he does on his own time is his own damn business," Sid said. I was grateful that at least a few of the guys didn't care if I...I mean, if one of the players was gay. "If there is a gay dude, then he's been here all along and it never hurt nothin' before, so who cares?"

"You should care," Kyle said. "You should all care." He glared at us. He was an intense guy anyway, but when he got pissed off, it was even worse. When he struck out, we knew not to even make eye contact with him. "That reporter's been going around questioning everybody and *Around Town* is on a mission to figure out who the faggot is."

"So let 'em," Tuna said. "Might shut you up finally."

"Yeah, it would be great. If they get the right guy. What if they don't? That kind of rumor will dog your ass the rest of your career," Kyle said bitterly.

That hit home for all of us. He was right. All it would take was for one gay rumor to attach itself to you, and you'd be wearing it like a nametag for the rest of your life. Didn't matter if it was true or not. Or, in my case, if it was temporarily true. A rumor would make it permanent in the public eye. Suddenly, Kyle wasn't the only one interested in outing somebody. Now everybody wanted to know, just to make sure they were safe from the wretched accusation.

Fresh panic ignited in my stomach as I remembered my little field trip after the game tonight. I couldn't bear to think of what would happen if I was spotted anywhere near a couple of gay men. Any other time I might have been able to explain it, bullshit my way out of it somehow. But now? With all the scrutiny and suspicion with the guys, it would be an open and shut closet. Henry Vaughn, Jr. was seen with a bunch of queens. He's the fag, Your Honor. Case closed. His punishment is to lose his career, his father, and his friends. A lifetime sentence with no possibility of parole.

"I'd like to out the bastard right now for screwin' up my ballclub," Boomer said. He'd been listening to our conversation while trying to concentrate on the game at the same time. "Y'all need to focus, dammit. You let me worry about the faggot. You just do your job. I'll take care of him, whoever he is." He said "take care of him" like he meant it in the mafia sense. I swallowed hard.

The game was not going well. We were down 2-0 in the seventh inning.

Oh God. The seventh inning.

A new surge of fear welled up in my stomach as I heard the beginnings of "Y.M.C.A." My "signature song" the announcers called it, because I always got up and led the fans in doing the arm movements. Friggin' "Y.M.C.A." was my signature song. How did my teammates *not* think I was gay?

I couldn't do it. I ducked into the clubhouse before the cameras could find me. I felt bad. I really did. I knew the fans were waiting. Little kids were looking for me. The radio announcers were probably wondering aloud where I was. I don't know, maybe I was making it worse, more obvious by not doing it, but I just couldn't. Not now.

I came out of the clubhouse in time for "Take Me Out to the Ballgame." I hopped up on top of the dugout and looked around at the fans. I made a zipping motion at my crotch and shrugged my shoulders, indicating that I was in the bathroom and that was why I had missed the song. The crowd roared its approval and I saw a bunch of kids giggling. Hitting home runs was great and all, but I swear I enjoyed playing around with fans more. "Take Me Out to the Ball-game" started up and I stood up on the dugout and conducted with my hands. It always got people to sing, which was so much fun. I leaned down into the dugout to yell at the guys.

"Come on, fellas! Sing along!" Boomer Wilkens gave me his usual annoyed look, but it wasn't his real annoyed look. It was a face that meant he was keeping up his stern appear-ance, but he really didn't mind my antics. I was the most popular player on the Baltimore Orioles – maybe even in all of baseball right now – and it was because of goofy stuff like this. The fans ate it up. It made the Orioles a more popular team overall and sold tickets, so Boomer was totally cool with it. He'd just never admit it. Sometimes he would mutter under his breath about me being an "asshole" and to "quit all this monkeying around," but I knew for a fact he didn't mean it. If he really meant it, he'd have screamed his head off and threatened my life.

"I can't hear yoooooou!" I taunted the guys as they sat in the dugout. Kyle glanced at me with annoyance. Tuna shook his head and waved me off, but he was smiling.

"Come on, Tuna!" Sid said and he actually got up, grabbed Tuna, and pulled him toward the dugout. Sid put his arm around Tuna and they swayed back and forth, singing like a couple of drunken sailors.

Kyle shook his head again, but he was trying not to laugh. Brady watched, amused, from the sidelines. I think he wanted to join them, but as a rookie, he was still trying to fit in and didn't want to make waves just yet.

The jumbotron showed Sid and Tuna singing and the

crowd erupted in laughter. The guys only sang a line or two, just for fun, and then sat back down in the dugout. I finished the song with the fans, took my usual bow, and then swung back down into the dugout.

I think we all felt better after the seventh-inning stretch. I know I did. For those few moments I was up on the dugout, it was easy to forget all the crap that was going on in my life.

It didn't last long.

Julio Rodriguez hit a long fly ball to right field. I know I should have caught it. It should have been an easy out, but it wasn't. I don't know what happened. I got distracted somehow and misjudged it. I ran as hard as I could, but I just couldn't get there in time. Rodriguez made it all the way to second. A double on what should have been the third out.

Shit.

I had to concentrate on what the hell I was doing. My contract expired at the end of the season and being popular with the fans was not a good enough reason for Boomer and the Orioles to keep me around. I felt like such an idiot. Getting distracted while out in the field was for little leaguers, and even then, your teammates gave you shit about it. Which they should.

My error, and I was officially charged with one, was one of those mistakes that just spiraled into disaster. The score was 2-1 in the eighth inning, so we still had a shot until I screwed up. We should have gotten out of a tight spot in the eighth. There had been a runner on second when Rodriguez hit the pop fly, but he only got to third because he, like everyone else, assumed I would catch the damn ball. And what excuse did I have? *Sorry, boys. I'm just kinda off my game 'cause I gotta meet up with some gay lovers after work.*

It was an ugly, ugly loss. 6-1. Against the Yankees, no less.

Every game that they won and we lost sank us further down in the standings. If they swept us in this series, we'd be in third place before we knew it.

"Henry, you coming or what?" Kyle asked.

"You guys are going out?" I asked.

"Yeah. I don't feel like going home. I need some fresh pussy to cheer me up," Kyle said. "You comin'?" The idea that fresh pussy no longer held any appeal and the fact that I had to see Sam instead depressed me in equal parts.

"Nah, I got some other stuff to do," I said.

"It's nice to see that somebody other than Tuna has enough sense not to go out drinking and carousing like a bunch of idiot college kids," came a familiar, unpleasant voice. I felt so bad for Tuna. I really did. I hoped someday he'd divorce that shrew and he could have some fun for once. But I knew if they ever got divorced, she'd squeeze his balls and leave him with nothing but his baseball jersey.

"Oh yes, ma'am," I said. "I don't know what's wrong with these guys, acting like little boys instead of men. Me, why I'm gonna go right over to church choir practice instead of that evil old bar." Kyle and Sid stifled their laughter. I took a mock step back from Emily's icy glare and shivered. "Ooh, it's getting kinda cold in here." Tuna smirked at me, but quickly put his arm around his wife and led her out.

"Damn," said Sid. "I'm telling you, that guy made me think long and hard before I proposed to my wife. I mean, Cindy's nothing like that crazy bitch, but I was like, what if they all change after you get married? Like the ring's got some kind of power that turns them evil." Sid shook his head. "Poor guy. Glad my wife lets me go out and play. Come on, Henry. I'm sure you can miss choir practice just this once."

"Nah, I'm gonna head out," I said, hoping they would just

drop it. I never missed a chance to go to the bar to pick up adoring female fans. I hoped to God they weren't suspicious.

"Come on, what do you gotta do that's so important?" Kyle asked.

"Jane, that's what I gotta do. Remember that hottie from last week? She's waiting for me now. So I gots to go!" I said, grabbing my stuff. Kyle shook his head and laughed. He bought it.

Thank God.

7

I took a cab over to Sam's place because I didn't want my car to be seen anywhere near a gay dude's house. Everybody knew my bright red Corvette with the license plate MLB PLYA. I paid the driver, who fortunately didn't seem to recognize me, and walked up to Sam's townhouse.

For the millionth time, I considered backing out and just going home. I sighed heavily and knocked on the door. If I just did what Sam wanted me to do, he'd have to research the pill, and he'd realize he was wrong. He'd figure out there was something in the drug and then he'd be forced to grovel and apologize. Yeah. It would be worth this field trip to get to see that.

The door opened and there stood a guy who was nearly as big as me. Tall, kinda muscular. Kinda cute, I supposed. He was no Brady Clayton, though.

He stood there for a moment, squinting. People looked at me like that all the time. He was trying to figure out where he knew me from. I had tried to disguise myself the best I could. I wore long black pants and a long-sleeved black shirt that covered up my muscles, which would hope-fully keep Sam and Jeremy from checking me out too much. Not that Sam hadn't pretty much seen the goods already. Ugh. I also wore a stupid cowboy hat. I felt like an idiot, but what choice did I have? Most celebrities wore sunglasses and a baseball hat when they didn't want to be recognized. I couldn't wear sunglasses because it was nighttime, and a baseball cap wouldn't exactly conceal my identity, consid-ering what I did for a living.

I started to worry that I might have the wrong address, but then I saw Sam sitting at the kitchen table. He shot me his usual look of distaste.

"Hi, Henry," Sam said, sounding as happy to see me as I was to see him. Jeremy's eyes opened wide with sudden recognition. It had taken him a bit to figure out who I was because he was seeing me somewhere totally different from where he was used to seeing me. Instead of being on televi-sion in an Orioles uniform, I was standing on his own doorstep wearing street clothes.

"You're..." Jeremy began. He turned around and looked at Sam. "Sam, how the hell do you know Henry Vaughn, Jr.?"

Sam stood up, crossed his arms, and stared at me. He clearly wasn't going to answer the question.

"Uh, I-I'm a patient of his. For the asthma trial. At Hopkins?" I said.

Jeremy and I both looked at Sam. He shrugged. "Confi-dentiality. I can't reveal a patient's identity to anybody. But since you told him yourself..." Sam just stood there, arms still crossed. It was clear he still couldn't stand the sight of me. It was a big mistake to come here. I really didn't want to know what he had in mind for tonight.

Jeremy's eyes opened even wider. "You mean, he's the one who thinks he's-"

Sam nodded slowly, enjoying every second of this. Jeremy looked at me in amazement. It was awkward and embarrassing. I just stood there at the door.

"Oh, um. I'm sorry. I'm sorry!" Jeremy said finally. "Please, um, come in." He seemed really flustered all of a sudden. He was obviously a little star-struck. It was kind of cute. It was certainly a better reception than the one I'd gotten when I first met Sam. It was funny. Jeremy was acting just like some of my female fans. Kinda shy and nervous about talking to me. I don't think it had ever occurred to me that I might have gay fans.

Sam's townhouse wasn't much to look at outside, but inside it wasn't bad at all. Nowhere near as neat and clean as I'd expected a gay guy's house to be. I had envisioned fresh vacuum cleaner lines on the carpet, fancy art on the walls, and the scent of flowers in the air. His house just looked like any other guy's place. Mail and other papers strewn on the table, a few clothes on the floor, and a trashcan overflowing a bit. Except for the medical magazines on the coffee table, it was kinda like my place. Of course, my place was a lot bigger.

Sam walked over to where Jeremy and I were standing in the living room and said, "Henry, this is Jeremy." I was about to shake his hand, but Sam grabbed Jeremy and kissed him passionately, obviously for my benefit. I'd more or less expected it, but it still annoyed me. I shook my head as I watched him make out with Jeremy for a few seconds. I didn't find it erotic in any way, mainly because I despised Sam, but it didn't disgust me the way it would have just a few days ago. Jeremy gently but firmly pushed Sam away.

"Come on now, be nice," Jeremy said and looked at me apologetically. I tried to hide my irritation so as not to give Sam the satisfaction, but he still smirked at me.

"You want a beer?" Jeremy asked.

"I'd love one." Yes. Alcohol would be very helpful right about now. Jeremy walked through the swinging door to the kitchen and came back quickly with three beers. Meanwhile, Sam flopped down on the couch in the living room. I sat in a chair as far away from him as I could.

I gratefully accepted the beer from Jeremy, who then sat on the couch next to Sam. Sam put his arm around Jeremy, but this time I think he did it out of genuine affection for the guy and not just to annoy me. I had to admit they made a cute couple. It was kind of sweet the way they looked at each other. They were obviously very much in love.

"Look, Sam told me about your, um...situation. I mean, I didn't realize it was you until now, but... I just want you to know that it's not the first time I've heard about something like this happening." I raised an eyebrow at him. "Well, not the whole drug thing. I admit that's kind of a first. I just mean, I've known a lot of guys over the years who were, shall we say, a bit confused."

"I'm not confused!" I said, a little more forcefully than I'd intended. After all, the dude was just trying to help.

"Don't you dare yell at him!" Sam said. He sat up in front of Jeremy like the hero in a movie stands in front of the girl to protect her.

"I'm sorry. I didn't mean anything by it," I said.

"Yeah, well, just watch it, Nancy," Sam muttered.

"Dude, could you just cool it with the girl names already? This whole thing is hard enough as it is."

"I know! See that's what makes it funny, Mary Lou."

Jeremy punched him on the shoulder. I hoped it hurt. "I'm just saying that sexuality is a complicated thing. It's not as clear cut as you might think," he said.

"I know my sexuality. Believe me. And I don't swing that way," I said irritably.

"Don't swing much at all, lately," Jeremy muttered. He shook his head and took a sip of his beer. I felt bad. He was trying to be on my side, but I was losing him.

"Why do you have to say it like that? Like being gay is such a horrible, awful thing? You act like you're all hot shit and you think gay guys are beneath you," Sam said angrily.

"He should be so lucky," Jeremy said under his breath. That got a smile out of Sam and I felt like they were both ganging up on me.

"Look," I said wearily. "I really don't know what you want me to say here. All I know is the truth. I've been straight my entire life. I've banged dozens of women and I don't ever, ever remember being attracted to a man before I took that pill." I looked at Jeremy, hoping maybe I could convince him, as I'd pretty much given up on Sam. "I took the pill. I went to bed that night and had wild, animal sex with a woman. The very next day, I went to work, saw Brady Clayton naked in the clubhouse, and got a—" I thought I could say it out loud. I really did. I figured if I confessed the most horrible, awful, humiliating moment of my life, then Jeremy would understand that I was not making this up. "A-a-"

Jeremy held up his hand to save me from myself. "Stiffy," he said for me. I nodded with relief. He leaned back in his chair and said dreamily, "Man, that Brady is *hot.*" Sam narrowed his eyes at Jeremy, which was bullshit because Sam had said the same thing about Hot Rookie just the other day. Then Jeremy looked at me and I did see some sympathy in his eyes. Maybe I could convince him.

"Dude, I work with that guy every day," I told him. "I've seen him, and all the other guys, naked a hundred times. And never..." I just threw up my hands in frustration.

Jeremy looked over at Sam. "I gotta admit that does seem rather strange."

Sam just rolled his eyes. He'd heard my whole song and dance before and he still wasn't buying it, but Jeremy? He was on the fence. And Sam loved Jeremy, so maybe I still had a shot.

"Come on," Jeremy said. "Tell him the real reason you brought him here." I hated to think what further torture Sam had in mind for me. My eyes opened wide and Jeremy laughed softly at my worried expression.

"All right, all right. Look, Betsy. I want you to meet my friend, Thomas. If anyone can help you with your little problem, it's him. He's like the patron saint of closet queens," Sam said.

"I'm *not* a closet..." I just couldn't say queen. Not when I was referring to myself. "I'm not in the closet."

"Hen, I mean, Lillian..." Sam began. I drank a big swig of my beer to quell the urge to deck him. "What happened to keeping an open mind? That you would consider the fact that you might really be gay? That is the main reason you're here, isn't it?"

"Yes, Sam," I said, gritting my teeth. "I'm here because I am so incredibly open to the fact that I just might really be gay." Sam smiled his smug smile. I shotgunned the rest of my beer.

"So where is this guy?" I said, looking toward the door.

"Not here. We have to go meet him at work."

And that's how I found myself in the backseat of Sam's ratty old Ford, going God knows where to meet God knows who. We ended up in some back alley in downtown Baltimore. It was kinda scary, but then, most of downtown Baltimore is at night. I hate to say it, but the depictions of Baltimore on TV shows like *Homicide* and *The Wire* are fairly accurate. Sam parked his car and he and Jeremy got out.

"Where the hell are we?" I asked as I climbed out of the backseat. I found it highly disturbing that neither one of them answered my question.

We went to the back door of some building and Sam opened it with a key. He led me up a dark, windy staircase like something out of a horror movie. When we got to the top, Sam turned around and grinned at me. Not quite an evil horror movie grin, but it was close. I really, really didn't want to know what was in there.

Sam opened the door to reveal some kind of backstage area with lots of makeup tables and mirrors. There was a lot of activity going on and there were a number of men in various stages of undress. Those that were dressed, were dressed in, well, *dresses.* People were scurrying around, grabbing at wigs, and borrowing each other's clothes. The smell of makeup and hairspray was strong.

The last thing I wanted was for Sam to know he'd gotten a rise out of me, but I couldn't help but stare in horror at what I was seeing. Seriously, what the *hell?*

"Hey Adam, where's Thomas?" Sam asked a guy wearing makeup but no wig. Somehow, he looked creepy and friendly at the same time.

"I don't know. He was here a minute ago," Adam said as he looked in the mirror, applying his lipstick. *His* lipstick. Too weird.

"Thomas! Tom! Where the hell are ya?" Sam yelled as he looked around for his friend. I looked around at all the activity going on. So many conflicting emotions tumbled around inside me. I had been extremely attracted to women, then suddenly I had become attracted to men, and now here I was surrounded by men dressed as women. It was almost more than I could handle. There was one guy over in the corner who was fairly ripped. He had muscle tone similar to the athletes I knew. And yet he was wearing a skirt and putting on a wig. It was confusing. It was like my body didn't know how to react. It was kind of a weird, unsettled feeling. Kind of like when you're a preteen and you first start having feelings for the opposite sex. It's pleasant and exciting and confusing all at once. An experience we all go through. So why did I have to go through it twice?

I tried to look around at everybody while keeping my head down and the cowboy hat over my eyes so I wouldn't be recognized. This place was nuts. I was about to grab Sam and demand that he tell me where I was and what was going on when I suddenly saw it. There it was, up on the wall, mocking me.

A shiny mirror in the shape of a hippopotamus.

Oh, sweet mother of fuck, I was standing in the middle of Club Hippo.

"Welcome to hell," Sam whispered. I would have punched him right then and there, but I was just too stunned to move.

A flamboyant guy who made Liberace look like John Wayne came floating by. He was dressed as Liza Minnelli and he looked pretty convincing. He put an arm around Sam's shoulder and kissed him on the cheek.

"Hi, sweetie," said Drag Queen Liza.

"This is Ben Harford. Ben, this is Henry." Ben extended his hand rather daintily toward mine and, for a horrible moment, I wasn't sure whether to shake it or kiss it. I decided to shake it. Rather forcefully. Ben winced a bit, but smiled. I was overcompensating, trying to show off my force, and I think he knew it. He was gracious enough not to call me on it like Sam would have. Ben stood back and looked me up and down.

"That's a nice back porch ya got," Ben said. Whatever the hell that meant. I wasn't sure I wanted to know. Sam startled cackling.

"Oh, he doesn't speak shebonics," Sam said. Then slowly and deliberately, like he was speaking to a foreigner, he said, "He said you have a *nice ass*." I groaned inwardly.

"There's Thomas. Over there," Jeremy said, gesturing to a guy across the room. In a wig. Of course.

"Thomas! Get over here, would you?" Sam shouted. Thomas obliged, bounding over toward us like an eager puppy.

Wow. The first thing I noticed was that Thomas had the most beautiful eyes I'd ever seen on a man. It wasn't just the color, though they were an absolutely gorgeous shade of light blue; it was the fact that they were so warm and friendly. I found myself at ease around him before he even spoke a word.

"Henry, this is Thomas Palmer," Sam said. I went to shake his hand and Thomas quickly pulled off his wig and tossed it on a table. He grasped my hand in both of his and looked me in the eye. My heartbeat quickened. He was very handsome.

"Very nice to meet you, Henry. I'm so glad you came here tonight." His voice was gentle and sweet. His eyes were filled with concern, which I found very touching since we'd only just met. I understood what Sam had meant when he said Thomas was the patron saint of gays in the closet. He could see the fear in my eyes and he didn't think it was amusing like Sam did. I must have looked completely overwhelmed, because Thomas looked around the room and then back at me. "Maybe this wasn't the greatest place to bring him, Sam."

Sam shrugged. Thomas seemed to genuinely care that I was upset, and I was grateful for his kindness. I swear, I looked into his eyes and suddenly I felt like everything was going to be okay. For the first time since I took the pill, I wasn't afraid. If only for a moment.

Also, did I mention how handsome he was?

He wasn't smoking hot like Brady, but he was very cute. It occurred to me that he was the type of guy who girls would call "sensitive," but in a good way, not in a wussy way. The soft yet strong type. It was kind of fascinating. My foray into gay life was giving me invaluable insight into what women wanted. I could see now, if only temporarily, what girls saw in us. This was gold. I'd have to remember this for the next time I went to pick up a chick.

"So, Sam tells me you're having kind of a rough time lately. You know, trying to figure things out," Thomas said gently. "I know it can be really confusing sometimes."

My usual response to that was to bitch and moan about how I wasn't really gay, but Thomas seemed so nice and understanding that I didn't feel defensive around him.

"Yeah. It's confusing to say the least. I know nobody believes me, but I'm really not gay. It really is just the pill I took," I told him.

"Pill? What pill?" Thomas asked, first looking at me, then at Sam.

"You didn't tell him?" I asked Sam.

"Of course not. I told you, I can't reveal anything medical. All I told him was that I met a *minor* celebrity who was confused about his sexuality. And that you were kind of an asshole."

"Sam," Thomas said firmly and shot him a warning look. I was really starting to like this guy. "What pill did you take?"

I sighed wearily. Thomas seemed really sweet and I knew he wouldn't make fun of me, but I also knew he wasn't going to believe me. I understood, though. I wouldn't have believed me, either.

"I'm straight. Like, honestly straight. Was never attracted to men ever in my life. Then I took part in a clinical drug trial at Hopkins..." I still didn't want to admit that I had asthma, especially to a cute guy, but that was really the least of my problems, "...to treat my asthma. I took the pill they gave me, and ever since I've been attracted to men."

Sam rolled his eyes. Thomas nodded thoughtfully and said, "I see."

"It's okay if you don't believe me. I wouldn't," I told him.

"This all must be really hard on you," Thomas said and I think he really meant it. It was wonderful. I knew I had been kind of an asshole with Sam, but I really was going through an awful lot. It wasn't like I could talk to my friends or my dad about what was going on, and the only people in the world who knew about this, until now, were Sam and Jeremy. They weren't exactly my biggest fans. It felt so good to have somebody on my side.

"Thomas, shake a leg already!" somebody called out.

"Yeah. I gotta get ready to go on. Look, Henry," I was surprised at how my heart flipped a bit when he said my name. "I'd love it if you'd stay for the show, but I understand if you're not comfortable with it. The drag scene's not for everybody, even if you are gay. Even Sam's not really into it; he just comes because we're good friends." Thomas smiled at Sam, who actually smiled warmly back. They were obviously very close.

"So who are you tonight?" Sam asked.

"Oh, I'm not headlining," Thomas said. "Just one of the showgirls this time." I winced and instantly regretted it. I hoped Thomas didn't notice, because I really didn't want to offend him. It's just that he was so *cute*. I hated the idea of him in a dress. I wanted him to stay the way he was. Handsome and sweet and *male*.

Did I really just think that? I seemed to be sinking lower and lower into this...I don't know...alternative lifestyle. I must have shown my confusion and stress because Thomas had that concerned look for me again. "Maybe you should take him home, Sam. This really is a bit much."

"What?" Sam said, wearing an innocent look that fooled no one. "I figured he might as well jump right in. You know, like in a pool." He made a diving motion with his hands. "It's harder to get into icy cold water one toe at a time." Sam punched me in the shoulder. "Just dive right in and join the fun, Alexandra!"

"Knock it off, Sam," Thomas said sternly. He looked back at me with those big, warm blue eyes and my legs turned to Jell-O.

Oh, God. I was totally crushing on Sam's friend. How did mean old Sam get a sweetheart like Thomas for a friend anyway?

"Everything will be okay, Henry. I promise. We'll sort out whatever's going on with you." I couldn't believe how utterly sympathetic Thomas was to my plight. I knew he thought I was just deeply in denial and he didn't believe for a second that some drug had turned me gay, but he didn't judge me. He knew I was in pain and that was all he needed to know to want to help.

I couldn't take my eyes off him, but it was partly because he was half dressed as a woman. It was just really weird.

Thomas looked down at his clothes and smiled, not taking offense.

"This isn't my real job. I'm actually a radiographer. You know, x-ray technician. I just do this for fun and for a couple extra bucks."

I nodded, relieved to hear his rational explanation. He really was adorable. With Brady, I'd mostly just been hot for his body. Thomas was different. He was so handsome and kind and easy to talk to that I found I liked the whole package. I don't ever remember feeling that way about a woman.

That thought scared me. A lot.

"Come along, ladies! Only fifteen minutes until show-time and I see more hot dogs than hot chicks! Now get dressed!" came the high-pitched squeal of an incredibly gay man. I mean, they were all gay here, but *damn*. I had to admit, I had expected all gay people to be like this guy. Just screamingly, flamingly queer, but so far this guy and Liza Minnelli were really the only ones who were like the gays you see on TV. I didn't know Sam was gay at first and I doubt I'd have known Jeremy was if I didn't already know he was Sam's boyfriend. I'd never have guessed Thomas was gay; at least once he had removed the wig and the dress. But this guy? You could tell he was gay from space. Thomas laughed as the queen brushed past us in a rainbow blur, but then seemed to consider my feelings.

"I know it's kinda crazy around here," Thomas said, looking around again at all the activity in the room and probably seeing it from my perspective. "It's okay if you don't want to stay." Thomas put a gentle hand on my arm. I was surprised, even pleased by his touch, but I tensed up. I couldn't help it; it was a reflex. Thomas dropped his hand immediately. I felt terrible, but he smiled warmly. He understood my discomfort and I was so, so grateful that somebody finally did.

"No, it's okay. I'd like to stay. Only, I'm not sure if it's safe. I really can't be seen in a place like this. See, I'm a-"

"Oh, of course! You're right. That's all you need is to be seen at Club Hippo," Thomas said, shaking his head and laughing at himself. "Especially with all the media circus surrounding the team."

I looked at him in astonishment. Thomas hadn't given any indication that he knew who I was and I knew Sam didn't tell him. He had recognized me and never even blinked. Was it possible that he was a baseball fan? I was honored that he'd recognized me, but then I remembered today's game and hoped he hadn't seen it.

"Rough game today," Thomas said softly.

Shit.

"You'll get the Yanks tomorrow. I know it! And look, if you do want to stay, there's a dark corner table in the back. Nobody'd ever see you down there."

I guessed it would be rude to make Sam and Jeremy take me home instead of staying to watch their friend.

Bullshit.

Thomas had looked me in the eye and said he would love it if I stayed. That's why I stayed, though I hated to admit it to myself.

Thomas led Sam, Jeremy, and me down to the club area. I couldn't resist checking out his "back porch" while he was walking down the stairs in front of us. Yeah. Even his ass was adorable.

I kept my head down while we walked through the bar area and soon we were safely in the dark of the club.

"I gotta get back up there," Thomas said. He shot me a

concerned look. "You okay? Are you sure you're, you know, comfortable with this?"

I nodded, even though I was extremely uncomfortable being in a gay club preparing to watch a drag show. I was really curious to see Thomas perform, though, and I hoped I would get to see him again after the show.

Thomas went to touch my hand, then thought the better of it. He probably thought I would flinch again. I wouldn't have. "See you guys after the show!" He did tap my hand once as he got up to go. I watched him walk back up the stairs. I couldn't help it. He was gorgeous. After Thomas disappeared up the stairs, I turned back around to see Sam and Jeremy staring at me. I guess they saw me watching Thomas.

"Um, he seems nice," I said.

Sam stared at me accusingly. I don't think he liked the way I was looking at his friend. He did seem to have some measure of sympathy, though, because he asked, "You all right there, Christina?"

"What do you care?" I don't know why I answered when he called me girl names, but I always did. I looked around at the club, tables full of happy same-sex couples, friends, and there was even a group of bachelorette party girls. Funny how straight girls can go to a gay club and nobody thinks twice. If a guy goes to one, then he has to be gay. Either that or there's something seriously wrong with him. The fear began to well up in me again that I might be spotted here.

A waiter walked nearby and Sam flagged him down.

"Uh, hi. Yeah, can we get a couple of Heinekens and..." Sam pointed to me to give my order.

I dropped my head down and said, from underneath my hat, "I'll take a shot of Peach Schnapps and whatever's good on draught."

"Peach Schnapps?" the waiter asked. Figured. Even in a gay bar, my drink order was weird.

"Yes, Peach Schnapps. Make it three shots. Thanks." The waiter walked away and I looked up. "Just try it. You might like it."

Sam shrugged. I rubbed my temples wearily. I hoped the drinks would get here soon. The stress was really starting to get to me.

"You okay?" Jeremy asked.

"No. Not really. But there's nothing I can do," I said.

"Yeah, yeah. Your life is so terrible," Sam said.

"It is, dammit. Right now, it is. You know, you don't have a clue what I'm going through. Maybe nobody gives a shit if you're gay at the hospital, but where I work it's a huge deal! At least Thomas seems to sympathize with me."

"That's why I brought you here, Henry," Sam said softly. He actually sounded a bit sorry for me for once. "I'm no good with these kinds of things, but I knew Thomas would take good care of you. He knows what to say. What to do. I don't."

"You promised you would research the pill, Sam. You promised. That's what you're supposed to do. I never said you had to believe me about the drug, but a deal's a deal."

He nodded. "I know, I know."

"What if there's no cure? I can't hide this *condition* forever. I kinda have a reputation, you know, with the ladies. People are gonna notice if I stop picking up girls."

"Just pick up a chick in front of your friends and then pay her to go home. Kinda like reverse prostitution," Sam said.

"I can't do that! What if she talked to the tabloids? Seriously, what am I gonna do? I go out with the guys a few times a week and we get girls."

"Gross. You're a slut, Amy."

"I am not. Girls are sluts. I'm a stud. It's not fair, but it works for me."

"Well, if all else fails, bring home a girl, close your eyes, and think of Matthew McCona-hottie."

"I'm not gonna...." Sam had a point. Matthew McConaughey was kinda hot. That would almost work. The idea of hot, male movie stars was a foreign concept to me. Before, I had been all about Megan Fox, Cameron Diaz, and Halle Barry. They had occupied my thoughts during many a shower in the past. I thought about who was hot. Brad Pitt? No, not really. Harrison Ford? Nah, too old. Channing Tatum? Oh, yeah. He was more my type.

My type. Oh, God. I had a type now? I actually groaned aloud. "No way. I can't do that."

The waiter arrived with the drinks. Sam sipped his shot of Schnapps hesitantly.

"Ugh, it's awfully sweet!"

"I know. It's deeeelicious!" I said. "Come on now, drink it down. You too, Jeremy." I handed Jeremy a shot. He also grimaced at the sweetness, but he chugged it all. The lights started to go down and a spotlight hit the stage. Dread settled in my stomach as I remembered what we had been waiting to see. I didn't think I was ready for this. I knew I wasn't ready for this. There were a lot of things in life that I wanted to see before I died, but a bunch of men dressed up as women prancing around the stage was not one of them. I guessed it was too late to change my mind now.

"Ladies and ladies, gentlemen and gentlemen, please welcome to the stage, Miss Gay Maryland, Teri Pearson!"

A black guy strutted onto the stage wearing a bikini and a Miss Gay Maryland sash. The crowd cheered. I just groaned. I'd had a lot of *how in the hell did I end up here* moments since I first turned queer, but this one had to be the worst. I thought of my teammates. I couldn't imagine what they would do if they knew I was here. My life as a girl-crazy, sexy, star athlete seemed a million miles away as I watched this guy in a bikini stand on the stage lip-syncing to some Whitney Houston song.

There was one thing I found baffling and fascinating at the same time. This guy in a bikini; you would swear he was a woman. At least from the neck down. I mean, *wow*. I suddenly had new sympathy for people like Eddie Murphy who ended up with a dude and didn't realize it. I couldn't help but be transfixed by the performer's crotch. It was like some magician's trick.

"Good God, where does he put it?" I asked.

"Special underwear and tuck, tuck, tuck, my friend," Sam answered. I shook my head in disbelief. It really was something to see. That was almost worth the price of admission right there. Miss Teri Whatever began walking around as she "sang." There were lots of people giving her dollar bills, but they didn't stuff them anywhere like strippers did. Thank God. I tensed up as Teri came near us. I was quite happy hiding out in the dark, thank you. For once, I didn't need any attention drawn to me. Jeremy took out a dollar bill and held it up and Teri wandered over to where we were. I held my breath, praying that the spotlight that followed the performer around wouldn't land on me. Teri wandered safely off after briefly visiting with Jeremy, in search of more dollar bills. I noticed that she/he was sure to look each person in the eyes and "sing" a few notes to them as she took their money. It was kind of sweet in an insane sort of way. That seemed the best way to sum up this whole trip to gay fairyland. Sweet, yet insane.

Teri/Whitney Houston finished her song and exited the

stage. One down, who knew how many to go. I heard the familiar strains of the song "Copacabana" start to play. Before I knew it, the stage was loaded with showgirls in skimpy outfits with elaborate feathers like you would see in Las Vegas. One of the showgirls looked awfully familiar.

It was Thomas.

My heart beat a little faster when I saw him. I shook my head as I watched him dance with the others. He had been so handsome just a few moments before and now there he was, dressed up like a woman. I had a hard time understanding why people were into this kind of thing. If you were gay, didn't that mean you were attracted to men dressed like men? If you wanted someone dressed as a woman, why not just go for the real thing? And if you were a lesbian, why would you be attracted to lesbians who looked so butch and dressed in men's clothing? So many things about being gay that I didn't understand. I didn't want to understand.

I couldn't help but focus on Thomas. Okay, so he was dressed like a girl. But on the plus side, the outfits were pretty revealing. I was pleased to see that he didn't really look like a woman, no matter how he was dressed. Even Eddie Murphy would have known the difference. You could really see Thomas' muscles and his chest, while covered in a bikini-like top, still looked male. I refused to look at his crotch. If he looked like a woman down there, I didn't want to know about it. I wondered what he would look like shirtless in a good old-fashioned pair of jeans.

I suddenly broke into a cold sweat. *What was I doing?* It scared the hell out of me to see how easily I could just slip into fantasizing about men. First Brady, now Thomas. It almost seemed natural to me and that was the last thing I wanted. It wasn't natural. At least not for me.

I glanced up to find Jeremy and Sam staring at me. I realized I was drenched in sweat and breathing heavily. Sam actually looked worried.

"You breathing okay?" he asked. "Did you bring your inhaler with you?" I nodded. I knew my symptoms were panic-related and not asthma, but I figured it couldn't hurt. Say what you will about the people in this bar, I bet not one of them would judge me or think I was less of a man for using an inhaler. There was a sense of freedom in that as I whipped out my inhaler and took a nice deep hit, right there in plain sight. It didn't help much.

The next performer stepped out on stage. I really didn't think I could take much more of this. Thomas was right. It was too much. This whole thing was just too, too much.

I sighed wearily as I prepared to endure another gender-bending performance. I recognized this guy. It was Ben, the one who had told me I had a nice back porch. I couldn't help but feel flattered by that. Ben stepped out on stage, ready to do his best Liza Minnelli impression. The crowd went crazy over him. He sang, or "synced" "New York, New York." You couldn't go wrong with that one, I supposed. I had to give Ben credit. He was an incredible performer. He was working with a live concert version of the song and his lips matched every giggle, every little sound that Liza had made on the recording. I mean, he knew it cold. The song started out slowly, then built to a great crescendo.

It was mesmerizing. It truly was. I just couldn't believe the crowd's reaction. They were really getting into it. Clapping, cheering, some of them lip syncing along. I couldn't help but feel a little jealous of him. Ever the attention whore. But honestly, it was more than that. I just always thought it would be kind of cool to perform: to sing and maybe even dance a little. Ha! I should tell that to Sam. He'd be more convinced than ever that I was a closet queen. Uh, yeah, Henry? The whole *I secretly want to sing and dance* thing? Yeah, that's number one on the *you might be gay if...* list. Straight guys don't exactly sit around fantasizing about performing on Broadway. Not that I did.

Okay, I did. A lot. Always had.

And I'd never, ever told a living soul about that. I'd always thought about what it would feel like to be onstage somewhere, singing my heart out. I have a pretty good voice. At least, I think I do. It's not like I ever sang in front of anybody, unless you count "Y.M.C.A." My secret fantasies about doing theater really scared me. What if that did mean I was gay? I mean, I know that alone didn't prove it, but considering what was going on in my life, it couldn't be a good sign. No. I was reading too much into it. But what if I wasn't? I felt the panic start to well up inside me again. I'd never tell Sam or even Thomas, but I was absolutely petrified that maybe I had been gay all along.

I hated Sam for forcing me to come here. This was exactly what he wanted. To make me start believing that I might actually be gay. Well, mission accomplished. Jeremy and Sam were both waving dollar bills in the air, trying to get Ben/Liza Minnelli to come over to our table. She/he started coming over to us right as a new grip of terror seized my throat. The fear that I might really be gay and the horror that my life as I knew it would be over if anyone found out began to completely overwhelm me.

Then the spotlight hit me.

I was completely bathed in light, thanks to the glow that followed Liza Minnelli. If anybody in that place watched baseball or even the news, then my life was over.

I jumped up and ran out of there and vowed never, ever to go near that place again.

8

I barely slept at all, worrying that someone had seen me at Club Hippo last night. I literally shook when I turned on the news and scanned the internet for headlines with my name. So far, nothing.

My relief was short-lived, however, as things were more intense than ever at the clubhouse. Kyle was in a worse state of pissed off than I'd ever seen him, which was saying a lot. As I'd predicted, he'd gotten a lot of flak for his comments about gays. Bad enough that he'd made it clear that he was unhappy about a gay guy on the team, but he had used the word *fag*. Now he had GLAAD and all these gay groups up his ass for an apology. Oh man, was he mad as hell when he heard about that.

"Hell no!" Kyle screamed when Tuna made the mistake of telling him what he had heard on the news. "I ain't apologizing to no faggots! They don't belong in sports anyway. They belong prancing around onstage or doing fashion designer stuff or whatever it is they do." I tensed up at his mention of gays and the theater.

"Kyle's right. Gays belong on Broadway or at the ballet,

not on a professional sports team," Tuna agreed. I was shocked. I hadn't expected that attitude from Tuna, who rarely had a bad word to say about anybody. "Let them take their pansy-asses back to San Francisco where they can wear dresses all day if they want to. Now I'm going home to my *heterosexual* wife who better be wearing pearls and have dinner on the table waiting for me. No woman of mine is gonna work for a living! And whose idea was it to let women vote? And who says it's okay for Negroes to drink out of the same water fountain that I use for my lily white lips?" Sid and I laughed uproariously. Not only were Tuna's words ridiculous, but his impression of Kyle was spot-on.

"Anything else?" Kyle said, glaring at Tuna.

"Spicks are only good for landscaping and washing dishes." He paused, then added, "And children should be seen and not heard. Okay, I'm done."

"You think this is all just a big joke, don't you?"

Tuna nodded. "Well it's pretty damn funny that you're gonna have to write 'I will be nice to gay people' 500 times as penance." Kyle suddenly grabbed Tuna by the collar. Sid and I both charged forward and pulled Kyle off him. Tuna straightened out his shirt. "Calm down, boys," Tuna said, then lisped, "Oh, yeah. Everybody wants a taste of Tuna." Sid and I laughed at that, but Kyle lunged for Tuna again. I managed to hold him back, but barely.

"I'll kill you, you fucking faggot!"

"Dude, chill out already!" I said. "You're making way too much of this whole thing."

"Oh I am, am I?" Kyle said, fixing his angry glare on me. "We're the laughingstock of the whole sport, you know that? You want to be known as the gayest team in major league baseball? You've heard those other guys talking. Everywhere we go, people are talking about us having a queen on the team."

"Queen on the team. Sounds like a movie title," I said.

"Yeah? I think it's you. You're the one always dancing around, making a fool of yourself," he said, cutting through the heart of my deepest, darkest fear about myself. That my secret love of performing, coupled with my recent, uncontrollable attraction to men had nothing to do with the pill. Good thing I loved performing, because that's exactly what I was doing. My act of hiding my crippling fear of being found out was Oscar-worthy. I rolled my eyes and laughed.

"Oh, yeah, Kyle. It's definitely me. I always thought you and me," I said, winking at him, "had something kind of special." I sidled up to him while the guys cracked up. My gut reaction had been to scream and yell and deny that I was gay, but that was "protesting too much." When you joked around, you showed confidence even if you really had none.

"Yeah, Henry, I always knew it had to be you," said Sid, shaking his head and chuckling. Tuna was laughing, too. It was like the very idea that I, Henry Vaughn, Jr., the athlete who probably held the league record for most women in his bed in a single season, could be the gay guy was the most preposterous thing they'd ever heard. It was awesome. Even Kyle cracked a smile, as if he understood how stupid he was being.

"What the hell is so funny?" Boomer Wilkens roared as he charged into the clubhouse. "You guys stay outta here," he yelled just before slamming the clubhouse door on the reporters who were trying to come in to grill us about yet another loss. Boomer turned to look at us with even more than his usual fury. Uh-oh. Dad was home and we were all in trouble. "You know what's funny? You know what's a joke?" he yelled as he paced up and down the room like an army drill sergeant. "That performance out there, that's what. That was a joke. And you guys think it's funny, don't you? Don't you? You guys are a complete disgrace out there. We're in third place now. Third! The fans are starting to turn on you, ya know that? They're having flashbacks of all the years the Orioles sucked and they can see us sinking back into that hole again. What the hell do you guys have to say for yourselves?"

Silence. Crickets. Boomer stared at us and we knew the question was not rhetorical. He expected answers and, truthfully, he deserved some. I was usually the most outspoken member of the team, so I'd figured I better step up. I was about to speak, but Jackson Peters beat me to it.

"You're right, Boomer. I don't know what else to say except that you're right," Jackson said.

"You're damn right, I'm right!" Boomer screamed louder than I had ever, ever heard him yell. Hoo-kay, I was glad I hadn't spoken up. "There is no excuse for this bullshit. None! And I know what the problem is. We all know it. There's no reporters and no queer hugger gay rights groups here, so let's just call a fag a fag, okay? And we got one somewhere in here and I want to know who the hell it is!"

"Finally!" Kyle said and Boomer whipped his head around so fast it made Kyle jump. Boomer fixed his menace on Kyle, so he had to start talking quick. "This guy, whoever he is, is screwin' up the whole team. The sooner we figure out who it is, we can stop being paranoid and accusing each other. Look, we all know there's been a sort of an unspoken Don't Ask, Don't Tell policy in baseball. If you're gay, shut up. Nobody wants to know about it. I know I don't. I don't even want to think about it!" I saw Jackson and Carlos nodding their heads, grimacing. I looked from

Kyle to Jackson to Carlos. Their looks of disgust were so ugly.

I guess I used to look like that.

That used to be exactly how I felt. I hadn't wanted to know about gay stuff either. Now I thought about it all the time because I had no choice. I wondered again if maybe this was some punishment from God to teach me a lesson. Sort of like *A Christmas Carol*. Instead of ghosts, I got fairies.

"But look, we didn't ask, but somebody told," Kyle said, continuing his rant. "Somebody leaked something to the reporters and now we know there's a gay guy on the team. Too late to go back now; it's out there. So we need to know who it is so we can figure out what the hell to do, because this whole thing is killin' us. It's just *killin'* us. Ain't you people sick of losing? 'Cause I sure as hell am!"

"Well?" Boomer said, eying each one of us suspiciously. "The only way we're ever gonna get back on track is if we figure out who it is, so fess up, dammit!" He walked down the line, continuing his drill sergeant routine. It was crazy. This whole thing was just nuts. It was like one of us had been caught cheating: corking his bat, shooting up steroids, or betting on baseball. They were acting like being gay was a horrible crime. I guess in professional sports, it was.

As I listened to Boomer berate us, I thought of Thomas. Kind, sweet, understanding Thomas. I found myself wishing I could talk to him. He would understand how terrifying all this was. Sam would understand, too. He just wouldn't care. But Thomas would be so comforting. Like a schoolgirl with a crush, I wondered if Thomas had thought about me at all since last night. I doubted it. Who was I kidding? He was kind to everyone. I was nothing special to him.

"Come on, dude. Seriously," Kyle said, looking around. "Just tell us already."

"We're gonna find out sooner or later. You know that," Boomer said.

"Oh yeah, I'm sure whoever it is will just speak right up now. What's he got to lose?" I said, my fear starting to give way to anger. "Oh, that's right. Everything!"

"Oh, shut up, Henry," Kyle said. "This is the only way to put all this bullshit behind us and you know it."

"And you know damn well that Boomer will get the guy kicked off the team for being a fag, no matter what his contract says. You know that, right?" I forced myself to use the word "fag" in order to keep up appearances. It was already hard to remember a time that I had used that word so casually. It damn near killed me now. Now, when I heard the word, all I could think of was Thomas. I felt actual pain in my chest just thinking of anybody calling him that. He was really sweet and didn't deserve that. I guess nobody really did. Kyle glared at me, but didn't say a word. He knew I was right. Boomer stood there, arms crossed, and didn't dispute my accusation that he'd kick the guy out. "So why in the hell would he speak up?"

"Henry's right," Kyle said. "Nobody's gonna cop to it. But that don't mean we're not gonna find out who it is." Kyle's menacing glare matched Boomer's.

The guys eventually gave up for the night, realizing nothing was going to be resolved. There wasn't going to be any confession, but that didn't mean they'd give up the witch hunt.

WE HAD a seven-day road trip ahead of us. I'd hoped that maybe getting away from the clubhouse would help, but we simply packed up all the tension and took it with us on the road. It was the most depressing bus ride I'd ever been on in my life. The trip from Baltimore to Philly wasn't exactly inspirational. I stared out the window at some of the most rundown neighborhoods I'd ever seen. I supposed I should have been grateful that I had it so much better than those people. As if a scenic bus tour through Skid Row wasn't enough, fights kept breaking out on the bus.

Now that we were all stuck in a big, metal box together, everybody was angry and tense. Sure, travel was always a bitch for us, but it was part of the job and we made the best of it. We'd joke around, rag on each other, sometimes even play cards to pass the time. A long bus ride could actually be fun with a bunch guys goofing around, acting like kids on their way to camp. Not anymore. Right now, the guys were obsessing over whether the man sitting next to him might be gay or worrying that they themselves might be accused. The prospect of being falsely outed was horrifying enough, but now we knew for sure the gay guy would be kicked off the team. What if one of the other guys did get outed and was kicked out? Could I just stand by and let that happen?

My cell phone started buzzing. I glanced down at it, expecting it to be my dad. It was a number I didn't recognize. I usually don't answer if I don't know the number, but I was eager for any distraction I could get.

"Hello?"

"Is this Henry Vaughn, Jr.?" It was an older guy, maybe my dad's age. The voice was unfamiliar.

"Uh, yes. Who is this?"

"It's Peter Angelos!" Oh God. What did the owner of the Orioles want with me? "What the hell is all this crap about there being some queen on the Orioles?"

"Wh-what did you say?"

"And who the hell cares anyway?" Mr. Angelos continued. "Don't we all experiment with stuff like that in college? I once banged four or five guys on the varsity football team. Does that make me *gay*?"

"Uh, sir, I don't-"

The guy laughed, suddenly sounding much younger.

"I'm just screwin' with ya, Henry. This is Thomas Palmer. From last night?"

I threw my head back and laughed heartily. He got me good. *Classic.* Totally something I would have done. Some of the guys looked up to see what was so funny, but they saw I was on the phone and just ignored me. Tuna was sitting right next to me, talking to Sid as they tossed a Nerf football back and forth. I was glad he was otherwise occupied so I could talk on the phone.

It took a few seconds for my heartbeat to slow down from the brief scare I'd had when I thought I was talking to Peter Angelos, but then it sped back up again when it registered that I was talking to Thomas.

"I hope you don't mind me calling you," Thomas said.

"No, no. Not at all. What's up?" I tried to sound casual, but my heart was still racing. I didn't want to get used to being gay, but I loved the rush I felt when I met Thomas last night and the way I felt now just hearing his voice.

"I just wanted to check to make sure you were okay. I feel awful about what happened last night," he said.

It took me a moment to remember what he was talking about, as the whole trip to the club had been a nightmare. Well, except for meeting him. I remembered I ended the night by scampering off like a frightened squirrel when Liza Minnelli had come too close to me. Shit. I hoped Thomas didn't think I was less of a man for running off like that, but then I remembered that he'd been the one in the showgirl outfit.

"Oh, you know. It's okay."

"Sam and Jeremy said nobody even looked up when you left. Nobody saw you there. I just wanted to tell you that because I'm sure you're worried about it."

"Thanks. I appreciate that. That does make me feel better." It amazed me how Thomas seemed to understand my position and didn't take offense at all at my having to hide all the gay stuff. Sam just got pissed about it, but Thomas appreciated what a dangerous position I was in.

"How's everything going with the team?"

I desperately wanted to tell him about all the ugliness that had been going on in the clubhouse. How Kyle and Boomer were hell bent on finding out who the gay player was. How terrified I was. Thomas was so kind and his voice was so soothing. I wanted more than anything to be with him, to have him look at me with those beautiful eyes of his. Those eyes that contained no anger, no judgment. Only kindness and concern.

"Not great. Things are pretty intense right now," I told him, lowering my voice and glancing around at the guys on the bus. Nobody was paying any attention to me, but I knew I still had to be careful.

"Oh, you can't talk now, can you? Where are you?"

"On the bus to Philly."

"Oh, man. I don't want to get you in trouble. I'll let you go."

"No! No, it's okay. I just can't, you know…"

"Talk about anything rainbow-colored. Gotcha," he said, laughing. "Look, maybe we can get together sometime when you get back. I know you must be going through a really tough time and I don't want you to go through it alone."

"Thanks, Thomas," I said quietly. I took the risk of using his name because I wanted to say it out loud. Shit, when had

I turned into a 13-year-old girl? Next, I'd be doodling his name in my notebook.

"Call me anytime, Henry. You should have my number on your cell." He laughed, and added, "You can save it on speed dial under the name Titty Tanya or something."

I laughed. That was actually a great idea.

"Thanks," I said. "I really appreciate this. I guess I really do need some support right now."

"I know. We'll talk soon." Thomas hung up and my heart did cartwheels inside my chest. I was excited that he had called me, but I knew I was making this out to be more than it was. He was known for being the protector of those struggling to come out of the closet. That's what he was doing with me. He thought I really was gay, so he was just trying to be nice to me like he was with everyone else. He just had a soft heart. He didn't feel anything special for me.

Did he?

"Who was that?" Tuna asked. Damn. I had nearly forgotten that he was sitting next to me. I hoped I hadn't said anything incriminating, but I was pretty sure I hadn't. I had been very aware that I was surrounded by a busload of gay haters the whole time I was on the phone.

"Oh, just my boyfriend. You know," I said. Tuna shook his head and laughed. Amazing. The more I joked about being the gay one, the less people suspected me. It gave me a little thrill to say out loud that Thomas was my boyfriend, which was incredibly stupid. I mean, sure, I thought he was cute and all, but it's not like I wanted to date the guy. Or any guy, for that matter. When the drug wore off in a few weeks, I'd be straight again and that would be that. At least, I hoped it would wear off.

❧

THE FIRST GAME in Philadelphia was a nightmare. The Phillies had sucked so far this year and they should have been easy to beat. Their team was on edge because they were dealing with an embarrassingly bad season so far; they were 25 games out of first place in their division. Our team was tense for all the obvious reasons, so when the two teams came together, it wasn't pretty. In the first inning, our guy had involuntarily hit the batter with a pitch. I mean, shit. Of course it was an accident. There were runners on first and second with one out. Why would he load the bases on purpose? Words were exchanged, and their guy plunked Sid in the next inning. Boomer had to hold us back from clearing the bench on that one. The umpire issued a warning, which meant the next idiot that tried anything like that would be ejected. Things calmed down until the eighth inning when Kyle was up to bat. Apparently, he was bitching under his breath about balls and strikes. We were in a tight spot; it was 8-7 Phillies and we needed to rally and quick. After a called strike three, Kyle threw down his bat in disgust. The Phillies catcher made some remark about Kyle being "a girl like the rest of the fairies on our team."

He picked the wrong guy to screw with. Kyle tackled him; I mean he took his ass *down*. You better believe that cleared the benches. We all rushed to support Kyle and the Phillies all rushed to their catcher's defense.

The fight made all the sport shows that night and we were all glad of it. We wanted the Orioles to be known as bad motherfuckers, not a bunch of queers.

The guys were all pumped up on testosterone by the end of the game. Which we lost. To the Phillies. Shit. Nobody wanted to go back to the hotel room so we decided to go out. I needed a drink desperately, but I was worried about going to a bar. The guys would be picking up girls and they would be suspicious if I didn't. Even some of the married guys took girls back to their hotels, which I think sucks balls. I was no angel, but I never lied to a girl to get her in bed and if I was married or had a girlfriend, I sure as shit wouldn't cheat. Sid was a newlywed and, so far, hadn't cheated and I hoped he never would. He was a good guy and his wife seemed nice. Of course, Tuna's wife was a raging bitch and he still didn't cheat on her.

I took a cab to the bar and couldn't resist calling Thomas on the way. I was nervous about calling and hoped I didn't seem too eager. My anxiety vanished when he picked up the phone and his first words to me were:

"Are you okay? I saw the game. Did you get hurt?" *No, but if I did you'd be the first one I'd want rubbing my owie.*

"No, I'm fine, really." I was glad that as long as I was safe in the cab, I could say whatever I wanted. The cabbie would just assume I was talking to my wife or girlfriend. He was Indian or Pakistani or whatever and probably didn't follow baseball anyway. I doubted he knew who I was.

"Man, you guys are really on edge. Sorry you lost. At least it was a close game."

"Thanks for watching." At least during this game, I'd looked manly and tough. Much better than my last game with my awful fielding error.

"Oh, I never miss a game. I'm a huge fan. I'm just so glad you're okay. That looked like a nasty fight."

"Yeah, I'm fine. It's really no big deal."

"How's everything else going?" he asked.

"Oh, you know. The same. And now I have to...well, some of the guys are going out for a drink. I'm not sure..." I lowered my voice. "I'm not sure what to do about, well, usually when we go out, we pick up girls..." I glanced at the cabbie, but he was fiddling with the radio and wasn't paying any attention to my conversation. "I'm kinda nervous about going out with the guys tonight. We're just going out for a few drinks, but you know, it's hard to..."

"Keep up appearances," Thomas finished for me. "I know it can be tough. Just do your best to stay relaxed. Have a few drinks and just be your usual self. Nobody suspects you and nobody has any reason to, okay? They've never noticed anything before; they're just on edge because of the rumor."

"But they never noticed anything because I wasn't...I mean, I'm not really..."

"Oh, right. The drug and all," Thomas said. He'd forgotten all about it because he didn't believe me. "Well, still, just be yourself and you're gonna be just fine." I gave him a lot of credit for humoring me about the drug making me gay. He didn't believe me, but he didn't make fun of me for believing it. He sighed. "I can't imagine how scary this must be. I mean, it's hard for anybody trying to figure out, you know, who they are, but on a sports team, it's got to be really tough. I wish I could be there with you so you wouldn't have to deal with this alone."

I wished he was here with me, too. For just a moment, I fantasized about what it would be like to take Thomas back to my hotel room instead of a girl. As pleasant as that thought was, I forced myself to stop thinking about it. I didn't want to encourage this whole gay thing any more than I had to. Once I turned straight again, I didn't want to have to recall the times I'd been thinking sexual thoughts about men. When this was over, I would just pretend it had never happened. Still, it was hard to get around the whole attraction to men thing, as much as I tried to avoid it. I'd always been highly sexual, and I couldn't turn that off just because it was men that aroused me instead of women. When I jerked off, I had to think of men or I couldn't come. I tried to make the thoughts as fleeting as possible. I allowed the vision of a hot guy to flash through my head long enough to help me finish, and then I would try to forget about it once I had gotten off. It was awful.

When I went back to being straight, I wouldn't ever be able to look Brady Clayton in the eye again.

"I'll be all right. Don't worry about me," I told Thomas. The truth was, I loved that he was worried. Nobody worried about me. I'd never had a girlfriend who called to make sure I was okay when I got hurt during a game. My dad was a "walk it off" kind of guy. Unless I fell and broke my cock, the girls I took home didn't care if I was injured. It was a good feeling to think that Thomas would be at home tomorrow, watching the game, cheering me on and worrying if the game didn't go well. I wondered if it might be possible for Thomas and me to be friends when I was straight. I guess not. It would be too big of a risk if people knew I had a gay friend. Too bad. I didn't have a whole lot of close friends.

"I gotta go. I'm at the bar."

"Okay. Just relax and everything will be fine. Call me if you need anything, okay? It can be two in the morning. I don't care. I know I'm probably the only one you can talk to about this right now, and I want you to know you can count on me, okay?"

"Thanks. Thanks, really. A lot." This guy was amazing. He barely knew me, and yet he had my back more than people I'd known my whole life.

I leaned forward and handed the cash to the cabbie. I always tipped guys like this very generously. It was a pretty tough life they had, driving strangers around all night. It must be incredibly dangerous, too, especially in downtown Philly.

"Thank you. Thank you very much!" the guy said in a

thick, foreign accent. "Uh, is okay?" he asked as he pulled out a piece of paper. He handed me a pen. "Autograph, please? Is for my son. He is very big baseball fan." Wow, so the guy did know who I was. I glanced at a photograph of the guy's kid that was taped to the dashboard. He was adorable. I wished I had a baseball or something else to sign for him.

"Oh, wow. Sure! What's his name?"

"Ravi. R-a-v-i." I signed *To Ravi, all the best to you, Henry Vaughn, Jr.* I handed it back to the cabbie.

He nodded politely. He looked so excited. I'm sure he hated being away from his kid all night, but now he would have something cool to give Ravi in the morning.

"Bout time you showed up," Kyle said when I got to the bar.

"Gimme a break. I was dealing with adoring fans, okay?" I was very happy to see a shot of Peach Schnapps and a beer already waiting for me.

"Mmmm, mmm," Kyle said, eying up some girl in a shiny, tight outfit sitting at the bar. I followed his gaze and pretended to check her out along with some other chicks in the room. I was already bored. It wasn't going to be easy to keep up appearances.

"So you up for wild night on the town, Tuna?" I said, still looking around the room at the ladies.

"Nah. Just gonna have a few drinks is all."

"Come on, man. You gotta live it up while you're away from the old mace and chain," I said. "Ball and chain" just wasn't strong enough to describe Mrs. Tuna. That bitch was scary.

"She's not that bad. Really," Tuna said with affection. He

did love her. I had no idea why, but he did. "Seriously, she's different at home. You guys just never really get to see the good side of her." I guess that was true. I knew she was involved in a lot of the Orioles' wives' charity stuff, so she couldn't be a complete shrew.

"I'm getting another drink," Kyle said. He didn't ask us if we wanted anything because he was only going back up to the bar to talk to the girl sitting there. I glanced nervously around, not sure what to do. No way could I walk out of there without a girl on my arm. I never left a bar without a lady friend for the night. But what in the world would I do with her once I got her back to the hotel room? I wasn't sure I could perform. Then again, I hadn't had sex since I took the pill so it might not be that difficult. Still, fear knotted up my stomach and I downed half my beer in one gulp. Maybe if I got the girl drunk enough, she'd just pass out and I wouldn't have to do anything. I remembered Tube Top girl back at Max's at home, the one who couldn't hold her liquor. Where was she when I needed her? I spotted a girl over at the other end of the bar who was putting away drinks pretty fast. She had definite potential. I downed the rest of my beer and sauntered up to the bar next to her.

"Next one's on me," I said, hoping whatever she was drinking had very high alcohol content.

"Thanks!" she said, smiling at me approvingly. I hoped she recognized me. That always made these things go quicker. Actually, no. It would probably be better if it took me a while to convince her to go home with me. More time meant more alcohol. "You're a real hottie. How would you like to take me home?"

Shit.

"Sure, let's go!" I said, louder than necessary. I took her by the hand and helped her down from the barstool. It was strange to be so gentlemanly, knowing full well there was nothing polite and genteel about taking a random girl home from a bar to screw her.

A sudden wave of loneliness washed over me. There was nobody here who had any clue what I was going through. I was eager to get back home to Thomas and, hell, even to Sam, because at least he knew about my problem. It was tiring and stressful having to keep up appearances all the time. I wondered how people could stay in the closet and endure years of this. I could never have done it. Hopefully, I only had a few more weeks of this and then the pill would wear off. It seemed like an eternity.

I projected as much confidence as I could as I led...I still didn't know her name...whoever...out of the bar. I winked at Tuna and Jackson. Kyle was nowhere to be seen. Dammit. He was probably in the can. Figured. The one guy who was gunning to find out who was gay and he wasn't there to see me leave with this hot lady. Oh, well. He'd ask where I was and Tuna or somebody would fill him in. I had witnesses, dammit.

We got in a cab and started making out. I was grateful we had a different taxi driver than I'd had earlier. I didn't want to scandalize poor Ravi's dad. It was uncomfortable kissing her, but not too awful, I guess. It just felt kind of weird. It felt like work.

We kept kissing and I felt her up a bit, but nothing was happening. I mean, I wasn't hard at all. *At all.* I started to sweat. This wasn't going to be easy. I'd had a knot of fear and anxiety in my stomach ever since I set foot in the bar, knowing what I had to do. I had to pull myself together or I was in for a truly embarrassing experience.

The cabbie winked at me as we left the taxi, like he was proud of me for getting lucky that night. Great. I was even getting pressure from the cab driver to perform well. We stumbled into my hotel room and I suddenly wished I hadn't had so much to drink. I felt dizzy and a little sick and I wasn't sure if it was the alcohol or the stress.

As we stumbled onto the bed, I realized there was no getting out of this. This was happening. It was happening now. She took my shirt off and I pulled off her dress. She made noises of approval as she ran her hands over my chest. She started to head south and I panicked and grabbed her hand. I tried to cover by kissing her hand, which was ridiculous. I just couldn't have her touch me down there only to find out there was nothing whatsoever going on with my dick.

After all the kissing and rubbing in the cab and now here, it still wasn't working. Terror caught in my throat and I tried to think of something, anything, that would get me out of here. Pulling a fire alarm. Suddenly acting like I was passed out drunk. Faking a heart attack. An asthma attack! That could work. I had my inhaler in my bag. I could...no. I couldn't do that. Somehow, having a geeky asthma attack in front of a hot girl would be almost as embarrassing as not being able to get it up. I rubbed my hands over her breasts and waited, hoped, prayed, for something to happen. I kissed her, touched her, and finished undressing her. She was getting impatient. I could feel it. I could argue that I wanted to take my time, be a gentleman, be a kind and attentive lover.

She'd never go for that. Who were we kidding? This was a one-night stand. It was sex. Not making love. She pushed me down on the bed. It was go time. This was about to be the most humiliating moment of my life. She would realize I was still soft and she'd probably storm out of there, calling me a....

Oh no.

She didn't seem to know who I was, but what if she did? Or what if she recognized me on the news tomorrow while we were still in town with the Phillies? She'd hear about the gay rumor and she'd tell people about her experience with me in bed. I started breathing heavily, the beginnings of a full on panic attack. She mistook my heavy breathing for passion and started kissing me, depriving me of badly needed air. I thought I was going to die. Really, literally die right there. And for a second, I was okay with that.

I realized how ridiculous that was. There was only one thing I could do that had even a remote chance of saving my reputation, my career, my life. It was something I had been avoiding since I took the drug, but I knew I had no choice. It went against everything I had ever believed about myself and about the world. It was everything I was never, ever supposed to do. It had been drilled into my skull since I was a kid. It was bad. It was wrong. But I had no choice.

I closed my eyes tight and I imagined having sex with a man.

9

Now I was pissed. I got through it all right, I guess. I don't think the girl suspected anything. I never did find out her name. I survived the ordeal, but it could have been worse. It could have been much, much worse. I decided I was through playing games. I wanted answers and I wanted them right now. I called Sam from my hotel room, where I would be free to cuss him out with nobody overhearing. We were finally heading back to Baltimore and the first item on my agenda was to kick Sam's ass. I called him at work so he wouldn't be able to yell back.

"Sam Aubrey," he answered the phone politely.

"It's Henry."

"Oh."

"For your sake, I hope you've been looking into what's in that drug."

"I have, Henry. A little. Look, it's been crazy around here. We have a really heavy patient load and with this clinical trial..."

"Has anybody shown up with...does anybody else have any, you know, side effects?" That was my best hope. That somebody else had come in and admitted they were having confused feelings or whatever. Then Sam would have to believe me.

"No, Henry," Sam said, sounding weary and annoyed. Poor little thing, was I getting on his nerves? He was seriously lucky I wasn't a bully or I would have beaten him up by now. It made me crazy that he refused to take me seriously.

"Did it ever occur to you that maybe there are other patients going through this and they're just too embarrassed to tell you?"

"No, not really." I felt my blood pressure rise every second that he dismissed me.

"All right, you listen to me, you little sonafabitch. I want answers! It's your job to deal – nicely - with patients who are having trouble with the drugs you give them. I am suffering with a *severe* side effect here, and you are the one who's responsible. If you don't start taking me seriously, I'm gonna have a little chat with Dr. Gallon and tell her what's going on and how you've been treating me."

Sam scoffed. "Yeah. You're gonna go talk to Lucy Gallon and tell her you're gay." Dammit. Called my bluff. Screw him.

"Look, just take an hour out of your precious busy schedule and look at what's in the drug and any possible side effects it might cause. I will meet you tomorrow for lunch or something and we can talk about whatever you find." I must have really been lonely and scared to actually suggest going to lunch with Sam. "I can't go on like this, Sam. You don't understand what I'm going through here."

"You think I don't understand what you're going through," Sam said, sounding almost as tired as I felt. He was probably right to be a little annoyed with me on that one. I was sure he'd been through some shit in his life as a gay man.

"Well, maybe you do. Then why don't you help me?" I said. I hated how pathetic I sounded, but I really needed him to give me a break here.

"I'll see you tomorrow, Angela," Sam said, sighing.

I MET him for lunch the next day in the cafeteria at Johns Hopkins. At first, I was relieved that he was finally going to research the drug, but then I started obsessing over what he might find.

Like, for instance, nothing.

I found Sam in the cafeteria and we went to get our food first. It was excruciating having to wait in line right next to him, dying to know what he had to say. He seemed in no hurry and I wondered if he was moving slowly on purpose, just to torture me. Probably. Prick.

We finally sat down at a table. I sighed and looked down at my cheesesteak sub and fries. I was really hungry, but my stomach was tied in knots and I wasn't sure that I could eat. I was about to demand that Sam tell me what he found when somebody else sat down at the table with us. Dread filled my stomach, as I knew this meant we wouldn't be able to talk now. I almost groaned aloud until I looked up from my food tray and saw who it was.

Thomas.

He was the last person on earth that I ever expected to see here. So many emotions whirled through me so fast that I felt dizzy. Shock at seeing Thomas again. Relief that he was one of the few people who knew about my unique situation. Delight at seeing him in his scrubs. Wow, now I understood why women had such a thing for men in uniforms. It was unbelievably, undeniably sexy. Especially a medical uniform. Thomas looked like a white knight in blue scrubs, ready to save lives and cure people. Right that second, I wasn't totally sure I wanted to be cured of what ailed me.

"Hey, Henry," Thomas said, sending a jolt of electricity through my body as he said my name.

"Uh-ummm. Ummm, what are you doing here?" I asked, smooth and suave as always. Shit. I was never this tongue-tied in my old life. I wasn't intimidated by the underwear models or movie actresses I'd hooked up with. But this was different somehow.

"I work here at Hopkins," Thomas said, munching a french fry and grinning at me. I got the feeling he had wanted to surprise me by showing up for my lunch with Sam. He probably knew Sam hated me and that I needed somebody here who was on my side.

"You look different without, you know, makeup."

"Different better?" I had no idea how to respond to that without looking, well, gay, and without Sam making fun of me. I felt my face get hot. Was I blushing? I, Henry Vaughn, Jr. was *blushing?* What the hell? Thomas noticed my discomfort right away and switched topics. "So, how are things? Adjusting any better?"

"No, not really. Being on the road was kinda tough."

Thomas nodded sympathetically. "Yeah, I bet it was."

I tried to look at Thomas without being too obvious. He was just so damn cute.

"I'm not really trying to adjust to anything. I'm just trying to get by. I know you guys don't believe me, but I'm not really gay." I took a sip of my diet soda.

"Yeah, well, I got news for you, Captain Feathersword. It's

not the drug," Sam said bluntly. "Did it ever occur to you that you might be in the placebo group?"

Placebo? No, it hadn't occurred to me. Shakily, I set down my drink. It bumped the edge of my lunch tray and I almost spilled it everywhere. Now I was glad I hadn't eaten anything yet because I felt like I could throw up. I must have looked as terrified as I felt, because Thomas looked alarmed at my expression.

"No," I managed to croak out. "Was I in the placebo group?"

Sam hesitated for several seconds longer than necessary, and then said, "No." I let out a shaky breath. Thomas looked pissed and was about to chastise Sam for screwing with me, but Sam continued. "However, I looked at each and every ingredient in the drug and there is nothing in it that's really all that unusual or could cause you to, you know, want to pick out matching towels with another guy."

Terror, coupled with fury, welled up in the pit of my stomach. I hated Sam. I hated him for what he was telling me and I hated the way he was telling me. My entire life and everything I had worked for and everything I had ever believed about myself was falling apart around me and he did not give a shit.

"That's not possible!" I said.

"And I interviewed a bunch of the other patients and so far you're the only one that went fruity," Sam said. He popped a french fry in his mouth, not a care in the world.

Thomas shot Sam an annoyed look, and then looked back at me with concern. I know he didn't believe it was the pill either, but he knew I did and that I was very upset. Sam's blasé attitude was twisting the knife and I was glad I wasn't the only one who was mad about it.

"This whole thing just makes no sense. No sense at all!"

"There's more. One of the ingredients is Clonazepam. It's used in a lot of anti-anxiety drugs. Maybe ingesting that reduced your anxiety about being gay. Sort of relaxed your inhibitions about it and made it harder for you to stay in denial."

"Do you really think that's what happened?"

"Maybe." Sam still didn't seem to care much either way.

I just sat there for a minute, letting it all sink in.

"What the hell am I gonna do?"

"You're gonna wait a couple more weeks until the drug wears off, then you'll know for sure. I can see that's the only way you're ever gonna be convinced of the truth," Sam told me.

"It'll be all right. We'll figure it all out somehow," Thomas said gently.

"I don't have time to figure it out! You guys don't understand," I said, then lowered my voice, "The rumor about the gay guy on the team has got everybody all paranoid and nuts. I mean, the rumors in the press started before, I, you know, turned..."

"Well, I guess they knew something you didn't," Sam said.

Giving up on Sam, I turned to Thomas.

"Look. I know this whole thing sounds crazy and I doubt that I would believe anybody if they tried to sell me the same story, but it's the truth," I said, looking directly into Thomas' eyes, hoping he would be able to see my sincerity. "I used to be with, well, sleep with lots of women. I mean, *lots* of women, okay? My whole life I've been, well, a...." I couldn't think of a good way to put this without making myself look like an ass.

"Slut," Sam finished for me.

"A womanizer," Thomas said, not unkindly. He looked a little amused. I nodded.

"Well, yeah. I guess you could call it that. I mean, my whole life I've been girl crazy. In grade school, high school, college, in the minor leagues...in the minors, I really tore it up. Girls dig athletes, and I was scoring some major-" I stopped myself before I said "pussy." I thought of Thomas as a gentleman and I felt weird talking vulgar around him. I saw Sam roll his eyes and Thomas still looked amused. "Anyway...and when I hit the majors, well, you know...."

"It got even easier to score some...time with your lady friends," Thomas said, smiling.

"Yes. Exactly. And then one day I visit Mr. Aubrey here and his band of voodoo thugs at Johns Hopkins," I said. "No offense." Thomas grinned and held up a hand to indicate none taken. "And the very next morning, I was, you know, attracted to...men. Seriously, Thomas. It was overnight. Like a light switch. I know it seems impossible, unbelievable, but that's really how it happened." I stared at him, searching for any signs that he believed a word I was saying. Thomas considered me for a moment.

"Well, I admit it seems crazy, but there's a first time for everything," he said. That was a good start.

"Are you serious with this?" Sam asked.

"I'm just saying it doesn't make sense that he never really had any homosexual feelings before that he can remember. Right?" He looked me and I nodded. "Think back, and be really honest with yourself here. Any confused feelings from when you were a teenager, any inkling of attraction for the same sex? I mean, you could be bisexual; did you ever consider that?"

"Wow. No, not really. It never really occurred to me because, seriously, I just never felt that way about, you know, guys." It was true. I didn't have any weird, confused feelings that I could remember. I used to only like women and now my feelings for men seemed just as strong and real. And not, you know, confused. First women, then men, but not both at the same time.

Right now, I didn't feel at all confused about how I felt about Thomas. I was crazy about him. No question about that. That both scared and exhilarated me. What scared me the most was that I could not remember feeling this way about a woman. Ever. That, combined with Sam's news about the drug did not bode well for my heterosexuality. Was it really possible that I really had just been in deep, deep denial?

Shit. Here I was, trying my damnedest to convince Thomas that I wasn't gay and now I was talking myself into thinking that I really might be.

"I suppose it's not entirely out of the realm of possibility that it was the drug." Sam was about to yell at Thomas for even thinking that, but Thomas held up a hand to stop him. "No, seriously. Think about it. Being gay is biological, right? I mean, nobody knows yet for sure what it is in your body that makes you gay, but you're born with it." He looked at me. "Usually. But think about transgender people. You take enough hormones and, even without surgery, you start growing breasts, your voice gets higher, etc. It's biological. So isn't it at least humanly possible that the researchers have accidentally stumbled upon something that causes homosexuality?" I was utterly delighted that Sam had no immediate retort to that.

"Yeah, and remember that Viagra was originally developed to treat heart disease," I offered, remembering that earlier even Sam had conceded that was a good point. "They sure weren't expecting the result they got on that one."

Thomas laughed. Yes! I finally had somebody who was truly on my side. And not just somebody. A nice guy who was incredibly handsome.

"Yeah, yeah, yeah. But look, there's nothing spectacular in the drug we gave you, okay? It's not all that much different than the other asthma drugs you've already been on. There was no miraculous development in the lab, no secret ingredient to give you gay superpowers." I glared at Sam. "I'm sorry, it just makes no sense and there's no scientific evidence whatsoever that the drug had anything to do with whatever's going on with you and there's every reason in the world to think that this is just who you are."

I let his words sink in a bit. What he said made sense and was far more logical than any explanation I could offer. But still, what he was saying didn't jibe with my experience. He could talk sciencey stuff all day; it still didn't explain how I could be straight my whole life and then just switch all of sudden.

"Then my life is over," I said, knowing that I sounded melodramatic, but at the same time, that was how I truly felt. Sam shot me a murderous look.

"I know it feels that way right now," Thomas said.

"Look, I'm sure it's rough on everybody who realizes they're, you know..." I still didn't like saying it aloud. "But it's different for a pro athlete. I mean, it's just not done. I don't see how I can survive as a gay major league ballplayer. I mean, the manager's already pretty much said when he finds out who the guy is, he's outta there."

"Asshole," Sam said, looking disgusted. Thomas shook his head sadly. I guess they faced this kind of stuff every day, but I didn't. Not yet. I figured I'd better start getting used to it.

"And Boomer's not gonna quit until he figures out who it

is. Him and Kyle McCracken. Kyle's really gunnin' to out somebody."

"I never liked that Kyle McCracken. He always seemed like such a jerk in interviews and even on the field," Sam said. I looked at him with surprise. He'd never mentioned being a baseball fan. "Yes, Susan, I do watch baseball. You know, in between painting my fingernails and curling my hair." I guess I deserved that. Sorry, I just never thought about gays being sports fans before I met Thomas and Sam. It shouldn't have surprised me, I guess. There were lots of women baseball fans and, as much as I'd like to believe they were all there to see me, some of them were really into sports.

"Yeah, Kyle never struck me as a nice guy either. And that was even before he said...what he said," Thomas looked more hurt than angry as he recalled Kyle's awful rant about gays. "I swear, no matter how many times I hear it, I'll never get used to that word." Sudden anger rose up in me and I wanted to punch Kyle for hurting Thomas like that. I felt guilty, too, knowing I'd probably said stuff like that in the past, but never on TV or to somebody's face. Kyle didn't give a shit who he hurt. "A shame he's such a jerk because he's not bad on the eyes," Thomas said.

I was surprised and a tad jealous at hearing that.

"Yeah, but he's nothing compared to that Tuna Manero," Sam said.

"Oh, Tuna is insanely hot," Thomas said.

"Really? Tuna?" I said. Thomas nodded eagerly. Too eagerly, dammit. "Wow, I never thought of him like that. I guess it's 'cause we're really good friends. What about Brady Clayton?" I couldn't resist adding to the conversation. I'd had all these feelings locked up tight and it felt good to finally be able to express them. Sam smirked at me. "Oh, shut up, Sam. You don't even have to be gay to think Brady's hot." Thomas laughed at that, which thrilled me.

"You got a point there. Brady Clayton. Wow, he is beautiful, isn't he? If anybody could turn a man gay, it would be him," Thomas said, smiling at me. "Maybe that's what did it!" I laughed with him. It was a nice moment that actually made being gay less scary. It amazed me to see how at ease Sam and Thomas were about being gay. It was so hard for me to imagine ever feeling that way myself.

"So I guess you guys are, you know, *out* at work?" I asked. Thomas nodded, still chewing a bite of his cheeseburger. When he swallowed, he elaborated.

"Yeah. I mean, my co-workers all know. Patients probably don't," Thomas said.

"No, I guess they don't. I mean, I never would have guessed..." I said, gesturing at Thomas. I felt myself blush again. Seriously. Blushing. I hoped he wouldn't notice. "And everybody's, you know, okay with it?"

"Pretty much. I wouldn't work there if they weren't. Life's too short for that crap."

I thought about my baseball career and how I didn't think the guys would ever accept me as a gay player. For a brief instant, that thought was actually a relief. My outing could be my "out." Meaning, I wouldn't have to play baseball anymore. I hated myself for even thinking that. I needed to never, ever forget how good I had it. I was a pro ballplayer, for shit's sake. Guys would kill to be in this position. I had fame, lots of money; what else could I have asked for? So what if it wasn't exactly my dream job? It was so much more than most people had. And it was more than I deserved.

I looked up from my lunch tray and noticed that Thomas was deep in thought.

"What?" I said.

"I was just thinking. I mean, my co-workers are totally fine with it and all, but I have a lot of older patients. I always joke around with them and they're really nice, but I wonder sometimes if they would treat me different if they knew. They're from a whole other generation, you know?" Thomas said. I nodded. I knew. Boy, did I know. I thought about my dad's friends. They sure would treat me differently.

"Yeah. It's amazing how fast people can change their opinion of you once they know," Sam said. Sam and Thomas exchanged a look of understanding. Thomas nodded and smiled gently at Sam. Something had obviously happened to Sam because he was gay. Something bad. Maybe I shouldn't give him such a hard time. The silence was uncomfortable so I decided to change the subject. Besides, there was something I'd been dying to ask Thomas.

"You like your job here? I mean, do you like it better than performing at the club?" I asked. He nodded.

"Sometimes he performs for the patients here, just not in drag. He does incredible impressions," Sam told me.

"Yeah. I know," I said, laughing.

Sam grinned. "Got ya, did he?"

I nodded. "Oh, yeah. He got me good. He does a mean Peter Angelos."

Thomas smiled. "There was this one old lady patient I had a few years ago. She came in for an x-ray to see if she'd broken her wrist in a fall. She'd lost her daughter to breast cancer just a few weeks before." He looked saddened at the memory. "Broke my heart. She was just so sad. So I start going..." and with that, Thomas launched into the most convincing impression of Jimmy Stewart I'd ever heard in my life. "Now you come on over here now, my dear, and we'll get your picture taken. Harvey's just about got the machine workin' again." I laughed aloud and even Sam cracked a big smile. Thomas looked me in the eye and my pulse quickened. "And she laughed. I mean, really, truly laughed. I never forgot that." Thomas started digging back into his food, unaware of the fact that I could not take my eyes off him. Sam glared at me. He noticed the way I looked at Thomas and he didn't like it. "So yeah, I mean, the drag stuff is fun and all, but the medical stuff is really my career. I like being in a job where I can make a real difference, you know what I mean?"

I nodded. "So, are you both out at home, too? I mean, I guess your parents know and everything," I said. Sam and Thomas exchanged another brief glance and I realized that whatever had happened to Sam most likely had to do with his family.

"Yeah. We're both out at home. Took me a little while, though. I was pretty shy about it, believe it or not. I used to be quite the shrinking violet," Thomas said.

"Now he's a loud-mouthed pansy," Sam said, smiling. It was nice to see he actually had a sense of humor once in a while.

"I finally got sick of hiding it. My mom and my sister were great about it. My dad had a really hard time, though," Thomas said.

"Yeah. I imagine it's hard on dads. Not exactly the life they pictured for their little boys," I said.

"No, *you're* what dads picture for their little boys! A major league ballplayer," Thomas said, grinning at me. I smiled weakly.

"Yeah. You got that right," I said quietly.

"It'll be okay, Henry. No sense in worrying about telling your dad now. You've got to get comfortable with it yourself first before you can even think about telling anyone. My dad didn't hate me or anything he just...it's like he just couldn't get his head around it. He couldn't accept it. It was a shock for him. He kept telling his friends that I had just broken up with a girl and that's why I never dated. Stuff like that. He just couldn't bring himself to admit to anybody that his son was gay." I could see the sadness of this memory in Thomas' eyes. I understood. God knows I understood. All you want is for your dad to be proud of you. "So one day I just snapped."

"Snapped?"

"I looked the old man in the eye and I said 'you can accept me or you can reject me, but you will never deny me again.'" The power of his words struck me. Wow.

"So what did he do?"

"He said he was sorry."

"Are you serious?"

"Yep. He said that he was sorry and that he was proud of me and wanted me to never forget that."

"Wow. You're lucky," I told him.

"You have no idea how lucky. He died of a heart attack six months later."

"Oh, wow. I'm-I'm sorry to hear that."

"Thank you," Thomas said. "I'm just so, so glad we made peace about it first, you know what I mean? I'd have gone through the rest of my life thinking he was ashamed of me and regretting the time we lost by not dealing with it all."

I nodded. My dad wouldn't be around forever either, but I thought it probably best to let him have his perfect fantasy son – the straight, macho ballplayer – not the gay son who had secret dreams of being an actor or singer.

"I don't think my dad will react...I mean, would react the same way. Doesn't matter anyway, I guess. Since I'm not really gay."

Thomas and Sam exchanged amused looks. Thomas clearly still didn't believe it was the drug. I sighed wearily and rubbed my temples, feeling a tension headache coming on.

"I'm sorry you're having such a hard time, Henry," Thomas said. He didn't look amused anymore, just worried.

"I just don't know how long I can keep hiding this from the guys, you know? It's exhausting. I went out drinking with them the other night. I did take a girl home..." I shook my head, remembering the near disaster that was.

"Did you take my advice?" Sam asked, smirking at me. No, I did not. I pictured being with a man, but it sure wasn't Matthew McConaughey. I couldn't look at Thomas. Not while remembering the fantasies I'd had about him while I was having sex with that girl.

"I don't want to talk about it," I said, feeling my face get hot. "And I sure don't want to do it again. I'll just have to figure out a way to get out of going out with the guys tonight."

"Then why don't you come hang out with us after the game?" Thomas asked.

"Thomas!" Sam said sharply, not even bothering to hide his annoyance.

"I have an early show at the club, and then we're just going back to Sam's place for a few drinks. Why don't you join us?" Sam was about to start bitching again, but Thomas stopped him. "Sam. Don't you remember how lonely you felt when you first realized you were gay?" Now I was about to argue, but Thomas cut me off as well. "Whatever's going on with you, Henry, I know you're upset and lonely and scared. There's no reason you have to go through this, whatever it is, alone. Come on, just come hang out with us and have a few drinks after the game."

"Fine," Sam said, scowling. He scrunched up the trash from his lunch and got up to throw it away. I hated the idea of spending time with that jerk and I was about to tell Thomas I didn't want to go, but then he turned to me and smiled.

"So see you maybe around 11ish after the game?" he asked.

I looked into those damn beautiful eyes of his and found myself nodding. "Can't wait."

10

I debated all day about whether or not I would actually show up at Sam's place that night. I was completely torn between wanting to see Thomas again and my desire to keep as far away from Sam as possible. In the end, my loneliness won out and I decided to go. I was stressed and miserable being around the clubhouse and whenever Thomas looked at me and told me everything would be all right, I believed him.

Thomas answered the door and I felt better just seeing him. He greeted me warmly and I suspected had I been anybody else, he would have hugged me. He didn't take that risk. Not after I'd flinched when he'd put his hand on my arm back at the Hippo. I felt bad about that. If only he had any idea how badly I wanted him to touch me.

Thomas gestured for me to come in. Sam shot me his usual look of irritation and didn't get up from his spot on the couch. Jeremy did get up to greet me. As he stood up, he pushed Sam on the side of his head, gently rebuking him for his rudeness to me. Sam glanced up at Jeremy with affection instead of annoyance, but he still didn't get up.

"Good to see you again, Henry," Jeremy said cordially. I nodded, shaking his hand.

"You want a beer?" Thomas asked me.

"Sure."

"Here. Come see what we got." I followed Thomas to the kitchen. He gestured at the fridge, so I peered in and selected a Clipper City, a local brew. Sam had good taste in beer. I'll give him that. Thomas took out a large bottle from a brown bag. He grabbed a couple of shot glasses and set them on the counter.

"What's that?" Thomas held up the bottle. Peach Schnapps. "No way!"

"Sam told me you liked it straight. So to speak."

"He made fun of me when he told you that, didn't he?"

Thomas laughed as he twisted off the top of the Schnapps bottle. "Yes. Yes, he did." He poured two shots and handed one to me. We clinked glasses and then downed the shots. Thomas looked at the empty glass. "You know, that's not bad."

"I know it's really sweet, but it goes down smoother than other shots."

Thomas nodded. "Shall we?" He gestured toward the living room where Sam and Jeremy were sitting on the couch, drinking beer. I made a face and Thomas smiled. "Don't worry. I'll smack 'im if he gets out of line. I know he's been mean to you and I'm sorry about that. He really is a good guy."

I nodded and followed Thomas into the living room. If Thomas liked Sam, then I supposed he deserved another shot. Thomas sat on the couch next to Sam and Jeremy and I sat on a chair across from them. Thomas poured me another shot and I downed it eagerly.

"Rough game today, huh?" Jeremy said. Sam smirked at

that, but Jeremy was being sincere.

"Yeah. It wasn't pretty." We lost 8-0.

Thomas, Jeremy, and I chatted about sports for a few minutes, while Sam just sat in moody silence on the couch. I drained my beer and Thomas brought me another one. I kept downing shots in addition to the beer and before I knew it, I was pretty buzzed. I couldn't help it. Alcohol was the only thing that seemed to calm my nerves lately.

Thomas leaned on his elbow and looked into my eyes in a way that gave me goosebumps. I found myself overanalyzing his every move, every glance, to see if he had any semblance of interest in me. He had a way of talking to people, really looking at them and letting them know they had his undivided attention, so it was impossible to tell if he had any kind of attraction to me. Still, when he looked at me like that, I allowed myself to imagine maybe he did like me the way I liked him.

"So when did you know you wanted to be a baseball player?" Thomas asked.

"I played ball in high school. Went to college on a scholarship. Got drafted. Then went to the minors."

"But when did you know? What made you realize that you wanted to be a major league baseball player when you grew up?" Thomas asked. I chugged another Schnapps as I thought about how to answer. I knew what he expected to hear. That I played baseball in the yard with my dad or that I saw *Field of Dreams* and it made me cry and that's when I realized I wanted to be a baseball player. Dad did play catch with me and I cried buckets watching *Field of Dreams*, but I wasn't about to admit that. But that's not what made me want to play baseball. Nothing in particular made me want to do it for a living. I was just good at it, so it seemed like a natural career choice. There was no magical moment in my youth when I felt inspired to pick up a bat and start pursuing my future. It just kinda happened. Thomas looked so eager to hear what I had to say that I wished I had a much better story to tell. Sam eyed me critically as I poured and downed another shot of Schnapps.

"Nothing. I never really wanted to play baseball at all." I couldn't believe I'd said that out loud. I glanced at my empty shot glass. I knew the alcohol was loosening my tongue and I should quit drinking before I said something I'd really regret. Against my better judgment, I poured another shot. I let it sit on the coffee table. For now.

"You never wanted to play baseball?" Thomas asked.

"Why not?" Sam asked. "Seems like a damn good gig."

"It is. It really is. And I'm grateful for my career. I really, really am. I just kind of wound up in baseball because I was good at it. Really, really good at it." Sam rolled his eyes. "No, I know. I mean, look, I don't mean to brag. Really. It just...it always came so easily to me. Athletics. It's not fair, you know? Not fair at all." I looked at Thomas instead of Sam while I spoke. Thomas was listening without judging me. Sam just assumed I was being an asshole. "I mean, I've seen guys work their asses off for years to be half as good as me. Wait, that doesn't sound right. I don't mean..." I couldn't stand the thought of Thomas thinking I was being an egotistical jerk. The alcohol didn't exactly help me put things eloquently.

"No, no. I get it. You're not bragging. You're saying you feel bad because other guys have to work so much harder than you," Thomas said.

"And they want it more! That's the thing." I downed another shot. I couldn't help it. Shit, this was like therapy. It felt amazing to get this stuff off my chest. I couldn't tell my dad stuff like this and I sure as hell couldn't talk to my teammates. "Like this one guy. I'll never forget his first day in the majors. He just walked around, all quiet. He was like in a daze, just looking around the stadium like he just could not wrap his brain around the fact that he was actually there. They say there's no crying in baseball, but let me tell you, that guy was holding some shit back." Thomas laughed. I looked into his eyes and tried to block out the fact that Sam and Jeremy were there at all. "I hit a grand slam once. To win the game. In the bottom of the ninth. And I didn't come close to feeling the way that guy did on his first day."

Thomas nodded sadly, contemplatively. I took one more ill-fated shot of Schnapps and blurted out, "The truth is, I've always wanted to be a performer."

Ohhhh shit. I hadn't really said that out loud, had I? When I heard Sam's laughter, I knew that I had. I couldn't believe it. That was something I barely even admitted to myself and here I'd just said it out loud in front of a guy who hated me.

THWACK!

Thomas smacked Sam, hard, on the back of the head. I was stunned at Thomas' fierce reaction on my behalf. Thomas, the eternal peacemaker, had just smacked his best friend for insulting me. I couldn't believe it. Maybe he did have some feelings for me.

"What kind of a performer?" Thomas asked me. What the hell. I'd come this far.

"Like singing and....stuff." So there you have it. That was my deepest, darkest secret that I'd never told anybody until that moment. I liked musical theater. Musicals as in Broadway and theater and 'jazz hands' and the fruitiest, fairiest, most gay profession ever in the history of mankind. Shit. I'd wanted this secret to stay shoved way down in my psyche where it belonged, not out in the open to provide more fodder for Sam to humiliate me with and call me girl names. I bet Liza and Judy would be among the next names he would call me.

"You mean like being a rock star or something?" Thomas asked, and I realized that so far, all I had copped to was a desire to sing. I hadn't outed myself as a theater wannabe yet. I could just cover and say, yeah, I like, wanna be the next Bono or Bruce Springsteen. Good, manly singers like that.

"No, I mean like musical theater." *Shit, shit, shit!* I glared at the Peach Schnapps and I wanted to scream *this is all your fault!* Sam laughed loudly, but ducked before Thomas could smack him again.

"So, have you been in any shows?" Thomas asked.

"I was Chicken Little in the second grade." Sam snorted at that, but I ignored him. "My teacher said I was the best she'd ever seen. I never did anything else after that."

"Maybe you should have," Thomas said. "Maybe you should try auditioning for something sometime."

I laughed. "Are you kidding me?" I'd never thought about performing professionally. Never. Hardly ever. Maybe once in a while.

"Maybe you should pursue that dream if that's what you want to do. I bet you'd be good at it." I bit my tongue so hard it hurt. I wanted to tell Thomas everything. I wanted to confess to him that I had wanted to be an actor and a singer for my whole damn life. I wanted to pour my guts out right there because I knew he would understand. I wanted to tell him that I wanted to be a Broadway performer. I wanted him to know that my dream role was Curly McClain in *Oklahoma*. The cowboy who sang and wore a cowboy hat and got the girl in the end. I wanted to confess to him that the secret safe that I had hidden behind my Mickey Mantle poster at home held my huge collection of Broadway musical CDs that I didn't dare put on my iPod. And I wanted to tell him that I was scared to death that all of those things meant that I really was gay and always had been. No straight man in the history of the world had ever owned the complete collected works of Rodgers and Hammerstein.

"Maybe you should just give it a shot sometime. I don't know, do a small show somewhere in the off season?" Thomas said. I laughed aloud at the idea.

"I can just picture my dad's face if I told him I wanted to sing in *South Pacific*." I jokingly sang a quick line from one of the songs. Utterly blank looks from Sam, Jeremy, and Thomas. "You know, "There is Nothing Like a Dame?" More blank looks. "I'm in Love With a Wonderful Guy?" Crickets. "Oh, come on. What self-respecting homosexual don't know the words to *South Pacific*?"

"Christ, you're an idiot!" Sam yelled at me.

"Kidding, just kidding," I said. I was kinda kidding. I guess the whole 'gays and musical theater' thing was a bit of a stereotype. I guess not all gays were into it, like Thomas said not all gays were into drag shows. Lots of straight people went to both kinds of shows. But still, I knew there was at least some degree of truth to most stereotypes, whether it was politically correct or not. Throw a basketball at the actors on a Broadway stage and your chances of hitting a queen were greater than 2-1 odds at the dog track. I felt very uncomfortable about being the only one there who did know the words to *South Pacific*. Screw political correctness: that made me the gayest man in the room. "Look, it's stupid. Just forget it. I should never have brought it up. It's not something I'd ever seriously pursue, so let's just drop it, okay?"

"It's never too late, Henry. Really. If it's something you really want to do, you just gotta do it!" I admired Thomas' optimism, but I didn't believe him. Of course it was too late for me. It was too late for me to take up theater when I was born to a man known as Henry Vaughn, Sr.

"I can't just do it, Thomas. It doesn't work that way. I've got an incredibly successful career as a ballplayer. It may have come easily to me compared to some, but I did work for it. And now I'm supposed to walk away and live as a starving actor?" I shook my head. "My life is pretty set now. I have a lot more than most people and I would be incredibly stupid to give that up. Shit, what do you think my dad would say? He wouldn't have to suspect I was gay. The whole musical theater thing," I punctuated this with jazz hands, "would be enough for him to disown me."

Thomas glanced quickly at Sam, and I knew the word "disown" had hit a nerve. "I-I just mean, my dad sacrificed a lot for me. My mom, well, we lost her when I was a kid, so it was all him for a while."

"Wow. I'm so sorry, Henry," Thomas said quietly.

"Thanks," I said, meeting his eyes. I forced myself to break away, but I could have stared at him all day. I wondered if Thomas had any idea about how I felt about him. I knew I was a good actor, but I hadn't really been trying too hard to hide my attraction to him. Maybe I really wanted him to know. Even if it wasn't mutual. It always feels good to think someone has a crush on you, even if you're not interested back. Sure, I had lots of fans with crushes on me, but that was a love affair with a poster and a fantasy version of me. I was pretty sure Alice from the bar had a crush on me, which was kinda sweet. It was especially flattering because she actually knew me in person and she still liked me for some reason. It was a good feeling, and I wanted Thomas to feel that way, too. I wanted him to know I adored him, even if he didn't feel that way back. "It's just, my dad worked really hard to get me where I am today and he's so damn proud of me. And I'm not gonna screw it up. Ever."

"I can understand that," Thomas nodded thoughtfully. "Are you any good?" My thoughts went straight to the gutter on that one and I had to stop myself from saying something like *come to bed with me and find out.* For a moment, I was afraid I'd said that out loud. I glanced at the Schnapps on the table. I had to cool it with that shit.

"Wh-what do you mean?"

"You know. Singing, acting. I mean, I can see you're a natural performer. I've seen you on the field," Thomas said. I shrugged. So I could field grounders and hit a few balls. That didn't mean I could act. "No, I mean, like, between innings and stuff." Thomas smiled at me, and my entire body warmed.

"Oh, you mean that stuff..." I laughed. He was referring to my antics with the fans. At first, I felt a little silly thinking Thomas had seen me on TV acting goofy, but his smile reassured me that like most of the fans, he enjoyed it. "Well, singing and dancing with the Oriole bird isn't exactly the same as a Broadway show."

"But it's not far off, Liza," Sam grumbled. *Liza.* I knew it. He looked bored and I didn't blame him. I disliked him as much as he did me, and I'd be pissed if I had to sit in my own home, listening to him drone on about his career aspirations.

"Can you sing? Don't be humble. Just tell the truth. We won't think you're being egotistical," Thomas said. Glancing at Sam, he said "Or at least I won't." I shrugged.

"Yeah. I guess I can sing," I admitted. My singing voice sounded pretty good to me in the shower, but what did I know? I had no idea if I was really any good.

"Well, let's hear ya, Celine!" Sam said, jumping up

suddenly. He rifled through a drawer, rustled up some sheet music, and thrust it at me.

Panic gripped me. The thought of singing in front of anybody terrified me, but it would be really awful to sing in front of these guys. Thomas would tell me I was wonderful no matter how bad I sounded. But I would know if he was lying. Sam would mock me mercilessly if I stunk. And the bottom line was that I didn't want to know. Just leave me to my fantasies and singing in the shower. This was a dream I had that I never shared, not just because I was embarrassed, but also because I knew it wouldn't come true. Now I wouldn't even have those remote fantasies if I found out I was terrible.

"No way!" I said. I tossed the sheet music back at Sam, accidentally hitting him in the face with it. That made me feel better.

"Please? I'd really love to hear you." When Thomas looked at me like that, I couldn't deny him anything. *Dammit.* I sighed heavily. I grabbed and downed one more Peach Schnapps before taking the music back from Sam. I skimmed it. It was *Unchained Melody*, that song from The Righteous Brothers. A great song, but couldn't we have started with something easier?

"Come on, Barbra. Let's do this thing!" Sam snatched the music out of my hand and put it on the piano. He stretched out his fingers dramatically.

"All right, but just a few lines, okay? I'm half drunk on Schnapps. I wasn't exactly prepared to do a Julliard audition today." Sam waved me off and started playing an intro on the piano. He was actually pretty good. Who knew the little prick actually had artistic talent? I cleared my throat and took a deep breath and started singing. I was afraid to see everybody's reaction, so at first I didn't look up as I sang. It was an incredibly romantic song, and I was very tempted to at least glance up at Thomas. I tried to resist the urge. At first, I didn't have any intention of singing the entire song, but I then found I was kind of getting into it. I loved singing. I did it all the time at home when I was by myself. This was such a powerful song and I found myself pouring all of my passion for performing, for singing...and for Thomas...into my voice.

Finally, I couldn't resist anymore. I looked up at Thomas just as I sang the part toward the end about *hungering for your touch.*

I inwardly hoped, prayed, that I wasn't imagining the intense look on Thomas' face. He stared deeply into my eyes. In that moment, it was like he knew I was singing to him. I held my gaze on him as I sang the part about needing your love, and then made myself look down at the paper as I finished the rest of the song. I was incredibly nervous about hitting some of the high notes at the end, but I think I nailed them.

The song finally ended. I took a deep breath and forced myself to look up to see everybody's reaction. Jeremy, Sam, and Thomas were all staring at me. Just sitting there, staring at me like they were enraptured. Or horrified.

"So...good?" I asked.

"My God, Henry..." Thomas said softly. It almost literally took my breath away – the way he looked at me.

"Henry, you have an absolutely incredible voice," Sam said as he stared at me with awe, almost dreamily. Samuel Aubrey, the uptight Johns Hopkins assistant who hated my guts actually said that and without a trace of his usual snarkiness. Maybe I did have some talent at this shit after all if I could make Sam, of all people, look at me like that. I mean, *damn.*

"Henry, you sounded amazing. I mean, just amazing!" Thomas said.

"Thanks." I knew he would have told me that no matter what I sounded like, but he really meant it. I could tell. Jeremy started applauding and the other two joined in. I felt my face get hot.

"Stop," I said, laughing, but I was enjoying the attention. I always did.

Sam seemed to warm up to me, slightly, after I sang. He was obviously impressed with my singing voice and I think he respected that I had the balls to actually sing in front of everybody. It was scary, but I was really glad I had done it. It was worth it to have Thomas look at me like that.

We all sat around the living room and talked for a while and Sam actually spoke civilly with me. He even laughed at some of my jokes and only called me a girl name once. I found myself feeling more relaxed than I had in a really long time, and it seemed to make Thomas happy that we were all getting along.

"Are you guys hungry?" Sam asked.

"A little," Thomas said.

"Yeah. I could eat something. Might be good to have something in my stomach besides alcohol. I feel a little dizzy," I said.

"Yeah, you were pounding the Schnapps pretty hard," Sam said. I waited for a Peach Schnapps joke, but it didn't come. Wow. Was I really that good of a singer?

"We got some chips and salsa and stuff in the kitchen," Jeremy said. He started to get up.

"I know where it is. I'll get it," Thomas said.

"I'll help you," I said, getting up and following him to the kitchen. I happened to glance back at Jeremy and Sam. Jeremy put his arm around Sam and Sam gave him a quick kiss. I found myself smiling. Thomas caught my eye and smiled and I knew we were both thinking the same thing. They were really cute together. I was finding it hard to stay annoyed with Sam. I guess I couldn't really blame him for not liking me. I was forever acting like being gay was the worst thing that could happen to me, so of course he was offended. I couldn't expect everyone to be as patient with me as Thomas was.

I followed Thomas through the swinging door to the kitchen, grateful to finally have a moment alone with him. He took out a small bowl for the salsa and a larger bowl for the chips and put them on the counter near me.

"The chips should be in one of those cabinets over there," he told me. I started opening cabinets to find them. "Henry." I turned around to face him. "That was really amazing, what you did in there. You're really very talented." I swallowed hard, trying to keep my heartbeat steady. I wondered if he could tell the effect he had on me. "I hope you'll sing again for me sometime."

"Anything for you, Thomas." I turned around and started looking for the chips again before I could say anything else incriminating. I finally found them and I opened the bag and emptied the chips into the bowl on the counter. Thomas handed me the jar of salsa and, as corny as it sounds, our fingers touched and I felt a shot of adrenaline course through my body. Our eyes met and I knew he felt it, too. The heat between us was more intense than anything I had ever known. It was like my heart had caught fire inside my chest. He looked at me for one breathless moment, then he leaned over and kissed me.

I damn near dropped the glass jar of salsa all over the kitchen tile.

I felt his stubble scratch my face, but it wasn't uncomfortable. It was manly, sexy. Thomas smelled faintly of some kind of men's cologne. His kiss was somehow soft and forceful at the same time.

He jerked back suddenly, as if realizing what he had done. I just stared at him, stunned. I was happily stunned, but he didn't seem to know that. He had no idea how hard I was restraining myself from pushing him against the refrigerator and planting my mouth back on his.

For one awful moment, poor Thomas thought he had completely misread my signals. He looked absolutely horrified at what he had done.

"Henry, I'm so sorry! I-I don't know what came over me." He looked so embarrassed that I could hardly bear it.

Shakily, I put down the salsa jar. I grabbed his hand in mine and said, "No, Thomas. Please. Don't be sorry. You're not wrong about...whatever this is between us. I mean, I-I feel the same way about you." The words were so hard for me to say out loud, but I couldn't stand for Thomas to feel humiliated for a second longer. He looked relieved that he hadn't made a complete fool out of himself after all.

The door swung open and Sam walked in. I dropped Thomas' hand, but it was too late. Sam had seen me, the guy who jumped back like he'd been stung every time a guy touched me, holding Thomas' hand and staring intensely into his eyes.

"What's going on here?" Sam demanded.

Thomas bit his lip, debating on what to say. He grimaced a bit, bracing himself for Sam's reaction.

"Um, I kissed Henry."

"You what?" Sam shouted. He turned around and glared at me, even though Thomas had been the one who'd put the moves on me. He turned back to Thomas. "Really? Really, Tom? *That* guy?"

The door swung open. "Hey, hey. What's going on in here?" Jeremy asked, bewildered, no doubt wondering what could have possibly happened that fast to get Sam all riled up.

"Thomas kissed Henry!" Sam informed him angrily.

Jeremy's eyes grew wide. He looked at Thomas, then at me, then back at Thomas. He tried so hard to stifle his laughter.

"It's not funny, Jeremy!" Sam cried, genuinely upset. I actually felt kinda bad. I knew he wasn't crazy about me, but I didn't see what the big deal was. To him anyway. I was the one who'd just kissed a guy for God's sake. I wondered if maybe Sam and Thomas used to be more than just friends.

"I know, babe," Jeremy said softly. I got the feeling that Jeremy didn't care what Thomas and I did, but he didn't like seeing Sam upset.

"Un-*fucking*-believable!" Sam muttered, and then stormed out. He went out the door on the other side of the kitchen and I heard him stomping up the stairs.

Thomas started to go after him, but Jeremy stopped him.

"I'll go talk to him," Jeremy said. He held up a mock angry fist at Thomas, who mouthed "sorry." Jeremy went upstairs to calm Sam.

Which left Thomas and me alone.

We exchanged slightly guilty looks and Thomas laughed softly. "I'm sorry, Henry. I didn't mean to attack you like that. I was already crazy for you, and now that I've heard you *sing*," he put his hand over his heart, "it'll be really hard for me to keep my hands off you."

"Then don't." I couldn't believe I'd been brazen enough to say that to him, but I wasn't sorry. I wouldn't have taken it back if I could.

Thomas sighed contentedly. He glanced toward the door

where Jeremy and Sam had disappeared, then he grabbed my hand and led me into the living room.

We sat on the couch together. It was wonderful to finally be able to sit so close to him. He looked at me with great fondness and concern.

"Oh Henry, I'm being so selfish. You're trying so hard to figure out who you are right now and the last thing I want to do is confuse you further."

"Too late," I almost whispered. "I really have no idea what's going on with me. All I know is that I haven't been able to stop thinking about you since the night we met."

Thomas gazed at me with this incredible expression of tenderness and desire. No one had ever, ever looked at me like that before. His lips were so close to mine that I could hardly stand it.

"So was that your first, you know, kiss?" he asked.

"With a guy? Yeah," I said, laughing softly.

"Now I wish I'd done a better job of it."

He glanced at the door to the kitchen, and then looked back at me. He hesitated only a second before pressing his mouth to mine.

Now that we both knew how we felt about each other, there was no reason to hold back. We wrapped our arms around each other and kissed passionately. Thomas was an incredible kisser. Each time he lifted his lips and pressed them back down sent a new ripple of delicious electricity through my body. I had never been kissed with such forceful passion before and I responded with equal intensity and eagerness. We simply could not get enough of each other.

Someone cleared his throat loudly. Thomas and I breathlessly broke apart and looked up. Neither one of us had heard Jeremy come back downstairs. He smiled wryly at us, then glanced back toward the kitchen door, and then back at us. The message was clear. Jeremy might not have minded catching us making out on the couch like a couple of horny teenagers, but we'd better knock it off before Sam came back.

"Is he all right?" Thomas asked, looking concerned.

"He'll be fine. He'll come around. He just needs some time to get used to...this," Jeremy said, gesturing at us.

"Yeah. Me, too," I said. Thomas turned his worried face to me.

"Are you okay?" he asked me.

"Yeah. Of course. Fine." And I really was. For now. I was buzzing on alcohol and I was on an emotional high from kissing Thomas. I knew the crash would come later. When I got home and sobered up, I'd probably realize what I had done and have a full-blown panic attack. I figured there were two kinds of men in this world: guys who had kissed another dude and those that hadn't. Right now, I was okay with the camp I was in, but later on I might not be. Still, I didn't want Thomas to worry about me. I knew he felt bad that he was supposed to be helping me to figure out my sexuality, not making it more complicated. He wasn't supposed to fall for me. But I was so, so glad he did. I reached over and took his hand in mine.

"Wow," Jeremy said, watching me hold Thomas' hand. "You've come a long way already." I felt my anxiety already start to creep up on me when he said that. Up until now, I'd been yelling at Sam and Jeremy about how I wasn't really gay, and now this. I squeezed Thomas' hand and smiled at him.

"Well, I better get going." I stood up and pulled out my cell phone to call a cab to come get me. "Thanks for everything, Jeremy. Please tell Sam, you know, I'm sorry. I really didn't mean to upset him." I genuinely felt bad about hurting Sam. I knew he had trust issues or whatever, and I didn't blame him for not trusting me. Thomas was right. Sam wasn't a bad guy. He'd obviously been hurt before and he was just cautious about letting anybody hurt him again.

Jeremy and Thomas spoke quietly to one another as I talked on the phone to the cab company. I wished I could've heard what they were saying. When I hung up the phone, Jeremy looked at me, then back at Thomas. He shook his head.

"Henry Vaughn, Jr.," he said. Jeremy looked at Thomas and offered his fist. "Niiiice." Thomas blushed as he bumped fists with Jeremy and looked at me sheepishly, which I found incredibly endearing.

The door swung open and Sam walked into the living room. We all turned to look at him. He still looked pretty pissed.

"Sam, I'm so sorry! I didn't mean to upset you," Thomas said.

"I know. I'm not mad at you," Sam said, glaring at me.

"Come on now, Sam. You know this isn't Henry's fault," Thomas told him.

"You know, I knew he had a thing for you, Thomas. It was so obvious the way he kept looking at you. I just never dreamed you'd like him back!" Sam said it as if the very idea was disgusting.

"If it makes you feel any better, neither did I," I said. I couldn't get over it. What did a great guy like Thomas see in me? I understood Sam's hateful feelings toward me more than I understood Thomas' tender ones. Sam glared at me again.

"Still think it's the drug?" Sam asked me bitterly.

"Sam," Thomas said quietly. Sam's expression softened a bit as he realized his remark had probably hurt Thomas more than it hurt me. Between upsetting Sam and worrying about me, Thomas felt bad enough.

"I think I'll wait for the cab outside," I said. I walked past Sam toward the door.

"Wait. Henry," Sam said. I turned to face him and he suddenly grabbed my collar and pulled me toward him with surprising force.

"Sam!" Thomas cried. Both he and Jeremy stepped forward, but I held up my hand to stop them. Sam was a lot smaller than me, so he wouldn't hurt me. Much. Besides, he had every right to be mad and if it made him feel better to hit me, I'd let him.

"Listen here, Betty," Sam spat at me. "You hurt him, I'll kill you. And I don't mean ha-ha I'm gonna kill you, I mean you will choke forth your last breath as you hang by your own jockstrap."

I stared into his face. He wasn't kidding. Sam shoved me away and then stormed into the kitchen. Jeremy shot me an apologetic look and then went after him.

Thomas walked over to me. He gently straightened out my shirt and inspected my chest for damage. I practically shivered with delight at his touch. The cab honked for me outside.

"I gotta go," I said.

Thomas nodded. He kissed me again and said, "We'll talk soon." He went into the kitchen to check on Sam.

I felt dizzy as I walked down the steps toward the cab. So much had happened tonight. I was more confused than ever about everything. I was so uncertain about my sexuality and I couldn't make any sense out of what was happening to me. There was only one thing I knew for sure.

I wanted to be with Thomas.

11

As I'd expected, I lay awake in my bed, thinking about everything that had happened. I kept waiting to break into a cold sweat when it finally sank in that I had kissed another man. I couldn't stop thinking about kissing Thomas, but so far, I felt nothing but exhilaration.

I couldn't believe how he knew all about my stupid dreams of singing and acting and he still liked me. I was a completely screwed-up mess right now and he seemed to understand completely. He was the sexiest, sweetest, most exciting man I had ever met, and I simply could not believe that he was just as hot for me as I was for him.

Rather than flipping out about how incredibly, well, *gay* I was being, thoughts of Thomas were occupying my mind.

Pleasant thoughts.

I also thought a lot about what Sam had told me about the anti-anxiety element of the pill and how I may have been in denial all along. I supposed he was right that I'd have my answer in two weeks or so. I was so confused that I wasn't even sure what to hope for anymore. I didn't want to be gay, but I did want to be with Thomas. So where the hell did that leave me?

I wished I had somebody, anybody, to talk to about it. It was like when you have an incredible first date with a girl and you really hit it off, you can't wait to tell your buddies about the great girl you met. You're all excited because you think you met The One.

Oh, God.

What if Thomas was The One? The One I was supposed to spend the rest of my life with? We'd only just met and I'd never felt this way about anyone. Not even close. Did that mean I really was gay?

I found myself thinking about my mom. I wondered if I would have been able to talk to her about all this if she was still alive. I liked to think I could have. I tended to idealize her as this perfect mother since she wasn't around anymore. She had been more patient with me than my dad ever was, that was for sure. I wondered if I could have told her that I was questioning my sexuality without her telling my dad. I bet I could have. I bet she'd have understood. I think she understood about my whole acting thing, too. When I did the Chicken Little play in second grade, she had told me she thought I had talent. I mean, yeah, all good moms would say something like that, but I think she meant it. That's one of my favorite memories of her. Mom smiling at me and telling me what a great job I did in the play. She had been so proud of me.

I knew I would have trouble sleeping, so I took a Unisom when I got home and I felt it finally start to kick in. The last thoughts I had before I drifted off to sleep were of Thomas. I wondered if he was thinking of me, too.

THINGS at the clubhouse were as bad as ever. Scratch that; they were worse than ever. We'd been playing badly and ticket sales were down. Fans were losing faith in us and who could blame them? You can only take so much losing before watching the games just isn't fun anymore and it's not worth the hundred bucks or so you shell out by the time you've paid for parking, beer, and hot dogs for the kids.

Kyle had made a few more unfortunate comments about gays to the media, and had been ordered by the front office of the O's to attend sensitivity training. I wasn't sure if he learned anything, however, as he continually referred to the workshops as Queer Camp or Be Friendly to Faggots School. I doubt the higher ups in the organization really gave a damn about sensitivity. More than likely it was just a PR thing to protect the Orioles' image. It was a dicey area, as the sports industry isn't exactly known for being gay-friendly, but they can't afford to ignore homophobic slurs either. Anyway, it served Kyle right and I was glad he was forced to go.

No doubt that as a team we were struggling, but I'd had a great couple of games recently. I knew I had Thomas to thank for it. I was happy for the first time since I took that stupid drug. Every time I stepped up to the bat, I gave it my all because I knew Thomas was watching at home.

I had another pretty good game tonight, at least compared to the rest of the guys. I went 2 for 4, with 2 RBIs. Good thing, because those were the only two runs we got and we won 2-1. It was a close one, but a win's a win.

I showered and changed into my street clothes after the game. It was a scorcher out. One of those nights where it seemed to get hotter after the sun went down. It was like 85 degrees out and it was 11:30 at night. I felt better after my shower, except for the throbbing ache in my ankle. I had managed to stretch a single into a double by sliding into second and my foot had turned the wrong way when it hit the base. Nothing broken or even sprained, I didn't think, but it hurt like a bitch. Our trainer came running out onto the field to take a look, but it was fine. To prove I was okay, I did some jumping jacks out there in the field. The fans went crazy. The laughter of the crowd; I swear it's better than an orgasm. My ankle hurt like hell when I did that, but it was totally worth it. Totally.

My good mood was destroyed when I heard the guys talking about going out. I knew I had to do it; it had already been suspiciously too long since I'd gone out for a drink. It practically made me sick to my stomach to think of having to take another girl home. The pressure was just too much, and it was so humiliating that I had so much trouble getting hard around women. Still, I knew I could think of Thomas and get through it.

But that was another thing. Having sex with a girl would have felt like cheating on him. It was stupid, I know. It wasn't like Thomas and I were dating, exactly. I didn't really know what we were. I certainly had no intention of sleeping with Thomas. That was a line I wasn't ready to cross. Not until I was a thousand percent sure I was really gay and maybe not even then. Still, I truly hated the idea of being with anyone else. But given what was going on with the Orioles right now, I had no choice but to keep up appearances.

Kyle, Sid, Brady, Jackson, and I headed out to the parking lot. I usually took a cab to the bar so I could drink my face off, but I decided to drive this time. If I had to sleep with a woman, I couldn't get too drunk. Besides, I wanted to call Thomas while I had a moment alone in the car. It was late, but I knew he would be awake. He'd have been watching the game.

It was a really long game tonight. It was a pitcher's duel, which isn't as exciting for the fans as a slugfest, so there weren't too many people waiting for us in the parking lot. It was a good thing, considering what happened after the game. As me and the guys headed to our cars, we ran into Joel Stone from the Texas Rangers. He'd had his own troubles with making gay and racial slurs in the media, but the Rangers hadn't forced him to undergo sensitivity training. Texas isn't exactly a hotbed of tolerance.

"Hey, girls," Joel said, and Kyle immediately stiffened. We all hated being disrespected because of having a gay guy on the team. Even me. I know it's not right considering, well, everything that was going on with me, but I couldn't help it. It was embarrassing that we were thought of as the gay brigade right now. As a sports team, we wanted to be thought of as rough and tough, an unstoppable force to be reckoned with, but the gay rumor combined with our losing streak just made us look like a bunch of fairies. I fucking hated it. We all did, but none more than Kyle. I was smart enough to just walk away. As much as I felt like bashing Joel's face in, I knew it was just not worth the trouble of getting into a fight. I kept walking and Brady and Sid kept going, too. Joel noticed I was limping a bit because of my ankle.

"Want me to carry you, sweetheart?" Joel said. *Shit.* Well, I couldn't just let that go, could I? I stopped walking and looked at him.

"Look, I know it's hard to resist all of this," I said, running

my hands seductively over my chest. "But try to control yourself, okay?" Fire practically shot out of his eyes after that
remark.

"What the fuck is that supposed to mean?" Joel yelled,
lunging toward me. I shoved him so hard he fell on his ass
and I was never so grateful for my fast reflexes. My
manhood had been in serious question lately and I had to
admit it felt good to fight. I wanted to pull him to his feet
and then punch him just to watch him hit the ground again.
Joel got to his feet and charged toward me. I couldn't wait to
take him out, but Kyle beat me to it. He landed a good
punch and before I knew it, Joel and Kyle were going at it. I
heard some cheers and looked over to see a few fans that
were waiting over at the parking lot. There were some kids
there, too, so I knew I had to stop this.

"Kyle, knock it off!" I grabbed Kyle and tried to pull him
off Joel, but Joel pulled harder. He wasn't done with Kyle yet.
He wrestled Kyle away from me and kept throwing punches.
I waited just a couple of seconds more so Kyle had a chance
to connect with Joel's face a few times before I grabbed him
and pulled him away. "All right, that's enough! Chill out,
man. Chill out. He ain't worth it. You're in enough trouble as
it is, Kyle. You'll get suspended; now cool it." Kyle kept trying
to lunge at Joel, but he knew I was right. He wasn't fighting
hard anymore, he was more saving face. He struggled a bit
in my grasp, but I knew if he really wanted to break free of
me, he could have. He was one crazy dude, especially when
he was mad. He knew he really could get suspended, so he
backed off a bit. "Come on. Let's go grab a drink." Joel
grinned maddeningly and I'd never wanted to smash someone's face more in my entire life. But I just kept walking
toward my car.

"Fucking faggots."

Keep walking, keep walking, I told myself. And somehow I did. I got into my car and revved my engine like all macho idiots do when they're frustrated. I managed to keep from banging on the steering wheel until I was out of view of the fans. I put on a CD of some of my favorite music to calm me down. It didn't cheer me up any because there was only one thing in the world that I knew would make me feel better.

I turned down the music and pulled out my cell phone. I actually screamed out loud when my phone started ringing at the exact second I was about to dial.

"Son of a bitch!" I yelled, my heart pounding. I was pissed as shit until I looked at the caller ID. Thomas. I forced myself to endure three more rings so as not to appear too eager.

"Henry? Are you okay? You're not hurt, are you?" I couldn't figure out how in the hell he could possibly know that I'd just been in a fight. "You didn't sprain anything, did you?" After a few more seconds, I realized he was talking about my earlier injury during the game.

"No. No, I'm fine. No problem," I said, trying to sound macho. "No big deal. My ankle's the least of my problems. Me and some of the guys just got in a fight." I said this both to sound manly to Thomas and because I knew he would worry. It was awful of me, but it was just so nice to have somebody who cared.

"God, Henry. Are you all right?" Thomas asked, sounding way more upset than I'd expected.

"I guess some of the Texas Rangers don't like the idea of there being a gay guy on our team."

Thomas was silent for a moment. "Henry, I'm so sorry you had to go through that. They don't suspect you, do they?"

"No. It's really no big deal." I thought about how I would feel if Thomas told me he'd been in a fight, especially if someone had threatened to hurt him because he was gay. That thought gave me a horrible, sick feeling in my stomach. Suddenly, his worry over me didn't seem quite so romantic anymore. "Really, Thomas. I'm fine. It was mostly Kyle getting into it with the Rangers guy."

"I really want to see you, Henry."

"I want to see you, too, Thomas."

"Are you sure? I was afraid you'd be upset about, you know, me kissing you. Once you had time to think about it and all."

"I can't stop thinking about it. I can't stop thinking about you. I thought I would freak out, too, but I didn't. I'm still confused as all hell, but I'm not sorry you kissed me, Thomas. Now tell me when I can see you so we can do it again."

Thomas laughed and I suddenly felt much better. More like my old self. I was never shy around women and I was happy to be getting some of my confidence back. Not that I had minded that Thomas had initiated physical contact – I'd always found it sexy when women were somewhat aggressive in bed – but you better believe the next time I saw Thomas, my hands would be all over him.

"Are you sure about this, Henry? I mean, if you need more time..."

Part of me was afraid that if I waited much longer, I would return to being straight and I would miss out on being with Thomas. That thought scared me more than being permanently gay did.

"I'm not sure about much these days, but I do know that I want to be with you as soon as possible."

"How about we meet at my place Saturday night? Game time is 1 p.m., so that should work, right?"

"That'll be great, Thomas."

After I hung up with him, I realized there was no way in hell I was going to have sex with some random woman. I really had no idea what I was thinking by getting into a relationship with a man or where the hell I thought it would lead, but I did know that Thomas cared for me and I would not hurt him by sleeping with somebody else.

I had to pick up a girl, so I would. I'd figure out something to do with her. This time, I really would fake an asthma attack if I had to. I cranked my music back up, feeling much calmer.

I parked my car at the bar and just sat there for a minute, looking at the neon lights in the windows. I used to love coming to this bar, especially after a win. It felt so good to be showered and clean after spending hours in the heat. Nothing tasted better than an ice-cold beer and a shot or five of Schnapps as I surveyed the bar looking for my next sexual conquest. I had felt like such a big shot, on top of the world. It was often the highlight of my day, being at this bar. The next morning was different. Harsh light of day and all that. I'd have the usual regrets as I looked at whatever I'd dragged home from the bar with me. If she'd already left, then I would just stay in bed alone and wonder what the hell I was doing with my life. It was lonely. But the very next night I would do it all over again.

I sighed. I couldn't very well sit in the parking lot all night.

I went inside to see Sid, Kyle, Brady, and Jackson already knocking back a few.

"Bout time, Henry. What the fuck?" Kyle said.

"And fine greetings to you, too, dear sir," I said. I smiled as I saw a fresh beer and a shot of Schnapps waiting for me. I grabbed the shot and poured it down my throat before I even sat down. "Ahhhh," I said, sinking down into my chair. The alcohol had barely hit my stomach and I already felt better. This was the fun part, the easy part. Just sitting here drinking with my buddies. Yeah. I could do this.

"I can't believe that son of bitch," Kyle muttered. "You shoulda let me fight him, Henry. I coulda kicked his ass."

"Probably. But it's not worth it, I'm telling you. You're in enough shit as it is. You want more sensitivity training? Joel's smaller than you. He'll go tell his mommy and next thing you know you'll be taking anti-bullying seminars called Arms are for *Hugging*!" I said, and I put my arms around him and gave him a squeeze.

"Screw you, faggot!" Kyle said, laughing. He pushed me away. He was kidding, I knew he was kidding, but I hoped nobody noticed that I had tensed up at the word "faggot." I couldn't help it. I'd jokingly called my friends "fags" count-less times in the past, just like my dad did with his friends. That seemed so long ago now. "I still wish you'd have let me nail that guy. I don't care if it gets me in more trouble. I would love to have that in the sports pages. *'Kyle McCracken in a street fight with Joel Stone. Stone is expected to be released from the hospital in 4-6 weeks and is learning to walk again.'*"

"In your dreams," I said.

"Well, the O's have got to earn some street cred back. Everybody thinks we're a bunch of pansies. This sucks! Don't that bother you?" Kyle asked.

"Yeah," I said, truthfully. It did. I didn't necessarily want the Orioles to have a reputation for being badass animals that liked to start street fights, but I wasn't crazy about being known as the queerest team in the league, either. I wasn't proud of feeling that way, but I couldn't help it.

"I'm gonna find out who the fag is and I'm gonna kill him," Kyle said.

"Dude, seriously," Sid said. "Take it easy. That's not even funny."

"He's right, though," Jackson said. "And you know he don't mean he's really gonna kill him. He just means we have to figure out who it is and just deal with him."

"Deal with him how?" I asked, casually taking a drink of my beer. I hoped I was as good of an actor as I was of a singer.

"I don't know. I guess it's up to Boomer," Jackson said. "I know he wants to figure out who it is before he's out of a job."

"What's Boomer's job got to do with a fag on the team?" It almost physically hurt me to use that word, but I had to. I had to make sure they never even suspected me. Still, I hated myself for saying it. I pictured Thomas every time I said it or heard it. Now that I had such a beautiful face to go with that awful slur, it wasn't so easy to just toss it around.

"Because the whole team's going to pieces because of this guy! We started off strong and now it's all falling apart. If we don't start winning, the first thing they're gonna do is fire the manager because that's what they always do," Jackson said. That was true. That was baseball's fix for everything. Get rid of the manager.

"And Boomer ain't gonna go quietly, either. His ass is on the line and he knows it. If he finds out who the gay guy is, he'll get him traded. Or worse," Jackson said.

"Worse?" I said. My hands were sweating and I nearly dropped my beer.

"He'll bust him down to the minors. Boomer don't play around. He's not a fan of the gaywads anyway, and this guy, whether he means to or not, is screwing up his career. He won't stand for it. I can't blame him," Jackson said. I hadn't really given any thought to the possibility of being sent down to the minors. That sure would be an effective way to get rid of the guy. But realistically, Boomer couldn't get away with it if the guy, whoever he was, was playing well. There's no law that says you gotta be hetero to play baseball. You could sue his ass for discrimination. But the slightest hint that you weren't performing well would give him an excuse to send your ass down to Triple A. Great. Like we weren't under enough pressure as it was. He'd get rid of the gay guy, but he'd make it look like it was because of the guy's performance.

"So I say we all gotta do whatever it takes to out this guy already," Kyle said.

"So fess up to it and get it over with," I said. Brady laughed at my joke, which earned him a nasty look from Kyle. Brady sobered up quick and I wanted to deck Kyle. I felt protective of Brady because he was a rookie. Also, he was hot.

"Screw you, Henry. This is important!" Kyle snapped at me.

"Is it? Is it, Kyle?" Sid asked. "Or are you just being an asshole about this whole thing? If everybody would just chill out about it, there'd be no problem. We're psyching ourselves out here."

"Exactly. I mean, I'm sorry, but I am the only one here who doesn't give a shit who's gay or straight on the team?" Brady asked. Damn, not only was Brady hot, but he was smart, too. And now he and Sid were on the good guy's side.

"Yeah, and maybe it's you," Kyle said to Brady.

"Don't be an idiot," Brady said. But he didn't deny it, I couldn't help but notice. I wondered for the millionth time if Brady was gay. It amused me to think of all the women who would be pissed to find out heartthrob Brady Clayton batted for the other team. I had to give Brady credit. It was an unwritten rule that rookies needed to keep their mouths shut, at least for the first few months that they were in the big leagues. It took balls for Brady to stand up to Kyle like that. "I'm just saying, Sid's right. You can't blame the fact that there may or may not be a gay guy in the clubhouse for us sucking lately. You know, this all got started with some vague rumor in *Around Town*. What if it's not even true?"

"That's just it. It doesn't even matter anymore if it's true," Kyle said. "The damage has been done. The only way to stop the rumor and save our reputation is to out somebody."

"So you'd be willing to out somebody who's straight just to stop the rumor," I said, shaking my head.

"Kyle's right. I mean-" I waved a hand, cutting Jackson off.

"Seriously. If I hear the word 'gay' one more time, I'm gonna puke up a rainbow. I need another drink," I said. I couldn't listen to any more of this. I needed to hurry up and pick up a girl and get the hell out of there. I'd figure out what to do with her later. Shit, I sounded like a serial killer. I went up to the bar and sat down, which I never did. I always just grabbed my drinks and went back to the guys.

"Heyya, Peaches," Alice said.

"Hey, Alice. How's it going?" I looked around the bar, trying to find somebody skanky enough to impress the guys. I got distracted by a guy in a muscle shirt, complete with muscles, so I turned back to Alice.

"The usual?" she asked. I nodded. "You okay? You look tired."

"I am. Very tired." It took a lot of energy to try to keep up appearances and my old, straight self had given me a lot to live up to. She watched me curiously. "What?"

"Nothing," she said. I knew I was not imagining her odd look. What if she was one of those chicks with an incredible gaydar?

"So hit me again, Alice," shouted an older guy down at the end of the bar. I expected Alice to pour him a drink, but instead she just looked over at him and said:

"I had a guy in here so drunk that he swore he'd been abducted by illegal aliens. They forced him to landscape and pick grapes for hours before they let him go," Alice said. I chuckled and so did the guy at the end of the bar.

"That's offensive. I love it. Use it, Alice," the guy said. He smiled and sipped his beer.

"Use what, Alice?" I asked. She turned around and blinked, surprised that I was still there.

"Oh, sometimes I try out my stand-up material here before I take it to open mic night."

"You're a comedian?" I asked. She looked a little irritated. I knew that look. I got that look from women a lot.

"Youuu've told me this before, haven't you?" I said. She nodded slowly. "Sorry." I really did feel bad. She was a cool chick and she was a lot smarter and classier than the girls I usually hooked up with. I had no idea what she saw in me. I really didn't. It was just the packaging, I guess. "I know I'm pretty obnoxious sometimes, but I don't mean it, okay? I'm sorry." I leaned on my arm like I was too tired to hold my head up and I just looked at her. She squinted her eyes and looked at me suspiciously.

"You're not one of those pod people, are you? I mean, you *look* like Henry Vaughn, Jr., but..." I laughed.

"I'm an asshole sometimes, aren't I?"

"Yeah, you are," she said, but in a friendly voice. She did a pretty good imitation of me, craning my neck, looking around the bar for my slut du jour. "Not now, Alice. I'm trying to score with someone who's actually attractive here." I felt like shit. I remembered how strongly attracted I'd been to Thomas when I'd first met him. It would have broken my heart if he had looked right past me at some other guy. And here I'd been doing this to Alice on a nightly basis. Not that she felt as strongly about me as I felt about Thomas, but still. There really was no such thing as a harmless crush. They still hurt when unrequited. I could be a real prick sometimes.

"I'm sorry, Alice. I don't mean to be a jerk. It just comes so naturally to me." That made her laugh.

"I know this about you. Now what's your problem tonight? Why are you still talking to me instead of, you know..." She jerked her head to the side, indicating the skankfest that was this bar after midnight.

"I don't know. I'm just not feeling it tonight."

"Yeah, you guys are awfully edgy." She glanced over at Kyle and the others, who were still involved in a heated discussion. I had no doubt they were still on the gay thing. "You guys have been really intense lately. What's the matter?"

"It's the, you know..." I made the limp wrist gay sign. Alice laughed and shook her head.

"You guys are still all worked up over that? Seriously, who cares?"

"I know. Guys are idiots." I glanced over at the guys, who were practically yelling at each other. "Some guys are over-protective of their macho image, what can I say?" Alice smirked at me. "I know, I know. But really. I don't care who it is. I just want to start winning ballgames again. But Kyle's turning this into a pink witch hunt." I lowered my voice mock ominously. "Everyone's a suspect." I brightened. "Except me, of course!" Alice laughed.

"It's definitely not you." So much for her gaydar. Good. Alice glanced at the clock.

"Five more minutes and I am out of here!" Dread washed over me as I realized once she left, I would have to either grab a slut to go or go back and sit with the guys. Neither option appealed to me at all. Alice whipped out her cell phone.

"Hot date tonight?"

"Nah. Car's in the shop so I gotta take a cab." I hated the idea of her paying for a cab, especially now that I knew she was a starving artist/comedian. I was about to offer to pay for a cab, but then I got an even better idea.

"Want a ride?" She gave me another *are you sure you're not one of those pod people* looks. Shit, was I that bad?

"Are you serious?"

"Sure, why not?"

"I'll tell you why not. You're wasting your time if think you're gonna get any action from me. You're cute and all, baby, but I am not a whore." See? Much classier than my usual girls. Even though she liked me and thought I was cute, she wasn't about to sleep with me since we weren't in a relationship. Good for her.

"Alice, I'm asking if you want me to give you a ride. We get in my car and drive until we get to your house, you say thank you and wave bye-bye and that's it. I'm offering you a ride. A ride *home*. That's all." She still eyed me curiously.

"You sure? I mean I don't have time to get breast implants before we get to the car." I sighed and she looked apologetic.

"I'm sorry. Look, that's really sweet. Sure. I mean, if you really don't mind." Alice glanced around, no doubt thinking she was keeping me from all the hot girls in the bar when, in fact, she was saving me from them.

"Trust me. I don't. Meet you out front in a few?" She nodded and went to work cleaning up the bar for the night.

I headed back to the table where the guys had stopped fighting long enough for Kyle to pick up a girl. Brady had one, too. I couldn't suppress a flash of jealousy at the girl who was lucky enough to go home with Brady. She looked very happy. I still wasn't 100% sure Brady was straight, but if he wasn't, he was damn good at hiding it. I hoped for his sake that he was straight; otherwise, he had a night of torture ahead of him with this girl he picked up. I knew from experience how much that sucked.

"Going home alone?" Kyle asked, with more smugness than suspicion. We often had contests to see who could pick up the hottest girl and he clearly loved the idea that I had struck out altogether while he clung to a girl whose bra and thong were clearly visible through her sheer, tight dress.

"Nope. I'm going home with Alice." I nodded toward the bar.

"Alice the bartender?" Kyle made a face and it pissed me off. Alice was a sweet girl and I hated that Kyle thought just because she wasn't supermodel gorgeous that she wasn't good enough.

"Yeah, you know she's always had a thing for me. Figured I'd give her a break." Kyle nodded and accepted this excuse easily. We both knew the next best thing to bedding a superhot girl was bedding a girl who had a severe case of fan worship. If you wanted your ego – and everything else – stroked good, take home somebody who'd been fantasizing about you for years. It's an experience you never forget.

I sat in my car and waited for Alice, immensely relieved that I didn't have to have sex with a girl tonight. I guess I'd been gay too long, because thoughts like that didn't even seem weird anymore. Alice knocked on the car door and I realized I'd forgotten to unlock it. I flipped the switch and she slid into the seat next to me.

"Thanks, Henry. I really appreciate this. I hope I'm not, you know, screwing up your evening plans here."

I laughed. "No, really. It's fine. I'm...tired." I waited until she had her seatbelt on and then I turned on the engine.

And was completely and utterly humiliated by what happened next.

As soon as I turned the key, the car was filled with the music I'd been blasting on my CD. It was "Luck Be A Lady" from *Guys and Dolls*. I quickly snapped it off and drove out of the parking lot. Maybe if I just acted like it never happened, it would be okay. Thank God, Allah, Buddha, Jesus, Muhammad, or whatever that I hadn't been giving one of the guys a ride home. Maybe Alice didn't notice. Yeah. I turned it off so quick that all she had heard was noise.

"Was that...*Guys and Dolls*?" Alice asked incredulously.

"Uh, um. I dunno. Radio." Alice poked the CD player eject button and pulled out a clearly labeled *Guys and Dolls* CD. "Uh, umm...well, uh...it's my mom's car," I stammered. It was all I could think of. I couldn't remember if I'd ever told Alice my mom was dead.

"Your mom drives a Corvette with a license plate that says MLB PLYA?" Alice asked dryly. Thoroughly embarrassed, I grabbed the CD out of her hands and tossed it in the backseat. I stared straight ahead, having no idea of what to say. There just...there was no fix for this. There went Alice's crush. It's hard to have the hots for a guy who's into showtunes, no matter how ripped his abs might be. God love her, she tried not to laugh. She really did, but she finally gave in and dissolved into giggles. She put a hand on my shoulder.

"I'm sorry, Henry. It's just..." She clapped her hands in delight. "I just always had this feeling that there was more to you than this macho crap."

"What macho crap?"

"Oh, you know. Always eying up half-naked women, showing off your muscles, showing off on the field. I mean, seriously, what are you compensating...for..." I saw the exact moment the recognition hit her. Her eyes grew wide and she clapped her hand over her mouth like I'd only ever seen people on TV do before. "Oh my God, it's you!"

"No, wait! It's not like that! I mean, n-n-n-ot really..." But it was no use. Her accusation had obviously horrified me and she knew it was true.

"Oh my God...of course it's you. Nice guy, single, cute, of course you've gotta be gay," Alice said, shaking her head. She laughed. And laughed and laughed.

"Yeah, well, you're just mad because you have a crush on me." I wanted her to feel as embarrassed as I was. It didn't work. She waved her hand dismissively.

"Oh, please. Everyone knows that." She wasn't one bit ashamed. Not even a little girlish blush. I guess I was the only one who blushed. *Dammit.* Panicking, I jerked the car over to the side of the road. The sudden motion startled Alice and she screamed. Good. At least I scared her a bit. I turned and faced her.

"Alice, seriously, you cannot tell anybody..." I said. I was terrified that my secret had gotten out this way. I had been so careful.

"Of course not, Henry," Alice said gently. "I hear how those guys talk. I know what those gorillas would do to you if they knew."

"Not to mention Boomer. He'd get me fired."

"You really think he would?"

"Or boot me down to the minors. Either way, no way he's keeping a gay guy on his team."

"But Henry, how is this possible? You're like the most raging hetero I've ever met!"

"Tell me about it."

"Then what...?" Alice looked at me, waiting for a reasonable explanation that I could not possibly provide.

"You know what? What the hell. I've got nothing to lose. You already know the worst part. Okay...okay...here's what happened." I closed my eyes and took a deep breath. I couldn't believe I was about to tell this crazyass story to another human being. I opened my eyes and looked at her. "I've got asthma and I have to use this stupid inhaler." Alice started giggling. "Shuut uuuup!" I whined.

"I'm sorry, I'm sorry. It's just I cannot believe the great superhero Henry Vaughn, Jr. is an asthmatic." I glared at her and she put her hand up in apology. "I'm sorry. Really." If she was laughing at me for this, what would she say about the rest of the story?

"You know what? Never mind." I started up the car and got back on the road. "Which way to your place?"

"No, Henry. Please. I'll be good. I promise." I didn't say a word to her for the rest of the ride to her apartment, except to ask for directions. I pulled into the parking lot and waited for her to get out. She put her hand on my arm.

"Henry," Alice said softly. I turned to face her. "Please. I want you to be able to confide in me. I won't tell anyone. I swear. I've seen all the ugliness that's been going on with the players lately. If you're the...if it is you, then you must have been going through hell these last few weeks." I sighed. She looked genuinely concerned and I was really tired of bearing this burden alone. I leaned back in my seat and stared straight ahead.

"So, I've got asthma, okay? And, for *obvious* reasons, I didn't want anyone to know about it." She looked guilty. Good. "So I took part in an experimental drug trial to see if I could just take a pill instead of having to rely on my inhaler. So I took the drug they gave me and the next morning I was...I found myself attracted to men." I said the last part as steadily as I could. It was so embarrassing, I couldn't look at her. The silence was killing me, so I sneaked a glance at her. She looked at me the way I would look at her if she told me she drank a magic potion that turned her into a lesbian overnight.

"Well, Henry, I...I really don't know what to do with that," she said finally.

"Yeah," I scoffed. "Me neither. I don't blame you if you don't believe me, but that's what happened. It's insane, I know."

"Well, it's absolutely crazy. But Henry, it's not as crazy as you actually being gay!"

"So...you don't think I really am?"

"Do *you*?"

"Well. I don't know exactly."

Alice nodded thoughtfully. I gave her a lot of credit for taking this as seriously as she was. "I mean, it seems impossible that I could really be gay. But it just...seems so real, you know? I mean, I was horrified at first, but now...it kinda feels right. So I don't know what to think. I mean, Sam – that's the research assistant at Hopkins – he said the drug is designed to stay in your system for a month."

"And it's been how long?"

"Three weeks. And there's been no change whatsoever."

"Wow."

"Yeah. At first I was completely convinced that it had to be the drug, but...it seems less and less likely now."

"Does Sam know about what's been happening to you?" Alice asked.

"Oh, yeah. He knows."

"Wow." Alice laughed, but quickly stopped. "I mean, I'm sorry for laughing..."

"No, no, really. It's fine. I was way too sensitive earlier. I mean, this whole thing is ridiculous. How can you not laugh?"

"Yeah, I just..." She started laughing again. "I mean, that must have been an awkward conversation to have with the assistant guy."

I laughed, remembering that day well. "It was."

"So you think you might really be gay?" She eyed me curiously but completely without judgment. I actually felt good about talking to her about this. It was great to talk to somebody who knew me before any of this happened.

"I don't know. At first, I was totally convinced it was the pill. It was just so sudden, you know? I go to bed with some girl, like usual, and then bam! I wake up the day after taking the drug and suddenly I'm gay."

"Yeah. That was sudden. In all the time I've known you, you've never shown the slightest indication of being gay. At all. Ever."

"Yeah, but...isn't it possible? Lots of gay guys are in denial for years and years. They get married and have families and all that before they realize the truth about themselves. The way I grew up, the way my dad is and all, I couldn't even consider the possibility of being gay. It just – wasn't possible. He'd never accept me, so maybe I've been gay deep down all along and I just never knew it."

Alice nodded, but still didn't look particularly convinced. And why should she be? After all, she'd seen me fuck my way through that bar for the last several years. What I was saying didn't particularly add up.

"The way you're talking, it almost sounds like you want to be gay," Alice said. I wasn't sure how to respond to that, because I wasn't even sure myself anymore. Wide-eyed, she asked, "Do you?"

"I don't know. I guess I'm just trying to accept my fate here. Besides, there's this...this g-g-guy..." The moment the words were out of my mouth, I wanted to stuff them back in and choke to death on them.

"Really?" Alice asked quietly but with great interest. "You met someone? Tell me about him." She seemed to get how awkward and uncomfortable it was for me to say that out loud. She treaded carefully.

"He's a friend of Sam's. His name is Thomas Palmer."

"Wow," Alice said softly.

"What?"

"I wish you could see your face right now. You're really crazy about this guy, aren't you?"

"Yeah." I laughed. "I am. Is that the most insane thing you've ever heard? I mean, the thing is, I've never felt this way about anybody...like, not even a girl. Ever. This is just different."

"Wow. That's so sweet. I'm jealous!" She laughed, but I saw the hint of truth in her eyes. "So does he feel the same way?"

"Yeah. He seems to, believe or not." I shook my head, still not believing it myself. "We kinda have like our first date Saturday night. I'm going to his place." Alice raised an eyebrow and I felt myself blushing again. I hoped the car was dark enough that she couldn't see it. "N-n-o it's not like that. I mean, I don't ever plan on sleeping with a guy. It's just

I can't risk letting any of the guys find out, so right now it's just safer to meet at his place."

"Yeah. You're probably right," she said wryly. Alice knew about my huge sexual appetite and I don't think she believed I wasn't going to have sex with Thomas, but I knew I wouldn't. That was a step I didn't know I'd ever be able to take.

"So, what does he do?" My mind immediately took "what does he do?" to mean what did he do sexually. I found myself thinking of all the things I wanted Thomas to do to me. Thank God I came to my senses and realized what Alice was actually asking before I completely embarrassed myself by offering way too much information. "Um...uh...ah he's-he's a radiographer." Alice grinned at me like she knew what I had been thinking. I blushed harder. "You-you know, like an x-ray tech. He works at Johns Hopkins. He looks, like, amazing in these blue scrubs he wears."

"Ohhhh, I love guys in scrubs!" She leaned back in her seat dreamily.

"Right? I know!" I said excitedly. I couldn't believe I was actually having this conversation with her. "He's also a drag queen."

"You're kidding. That's awesome! Have you seen him perform?"

"Once. He just does the drag stuff on the side or whatever. It was...an experience to see that."

"Where does he work? The Hippo, I guess?" I nodded. "Wow, I'd love to see him perform sometime."

"Yeah. I'd like to see him perform again, too." And I meant it. I still wasn't crazy about Thomas in a dress, but he was incredibly sexy when he performed on stage. "It's just...I have to be really careful about going to places like that."

"Oh, yeah. I guess you do. Wow. I just...I'm having so

much trouble picturing you with a guy. I mean, Henry Vaughn, Jr. Gay. I never would have thought it in a million years."

"I know. It's crazy. But man," I said, laughing and banging on the steering wheel. "If you could see some of the thoughts that run through my head? I mean, we're talking really, really, gay."

She laughed and looked at me in wonder, shaking her head. "Just so weird. And sudden."

"I know...but, thinking back, I guess there were other signs. Like the Peach Schnapps thing. Kinda girly, don't you think?"

"Well yeah, Peaches. That's why I make fun of you for drinking it. But that doesn't make you gay."

"But there's...other stuff." Why was this next part even harder for me to admit to her than the gay thing?

"Come on, you can tell me," Alice said. I hesitated, sighed. "Henry, you just admitted to me that you're attracted to men and that there's a great guy that you really want for your boyfriend. What could be harder for a guy like you to admit than that?"

"I know, I know. Okay, look. It's just that...it's not that I don't like playing baseball. Well, sometimes I don't, but nobody likes their job all the time, right? Shit, I never told anybody this in my whole life and now I'm about to tell the fourth person this week."

"Who else knows?"

"Thomas," I said shyly. "And Sam was there, too," I said with irritation. I couldn't wait to see Thomas Saturday night without Sam and his disapproving looks. "And Sam's boyfriend, Jeremy."

"So what is it already?" Alice asked.

"All right. Deep down I always wanted to be a

performer." I closed my eyes and said the next part really fast to get it over with. "To sing and act on Broadway and stuff like that."

Alice didn't miss a beat. "I think you'd be really good at that, Henry."

I turned to her, astonished. "You do?"

"Sure. Henry, anybody who's ever seen you at an Orioles game knows you have more fun clowning around and revving up the crowd than you do playing the damn game. You're a natural performer."

"Wow. Thanks. But be honest here, and all political correctness aside, my lifelong dream of being on Broadway is a pretty big sign that I've been gay all along, right?"

"Well, I don't know. That is a pretty big stereotype."

"Come on, Alice. It kinda does tip the scales, doesn't it?"

She laughed. "Well, maybe. I don't know. So you're pretty sure now that it isn't the pill? That you're not gonna, you know, change back or anything?"

"I don't think so, Alice. I really don't. I guess I'm okay with it. It's the worrying about what would happen if anybody found out that's horrible. Worrying about if the guys find out or if my father finds out." I closed my eyes and groaned. "My father. Man, it would kill him. Well, he'd kill me, then it would kill him. So I'm freaking out about what will happen if people find out, but on the inside? On the inside, it feels kinda right, you know?"

"Incredible. Just incredible," Alice said, shaking her head. She looked up at me, smiling. "Meeting Thomas has a lot to do with why you're starting to be happy about being gay, doesn't it?"

I nodded and said softly, "It has everything to do with it. But I don't know how long I'm going to be able to keep this up. You know, keeping this a secret. A lot of the guys want to figure out who the gay guy is and get him out so we can save the reputation of the team or whatever."

"That's awful. Men can be so stupid!"

"Yes. Yes, we can." I rubbed my temples. It gave me a stress headache just thinking about having to act straight around the guys. It was so damn much work. "It's exhausting. I mean, you know how I take girls home all the time from the bar. They're gonna start suspecting something if I stop. Oh, by the way..." I said, turning toward her and giving her an apologetic look. "I kinda told the guys I was taking you home tonight. You know, to-"

Alice gasped.

"I'm sorry, Alice! That was horrible of me. Look, I'll tell them that you only wanted a ride home and that you turned me down."

"No, no, it's just that I got a great idea. I can help you! I can be your beard!"

"You can be my what?"

"You've never heard of a beard?" I shook my head.

"It's like when a gay guy doesn't want to come out of the closet so he has somebody act like his girlfriend so nobody gets suspicious. I could do that. Let people think we're dating! That way you don't have to answer any questions about why you're not screwing every girl you see."

"You would do that for me?"

Alice shrugged. "Sure. It's not gonna hurt my reputation any to be dating Henry Vaughn, Jr." She looked excited at the idea, which worried me. Sure, it would make my life a hell of a lot easier if people thought she was my girlfriend. But I knew Alice kind of liked me and I didn't want her to get hurt. She wasn't stupid. She knew I was gay and she knew what she was doing. Still, I felt like I was using her, even though she had offered.

"I don't know. Are you sure about this?"

"Sure, why not? I mean, I'm not gonna do it forever, but at least it will give you some time to get your head on straight and figure out what's going on."

"Yeah. I guess that could work."

"So what are you gonna do with Thomas tomorrow night?"

"I don't know. Just hang out. Order in, have a couple of beers, I guess."

"Henry, I've never seen you look so happy. I'm so excited for you! You have to promise me you'll call me after your date. I don't care how late it is. I'll be working so I'll be awake."

"I'll call you. I promise. Thanks, Alice. This is really nice. I mean, I don't really have anybody I can exactly talk to about this, so..." Alice nodded, understanding.

"So do you think you'll kiss him? Do you think he'll kiss you?" Alice asked excitedly. This must be what conversations between teenage girls were like. It was kind of fun.

"Well, we kinda already kissed."

"You did? That's adorable!" I was already feeling better about this whole Alice-as-my-girlfriend thing. She seemed totally on board with me being gay. She actually seemed to like me better as a gay dude. Maybe this whole thing would work out. I told her how I accidentally confessed my theater dreams and how Thomas hit Sam for laughing at me.

"Oh, that is so sweet!" Alice gushed.

"I know. He's like the nicest guy ever, so when he did that, I started hoping maybe he did have a thing for me. Then he and Sam made me sing for them."

"They got to hear you sing? I want to hear you sing!" I looked at Alice and shook my head. That would be a very bad idea. Not to be horribly cocky, but I didn't want her to have another reason to have a crush on me. I still wasn't entirely convinced that I had enough talent to make it as a singer, but all I knew was that my singing had made Sam practically swoon over me. And that guy couldn't stand me. Talent was sexy, no doubt about it. I practically went weak in the knees when Thomas performed, even if he was in a dress.

"No way!"

"Come on, Henry! Please?" I shook my head.

"Not tonight, dear. I have a headache. Sometime, though. I promise, okay?" Alice sighed but nodded.

"So anyway, you sang and then what?"

I told her about what happened in the kitchen, how Thomas and I just locked eyes and he impulsively kissed me.

"Oh, that is so romantic..." Alice said dreamily. I thought so, too, but I'm a dude so I couldn't admit it. I was glad she'd said it, though.

"Yeah," I said. "Wow. I feel so much better. I guess bartenders really are like shrinks. I feel like I owe you a hundred bucks for sitting here listening to me ramble."

"This one's on the house, baby. I'm so happy for you, Henry. It'll be fun being your fake girlfriend, but I also like being your real friend."

It's funny. It took being gay for me to realize what a great girl she was. To think, all this time we could have been friends. Better late than never, I suppose.

"You better go get some rest. You look exhausted."

"I am. Thanks for the ride."

"Thanks for the therapy session," I said, grinning at her. She got out of the car. "Flip the lights when you get inside so I know you're safe."

Alice nodded. "Bye, *honey.*"

"See ya later, *sweetheart,*" I said to my new fake girlfriend. She started to walk away, then turned back and leaned into the window of my car.

"Hey, I just thought of something. If you're the gay one, that means it's not Brady Clayton. Yes!!!!" She pumped her arm in the air. I laughed and nodded.

12

I fidgeted in the backseat of the cab like a kid on a long car ride. I simply could not wait to see Thomas again. It was excruciating getting through the ballgame because all I could think about was him. I was really nervous, but I promised myself I would be more forward with him this time. Thomas had really put himself out there when he first kissed me and I didn't want him feeling all the pressure in this relationship. Besides, I'd always been forward with women and I didn't see why that should change now that I was...whatever I was. My plan was pretty much to grab him and kiss him the moment I saw him, no matter how nervous I was.

Once I got to his apartment door, I took a deep breath and wiped my sweaty palms on my jeans. I knocked and my heart pounded in my chest as I waited for him to answer. When he came to the door, I felt a surge of adrenaline when I saw him.

Thomas looked so sexy in his jeans and simple T-shirt. When he smiled at me, I felt my nervousness disappear. There was only happiness and excitement now. He shut the door behind me and then seemed a little unsure of what to do next.

That was my cue. I wrapped my arms around him in a warm embrace. I breathed him in. The scent of his cologne brought back vivid, pleasurable memories of our first kiss.

"God, you smell good. What is that?" I asked him.

He grinned shyly and answered, "Obsession."

"Mmmmmm. Obsession indeed," I murmured seductively. I leaned in and kissed him. I felt his body relax into mine as we kissed and I rubbed his back. Kissing him was so exciting and so familiar at the same time. Holding him in my arms was like coming home.

I sighed contentedly. "Much better. I've been waiting to do that for so long."

"Me, too," Thomas said. His clean-shaven face was slightly red from where my 5 o'clock shadow had scratched him.

"Sorry. My beard left a mark," I said, using that as an excuse to kiss the red spot on his face, which probably just made it worse.

"Worth it," Thomas said, rubbing my scratchy face with his hand. "It's sexy."

I smiled, pleased with the compliment. We just looked at each other for a moment. Funny how the silence wasn't awkward. We felt so comfortable with each other already. We just liked looking at each other, being together.

"Come in. Sit down. You must be exhausted." Thomas led me to the couch.

I sat down and looked around at his apartment. It looked like a guy's place. Simple, functional, no frills, but clean. I don't know what I had expected. Fancy interior designing? I knew that was a gay stereotype, but still. It still surprised me to see how much gay guys were just *guys*.

Nobody would ever have guessed that a drag queen lived here.

"Want a beer?" Thomas asked.

"Sure. I'd love one."

Thomas went to the fridge and peered in. "What kind do you like? I got Guinness, Rolling Rock, Yuengling?"

"Yuengling works. Thanks!" He came into the living room with a Guinness and a Yuengling. He also put down a couple of shots. He sat down on the couch next to me.

"Schnapps! You're the best!" We clinked shots and downed them. He grabbed his bottle of beer and took a swig. "You like the dark stuff, huh?" Thomas nodded as he swallowed a mouthful of Guinness. "Not me. Too bitter."

"Yeah, that's what Sam says, too. I love the stuff." Thomas leaned back and put his feet up on the coffee table. He gestured at me to do the same. "Relax. Make yourself comfortable." I couldn't believe we were allowed to put our feet up on the coffee table. Just one of the many differences that came with dating a guy. *Cool.* I wondered what the policy was for burping and farting in front of each other?

"Wow. This isn't exactly how I pictured it would be like, dating a guy," I said, gesturing at the beer and the feet on the coffee table. As soon as I said it, I regretted it. I mean, were we dating? It's not like it was anything official. "I-I mean not that we're dating...we-we're just...I-I mean for all I know, you could be seeing somebody else..."

"I'm not," Thomas said quickly. He put a hand on my shoulder. "There's just you." I let out a nervous breath. "Henry, I think you're an amazing guy. I can't believe that you even agreed to go out with me. You're out of my league, no pun intended. You're out of most people's league." I shook my head and was about to protest when he squeezed my shoulder. "But I just want to make sure we take things really slow here, okay? You're the only man I'm interested in. I promise you that. But you've been through so much lately, I just want to make sure you don't do anything you're gonna regret."

"Like what?"

"I just mean, this is a really confusing time for you. Just a few weeks ago, you were sure you were straight. From what Sam says, you were *really* sure. I just...I would feel terrible if you like, I don't know, experimented with...you know...gay stuff and then realized that you weren't."

"You're not an experiment to me, Thomas," I said, looking him in the eye.

"No, no. I know that. I just...let's take things slow, okay?" I nodded. Thomas was such a great guy. I didn't deserve him. And he thought I was out of his league?

"So are you sick of baseball or do you want to watch one of the games? There's a bunch on right now," Thomas said, picking up the remote.

"I wouldn't mind checking out the Indians/Yankees game." Thomas flipped the channels until he found the game. It was just getting started. "Thanks. So you're a sports fan, huh? Any besides baseball?" I asked.

"I love football," Thomas said. You'd think I'd know better by now, but it still surprised me to know that gay guys watched sports. He sighed. "Henry, I need to tell you something." He turned and looked at me. He looked somewhat serious, but there was a mischievous glint in his eye. "Before our relationship progresses any further, I think it's important that you know." Thomas took a deep breath. "I'm a Steelers fan."

"Ohhhh, it burns!" I said, grabbing my stomach. Thomas burst out laughing.

"I know. I know! It's just that my Dad was from Pennsylvania, so growing up..."

I shook my head. "You think you know somebody...oh, well. I'll make you a Ravens fan yet, young man."

"Many have tried, darling. No one has succeeded," Thomas said. I knew he was joking, but I liked when he called me "darling." "Have you eaten yet? You hungry?"

"Starved." I was feeling light-headed, both from the alcohol on an empty stomach and from the company. The more I got to know Thomas, the more I adored him. I couldn't remember the last time I'd felt so relaxed. So happy.

Thomas went to the kitchen and returned with a bunch of food delivery menus. After some discussion, we settled on pizza and buffalo wings. Thomas called in the order, then sat back down with me on the couch and put his feet back up on the coffee table. He sat next to me for a moment, and then put his arm around me. I felt my shoulders relax at his touch.

Thomas kissed my cheek and murmured, "I'm so glad you're here."

"Me, too." There was no place in the world I would rather be.

Thomas kissed down my cheek and started kissing my neck a little. I was surprised at how much it turned me on. In the past, I usually just hopped into bed with a woman and did just enough foreplay to get her ready to go and that was it. There was something so sexy, so sensual about how Thomas and I were taking our time. It wasn't just that I was nowhere near ready to have sex with a man. I had the feeling Thomas wasn't the type to sleep with a guy on the first date. Just like with Alice, I really respected that.

I moaned as he continued kissing the sensitive skin on

my neck. It felt so good. It was all the more exciting because I was absolutely crazy about the guy who was doing it. Thomas' mouth traveled slowly from my neck up to my mouth and soon we were making out pretty heavily. I found myself already rethinking my vow not to sleep with a man. I didn't know how long I would able to resist going all the way with Thomas.

We came up for air for a second only to see that the Yankees had hit a two-run shot.

"Dammit!" Thomas yelled at the TV. Oh, thank God. After the whole Steelers debacle, I was afraid to find out he was also a closet Yankees fan. We would've needed a serious talk about that one.

"Son of bitch!" I yelled, too. "The Indians will rally. They got the top of the order coming up next inning."

"I hope so. Now that I'm dating you, I got extra reason to hate the Yankees," Thomas said. So we were dating, even if not publicly. *Cool.*

The game went to commercial while the Indians changed their pitcher, so Thomas turned to me and we started kissing again.

There was a knock at the door, meaning the food was here. Thomas broke off the kiss and stood up. He looked down at the front of his jeans, where he was sporting an impressive hard-on.

"Shit!" Thomas said, laughing as he glanced at the door. I laughed, too. Score another point for dating a guy. Now I was no longer the only one in the relationship who had that problem. Thomas untucked his shirt, and then headed to the door to get the food. I ducked into the kitchen under the guise of getting another beer. I couldn't risk being seen by the food delivery guy, who might recognize me. I made a mental note to pay Thomas back for dinner. I hadn't meant to stick him with the bill, but I just couldn't take the risk of answering the door. I waited until I heard the door shut to come out of the kitchen. I set down a Guinness for Thomas on the coffee table, then dug into my wallet for some cash.

"No, no. I got it," he said. Another point for dating a guy. I didn't always have to pay for everything! A nice thought in theory, but no way was I letting him pay.

"Here, take it. I know that hospital doesn't pay you what you're worth and, believe me, the Orioles pay me way more than I am." I thrust the cash at him and he knew I wasn't going to take no for answer.

"Thanks, Henry."

We settled back on the couch and ate dinner. Thomas had kept me so busy earlier that I had forgotten how hungry I was until I smelled the food.

"This is soooo good. Where's it from again?" I asked.

"Mikie's Pizza."

"Oh, cool. Man, these wings got some kick to 'em, don't they? *Damn!*"

Thomas laughed as I took a big swig of beer. "Yeah they do. You like spicy stuff?" I nodded. "Me, too. You ever go to Nacho Mama's in Canton?"

"Are you kidding? I love that place." Nacho Mama's was a quirky little place nearby where they have a warning printed on the menu that they will play Journey at 10 p.m. and they ask you to report any Elvis sightings. They also have delicious Mexican food and their famous Hubcap Margaritas that you drink from a big hubcap. Well, you and three or four of your friends with straws.

"Me too. We should go get a Hubcap Margarita sometime."

I hesitated before answering. "Yeah. Yeah that would be great." And it would be great. It's just that it was hard for me to imagine ever being out of the closet enough to actually go out on a date with him in public. And that sucked, because I really, really wanted to. I would be so proud to have this incredibly handsome man on my arm.

I finished eating, chugged the rest of my beer, and then sat back on the couch. We just relaxed and watched the game for a little while. The damn Yankees were still winning. I accidentally belched and was about to apologize, when Thomas spoke up.

"Nice one," Thomas said, without lifting his eyes from the TV. Yep. Dating a dude was cool.

We watched a little more of the game. Pretty soon, we were making out again. Our kissing became more desperate, more passionate, and I knew we couldn't stay at this level of arousal for much longer without some release. I kissed Thomas' mouth, then neck. I pushed him onto his back and I climbed on top of him. I wanted so much to please him. As I kissed him, I slid my hand down to his jeans and started to unzip him.

"No, Henry. Don't." Thomas managed to say between kisses. He pushed my hand away. I looked at him in bewilderment. I mean, sure I was new to the whole gay thing, but surely he hadn't expected us to do all this hot and heavy petting without going any further. I wondered if I had violated some unwritten gay rule by trying to touch him.

"What? Am I doing it wrong?"

"No!" he said, laughing softly. He looked at me like I was the most adorable thing he'd ever seen. "No, of course not. It's just...Henry, I just really don't want you doing anything that you're going to be sorry for later."

"Thomas, how could you think I would be sorry about this?" I asked him.

"Because you're not even totally sure you're gay."

"It's been almost a month since I took the pill. It's almost completely worn off. Even my asthma symptoms are back."

It was true. I had to admit, the drug had worked pretty well at first and I'd barely had to use my inhaler for a few weeks, but my lungs had felt noticeably tighter the last few days. I'd made sure I took a hit before I came here so I wouldn't look like a giant dork in front of Thomas. Not that he would ever think that. He'd just give me a worried look and ask if I was okay. My asthma symptoms were back, but I was just as gay as I was after I first took the pill. It seemed more and more likely every day that Sam's theory about the pill was right. It had lowered my inhibitions and forced the truth about my sexuality to come out. So to speak.

"I just don't want to, you know, go too far with you until you're totally sure you're gay. So it's been about three weeks since you took the pill, right?" I nodded. "Then let's just wait one more week, just to be sure." Thomas put his arms around my neck as he looked up at me. I loved having him on his back. I couldn't imagine having to wait another week to see him naked.

"You don't really think I'm gonna suddenly turn straight, do you?"

Thomas looked like he wasn't sure what the right answer was. "Well, no. Not really."

"I don't think so, either. I have a feeling Sam was right about the whole anti-anxiety thing. I was probably deep in denial because of my dad and upbringing and all. I don't know."

"But that's just it, baby," Thomas said tenderly. "You're not sure."

"But even if it turns out I'm not gay, Thomas, I'm not gonna be sorry we fooled around."

Thomas looked at me wryly. "Yeah. You say that now.

Cause you're thinking with this," he said, grabbing my groin through my jeans.

"Ohhhhh..." I moaned, rolling my eyes back with pleasure. Thomas winced, but started laughing.

"Sorry, Henry."

"They're turning blue, Thomas..."

He laughed again and shot me a guilty look.

"I know, baby. I know." Thomas looked so conflicted, tortured even, over what to do. I knew he felt bad getting me all riled up and then refusing to go any further, but he was obviously very concerned about me having horrible regrets about doing anything sexual with a dude if it turned out I was straight.

"Maybe...maybe I can just do you."

"How is that better?"

"I don't know. It just is. That way, you know, if anything changes, you won't have to admit to yourself that you actually *did* anything." Warped logic, but whatever. It was a start. "Yeah," Thomas said, more to himself than to me. "It's okay if I take care of you."

My cock was throbbing with need so I was too weak to argue, but once Thomas got me off, I would seduce him into letting me take care of him. Oh, yeah. I had my ways.

Thomas grinned at me mischievously and I felt a flash of delicious anticipation. Now that he had made up his mind he was going to pleasure me, he seemed enthusiastic rather than worried. He pushed me off of him. I wasn't a small guy, but Thomas was pretty strong. I found it so sexy when he took control. He started by pulling off my shirt.

His eyes grew wide and he sucked in a sharp breath and let it out slowly.

"What?" I asked, knowing damn well what. I'd been *dying* to show off my physique to Thomas. I worked out a lot and I had some pretty impressive muscles, if I did say so myself. I loved showing them off, but I refused to be one of those douchebags who took his shirt off every chance he got. I had bided my time, and now Thomas had been the one who took off my shirt.

"I just...I never dated an athlete before." He ran his hands over my chest with admiration. It was wonderful. Lots of people admired my body, but Thomas' was the only opinion that really mattered to me. I had never wanted to impress someone so much in my life. "Henry, you are a work of *art!*"

"Thanks, Thomas." He was momentarily distracted from his mission while he admired me, but then he remembered the task at hand. He pushed me onto my back on the couch and pressed his mouth to mine, kissing me passionately. He started kissing my neck again, which he already figured out drove me nuts.

"Oh, God. Thomas..." I moaned. It felt a little strange to my own ears to be calling out a man's name in the throes of sexual passion, but then I usually avoided calling out anybody's name for fear of saying the wrong one.

Thomas was so strong, so masculine, as he climbed on top of me, kissing me, sliding his hand further and further down my body.

I was completely at his mercy. I loved it.

He fumbled with my zipper. I was so hard it was difficult to get the zipper down, but he finally did. He pulled out my cock and I gasped out loud. He slowed down a bit and looked a little worried, like he thought I might be suddenly freaking out over what we were doing. He had nothing to worry about. It was a sharp gasp of pleasure, not regret.

"Tell me if you want me to stop," Thomas said. I gave him a look that said *you're rubbing my dick, you think I'm gonna tell you to stop?* He laughed. "Just tell me if you get uncomfortable, okay?" Poor Thomas. I don't think he liked breaking in gay virgins. I leaned my head back on the couch, loving what he was doing to me. Rubbing me, kissing me. My whole body tingled with pleasure. I learned something about getting a hand job from a guy.

They know what they're doing.

They've got one of these things, too. They've probably touched it a million times so they know how to do it just right. Thomas rubbed my cock with one hand while his other hand was behind my head, pulling me toward him as he kissed me passionately on my mouth and my neck. I couldn't stop moaning and calling out his name. I don't ever remember being so loud during any sexual experience, but I couldn't help it. I couldn't ever remember feeling this good. Thomas looked at me fondly, clearly enjoying my pleasure and proud to be the cause of it.

It didn't take me long to finish. It was the most powerful orgasm I'd had in a long, long time. I was glad I was gripping the couch and not his shoulders when I came, because I probably would have hurt him. I lay back, breathless, panting. He cleaned me up with some tissues and rinsed his hands with hand sanitizer. He looked at me with a mixture of joy at seeing my pleasure and his usual worry.

"Thomas, I'm not ever gonna be sorry you did this," I said, pulling him close to me for a kiss. "Thank you." I whispered into his ear.

His cock was so hard it was practically bruising my stomach. This was ridiculous. He couldn't possibly expect me to leave him in this state. I looked down at his groin and then back up at him. "Thomas, I can't just leave you like this. It's-it's-it's...mean!" I sputtered, not being able to think of a better word. I wouldn't leave him unsatisfied and frustrated.

He was going to come whether he liked it or not. "Please," I said to him, practically begging. "Let me do this for you."

He looked at me, torn between his concern for me and his sexual desperation. He sighed and then began unbuckling his jeans.

That's *better*.

I reached for him but he gently pushed my hand away. As a sort of a compromise I guess, he put one hand on my naked shoulder and jerked off with the other. Dammit, he was so stubborn! For the first time, I noticed he was left-handed. I guess that was the hand he used on me, but I was too wrapped up in my own pleasure to notice.

Thomas grunted softly with his eyes closed. I hoped he was thinking of me, imagining that it was me touching him. I never thought it would be hot to watch another guy beat off, but it was a turn-on to see Thomas' face contorted with pleasure. I wished so much it was me doing that to him. It took him even less time to finish than I did. More tissues, more hand sanitizer. He turned to me. "Thanks," he said, trying to catch his breath. He was visibly relieved.

"For what? You didn't let me do anything," I said, terribly disappointed. I had wanted to touch him so badly. I wanted to make him feel as good as he'd made me feel.

"Believe me, you did plenty," Thomas said, looking at my muscular chest. I put my hands on his shoulders and kissed him gently.

"At least take your shirt off and let me see you."

"No way! I'm not following...that!" Thomas said, gesturing at my chest. Okay, lose a point for a gay relationship. When you're dating someone of the same sex, I guess there were inevitable comparisons. In a lesbian couple, somebody had to have the bigger tits.

I hated that Thomas felt inadequate around me. I loved

his body. He looked incredible, whether he was in scrubs or in jeans and a T-shirt. He was an x-ray tech, for God's sake. I didn't expect him to look like me or my teammates. I wished I had the words to tell him how hot I was for him. How I was more turned on by him than I had ever been by anyone.

"Please? I want to see you." He looked at me, considering. He was hedging and would give in. I could see it. It thrilled me to know that he was as helpless to resist my requests as I was to his. He grudgingly pulled his shirt over his head.

"Happy now? Nothing to see here," Thomas said.

"Ohhhh, I disagree," I said, running my hands over his deliciously naked chest. He looked wonderful. Sure, he wasn't as built up as I was, but he had muscles and I thought he was incredibly hot. He had that sexy little trail of hair that led to his belly button and further south. I kissed him on the mouth, on the neck, and wrapped my arms around him. I murmured in his ear about how crazy he made me in his scrubs, jeans, and shirtless, and how I couldn't wait to see the whole package sometime soon. He smiled shyly.

"So!" I said brightly, sitting up and acting as if we hadn't just been rolling around on the couch like a couple of horny teenagers. Thomas laughed. I put my shirt back on and he did the same. Now that our sexual needs were relieved...for now...we could just relax and enjoy each other.

"So..." Thomas said.

"Tell me about performing." I put my feet back on the coffee table.

"What about it?"

"What does it feel like to be up there onstage?" Thomas looked at me knowingly. He knew about my theater dreams and understood why I was asking.

"Fun. Just a whole lot of fun. I mean, the best part is when you've got a great crowd who's into it, you know?" I nodded. It sounded like heaven for an attention whore like me. I mean, except for the whole 'guy in a dress part'. "But the thing about performing, as far as I'm concerned, is that it's just for fun. I mean, I really enjoy it, but I'm not the kind of person where it's in my blood, you know? Like I have to do it. I have a blast with it, but if I couldn't do it anymore for some reason, it would be okay. I'm not like you, Henry."

"What do you mean?"

"I do think it's in your blood. Performing. I think it's something you were meant to do. You've got the talent. I'm sure of that."

"You really think so?"

"I've heard you sing!" Thomas said, dramatically putting a hand over his heart. I laughed. "And I think you've got this great comic ability, too. Timing, you know? The way you joke around with the fans, dance on the dugout, and all that. You're more, I don't know, *you* when you're doing stuff like that than when you're actually playing the game."

I loved how well he really understood me. I'd always known that about myself, but I had tried to ignore it. Playing baseball was easier, safer. More socially acceptable for a guy. And it made my father happy and proud of me. My love of singing and acting was a secret that I tried to keep hidden even from myself, but Thomas could see completely through me.

He got up to go to the kitchen to get a beer. He held one up to me and I nodded. He cracked open a Guinness and handed me a Yuengling.

"You ought to try performing at the club."

"Doing what?" I asked, picturing karaoke or something. He just looked at me and then I realized what he meant. "Are you out of your friggin' mind? I'm not doing drag!" I yelled before I realized how offensive I was being. I mean, he performed in drag all the time. Thomas just laughed.

"No, no; think about it. It's perfect. You could just do a number just to see how you really feel about performing. About really giving it a shot as a career. In drag, nobody would recognize you. You could perform in plain sight and nobody would have a clue it was you. You wouldn't even have to sing, just lip sync." I shook my head and he laughed. "Man, I would give *anything* to see that."

"Yeah, I'll just bet you would." The idea of singing in front of people both excited and terrified me. The idea of performing in drag and lip-syncing held no interest for me whatsoever. "I'd love to see you perform again. I just wish it wasn't so risky for me to go to the Hippo."

"You don't have to go there to see me perform. I've got the perfect song for you. I'm gonna dispense with the dress, though." Thomas got up to put on a CD. My own personal show from Thomas. What could be better? I settled back on the couch and got comfy, but then he said, "And I'm not doing this alone, Mr. Future Broadway Star."

I recognized the song from the very first note. It was "The Wallflower (Dance with me, Henry)" by Etta James. It's a cool song where the girl keeps asking Henry to roll with her, meaning dance, if he wants any romance from her. My mom used to play that song for me because it had my name in it.

Thomas was a spot-on lip syncer. He didn't miss a word. I wondered if he had learned this song just for me, or if he'd ever performed it at the club. He was incredibly sexy, seductive as he performed for me. And it was so, so much better without the dress.

"See, this," I said pointing at him. "*This* is what I thought it would be like dating a guy." He missed a few words from laughing, but then continued the performance. He pulled me up off the couch and danced with me. It was ridiculous and hilarious and fun. I did love singing and dancing and doing it with him was just joyful. There was no other word to describe it. There's a point in the song where the guy, well, Henry, sings a bit. Like he's agreeing to dance with her or whatever. I started mouthing the guy's part to Thomas' girl part, and he was delighted that I knew the words. I dipped him as the finale of our dance, but we were laughing so hard that I dropped him. I loved the position I had him in as I straddled him while he was on the floor. I planted a big kiss on his mouth before I helped him up.

We collapsed back on the couch, laughing. It was wonderful watching him perform just for me. Talent is sexy, and Thomas Palmer was wonderfully talented.

"That was great, Thomas. I love that song. My mom used to play it for me."

Thomas leaned on his elbow and looked at me. "What happened to her?" he asked gently.

"Cancer. I was ten."

"Wow. I'm really sorry, Henry."

"Thanks. Me, too."

"So, do you get along with your dad pretty well?" Thomas asked.

"Yeah, I guess. He did the best he could."

"I'd say he did a pretty good job."

"If he could see me now..." I said, shaking my head.

"He'd be pretty upset, huh?"

"That's an understatement. He's, shall we say, old fashioned."

"He must be pretty proud of you."

"He is. Well, he's proud of his macho, major league baseball-playing namesake. I don't think he'd be too proud to see the new singing, dancing, super-gay Henry Vaughn, Jr."

Thomas nodded. "Do you think you'd ever tell him?"

"I...wow. I don't know. I don't think so. I mean, I can't imagine doing that. Ever. What if he disowned me? Wait, can you even disown a grown man? I guess not. I mean, it's not like he supports me anymore. I send him money. But what if he never spoke to me again?"

"You really think he wouldn't?"

"I don't know. I'm honestly not sure." I couldn't imagine life without my dad. I would feel like an orphan, no matter how old I was. I didn't want to talk about this anymore, so I just rested my head on Thomas' shoulder. He stroked my hair affectionately. It was the most calm and content I think I'd ever felt in my life. I hated for the night to come to an end, but I knew if I didn't get out of there soon, I would fall asleep and poor Thomas would never get rid of me.

"I better go. It's getting late."

Thomas nodded. I called for a cab and we put the time waiting for it to arrive to good use. I pushed his back against his front door so I could make out with him. My palms were pressed flat against the door and my mouth was pressed against his. He cupped my face as he kissed me.

"Good luck at the game tomorrow. I'll be watching. Oh, and darling," he said, lovingly tracing his fingers under my chin. "Don't be afraid to do the 'Y.M.C.A' for the fans. It doesn't mean anything."

I laughed, mostly at myself. "I know, I know. Thanks, Thomas. For everything." I kissed him one more time before I headed out.

I could barely sit still in the cab and it wasn't just because my dick was hard as a rock from my recent makeout session with Thomas. Good thing it was dark out or the cab driver would have been really flattered by my standing at attention for him. I was antsy because I was dying to go home and talk to Alice about my date. I was so grateful for her friendship. I'd just had the most incredible date of my life. If not for Alice, there would have been no one to tell.

I went upstairs and stripped down to my underwear since I hate pajamas. I lay down in bed and called Alice.

"Henry! How was it? It's really laaaaate..." She said that last part in a singsong voice, like she wanted to know what Thomas and I were up to until 1 a.m. I laughed.

"It was amazing, Alice. It really was."

"I'm so glad! Tell me everything." So I did. I recounted everything. How much fun we'd had just hanging out and drinking beer. I even told her about what Thomas had done for me and she loved the part about how he wouldn't let me touch him. Glad somebody did.

"Awwww, he sounds so sweet!" Alice wailed into the phone. "I want to meet him. Can I meet him?"

"Sure. I don't see why not. Now, it's late, lady. Go to bed," I told her.

"I'm still at work."

"Don't sound like you're working too hard right now."

"That's 'cause I'm not. I had to run outside to talk to you," Alice said. So wait, she was just standing outside on the street in Baltimore in the middle of the night? She was gonna get mugged or raped or something.

"Girl, get your ass back inside! It's not safe outside at night. I can't believe you haven't been ducking bullets yet." Alice laughed, so I ordered her more sternly. "Go inside. I mean it. Don't make me come down there!"

"Yes, Dad," she said. I heard the door swing open, so I knew she had done what I asked. "I'm so glad things went well for you tonight. I'm so happy for you and I can't wait to meet...you know who."

"Cool. Thanks for gossiping with me. So I guess I'm like your gay best friend now, huh?"

"Exactly. Hey, I better go. I'm getting unfriendly looks from my coworkers. Good night, *Henry*." She said the last part loud enough so people would know she was talking to me. The public beginning of our fake romance.

I fell asleep that night thinking about my very real one with Thomas.

13

I decided to go see Sam at the hospital on Monday. I still felt kinda bad about how we'd left things the last time I saw him. More importantly, Thomas really liked Sam and I didn't want to screw up their friendship. I figured I would talk to Sam and make sure he was okay with the whole me and Thomas thing. The last time I saw him, he'd been threatening my life for kissing his best friend.

I found him in the Johns Hopkins cafeteria around the same time I had met him the last time. He looked very surprised to see me and I swear I saw a flash of guilt in his eyes. Was it possible he was actually sorry for being mean?

"Thomas isn't coming to lunch today. He's got too many patients."

I was a little disappointed that I wouldn't get to see Thomas, but of course that wasn't why I'd come.

"Actually, I came here to see you." Sam shot me a suspicious look. "It's nothing bad. I just wanted to see how you were and, you know, apologize for..." I wasn't exactly sure what to apologize for. I refused to say I was sorry for kissing Thomas. I wasn't. "...for upsetting you the other night."

"Yeah, well...maybe I did overreact just a little bit, Loretta." Okay, so he was still calling me girl names, but there didn't seem to be much hostility anymore. Now it was more like he was teasing me rather than really trying to insult me. "I just...I don't want him getting hurt." Sam looked genuinely worried, which made me like him more. Anybody who was protective of Thomas was okay in my book.

"I'd never hurt him, Sam."

"Maybe not on purpose. But what if you're not really... you know." Sam looked around to make sure nobody was listening, and I really appreciated his discretion. "Look, do I think it's the pill? No. Do I think you're confused? Yes." Fair enough.

"I didn't mean to fall for him. Believe me, I never expected that to happen. Like, ever. But I really care about him, Sam. A lot."

Sam looked me in the eye and sighed. He could see I was sincere about my feelings for his friend.

"I know you do. I guess he is pretty irresistible," Sam said, smiling with pride.

I couldn't help but ask him the question that had been burning in my brain since Sam first introduced me to Thomas.

"So, did you two ever, you know, date?"

Sam laughed. "No, no. It was never like that with us. We're more like brothers. I'm like his very...protective... brother," Sam said, shooting me a warning look. "Thomas has helped me through so much shit in my life. He's always been there for me, so you better believe if anybody messes with him, I will make sure they suffer. I don't care if they are bigger than me."

I could see that he meant it, too. He looked really sad as

he remembered whatever it was that Thomas had helped him through.

"What happened to you, man?" I asked as gently as I could. "I mean, I can tell it was something pretty bad."

"Yeah," Sam said, looking more depressed than I had ever seen him. "I just...I don't really like talking about it."

"Oh, yeah. Of course. Dude, I'm sorry. It's none of my business. I shouldn't have –"

"No, it's okay." Sam actually reached over and squeezed my hand briefly. "It's okay. I don't mind if you know about it. I trust you. I just don't like talking about it. Ask Thomas. He'll tell you. Tell him I said it was okay."

I nodded. I was really honored that Sam trusted me with his secret, but I could see that this conversation was really bumming him out. So I changed the subject. To me, of course.

"Soooo," I began smugly, "I know Thomas has helped a lot of people with their, you know, closet issues and such. Am I the first one he actually fell for?"

Sam rolled his eyes and grudgingly admitted, "Yes, Ellen, you are. It figures. Though I guess if Thomas likes you, you can't be a complete and total asshole."

"Stop. You're gonna make me cry!" Sam chuckled and it was nice to see him smile again. "Sam really, in all serious-ness, I have no idea what Thomas sees in me either. If it makes you feel any better, I *know* he's too good for me. But I'm glad he doesn't seem to know it. He's really helped me relax about the whole gay thing."

"Oh, I hear he relaxed you quite a bit."

No way. Thomas hadn't told Sam about...had he? Sam's smirk confirmed it. I felt my face get hot.

"Oh my God. You're blushing. You're actually blushing!" Sam practically shouted. He still enjoyed watching me squirm, so I guess not that much had changed. "And you said you wouldn't hurt him. You dropped him on the floor, you klutz."

"I cannot believe he told you all this!"

"Oh, he tells me evvvverything." Sam could see I was getting really irritated with Thomas, so he said softly, "Oh, don't be mad at him." I got the impression that he didn't want to come between me and Thomas any more than I wanted to interfere with their friendship. "He was just really excited about his date with you and wanted to tell me all about it. He was like a damn teenage girl. 'Oh, he's soooo cute, Sam. And so sweet. And so funny! Did I tell you how funny he is?' " Sam said, rolling his eyes. " 'He was so *romantic*. He actually kissed me first this time!' Vomit." Sam pretended to be annoyed, but he clearly thought it was cute that Thomas was so excited. He also knew I made Thomas happy, so he couldn't really hate me anymore. It gave me a huge thrill to think that Thomas had called Sam and told him how great our date was. I could hardly be mad at Thomas for telling Sam all the details. Hadn't I done the very same thing with Alice?

"Did he tell you he took my shirt off?"

"Are you kidding? I got a play-by-play of every bulge, every ripple..."

I pumped my fist in the air. "Yes!"

Sam laughed, then raised an eyebrow. "His description was hardly necessary, as I am familiar with what you look like with your shirt off."

"Oh, yeah." It seemed so long ago that Sam had examined me at Hopkins.

"All the guys in the world and he hadda pick you," he said, shaking his head. I nodded proudly. "Well, I better get back to work." Sam stood up to put his tray away and throw out the trash from his lunch. "So, you know, let me know if anything...changes." He still didn't believe it was the drug that had made me gay, but now that Thomas was involved, he had more reason to be concerned about the off chance that it might be.

"I really don't think it will."

Sam nodded and started to head back to his office. He turned back around. "It was actually almost nice to see you, Georgina. I'm glad to see you're doing better, you know, with everything that's going on. And, Henry, really. If you need anything, anything at all...call Thomas. He actually gives a shit."

He smirked at me and walked away. Maybe I was imagining things, but his smirk looked more like a real smile this time.

14

The asthma pill had clearly worn off, as I had to keep sneaking into the clubhouse to take hits of my inhaler during the game. It was only about 24 hours until it had technically been four weeks since I'd taken the pill, and I knew it was just a formality to wait one more day to be sure the pill hadn't caused my homosexuality.

It clearly hadn't.

I had to face the truth that I really was gay. When I was with Thomas, I was fine with it. More than fine. I loved it. I was so happy when I was with him that I didn't care about anything else. It was here in the clubhouse that I hated it. I was scared to death all the time and people were always saying nasty things about gay people. It was awful. I wanted to hurry up and get the hell out of there so I could see Thomas to be reminded of all the reasons that it was okay that I was gay.

When I got to his place, I immediately spilled my guts about all the stress and ugliness that was going on in the clubhouse. Thomas was wonderful. He rubbed my back and shoulders and listened with compassion while I vented.

"It's so awful there right now, Thomas. What am I gonna do if anybody finds out about me? It's...it's been a month now, you know. So I guess I'm really..."

Thomas nodded. He stopped rubbing my shoulders so he could look at me. "Are you okay?"

I nodded. "Yeah. I think so. It's still gonna take some getting used to. But I know you're gonna help me with that." I leaned over and kissed him. Warmth spread throughout my body as he wrapped his arms around me. He always made me feel better. Always. The full magnitude of my sexuality hadn't quite hit me yet. There was so much to think about. So many repercussions. My life would be so, so different from now on. But there was no point in denying that I was gay anymore. Right now, with Thomas' lips on mine, I didn't have much interest in denying it anyway.

We settled back on the couch and put our feet up, just enjoying being together. I kept trying to put the craziness of the ballpark behind me, but I couldn't. Thomas noticed. He always seemed to know what I was thinking.

"It'll be okay, hon."

"I know. I'm just..." *Scared*. But I didn't want him to know that. I wanted him to think of me as manly and brave. "...worried about everything." I suddenly remembered Alice and felt a lot better. She would keep me safe. With her as my girlfriend, the media might leave me alone. "I almost forgot to tell you. I have this friend, this really sweet girl, who knows all about you and me. I just had to brag to somebody that you were my guy and I knew I could trust her."

Thomas smiled at me and I felt my pulse quicken. God, I loved when he smiled at me.

"She wants to meet you, if that's okay."

"Of course! I would love to meet her."

"The best part is that she offered to be my...what's the word when a gay guy has a fake girlfriend so nobody suspects him of being gay?"

Thomas' face fell. "Beard," he said, sighing wearily.

"Oh. That's not a good thing, is it?"

"Well, no, not really." Thomas took my hand in his. "Look, I understand how dangerous a time this is for you. I know you really could lose your job if anybody found out. Or even if you didn't, those guys could make your life a living hell if they knew. It's just...I hate hiding, Henry. I really, really hate it. It goes against everything I believe in."

"I understand, Thomas. I just can't tell anybody. I can't –"

"I know that, hon. I don't expect you to come out or anything. Not yet anyway. Look, the decision to come out of the closet is very personal. I wish with all my heart that everybody who's gay would announce it to the world and be proud of it, but even I understand that it's not that easy. Not in a line of work like yours." Thomas squeezed my hand. "I don't believe in pressuring people to come out, and I sure as hell don't believe in outing people against their will like your teammates are trying to do." He said that last part bitterly. He really was the patron saint of gay people. "Even if you never came out, it would be amazing if you could go on television and make some kind of statement in support of gay athletes. You wouldn't have to say that you were one; just that there's nothing wrong with it and that you fully support any players who might be gay."

I could see that would be a dream come true for Thomas if I did that. I would be his swashbuckling hero. His brave white knight. I swallowed hard. I knew I could never be that strong.

"Hey," he said gently. He looked concerned as he saw the

fear on my face. So much for being his courageous hero. "I'm not asking you to do that, Henry. You could lose your job over it. I know that. Baby, we can use your friend for now. Anything to keep you safe from the media and help protect your job. I promise I will respect your choice about coming out, even if it means that you never tell anyone. But you have to know that..." Thomas let go of my hand and swallowed hard. "I won't hide forever. N-not even for you."

I could see that it hurt him very badly to say that last part. I felt terrible about what I was asking him to do, even temporarily. Thomas was so devoted to helping gay people to be proud and to deal with their homophobic families. Of course, he wouldn't want to hide that he was gay. He was very passionate about gay acceptance. He wanted to change the world. I was so proud of him. He was so brave. Not like me. Not like me at all.

"I hate hiding you, Thomas. I hope you know that," I said as I drew him into my arms.

"I know, Henry. I know." Thomas spoke soothingly in my ear as he massaged my back. I had known him such a short time and I already couldn't imagine living without him. But now I knew it would eventually come down to an ultimatum: either I came out or I would lose him. Both thoughts terrified me. I just couldn't deal with it. Thomas had said we could use Alice for now, so we would. "But I need for you to understand something. I will never, ever ask you to come out or do anything you're not comfortable with. But you have to promise me that you won't ever lie to anyone about me being gay. You don't have to volunteer the information and, for now, you certainly don't have to say that I'm your boyfriend. But I don't want you ever telling anyone that I'm straight, okay? If anybody ever asks, don't lie about who I am, what I am. Okay?"

I nodded. I could see how important this was to him. It scared the hell out of me. The idea that, if asked, I would have to admit that my "friend" was gay. I supposed I would cross that bridge when I came to it. If I came to it.

"You need to make sure you tell...wait, what's her name? Your friend?"

"Alice. Alice Beckford."

"Tell Alice I really appreciate all her help and that I can't wait to meet her. And Henry? We have to make sure that this doesn't interfere in her life too much, you know? I mean, what if somebody else wants to date her?"

"Oh, yeah." I felt bad that the thought hadn't even occurred to me. Typical of me. Thinking of myself and nobody else. Shit. Alice was a smart, pretty girl, and I had no idea why nobody had snapped her up already.

"Just make sure she knows that we don't want to get in her way, okay? She can back out any time, no hard feelings, right?"

"I'll tell her." Typical Thomas. Thinking about everybody else's feelings.

"Speaking of friends...I hear you paid one of mine a visit." Thomas said, brightening a little.

Oh, yeah. Sam. Okay, so I wasn't totally self-serving all the time. I had gone to see Sam to make sure he wasn't still mad. I thought about other people's feelings. Sometimes.

"Yup. Oh my God, Thomas. I cannot believe you told him about-"

"I'm sorry. I'm sorry, Henry! He's just, you know, my best friend. I-I just wanted to tell-"

"No, no," I said, laughing. Thomas looked so guilty that I had to let him off the hook. "I can't be mad. I told Alice, too. Everything. I mean, *everything*. It's okay. It's just, you know

Sam. Anything you tell him can and will be used against me."

"Did he make fun of you? I'll kill him!"

"No, no, it's okay. We made nice. Pretty much. I guess he's not that bad." I leaned on my elbow on the couch and looked at Thomas. "So...what happened to him? I know it was something bad. He told me to ask you. He said he didn't want to talk about it, but he said it was okay for you to tell me."

"He did?" Thomas asked, looking genuinely surprised. I nodded. "Okay, well..." Thomas looked sad. I guess he didn't like talking about it either. "I actually met Sam before he started working at the hospital. He came to the Hippo on his 21st birthday. All alone. I can always tell when somebody's never been in a gay bar before. So I went up and introduced myself to him and we just talked for a while."

I smiled just thinking about that. I could so clearly imagine Sam, looking lonely and scared, and Thomas going up to him with his warm eyes and gentle voice, making him feel comfortable. That was what he did best.

"We stayed 'til closing and just talked and drank. He told me everything that had happened to him." Thomas paused for a moment, remembering. I saw fondness as he remembered the night he met one of his dearest friends, but also sorrow at what Sam had told him. "Um, well, he...when Sam first realized he was gay, he told his parents. And they...well, they abandoned him."

"Oh, my God," I whispered. "Both of them? Even his mother?"

Thomas nodded. "I know. It's-it's just so awful." He looked at me and I saw such pain in those eyes that I adored. "The thing is, his mom and dad weren't like religious nuts or anything. He had absolutely no idea that they would react that way. They...they kicked him out of the house right away. He was fifteen years old."

I sucked in a breath. I wanted to take back every nasty thing I had ever said or even thought about Sam Aubrey. He could call me any girl name he wanted for the rest of his life. Dear God.

"He spent the next few years in foster homes. He was bullied horribly in high school. The kids actually mocked him for having parents who didn't want him because he was a..." Thomas couldn't bring himself to use the word the bullies had used. "Because he was gay. He-he...even tried to...there were, you know, attempts..."

I squeezed Thomas' hand and nodded to let him know I understood. He didn't have to say out loud that Sam had tried to kill himself.

"So, as soon as he was old enough to go to a bar, he went to the Hippo, hoping to find people like him."

"And he found you." Thank God for that. Now I understood why Sam cared so much for Thomas and why he wanted to kick the living shit out of anyone who would possibly hurt him.

"Sam hated being gay. He felt like it turned everybody against him." Thomas smiled softly. "Then he met Jeremy and he didn't seem to mind so much."

"I know exactly..." I said, punctuating my words with kisses, "how...he feels..." Thomas smiled at me.

He rubbed my cheek with the back of his hand, and said "You look tired. You better get home and get some rest. I'm sure tomorrow's game will be better."

I nodded, feeling even more tired just thinking about today's game. Another ugly loss.

"You'll have to, you know, wear your baseball uniform for me sometime," Thomas said seductively.

"Really?"

He nodded and I felt myself start to get hard. "Only if you wear your scrubs. Mmmmm. So I can take them off..." I said, then I kissed him. I started to run my hand down the front of his pants, but he stopped me. As usual. Shit.

"Not tonight, baby. It's late and you look so tired. Next time, I promise."

"And you'll let me...take care of you? You promise?"

"We'll see," Thomas said, but the glint in his eye told me that was a yes.

15

My dad came to the game yesterday, which was nice. I always tried to take him out for a beer afterwards, so I ended up going out with him instead of Thomas. Naturally, the subject of the gay guy on the team came up and I knew I should have taken the opportunity to sort of ease him into my newfound acceptance of homosexuals. I could have just said something casual like "I don't know. I guess it's not really a big deal if one of my teammates is gay." But no. I kept changing the subject every time it came up and I hated myself for it.

It was nice hanging out with my dad, but it made me crazy that I couldn't go see Thomas, especially after he'd pretty much promised the next time I saw him we could fool around. And this time he would actually let me participate. I got so excited I could barely walk every time I thought about all the things I wanted to do with him. To him. I'd been walking around with a near constant boner for the last 24 hours and I knew Thomas was the only cure.

I felt I couldn't wait a second longer. I texted him during today's game and told him to eat dinner without me and I'd grab something on the way. I told him we were going straight to dessert when I got to his place.

Easy, Tiger, he'd texted back. But then he wrote: *Can't wait.*

I actually drove to his place this time. I didn't have the patience to wait for a cab. I also brought an overnight bag. I guess it was presumptuous, but I figured we'd play it by ear and Thomas could kick me out if he wanted to. But I didn't think he would. If he thought I was ready to spend the night at his place, he'd probably let me.

I charged into his apartment the moment he opened the door. I shut the door behind me and before he even knew what hit him, I had his back against the door and my mouth on his. When I finally broke off the kiss, Thomas was panting harder than I did when I was in the middle of an asthma attack.

"God, Henry!" He laughed and looked a little flushed.

"I missed you."

"I can see that. Baby, you know I want you. Bad," Thomas said, eagerly running his hands over my chest. "But we still need to take it slow. I don't want you doing anything you're not ready for, okay?"

"I'm fine, Thomas. I know what I'm doing."

"Still. One step at a time, okay?"

"Whatever you say," I said. Then I grabbed him around the waist and slung him over my shoulder. I'm pretty strong, but Thomas was a big guy. He was tall and somewhat muscular, so it was an effort for me, but I did it.

I carried him to the bedroom and flung him down on the bed.

"You're a Neanderthal, Henry," Thomas said, breathless, laughing.

"You know you love it," I said. I climbed on top of him and he looked up at me with eyes full of desire that I could not wait to fulfill. I was excited but also nervous. I'd never wanted to please anybody so much in my life. I hoped I would do a good job despite the fact that I had never touched a man sexually before.

I took off my shirt and Thomas stared at my chest. He ran his hands over my biceps and abs. His touch made me shiver with anticipation. "I feel like I'm in bed with a Greek god..."

"That's a bit of an exaggeration, darling," I said, but I loved the way he admired me. I was so glad that I turned him on. "Come on," I said, tugging at his shirt. "Off with it before I tear it off."

Thomas groaned and grudgingly pulled his shirt over his head. He was still really self-conscious about his body. I wished he would stop comparing himself to me. I didn't compare him to anybody. There was no comparison. I only had eyes for him.

"Thomas, you're the hottest guy I've ever met." He rolled his eyes, not believing a word I said. "Baby," I murmured in his ear. "I have to jerk off like ten times a day just thinking about you. You drive me *crazy*."

I fumbled with his belt and he fumbled with mine. I couldn't wait to get him completely naked. I wanted to see every inch of him. I pulled off the rest of my clothes and yanked off his jeans and underwear.

He looked incredible.

Seeing Thomas naked in bed, erect and ready to go, was probably the sexiest thing I'd ever seen in my life. I looked him up and down. I shook my head.

"What?" Thomas asked, looking more self-conscious than ever.

"All this time you're bitching about my muscles...you knew damn well your cock was bigger."

Thomas grinned mischievously and arched an eyebrow in a way that I found sexy beyond all reason. Oh, yeah. He knew. Guys always noticed that. Even straight guys look and compare themselves in the shower. If they say they don't, they're fucking liars.

"You just relax. Relax and let me take care of you," I told him. I kissed him and he ran his hands over my chest. I kissed his mouth, his neck. I kept kissing down his chest, slowly, further and further down. His body suddenly tensed and I could pinpoint the exact millisecond that he realized I had no intention of using my hands to get him off.

"Wait! Henry!"

I rolled my eyes, but I had expected this battle. I kissed my way back up to his face, looked him in the eye, and waited for his argument.

"Baby, you don't have– "

"I know, honey. I want to," I said. I kissed him over and over. "I want...to do this...for you...and you're...going...to let me..." I knew once I had him in my mouth that he would be completely helpless to argue. All guys were. You can't think rationally in the middle of a blow job. But I had to get to that point. "Thomas, I'm an adult. I know what I'm doing. And I'm going to do it."

Thomas looked into my eyes, worried that we were going too far but having a really hard time resisting me. I loved that. I wanted to be irresistible to him.

"Just relax," I told him, massaging his shoulders. "Relax, and let me do this for you. Please."

He sighed. "Only if you're sure. And you can stop if you're uncomfortable, okay? Even in the middle. If you change your mind-"

"Duly noted. But I won't."

I started kissing back down his chest.

"Wait!"

"Thomas, I swear to God..."

"No! It's just...I don't want you to have to swallow." He leaned over to grab a box of tissues on his nightstand. Watching him stretch out like that, naked, made my cock throb even harder. I wanted him so bad. He tossed the box of tissues toward the foot of the bed. "I'll try to warn you before I come." He flopped back down on the bed.

"Okay, go."

I chuckled and shook my head.

I started over, kissing his mouth. I massaged his shoulders at the same time, trying to get him to calm down and quit worrying about me. I felt his body, slowly, start to relax. Finally, I kissed down his beautiful, naked body.

He gasped sharply when I finally took him in my mouth. I knew I was pretty much home free now. Thomas was under my control, right where I wanted him to be.

Then all of a sudden it hit me and I could not believe what I was doing. It was something that I never, ever thought I would do. Something that, as a man, I wasn't supposed to be doing with another man. This was a straight guy's worst nightmare. Guys tried to scare each other with it all the time. They'd ask, "Gun to your head, do you suck a guy's dick?" "Would you do it for a million dollars?" "What do you think really happens in prison?"

I was stunned at how forcefully the fear hit me. I felt cold sweat start to break out on my back. Thomas was right to be so cautious. This was too much, too soon. I wasn't ready. Maybe I never would be.

Then I heard it.

Thomas' voice. Moaning and calling out my name.

And, just like that, the fear vanished. His voice soothed, calmed, and excited me all at once. I remembered I wasn't with some random guy and this sure as hell wasn't prison. I was with the man I adored more than anything in this world. The sweet sound of Thomas' voice reminded me exactly why I was doing this. I cared deeply for him and I wanted to please him so badly. By the sounds of ecstasy he was making, I knew I was doing a good job. Suddenly, it wasn't weird or uncomfortable at all anymore. It felt right. Natural.

Thomas hoisted himself up on his elbows for a minute. I felt a little self-conscious at first, but then it was kind of erotic having him watch me suck him off.

"God, Henry. Your body is *amazing*," Thomas said, still watching me. He rolled his head back and moaned, "Ohh-hhh, Henry. Watch out, hon. I'm almost there..." He barely managed to croak out the words before his body shuddered into a violent orgasm.

I had never been more aroused in my life.

It was just the way he sat up and looked at me, my body, and then lost control seconds later. I had never felt more desirable, more like a man, than I did at that moment.

I wiped my mouth with the tissues, but only because it was what Thomas wanted me to do. Funny how there was nothing gross about it. I mean, it was *Thomas.*

I crawled back up to lie down next to him. He lay on his back, panting for a moment, and then rolled over on his side and looked at me. His eyes had this wonderful sleepy, satisfied look and I knew I had done well.

"Henry," he said, laughing. "Are you sure you've never done that before?"

"Oh, I'm sure," I said, laughing, too. I touched his face

and said softly, "You're the only one." He smiled at me. We both knew I was talking about more than blow jobs.

"That was amazing, Henry. Thank you for doing that for me."

I tucked his hair behind his ear. "I loved doing that for you." And it was the truth. It really was.

"Okay, MLB PLYA. Your turn." With that, he gripped my shoulders and pushed me onto my back. And then the sexiest man I had ever known proceeded to blow my mind.

I did spend the night. We fell asleep, naked, wrapped in each other's arms.

16

Not only did I tell Alice what Thomas and I had done in bed together, I didn't feel uncomfortable at all. Alice had zero hang-ups about gay people and she was really happy for me and Thomas. She and Thomas had both heard so much about each other that they were dying to meet, but I was kind of nervous about it.

I was so grateful to have Alice as my friend, but I felt bad that our relationship seemed to be so one-sided. Alice was always taking care of me, listening to me go on and on about my life. I made a mental note to take her out to a fancy dinner or buy her a nice necklace. Or both. Something to show how much I appreciated her friendship.

I didn't know what Alice was more excited about; meeting Thomas or going to a gay club. She'd never been. I was thrilled at the chance to see Thomas perform again, but I was scared to death to go back to Club Hippo. It was really dangerous for me. If anybody saw me there, I was done. The plan was to meet up with Thomas in the dressing room area before the show and then Alice, Sam, Jeremy, and I would sit at that table in the far corner again where it was dark and nobody should be able to see me.

I don't know why I was nervous about having Alice and Thomas meet. I guess I just cared a lot about both of them and really wanted them to get along.

"Chill out, Henry. If he's half as nice as you described him, we'll get along great!" Alice told me as we made our way upstairs to the dressing room. It was cool how much she was enjoying this. She was the type of chick who loved new adventures and going to a dressing room to see a bunch of drag queens was definitely a new adventure for her. "Hey, don't tell me which one is Thomas. Lemme see if I can figure it out based on how you described him." I shrugged.

We got to the top of the stairs and I opened the door. Alice's eyes grew wide as she took in the crazed scene of a bunch of men running around, half naked, with makeup and wigs on.

"Okay, figuring out which one is him is going to be harder than I thought," Alice said. I laughed.

"I know. I think even I'd have a hard time recognizing him under all the makeup and hair," I said, although I knew it wasn't true. I'd know those gorgeous eyes anywhere, no matter how much mascara and eyeliner surrounded them. I spotted him toward the back of the room and Alice followed my gaze.

"Found him," Alice said. "I can tell by *your* face." She squeezed my shoulder affectionately. I guess my face looked like Sam's whenever he saw Jeremy.

Thomas wasn't dressed. I mean, he had clothes on. Boy clothes. I guess he didn't want to frighten off my friend by meeting her while he was wearing a dress. Typical, thoughtful Thomas. He hurried over to us. Alice smiled warmly at him. Thomas grasped her hand in both of his, just the way he had when he'd first met me.

"You must be Alice!" Thomas exclaimed.

"And *you* must be Alice. Or at least that's what Henry calls you when you're on the phone with him," Alice said.

Thomas laughed. "Exactly! Speaking of which, I want to tell you how much I appreciate what you're doing for us."

"Oh, I don't mind at all."

"I promise our little arrangement with you won't last forever. I don't like hiding my relationship with Henry, but I don't want him getting hurt." Thomas looked over at me with concern.

"Oh, you guys are so cute together!" Alice said, looking at the two of us in wonder. She'd seen me take home so many women over the years and she'd never seen me with a guy. I knew she'd never seen me so happy before, either.

"Don't you have to get ready?" I asked. Thomas nodded.

"Yeah, I gotta get moving," Thomas said, glancing around at all the others who were nearly ready to go on.

"Good luck. I mean, break a leg." I hugged him and kissed him for luck. This was the one place where I could kiss him openly in public, so I did it every chance I got. I'd have to hide when I was down in the bar, but up here in the dressing room, everybody knew Thomas was dating Henry Vaughn, Jr. from the Baltimore Orioles. They were Thomas' friends, and we knew they wouldn't tell anyone. Call it the Pink Wall of Silence.

"I can't wait to see you perform!" Alice said.

"Likewise. I'd love to see you do standup," Thomas told her.

"That can definitely be arranged," Alice said. "Listen, I was thinking if you guys ever want to go out somewhere together, like to a restaurant or something, I could go with

you. I could pretend to be Henry's date. I know it wouldn't
be the same as a private date, but it would be something. At
least you two could get out once in a while." Thomas looked
at me and I nodded. That would work.

"That's really sweet of you, Alice. That would be fun.
Now, come on. I'll take you downstairs to your seats. Sam
and Jeremy are reserving a place for you way in the back."
Thomas quickly ushered us downstairs. He walked down in
front of us and Alice put her hand over her heart and
mouthed "*He's so cute!*"

I smiled and mouthed, "*I know!*"

Thomas took us to a table all the way in the back in the
far right corner of the club. It wasn't too dark yet, but it
would be once the lights in the club went down for the
show. Sam and Jeremy were at the table, having a few beers.

"Guys, this is Alice. Alice, this is Sam and Jeremy,"
Thomas said.

Sam stood up and shook Alice's hand. "So you're a friend
of Henry's," he said.

"Yeah, but you know, don't judge me," Alice said.

Sam laughed and said, "I like you already."

Alice sat down in a chair next to me. I sat with my back
to the rest of the place, so nobody would recognize me. I'd
turn my chair around when the show started.

"So, Isabel, you decided to grace us with your presence
again," Sam said, smirking. Alice looked at Sam, then back
at me. I had told her that Sam liked to give me a hard time,
but I don't think I had mentioned the girl name thing.

"Wait. Let me guess. You call him girl names to get back
at him for being such a homophobe, right?" Alice asked
excitedly. Sam winked at her and clicked his tongue and did
the handgun finger-pointer thing at her to show her she had
gotten it just right. "That...is...*awesome*! I call him 'Peaches'."

"For the Schnapps thing, right?" Sam asked, delighted to have a partner-in-crime in harassing me. Alice nodded enthusiastically.

"Al-iiiiiceeee!" I whined, but it was no good. She was locked on.

"Okay, so what names have you used already?" Alice asked, taking out a pen and a small notebook from her purse. I rolled my eyes and sighed.

Thomas squeezed my shoulder in support and I flinched.

I flinched.

I felt awful. I was just scared to death at being caught being here and I was a nervous wreck. I looked around at all the people in the club and, of course, nobody was paying any attention to us.

"I'm sorry," I said quietly to Thomas. He nodded, understanding. I took a risk and grabbed his hand and squeezed it. "Good luck tonight."

"Thanks," Thomas said, squeezing back. "See you all after the show!" He bounded away back toward the stairs and the dressing room. Alice turned to me after Thomas had disappeared.

"I really like him, Henry. He's so sweet. And I see what you mean about his eyes. They're *beautiful!*" I nodded, glad that Alice approved of my guy. Sam smiled at her. He had taken quickly to Alice - I think he found it easier to trust women - and now he liked her even more because of her sweet words about Thomas. I had told Alice all about Sam's horrible past, so she was especially kind to him.

"Hey, Alice," Sam said. Alice turned around. "No, I was talking to him," he said, gesturing to me. Alice giggled and high-fived him. I just shook my head. I had to admit they were kind of cute, even if they were ganging up on me. Alice seemed to bring out the kid in Sam.

The lights started to dim and the drag show began. Although the idea of guys wearing dresses still struck me as kinda weird, I had to admit that drag shows could be entertaining in a campy sort of way.

"Hey, Henry! Gimme a dollar!" Alice said, poking me in the ribs. She'd seen other people handing the performers money and she wanted in. I fished a dollar out of my wallet and she eagerly got up from her seat and approached the performer dressed as Lady Gaga. Normally, all you had to do was hold up your money and eventually the performer would sashay over and retrieve it from you. Alice didn't want to draw any attention to our table because of me, so she walked over to the drag queen herself.

"She's really getting into this, huh?" Jeremy said, shaking his head and laughing.

"Yep," I said, watching Alice dance with the performer. The queens were cool. They were very low-pressure, not like strippers whose goal in life seemed to be to humiliate you as much as possible in front of your friends. The queens would simply nod and smile, take your dollar, and kinda let you be unless you indicated you were up for more. Alice had no fear. She loved dancing for a few seconds with Lady Gaga before letting him/her go on to collect more dough. I suppose she was kind of an attention whore like me. *Cool.*

The next performer up was Ben. He did Liza Minnelli's version of "New York, New York" again. He was great, just like last time. It was another crowd-pleasing song that cost me another dollar from Alice.

My heart skipped a beat as soon as Thomas entered the stage. I hadn't seen what outfit he would be wearing and he was almost unrecognizable in full dress and makeup, but I could tell right away that it was him just by the way he walked. He did a kind of a 50s and 60s medley with a bunch of different songs. It was amazing how he could switch from song to song without missing a line. His lip syncing was perfection. I've said it before and I'll say it again. Talent. Is. Sexy. I was so proud of him.

One particular song in the medley caught my attention. It was the "The Wallflower (Dance with me, Henry)". The song we had danced to together in his apartment.

"Huh," Sam said snarkily. "I've seen him do this medley a bunch of times. *That's* a new addition."

While performing that part of the song, Thomas looked straight over in the corner at me. He lowered his heavily mascaraed eyes seductively as he sang/synced our song. He may have been dressed like a girl, but he was still my sexy man. Jeremy glanced over at me and smiled and so did Alice. I've had a ballpark full of fans chanting my name, but that experience had nothing on this one. It was a moment I wished could have lasted forever. The room was full of people, but he was singing only to me. It was over quickly as Thomas switched to another 50s song in the medley.

"Quick! Gimme another dollar!" Alice said, punching me repeatedly in the shoulder.

"Ow! Hang on," I said, digging in my wallet. Alice was so lucky she was a girl. I would have given anything to be able to walk right up to Thomas and give him a dollar myself. Alice followed my longing gaze toward Thomas, and she grabbed two bucks from me.

"I'll tell him the second one's from you," Alice said. She jumped up out of her seat and headed toward Thomas. I saw him wink at her when she gave him the first dollar, then smile broadly when she gave him the second one.

THE GAME WAS CALLED off early. It had been pouring down rain all day and it wasn't supposed to let up until sometime after midnight. I was thrilled at the idea of having a rare night off. Of course, the guys wanted to go out drinking and whoring, but I had the perfect excuse. I was going to see my new girlfriend, Alice Beckford, perform at open mic night at a comedy club. This was like 90% true. I was going to go there since I had the night off. I was even going to give her a ride to the club. The only part I left out was that she wasn't my girlfriend and that we would pick up my boyfriend on the way there.

I drove my huge Cadillac Escalade truck instead of my Corvette since the 'Vette was just a two-seater. I honked my horn outside Alice's apartment and she dashed out to the truck, breathless, trying not to get too soaking wet.

"Thanks for the ride, Henry!"

"My pleasure. If you're up for it, maybe after your show we can all go out to eat somewhere fancy. My treat." I had been looking forward to going out in public with Thomas and Alice ever since she suggested it.

"If you're buyin', I'm there," Alice said.

We picked up Thomas outside his apartment. He jumped into the backseat and shook his head like a wet puppy. Water droplets flew all over my truck.

"Hey, cut it out!" I said, laughing.

"Thomas, do you want to sit up front? I can-" Alice began.

"No, no way. Stay where you are. Stars gotta sit up front." Thomas said. "You ready for tonight? You nervous?" Alice nodded. "I know exactly how you feel. Well, you know you got at least two fans there with you tonight, okay?"

Alice didn't look nervous to me. I don't think I would be anywhere near as calm if I was about to perform anything, never mind standup comedy. You were a special breed if you could get up on stage all by yourself like that and try to make people laugh. She drew in a deep breath.

"I try not to think too hard about it before I go on. Here, I got a surprise for you, Henry," Alice said as she reached in her bag and pulled out a CD. "I saw Thomas perform and you're gonna see me perform tonight, so now it's your turn." She held up the CD and I couldn't believe what I saw.

"Is that...*Oklahoma*?" I asked. She nodded. My favorite musical. I couldn't believe she remembered.

"Yep. I've been listening to it and I'll even sing it with you, but you're gonna have to sing for me first. You promised you would sing for me sometime. Sometime is now, so get ready."

"You haven't heard him sing yet? Oh, you're in for a treat. You won't believe it. Seriously, Alice. He's incredible."

I glanced in the rearview mirror at Thomas. He was so damn cute. "But you're not biased or anything."

"Doesn't matter if I am. You've got serious talent. I'm not just saying that because I'm blinded by your biceps."

I chuckled at that. "So, Alice, what do you mean you'll sing it with me? You like...know the words?" I asked.

"Yep. I'll sing that sap Laurey's part with you, but I much prefer Ado Annie."

I could understand that. Laurey was the romantic heroine, but Ado Annie was the comic relief. I could see Alice doing Ado Annie quite well. Alice put the CD in the player and the overture started. I started feeling a little nervous.

Alice pushed the next button to go past the instrumental part to get to "Oh, What a Beautiful Morning." I really did love that song.

"Come on, Peaches. You're up." I looked at her, sighing heavily. A promise was a promise, and God knows she didn't ask me for much.

I took a deep breath and started singing along with the song. I kept my eyes straight ahead. I focused on the road more out of nervousness than concern for our safety while driving on the wet streets. I tried not to notice as Alice, very gradually, turned the music lower and lower until I was pretty much singing *a capella*. When I finished the song, she didn't say anything at first. I glanced over at her.

I confess I was a little disappointed that she didn't go all googly-eyed and swoony the way Thomas and Sam had when I sang for them, but she looked impressed.

Finally, she said "Daaaammmn, Henry!"

"Damn as in good?" I asked.

"Damn as in damn good! You sound amazing!"

"Told ya," Thomas piped up from the back.

"Do you really think so?"

"Yeah, Henry. You sounded great. Wow, I'm like really, really impressed," Alice said. She laughed. "Can you imagine what the guys on your team would say if they knew you could sing? Oh, and your *fans,* Henry! They'd go even crazier over you than they already do. Especially the women. Not that it would do them any good."

I laughed. "Yeah. I've thought about that so many times. What people would think if they heard me sing. I've always, always wanted to sing the National Anthem at a game."

Alice gasped. "Can you imagine? Oh, people would go nuts. Oh, you should do it, Henry!"

I scoffed. "Yeah. I can just see me broaching that subject with management." Then, in a falsetto high voice, I said, "Don't you see? I simply *must sing!*" I spread my arms out dramatically, then put them back on the steering wheel where they belonged. Alice burst out laughing.

"Yeah, I see what you mean. Maybe what say we let the gay rumors die down a bit before trying the whole 'let me sing for the people' idea," Alice said.

"Speaking of singing for people, dammit. You promised!" I said, pointing to the CD player.

"Yeah, yeah, yeah," Alice said. She forwarded through a few songs until she got to the one called "People Will Say We're in Love", which is a song that both the hero and heroine sing together. "I'm a comic not a singer, okay? So don't expect me to be as good as you. I only sing for funsies. You're the one who's actually good at it."

"Duly noted."

The song began and we sang it together, which was really fun. When did my life turn into a Broadway musical where my friends and I just started singing and dancing together out of the blue? I swear, between Thomas and Alice, I had taken to spontaneous performances with alarming ease. How on earth did it take me this long to realize that I was gay?

Alice really wasn't a bad singer at all. She had trouble hitting some of the higher notes, but she was a great sport about it. She just started laughing every time her voice gave out. It was such a pleasure to sing with her. I was able to imagine what it would be like to be singing onstage with a bunch of other actors and actually doing the show.

The thought gave me chills. Maybe I really had missed my calling. Well, it was too late now. A baseball player was what I was and what I'd always be known for. And I was lucky for that. I had nothing to bitch about.

Thomas applauded wildly in the back. I grinned at him

in the rearview mirror. He was always such an appreciative audience.

"Okay, fine. That song's all well and good," Alice said, fiddling with the dial. I knew exactly what song she was looking for. "Hah! Here it is. This one is sooo much better than that sappy one."

"Hey, I happen to like that sappy one."

"I swear, Henry. You get gayer by the minute," Alice said.

"I knoooow," I whined. She cleared her throat and proceeded to sing the most hilarious and entertaining version of "I Cain't Say No" that I had ever heard in my life. This chick had amazing comic ability and timing; there was no doubt about that. She was really, really good. Plus, she was totally right about that song being a lot more fun than the other one. It was sung with kind of a hick accent and Ado Annie is singing about how she can't say no when it comes to men. Whenever Alice got to a line about how rotten men were, she jokingly glared at me. When she got to a line that hinted about fooling around with a guy, she turned around and made eyes at Thomas while she sang. He was practically on the floor laughing.

When she finished, I whistled my approval. I would have applauded but, you know, steering wheel and all. It wasn't wise to drive with your knees in a rainstorm. Thomas laughed and applauded, though.

He tapped me on the shoulder and said, "You know how we said Brady Clayton is hot enough to turn a straight man gay? I think Alice is sexy enough to make me want to make a change."

I turned to Alice. "Hey, eyes off my man, *bitch!*"

Alice laughed and clapped her hands.

"That was awesome, Alice. Really awesome! I honestly can't wait to see you onstage tonight. You've got it, girl. You

really do," I told her. I meant it. She was really talented. I
was excited about having a friend who seemed to have the
desire to entertain as much as I did. I knew she understood
what it felt like to have a dream. All my life I'd avoided
telling anyone about wanting to perform, and here I had two
amazing friends in my life who supported me unconditionally.

"Thanks, Henry." She punched my shoulder affectionately.

The place was pretty small. It was more dive bar than
comedy club, but you had to start somewhere, I suppose.
Alice was a lot braver than I was. At least she was actively
pursuing her dream of performing. Thomas and I sat at a
table toward the middle of the place. There was no need for
me to hide in the dark this time. It was wonderful to be able
to sit at a table alone with Thomas.

Some of the bar patrons recognized me, which was fine.
A couple of young guys in their early twenties approached
me and asked for an autograph, so I signed a couple of bar
napkins for them.

"Listen, my girlfriend's doing her act tonight, so cheer
real loud for her, okay?" I told the two fans. I didn't know
whether I said that for Alice's benefit or for my own, as my
way of explaining why I was sitting at a table alone with
another man. I didn't look at Thomas when I said it. I really
hoped I hadn't hurt his feelings.

After the fans thanked me and went back to their table, I
ventured a look at Thomas. He was just looking around,
taking in the place, but he looked a little sad. I knew he
hated hiding and he didn't like the idea of me telling people
Alice was my girlfriend. Honestly, I hated doing it, too. But
what choice did I really have?

Thomas and I relaxed a bit more after drinking a couple

of beers. My beer was free, courtesy of the two fans who sent one over to me. I felt guilty. I made a mental note to grab some baseballs I kept in my trunk to sign for them if they were still around after the show.

The first two comics to perform were a man in his forties and a kid who looked like he was eighteen. They were really pretty awful, but Thomas and I cheered for them anyway. The silence in the room was too painful when nobody laughed. What balls they had to even try such a thing in front of all these people. It made me scared for Alice, though. I didn't think I could handle it if she bombed. That would be awful. I cared so much for her and I knew how hard she worked trying to make it as a comic. Well, she had at least two diehard fans in the audience tonight.

I felt my adrenaline surge when she walked – no, strutted, onstage. I had a feeling I was more nervous than she was. If she was scared, she didn't show it. She confidently strode onstage and adjusted the microphone to her height like I'd seen pro comics do on TV. The other two guys had seemed really nervous, and I think that put the audience on edge. You want your audience relaxed and ready to have fun.

"Soooo," Alice began, looking out at the crowd. "We got any drinkers here tonight?" Naturally, that got a lot of applause and hoots and hollers. Thomas and I held up our beers and cheered. "Yep. Me, too. That's what we Americans do. We drink. And we'll use any excuse we can find to drink. We even steal holidays from other cultures just to give us another reason to party. Anybody here get trashed for Cinco de Mayo?"

More cheers and hollers.

"And who knows what Cinco de Mayo is all about for Mexicans?" No one answered. "See? Crickets. That's what I thought. Nobody knows. It's Tequila Thursday, that's all we know, right?" Thomas and I laughed, and we weren't the only ones. I started to relax. She was doing okay. "And we have no shame, either. We love to hijack sacred holidays, too. The Irish have nothing on us when it comes to drinking on St. Patrick's Day."

That comment got lots of applause, too. I was so proud of her. I felt kinda bad for taking credit for being her boyfriend. Like Thomas, Alice was too good for me. She was smart and talented and amazing. She was my friend, though, for reasons known only to her. I was proud of that, too.

"Who knows who St. Patrick was anyway? Anybody have any idea? No. He's the patron saint of green beer, that's all we know. That's good enough for us in the ol' US of A!" More laughter and cheers. "What's next? We start taking over Buddhist holidays? The new tradition will be to rub the Buddha beer belly. We got plenty of those here in America. We'll be all up in the Hindu holidays, too. You know that god they got, Vishnu or whatever with the six hands? That's our excuse to do like six shots at once." Alice mimed doing six shots with hands flying everywhere, which got a big laugh. "There'll be no stopping us. We'll just drink our way through the calendar. What up? It's Diwali, mutha fuck-aaas!" Thomas threw his head back and laughed, clapping his hands. He wasn't the only one. Alice was killing. She was, by far, the best performer of the night.

I'd never been so proud and so jealous in my entire life.

Thomas and I met her "backstage" afterwards. Backstage was just a small, empty room with dusty chairs and one very excited woman. She ran into my arms and hugged me with such force that she almost knocked me down, which would have been embarrassing because I'm like twice her size.

"That's probably the best show I've had so far! I'm so

glad you guys came! It was such a great crowd tonight," Alice said.

"Don't give the crowd too much credit. That was all you, baby," Thomas said, taking his turn to hug her. I was so happy that the two of them got along so well, I could have burst.

"So what do you say, should we go out to eat and celebrate?" I linked arms with Alice as we walked back into the bar, but I was looking at Thomas.

"Sure, let's go!" Alice said excitedly. Thomas nodded and followed us out into the bar area. I knew it hurt him that I was walking around with Alice on my arm instead of him, but it couldn't be helped. It was just until we got out of the bar. It was hard for me not to be able to touch him, too. I wished Alice had driven so I could make out with him in the backseat.

We headed over to Ruth's Chris Steak House near the ballpark for a late celebratory dinner. I love me a good steak, but I'd never really had anybody to take to a fancy place like that before. I really should bring my dad here sometime. There's a guy who could appreciate a good steak.

Alice was so sweet. She kept excusing herself to the restroom during dinner so that Thomas and I could have a few moments alone together.

"This is nice," Thomas said. And it was. It really was. The way we were looking into each other's eyes, I couldn't help but think it must be obvious to people how we felt about each other. I glanced around at the other diners and nobody was paying any attention. I slipped my hand under the table and grabbed his. When the waiter came by to refill our water glasses, I tensed up a bit. However, instead of letting go of Thomas' hand, I grabbed it tighter. Thomas smiled at me and my heart just melted.

When we got in the car, all three of us were moaning about how we'd eaten too much. It was worth it, though.

"Thanks, Henry. This was so much fun," Alice said.

"It's my pleasure."

"Drop me off first." Alice said.

"We pass Thomas' place on the way."

"I don't care." Alice said through mock-clenched teeth. "Drop me off first." She turned around and winked at Thomas in the back seat.

"What, you trying to get me laid tonight?" I asked. Thomas laughed.

"Yeah. I'm your Wing Ma'am." she said. I didn't know if Thomas would let me have sex with him yet, but I was trying to wear him down. He was hell bent on taking this whole thing slow. Who knew? Maybe it would be the night for us. "Oh, hey. Before I forget..." Alice rifled through her bag on the floor and pulled out some CDs.

"Oh yeah! I got some for you, too." I reached into the center console and pulled out some CDs. We had agreed to trade. I would give her some musicals to listen to and she'd give me some standup comedy ones. Alice had never really been into musicals before, but she ended up liking *Oklahoma!* and she wanted to hear some more of my favorites. I wanted to lend her some more modern ones this time. I brought *Rent, Wicked,* and *The Book of Mormon.* I also brought *Kinky Boots,* which a musical about drag queens. I was going to lend it to Thomas, but it turned out he already owned it.

"Oh, these look cool. Thanks!" Alice said, flipping through the CDs.

I drove toward her place. The more I thought about it, the happier I was that she had insisted that I take her home first. I was really looking forward to continuing my date with Thomas.

"Come on, Thomas. Move up," Alice said, relinquishing her seat to him when we got to her apartment complex. He climbed out of the backseat. Alice leaned back in the window to say goodnight to me. "Thanks again, Henry. This was great."

I smiled and nodded. "Flip the light when you get inside so I know everything's okay," I said.

"I will. Have fun, you two!" she said, giving me a knowing look. She really was a great wing lady.

"Thanks for everything, sweetheart," Thomas said. He kissed Alice on the cheek before sliding into the front seat next to me. We both watched to make sure she made it safely inside. She flipped the light switch a couple of times, then I started to drive off toward Thomas' house.

"We need to talk about Alice," Thomas said, sounding unhappy.

"What about her?" I asked. "Don't you like her?"

"Are you kidding? I'm crazy about her. I think she's wonderful. It's just...Henry, I think she has a thing for you." I shrugged and nodded. "You *knew*? And you still let her pretend to be your girlfriend? Henry, this must be very painful for her."

"No, no. It's not like that. I mean she used to have a crush on me. A while ago. You know, before...everything. I'm gay, Thomas. She knows that."

"I don't know, Henry. Sometimes the way she looks at you..." Thomas said, looking worried.

"What way?"

"The way I look at you," Thomas said softly.

"No way," I said.

Thomas turned to me. "Henry, that girl would do anything for you. Don't you see that? She's doing this because she cares so much about you and she wants you to be happy. She's putting her own feelings aside for your sake and it's not fair to her."

"I do love her, you know. She's like my best friend. After you, of course."

"I know. But she needs to be allowed to meet somebody else. Someone who can love her in a way that you can't."

I nodded. I hadn't noticed anything about the way she looked at me, but Thomas had a point. It was a dangerous game, pretending to be in love with her. I don't know. Maybe deep down I had noticed it and I tried not to think about it.

"You're right. I'll be careful, okay?"

"We can't keep doing this forever, you know? Sooner or later..."

"I know. I know." I did know, but I didn't want to think about it. Thomas despised being in the closet and here I was, forcing him to hide. I hated hurting him like that. I hated the idea of hurting Alice, too. I knew Thomas wouldn't stay hidden forever and I didn't expect him to. I just couldn't bring myself to think of the day when I'd have to choose. Either tell people I was gay and we were dating, or lose him. I tried to put the thought out of my head. Thomas was okay with taking things slow. He didn't expect me to come out. Yet.

Maybe I wasn't ready to come out, but there were other things I was ready for.

Namely, I wanted to have sex with Thomas.

I was horny as hell and I also couldn't help but be curious. I'd always been, shall we say, adventurous in bed. I really felt like I was ready, too. It had been six weeks since I had taken the pill. I knew in my heart that I really was gay. I guess maybe I'd always known it, deep down. Either that, or the effects of the pill were permanent. I knew I was gay and I cared for Thomas deeply, so there really seemed to be no reason to wait to have sex. I knew it would take a lot of cajoling to get Thomas to let me do it with him, but hopefully, it would be him who "cain't say no."

17

We barely got into his apartment when I grabbed Thomas and kissed him. He broke off the kiss, laughing.

"Can I at least put my keys down?" Thomas asked. He tossed them over to the table. He missed. The keys fell to the floor with a clatter.

"There. Keys are down," I said and grabbed him again.

I kissed his mouth and then worked my way down to his neck. He had looked so handsome all night in his fancy dress shirt and slacks, but now all I could think of was getting him out of those clothes. He moaned softly as I kissed his neck.

"Tonight's the night, Thomas. I'm ready." I pressed myself against him so he could feel for himself how ready I was.

"Easy, babe, easy."

"Thomas, I want you so bad right now."

"I want you just as much. Probably more. I mean, look at you!" Thomas said. He slipped a hand inside my shirt and rubbed my chest. He unbuttoned a few buttons to get a better look. "I just don't think it's the right time yet. You're adjusting really well so far. I just don't want you to do anything you're not really prepared for."

I touched his face tenderly. "How much more preparation do I need? All I know is I adore you." He smiled and pulled me in for another kiss, which started out tender and became more and more passionate. Thomas started kissing my neck.

"Let's go to the bedroom." My eyes lit up with excitement, but Thomas put a hand up to slow me down. "But not, you know, actual sex. Not yet."

"Thomas-"

"Soon. I promise. I just want to be sure you're really ready."

"Thomas, I'm going away for an eight-day road trip soon. Don't you want to give me something to think about while I'm away?" I asked him as I slid my hand down his pants. He gripped my shoulders as I rubbed him.

"Ahh, Henry...Just think of it this way...you'll have something to look forward to when you come back."

I groaned. I knew there was no use arguing with him. He wasn't going to give in.

"But that doesn't mean we can't have plenty of fun in the meantime." Thomas unbuckled my pants. Before I knew it, he was on his knees and I had lost all ability to argue.

We made our way, eventually, to the bedroom and soon Thomas was snoring lightly as I held him in my arms. It had been an exhausting, exhilarating, wonderful evening. Although I was tired, I couldn't sleep.

I kept thinking about my date with Thomas...and Alice. It was great to be able to go out with him in public, but I kept replaying in my mind the hurt look Thomas had every time I held Alice's hand instead of his. I knew he was miserable being closeted when he was with me and I knew I had absolutely no right to make him do something that made him so unhappy. I remembered the look on his face when he told me how much he would love it if I would make a statement on television in support of gay athletes. I wondered how he would look at me if I went on television and announced that I was gay.

And that I was in love with him.

As I lay there, holding him and listening to him breathe, I knew that I loved him and I didn't want to hide him anymore.

I decided right then and there that I was going to come out of the closet. And soon.

IT WAS wonderful waking up with him the next morning. We sat at the kitchen table and ate breakfast and drank coffee. Just doing simple, ordinary things that couples did. I eyed him curiously as he opened a medicine bottle and swallowed a pill with his breakfast.

"What's that for?"

"High blood pressure."

I shot him a worried look. "You're awfully young for that, aren't you?"

Thomas shrugged. "It's no big deal. It's hereditary. My dad had it since he was in college."

"And he died of a heart attack."

"Don't worry, hon. I take medicine for it and I'm perfectly healthy otherwise."

I sat there at the table, admiring him.

"What?" Thomas asked, grinning at me. I wanted so much to tell him that I loved him, but I wanted to wait until the moment was right.

"Just think you're cute, that's all. I'm gonna miss you," I told him.

He nodded. "Me too."

Eight days on the road was a long time to be away from him. I would miss him terribly.

"Maybe we can get together for a little while tomorrow before I leave on Sunday."

"I wish I could. I can't tomorrow. At least not during the day and you've got a game at night," Thomas said.

"Why not? What you got going tomorrow afternoon?" He looked at me like he didn't want to tell me the answer to my question. "What? You going out with some guy? Tell me who it is so I can go beat him up."

"Going out with a bunch of guys, actually."

"Whore."

He laughed, but I noticed he still wasn't telling me where he was going. Now I was getting worried. Was he going out with another guy? He read my mind, like he always did. He swatted me playfully on the back of the head for even thinking that he was seeing somebody else.

"I'm going to the pride parade tomorrow, Henry."

"Oh. Why didn't you ever mention it?" I asked him. I thought he told me everything.

He put a gentle hand under my chin. "I didn't tell you because I didn't want you to feel bad. It's not like you could go, hon." True. The media would have had a field day with that one.

"I knooow, but..." I whined.

He patted my face, then got up to put his coffee cup in the sink. "Well, I gotta get to work."

I stood up to kiss him goodbye. "Did I ever tell you that you look hot in scrubs?"

He grinned at me. "Every time I wear 'em. Have a safe

trip, babe. Text me when you get there and call me when you get to the hotel."

"I will. Alice."

He smacked me on the back of the head again. I thought again about how happy he would be when I came out and we could drop the whole Alice routine. Thinking about that made me feel stronger, braver. Like maybe I really would have the balls to go public.

I thought about the gay pride parade Thomas and his friends were going to tomorrow. I wanted to go. I couldn't help it. I wanted to be there with Thomas and even Sam and Jeremy. Nobody would recognize me if I was more or less disguised in my usual Club Hippo gear: long-sleeved shirt, pants, stupid cowboy hat. It would be really crowded. I could blend in.

I couldn't wait to see the look on Thomas' face when I showed up at the parade. He believed so passionately in gay pride and acceptance, and having me show up there in support of that would mean so much to him. I couldn't wait.

THINGS SEEMED to be a lot calmer in the clubhouse these days, but I still felt kind of jumpy and nervous.

"So how are things with you know who?" Brady asked, winking at me. I froze. What did he mean by that?

"Uh. Who?"

"Your new girl. Alice."

"Oh, Alice! Oh, things are great. Really great. She's an awesome chick," I said, trying to still my slightly terrorized heart. I had to stop freaking out like this if I was gonna be serious about coming out.

"She is an awesome chick. I always-" He stopped and shook his head. "No, I better not say anything."

"What? You gotta tell me now. Else I'll beat it out of you."

"You might beat me up if I do tell you!" Brady said, laughing. "Okay, look. I just...the truth is I was just getting ready to ask Alice out when you beat me to it. Don't hit me!" He held up a hand, laughing. I stared at him, incredulous.

"Alice?"

"Yeah, Alice. Don't sound so shocked."

"No. No, I just...never realized you liked her." *Shit.* And Alice liked him, too. She had told me that many times. Thomas was right. I was keeping her from having a real relationship. But I couldn't tell her. Not yet. Soon. When I was ready to come out. Soon. Yeah.

"Yeah. I mean, dude. I'd never, you know..." he began. I nodded. Brady was a nice kid. He wasn't the type to steal another man's girl. "I just think it's cool that she does all this comedy and stuff."

"Oh, man. She rocks. You should have seen her the other night! She killed. She blew the other guys out of the water. She's going places, man," I said. Brady smiled and seemed glad that Alice was doing well. I guess I wasn't the only one who thought talent was sexy.

"That's great. She deserves it."

"Yeah she does. Well, she's clearly too good for me. If she ever wises up and figures that out, I'll tell her to give you a call!" Brady laughed and I fist-bumped him. Yeah, or if I ever get the balls to admit that I'm in love with a man.

18

I walked down the streets of Baltimore, a little nervous about where I was going, but very excited to surprise Thomas. I had on my long-sleeved clothes despite the heat, but I dispensed with the cowboy hat. I felt stupid enough wearing it at the Hippo, but it would be worse out here in the sunlight. I just wore a plain baseball cap and at least I could wear sunglasses now since I was outside. I hoped I would be able to find Thomas among all the people. Fortunately, I remembered him saying something about meeting Sam and Jeremy somewhere around North Charles Street and Mount Vernon Place.

There were lots of interesting things to see as I walked toward the parade area. I saw a guy ride by on a motorcycle with a big rainbow flag on the back. Wow. A flamingly out motorcycle dude. That guy had major balls, that was for sure. I saw a couple of lesbians walk down the street with their arms around each other. I'd have given anything to be able to do that with Thomas. Even just to be able to hold his hand in public would've been nice. I don't know. Maybe it was easier for women, but I'm sure it was still tough. Sam once told me it was hard when you're out in public with your boyfriend because you just never knew what people would do or say. Some people would smile at you while others might spit in your face. Or worse. Sam was really brave, though. He always had his arm around Jeremy in public, even after everything he'd been through in his life. Sam loved Jeremy enough to show it, no matter what might happen.

I thought about all the teenagers that got beat up in school for being gay. I felt sick every time I thought about that college kid that jumped off a bridge after some asshole had recorded him having sex with another guy. That was my worst nightmare. Being outed like that. I knew the awful knot of nearly incapacitating fear that kid had felt. I totally got why he felt like he had no way out. If only he'd had somebody like Thomas to lean on. Maybe he'd still be around.

Sam spotted me first. His eyes grew wide as he saw me walking toward them. It was kind of frightening how quickly he recognized me even with my hat and sunglasses on.

"Crackerjack disguise you got there, Francine," Sam said, folding his arms and smirking. "Nobody'd ever recognize you wearing a *baseball cap*." Thomas whirled around and his eyes lit up with astonishment. He gasped.

"Hen-" He stopped himself before he yelled out my name. Not that it would have mattered. It wasn't like he was gonna shout out my full name. He just stared at me in wonder. I could tell he wanted to hug me, but he couldn't. "I-I can't believe you're here." Then he whispered, "Thank you so much for doing this."

I lifted up my sunglasses a little so I could see him better. His beautiful eyes were so filled with pride and adoration that I wished I could have taken a picture of him right then and there. That was the look that I loved. The one that made my knees go weak. He looked so proud, so happy. If I had a snapshot of his face right then, I could look at it every time I felt my courage falter. I could be brave enough to do anything when I looked at that face.

I'm doing this because I love you, I wanted to say. But not here. Not with Sam and Jeremy and the crowd. But I would tell him soon enough.

"Did I miss anything?"

"No. Hasn't started yet," Thomas said.

"Parade hasn't started yet, but there's always plenty to see." Sam gestured to all the people gathered around. There was a wide variety of folks here. There were complete flamers, but there were lots more people that you'd never know were gay if they didn't have their arms around somebody of the same sex. Sam and Jeremy were like that and I suppose Thomas and I were, too. I hated that even in a place like this I was too chicken to show my feelings for Thomas publicly.

There were some oddballs there, too. Some hairy guys on motorcycles and some uber-butch dykes that looked like they could beat up the hairy guys.

I looked around and saw a couple of men pushing a stroller with a cute little Chinese girl in it. The two guys were clearly as enamored of her as they were of each other. They looked like a wonderful family.

I also saw a queer German Shepherd. Well, I suppose his sexual orientation was his business, but somebody had put a rainbow bandana around his neck and he didn't seem to mind.

I just looked around and marveled at the bravery of these people.

I noticed Thomas watching me watching the crowd.

"Pretty amazing, isn't it?" Thomas said softly. I knew what he meant. That was his gentle way of telling me that it would all be okay if I went public someday. I wouldn't ever be alone.

I lifted up my sunglasses again so I could look into his eyes. "Yeah," I said. "These people are so brave." Thomas nodded proudly. People worshipped me as a hero because I had a good physique and I had a job that was socially acceptable, but I'd never done anything remotely heroic in my life. Except for losing my mom, my life had been easy. I'd always been popular in school because I'd been born somewhat attractive and I was good at sports. Neither of those blessings had been earned. Baby, I was born *that* way. I had never done anything brave. And yet all these people were, as they say, loud and proud, despite the fact that half the country hated them for being different. I admired the hell out of them. These guys weren't taking the easy way out. They were refusing to stay hidden. They were heroic.

I took a small risk and put my hand on Thomas' back. "You're my hero, you know." I told him and I meant it with all my heart. He rewarded me with one of the sweetest smiles I'd ever seen. He was very proud, not just of being gay, but also for not being afraid to show it. Well, maybe he was afraid sometimes, but he never let the fear stop him.

I saw Sam look at me and then exchange a look with Jeremy. Was that, dare I say, respect I saw in Sam's eyes? He knew what a huge risk it was for me to be there and he knew I was doing it all for Thomas.

The parade began with a tall, black drag queen in a wedding dress atop a float. Yep. This would definitely prove to be interesting. Next up was a heavyset man in drag, who was clearly paying homage to Baltimore diva-legend Divine.

Divine was the guy in John Waters movies like *Pink Flamingos* and *Hairspray*.

I never realized how many gay support groups there were in Baltimore, but there were a lot represented in the parade. There was one called Baltimore Out Loud, whose members wore rainbow leis around their necks and cheerfully tossed out candy and strands of colored bead necklaces to the spectators. Jeremy caught a purple necklace and put it around Sam's neck. Sam kissed him on the cheek. They were happier than most of the married hetero couples I knew. I thought of Tuna and his scary wife and shuddered.

The next group got a huge round of applause. It was PFLAG – Parents, Families, and Friends of Lesbians & Gays. They were a bunch of cheerful moms and dads waving signs like "I love my daughter and new daughter-in-law" and "We are ALL family!" I actually felt a lump in my throat. These families were amazing. I couldn't fathom my father holding a sign like one woman held, which said simply "I love my gay son!"

Suddenly, Thomas bounded out into the street and engulfed the woman in a big bear hug. He held up her arm like they had just won a race.

"Thanks, Mom!" Thomas shouted and the crowd went crazy. I laughed and clapped my hands. Thomas ran back to where I stood and grinned at me like a little kid.

"Your mom's so cute!" I told him. She looked like a really nice lady. I wondered when I would get to officially meet her. Then I thought about having to introduce Thomas to my dad, so I quickly put that thought out of my mind.

Thomas went over to where Sam and Jeremy were standing. Jeremy had his arm around Sam. He was whispering something into Sam's ear, comforting him.

Thomas kissed Sam on the cheek and said softly, "We're

your family now. You know that." Sam nodded and squeezed Thomas' hand. There were tears in Sam's eyes. I couldn't even begin to imagine the pain he'd been through because of his family. I put my hand on his shoulder and squeezed it a little. He looked into my eyes and nodded, silently thanking me for my support.

More drag queens, more floats, more beads.

"Ow!" I yelped as something sharp hit me in the face. Sam cackled as I bent over to pick up the condom packet that had hit me in the cheek.

"Sorry, sweetie!" The drag queen yelled from the float. I waved to show it was okay.

"Poor baby," Thomas said, rubbing my face and laughing. I shrugged and put the condom in my back pocket.

"You never know. *Someday* I might even have reason to use this," I said.

"Oh, ha ha," Thomas said.

We turned back to watch the rest of the parade.

God help me, I never even saw the photographer from *The Baltimore Sun*.

19

I knew something was horribly wrong the minute I entered the clubhouse. I walked in and everybody just stared at me. Sid and Brady looked afraid and Kyle and Jackson just looked pissed.

"What's going on?" I asked, petrified to hear the answer.

"I knew it. I had a feeling it was you. I always said it was you, but everybody thought I was crazy!" Jackson said, shaking his head in disgust.

"Me what? What's your problem?" I tried desperately to steady my nerves. You know what they say about smelling fear. I had to calm down. I took an unsteady breath and waited for somebody to respond. Kyle came walking, no *charging*, toward me with fire in his eyes.

"You were right," Kyle laughed bitterly. "He's the faggot. It's so obvious now, I can't believe we missed it. He's always been the most flamboyant guy on the whole fucking team! All that 'Y.M.C.A.' bullshit. It was like he was flaunting it all over and we never even noticed."

"What the hell are you talking about? I ain't no fag!" My voice was shaky. I just couldn't control it. I had this horrible feeling like I was falling and I couldn't stop myself. It was like I was leaning over the railing of the Empire State Building and somebody just jerked it out from under me. That was my level of fear.

"Tell that to the entertainment reporter at *The Baltimore Sun*." Kyle opened his Orioles jacket to reveal an article from the Internet that he had taped inside the same way I showed off gossip articles about myself. The headline read 'Henry Vaughn, Jr. Attends Gay Pride Parade?' And there were pictures. I felt faint. That would be just perfect. They accuse me of being gay and I just swoon on the floor.

I had a moment of sheer, blind panic.

I swallowed hard and tried desperately to come up with an explanation. I somehow regained my composure enough to irritably snatch the article from Kyle's jacket. I faked a laugh.

"What the hell is this? Did you have this printed up on your computer or something?" I said, shaking my head. I was going to have to use every acting skill I had to get through the next five minutes, which I knew would be vital to the course of the rest of my life. I didn't even think about using this opportunity to come out of the closet like I'd been planning. I just shifted completely into survival mode.

I had to get out of this.

Kyle just glared at me. He could be really scary when he wanted to be. I couldn't believe I'd ever been friends with the guy.

"It's for real, motherfucker. Well?" Kyle demanded.

"Well, what?" I said, stalling. *I didn't know what.* Still in an utter state of panic, I tried to focus on the pictures. There were several of them of me with Thomas. There was one of Thomas touching my cheek, probably from when the condom had hit me in the face. There were a couple of photos of us just standing together. In most of the photos, I was wearing sunglasses. It's not like I was wearing my baseball jersey with Vaughn on the back. I could argue that it wasn't me. That was my only hope. "Are you serious? You think the guy in that picture is me?" I was relieved to note that my voice sounded steady. At least to my own ears, I sounded unconcerned, if mildly annoyed, by this silly accusation.

"You're not seriously gonna stand there and deny that's you in the picture!" Kyle said. Jackson was shaking his head. He didn't believe me either.

"Yeah, I'm gonna deny it 'cause it's not me!" I ripped up the pictures and shook my head like this whole thing was the dumbest thing I'd ever heard. I glanced around at all the guys in the clubhouse. I didn't see one person who looked like he believed me.

Suddenly, the door to the clubhouse burst open and a bunch of reporters came spilling in and I saw myself tumbling further and further into this nightmare.

"Sorry, Henry. I held them off as long as I could," Tuna said. He had such a look of fear in his eyes. Fear for what was happening to me.

John Sysantos, one of the regular sports reporters, came dashing up to me. "Would you care to comment on the reports that you attended the gay pride parade that took place on the streets of Baltimore this afternoon?" Sysantos asked as cameras flashed in my face. I looked up to see Boomer leaning in the doorway of his office, just staring at me. He would kill me for the media attention I had caused. My legs felt weak as I realized my career might already be over. I felt like I was literally seeing my life flash before my eyes. My reputation. My career. My father. It was all disappearing before my eyes.

Lucinda Mackleroy stepped up. She smiled at me and I saw a twinge of sympathy in her eyes. "Henry, would you care to comment on whether or not you attended the parade today and if you are, in fact, a homosexual?" she asked. She held up the photos from the internet story. Seemed there were plenty of copies readily available. It wasn't as if I'd ripped up the only ones in existence. The damn things were viral now. The Internet is forever.

"No. No, of course not." I inwardly coached myself to stay calm. I'd been through a lot of pressure situations on the field, but nothing had prepared me for the sheer surge of adrenaline that was coursing through my body right now. I felt like I could have a stroke or a heart attack at any minute. Of course, my lungs were also seizing up. I laughed and I hoped it sounded convincing. "I mean, yes, I would like to comment. I'm not gay. I mean, of course not. What do you think?"

Everyone stared at me. Waiting for me to continue, to elaborate. To convince them, because so far, nobody was buying it.

"So you just like to hang out with gay men socially?" John Sysantos asked. The question was bad enough, but his voice was dripping with sarcasm and disbelief.

"No. No way. That's..." I laughed bitterly. "Not exactly my kind of people, you know what I mean? Look, I can see that the guy in the picture bears a resemblance to me. Tall, muscular, good-looking. I mean, that's me all over, right?" I winked and laughed like I always did with the reporters. A lot of looks were exchanged in the next few seconds. Some shaking heads. They didn't believe me, but they were starting to realize that I wasn't going to cop to anything. "But that's not me."

"Are you sure?" Sysantos continued to press. "If you'll look closely at the picture, it really looks like..."

"Look, it's not me, all right? What the hell would I be doing at a place like that? Seriously, people! What would I be doing hanging around a bunch of fags? Look, we have a game to play, all right? No further comment," I said. As I stormed out of the clubhouse, I heard Boomer loudly ushering the reporters out the door.

I stumbled my way through the game that night in a complete daze. After the initial terror of the grilling by the reporters and other players had faded, the impact of what I had done hit me full force.

I had gone on television and called Thomas a fag.

Those horrible, disgusting words would be played over and over again on the news and on sports news reels. They would bleep out that horrific word, but everyone would know what I had said.

When I thought about how Thomas would turn on the television and hear those words coming out of my mouth, I wanted to die.

I wanted to absorb all the shock and the pain that he would feel. I wanted it to happen to me, not to him. My darling Thomas. I kept picturing his face from earlier today. How happy it made him when I showed up at the parade. Those eyes, looking at me with such fondness. Thomas, who never did anything but worry about my feelings and I had done this horrible, wretched, inhuman thing to him.

I managed to escape the ballpark after the game without talking to anyone. As soon as I got in the car, I called Thomas. I had no idea what in the hell I was going to say to him, but I had to talk to him. I had to tell him how desperately sorry I was.

He didn't answer.

I didn't expect to sleep that night, but I did. I was just so completely emotionally and physically exhausted that I actually fell asleep quickly. I was awakened by the sound of my cell phone ringing. Disoriented, I looked at the clock and saw that it was just after 10 a.m. Like a horrible nightmare, the last night's events came rushing back to me. My phone continued to ring and my heart lurched in my chest. *Thomas.* I grabbed my cell phone and didn't even look to see who it was.

"Hello?" I said hopefully.

"Henry?" It was a male voice, but not the one I'd been hoping to hear.

"Hi, Dad," I said, trying not to groan audibly. I couldn't deal with him right now.

"What the hell is going on? You're all over the news!" he said. I couldn't bear to turn on the television. I knew it was nonstop clips of my quote, mixed with clips of years of my on-field antics that suddenly "made sense" to people now that they suspected I was gay. If my dad had seen it, I knew Thomas had, too. "What were you doing in a place like that?" Hank demanded.

"Dad, I-I just....I..."

"Henry, tell me the truth. Are you a fag?" I winced at the word. The word that would follow me to my grave. Not because it was what I was, but because it was what I had said.

"Dad, I just can't...I can't talk about this now. I'll call you later." I clicked off the phone. I was just postponing the inevitable. I knew what had happened to Sam was going to happen to me. My dad would abandon me. I didn't care. I deserved it. As scared as I was about what would happen to me with my dad, with the Orioles, in the media, and all the other shit that was about to go down, none of it compared to how horrible I felt about what I said. The stress of being caught at the gay pride parade and being outed in front of the whole world didn't upset me anywhere near as much as the thought that *I could not believe I had done this to Thomas.*

I dialed Thomas' number, but he still wasn't answering. I was desperate to talk to him. I had to explain somehow. But how could I explain this? It wasn't like there was any excuse for what I had said.

From all the way upstairs, I heard a loud knocking on the door. I barely allowed myself to hope that it could possibly be Thomas. He could scream at me, punch me; I didn't care. I just wanted to see him. I threw on a T-shirt and went downstairs to answer the door. I didn't even bother looking to see who it was. If it was an axe murderer, at least he would put me out of my misery.

The second I opened the door, Alice flicked me, *hard,* in the middle of the forehead.

"Ow!" I said, rubbing my forehead.

"What in the hell is wrong with you?" Alice screamed at me. I had never seen her so angry. I don't think I'd ever seen her angry at all. She was like Thomas, calm and sweet most of the time. I hadn't even thought about how all this would affect her, but I should have known she would be furious. She adored Thomas. "How could you do this to him? What the hell were you *thinking*?"

I just shook my head. "I don't know."

Alice had been so proud of me for going to the parade. I had been on the phone with her for an hour yesterday morning after leaving Thomas' apartment. I told her that I was in love with Thomas and that I was seriously considering coming out. As always, she offered her unconditional support. She told me she would help me craft a statement for a press release or hold my hand while I made the announcement. Anything I needed, she was there for me. That was what real friends did. Real friends didn't knife the people they loved in the back. That was what people like me did.

"And Sam!" Alice yelled, storming into the house. I quietly shut the door and followed her as she raged. She spun around and glared at me. "You might as well write him off, 'cause he'll never speak to you again. Henry, how could you do this to him after everything he's been through?" Alice had a very tender spot in her heart for Sam because of the pain he had suffered with his family.

I had tried so hard not to think about him, but Alice was forcing me. Sam. Sam who hated me at first and with damn good reason. His own parents had abandoned him for being gay, so he had no tolerance for dealing with homophobic assholes like me. Yet he'd been stuck with me as a patient and I was sure I wasn't the only jerk he had encountered. He had no choice but to deal with whatever hate-filled crap people threw at him. Yet he had slowly come to trust me, against his better judgment. Thomas cared for me and that was enough for him to give me a second chance. What a horrible mistake that had been.

"Alice..." I began.

"Put some pants on and we'll talk."

I looked down and realized that when I got out of bed to answer the door, I had only put on a T-shirt and was still wearing the underwear I'd slept in. I really was a mess.

I came back downstairs in more decent attire and found Alice waiting expectantly on the couch.

Alice stared at me and simply asked, "Why?"

I put my head in my hands. "Because I was scared. I didn't know what to do. I was completely blindsided!"

Alice sighed. "That's true. You were."

"I just didn't have time to think! I never meant to say... Oh, God, I can't believe I used that word..."

"Neither can I." Alice said bitterly.

"Is it awful? Is it all over the news? I can't bear to turn on the television." She didn't answer, which meant yes. Dear *God*.

"Thomas won't answer my calls."

"Would you?" Alice asked. I just looked at her sorrowfully.

"And I have to leave for the road for eight days. I won't even be able to go see him!"

"Are you gonna be okay on the road with the guys all that time?" Alice asked me. She looked worried.

"I don't care! I don't even care what happens to me. I just want Thomas to be okay. Do you think he'll ever forgive me?"

"I hope so. I really do, but...this was so bad, Henry! Not even just the word you used, but you denied that you knew him. You lied about having gay friends. That was the one thing he asked you never to do!" Alice wailed.

"I know," I said quietly as I sank down on the couch next to her. I looked at her mournfully. "I love him so much, Alice."

Her expression softened like it always did when I spoke of my feelings for Thomas. She was the only one in the whole world who knew I loved him. Even Thomas didn't know. "Then you have to fix this."

"How?"

"I don't know. Just keep trying to get ahold of him. Don't give up. Maybe in a few days, he'll cool down. He's not exactly hot-tempered, you know."

"I know. He's the sweetest, kindest, most gentle soul that

ever walked the face of the earth and I ripped out his heart and crushed it with my cleat," I said.

Alice sighed wearily. She reached over and took my hand. "You made a mistake, Henry. It was a bad one, but I know you would give anything in the world to take it back."

"I would. God, I would! If I had it to do over again...I swear, Alice. I would look right in that television camera and tell the whole world that I love Thomas Palmer." I gasped. "Alice! I should do that! I should come out now and make a statement and-"

"No, honey. Don't do that. Not yet," she said, looking worried.

"Why not? It would fix this and Thomas-"

Alice squeezed my hand. "Henry, you're very upset right now and coming out, especially publicly, is a really, really big decision. You know how much you have to lose if-"

"I'd give it all up for him," I said softly.

"You really would, wouldn't you?"

"Yes. Yes, I would."

"But you may not have to. Just, please at least think it over for a few days before you do anything rash. You may be able to keep Thomas even without coming out. Just wait and see. Please." She looked at me pleadingly. She was really worried.

"Why are you so nice to me?"

She smiled wryly. "Well, somebody's gotta look after you while Thomas is mad."

"You're like a mother hen, Alice."

She put her hand over her heart and mock-swooned. "Oh, that's what every girl dreams of hearing from a hot guy! I'm like a *mother* to you..."

I winced. "I'm sorry, Alice. I didn't mean it that way. I mean, you do kind of remind me of my mom, though. She was sweet and kind and she was always fussing over me." Alice smiled softly, understanding. She knew how much I missed my mom. "And I know it's totally selfish, but I like when you fuss over me."

I sighed miserably. I kept thinking of what Thomas must be going through. What I had put him through.

"God, Henry. You look pitiful!" Alice said. She patted my cheek. "Good. Go to him looking like that and he'll have to forgive you."

"What if he won't see me?"

"He will, Henry. Give him time. He's hurting."

Alice got up from the couch and so did I. She gave me a warm hug. "Have a safe trip. Good luck and don't take any crap from those jerks on your team. And remember, the smartest two words in the English language for you right now are *no comment.*"

I laughed and nodded. "You're right." Alice squeezed my hand one more time before she left.

I called Thomas about fifteen more times before I left the house. He still didn't answer. Alice was right, though. I couldn't give up.

20

I felt lonelier on the road than I ever had before. It had more to do with Thomas' silence than the fact that most of my teammates weren't speaking to me.

There was a knock on my hotel door. I heaved myself wearily off the bed and answered the door to find Tuna standing there.

"Hey. What's up?" I asked.

"You wanna go grab a beer? I gotta live it up while I'm away from the wife," Tuna said, grinning.

"Yeah. Yeah, I guess you do. Sure, why not?" I grabbed my wallet and hotel key off the table and walked out into the hallway.

We walked in silence for a minute, then Tuna said quietly, "I don't care, you know."

"Care about what?"

"If you're...you know."

"Thanks," I said, smiling at him. *No comment.* Like Alice said.

"Look, it's none of my business, but let me just say one thing and I swear we don't ever have to talk about it again if you don't want to, okay?" Tuna said. I nodded, not exactly sure where he was going with this. "Look, my cousin is gay, okay? He had a really rough time when he came out, you know, with family and all. But we all just got used to it and kind of realized we were being jerks about the whole thing. There's just, there's nothing wrong with it, you know? I get that now. The point is, it was rough, but he's so much better off now that it's all out in the open. Sometimes it's a lot harder trying to keep it a secret. That's all I wanted to say. We can just drop it. It's done," Tuna said.

I nodded. It was like a mutual agreement. He knew I was gay and he didn't want me to bother lying about it anymore. At least not to him.

"I've never needed a drink so bad in my life!" I said.

"I hear ya. I'm buyin', so have at," Tuna said.

There were already a bunch of players down at the hotel bar. I saw Kyle, Jackson, and a couple of the other guys glaring at me. It was weird how they were mad at me for being gay. Like it was a personal insult to them. I think Kyle was just pissed because he never knew. Hell, I didn't even know myself until recently, so what was there to get all bitchy about?

At first, I didn't see that Kyle had followed me up to the bar when I went to get a Schnapps and a beer. I turned around and there he was.

He just shook his head at me and mumbled, "Cocksucker."

Cocksucker.

I was stunned at how that word just ripped through me. I didn't think there was a worse slur than faggot, but I think that was it.

I managed to just roll my eyes at him and walk away, but inside I felt torn apart. *Cocksucker.* Yes, I guess I was. I hated the way that disgusting word made it sound like I had blown some stranger in a gas station somewhere. It wasn't like that at all. I had been in bed with the man that I loved and I'd done it because I wanted him to feel good. And no matter how much Thomas worried that I would regret doing it, I didn't. Not then, not now.

I sat down with Tuna, Brady, and Sid, who seemed not to be offended by my gay cooties. I looked over at the other guys and the anti-gay coalition they had formed.

"I feel like I've been banished to the uncool table in high school," I said.

"Thanks a lot, asshole," Tuna said, winging a paper coaster at my head.

I put my head in my hands and looked really upset for a few seconds. I suddenly wailed, "Nobody's gonna ask me to the prom now!"

The guys at my table burst out laughing. I really had them going for a second. I think they thought I was about to have a nervous breakdown. I supposed they weren't far off, but I was feeling a little better.

"Yeah, laugh it up over there," Kyle shouted bitterly from his table.

"Oh, you're just mad because your little party over there is soooo lame," I said.

"This is all just a big joke to you, isn't it?" Kyle said. "You're dragging this whole ballclub through the mud, you fucking queer."

"Calm down, Kyle. That's enough," Sid said.

"It's all right, Sid. I'm not even gonna bother arguing because nobody believes me anyway." Then, lisping and examining my fingernails, I said, "I mean, I just don't get it!" The guys at my table grinned while the meanies at the other table just got more fired up.

"I don't care what you say. You're the faggot and I'm gonna prove it if it's the last thing I do!"

"If it's the last thing I do!" I repeated in a deep, mock-serious voice. "What are you, a cartoon villain?"

Kyle just shook his head, disgusted, while the rest of my table broke up laughing. I felt a little better. Not everybody hated me. Maybe I would survive this after all.

WE LOST the first two games of the four-game series to the Seattle Mariners. I wasn't sleeping much. I couldn't stop thinking about Thomas. I missed him so badly and I couldn't bear the thought of what he must be going through.

I had "no commented" my way out of countless interviews, so reporters in Seattle had stopped asking. Boomer Wilkens hated my guts, but so far, he hadn't really said anything to me. Half of the team wasn't talking to me, but at least I had a few guys who were still my friends.

Thomas still wouldn't answer my calls. I was starting to get really worried about him, so I called Alice and asked her to please go check on him and make sure he was all right.

"Tell him, you know..." I told her.

"I know, Peaches. I know," she said softly.

I went crazy for the next few hours, waiting for her to call me back and give me a report. Finally, my phone rang and it was her.

"Well?" I asked her, holding my breath. I was scared to death that she would tell me that he never wanted to see me again.

"I went to see him."

"And? Tell me the truth, Alice. All of it. How is he?" I asked.

"He's okay, Henry. But sad. He's just...sad," Alice told me. I closed my eyes for a second and sat down on the bed. My heart physically ached inside my chest.

"Did you tell him how sorry I was?"

"Yes. I told him you were a complete wreck over this. I told him that you never meant to say such a horrible thing, that you just didn't think until it was too late," Alice said.

"Good. Good. What did he say?" I asked.

"He...well, he's not ready to talk to you yet." I wondered if that was code for *he never wants to speak to you again*. "But he's really worried about you."

"About me? Why?"

"He's worried about how the guys are treating you on the road. And the crowds and everything," Alice said. Thomas did have reason to worry. I had heard some awful comments from some of the Seattle fans. I mean, most of them were fine, but there were a few assholes yelling some horrible things at me. A lot of fans think that since we're professional athletes, we just block out the sounds of the crowd. Nope. We can hear you motherfuckers loud and clear.

"Tell him not to worry about me. I'm fine. I can handle it." Besides, I deserved whatever was thrown at me. Who cared what those assholes thought anyway? Thomas' was the only opinion that mattered.

"Thomas said he wanted to call just to check up on you, he just...couldn't. He's not ready to talk yet." That meant there was hope. If he had at least thought about calling me, maybe I could still salvage our relationship. I didn't deserve a second chance, but I desperately wanted it.

"Do you think he'll see me when I get back?"

"I don't know. He-"

"Well, he's gonna. I'm not leaving his place until I get a chance to talk to him."

"Okay, Henry."

"And Sam? Did Thomas say anything about Sam?" I asked.

"Sam's...upset," Alice said slowly.

"And by upset, you mean...."

"Angry. Pissed off. But your bigger concern is Jeremy. He said...well, never mind what he said but seriously, watch your back. We're talking murderous rage here."

Wow. Jeremy was bigger than both Sam and Thomas, though not quite as muscular as me. Still, I bet he could kick my ass and I didn't really blame him. Jeremy had every right to be pissed at what I said on his own behalf. I mean, he was gay, too. But I knew he didn't care about his own feelings. He was pissed that I'd hurt Sam. If somebody did to my boyfriend, my Thomas, what I did to Sam? Forget it. I'd kill him. Sam had taken a long time to trust me, but he finally did. And look what had happened. I was just another in a long line of people to hurt him because he was gay. My self-loathing reached a new depth.

"Okay. Thanks for the warning. Thanks for all your help, Alice. I really, really, appreciate it."

"I know you do. How are you doing?"

"I'm fine. I'm okay. It's like, well, you really do find out who your friends are, you know? And it turns out I still have a few," I said.

"Good. Is Brady one of them?" Alice asked.

"Yeah. Yeah he is. He's been great."

"I knew it! He just seems like a good guy, you know? I'm so glad to hear he's not a jerk." *Shit.* She really did have a thing for him. I could hear it in her voice. And here she thought it was just a fantasy crush. She had no idea that Brady felt the same way about her. The second I came out of the closet, I was gonna hook the two of them up.

I felt a little better after I hung up with Alice. Thomas had, at least briefly, entertained the possibility of speaking to me again. All I had to do was somehow get through the next few days so I could see him again.

OUR STRING of road games finally ended. I headed over to Thomas' place very early in the morning, before he had to go to work.

I hadn't felt this nervous walking up those apartment steps since our first date. I wiped my sweaty palms on my pants and took a deep breath. I had thought about this moment for eight days and I still didn't have any idea of what I was going to say. I knocked on his door and I actually gasped slightly when he answered almost right away.

Thomas stood at the door, looking at me. He was dressed in those blue scrubs that I loved.

His face. Oh, God. The look on his face. It was worse than I had imagined.

Thomas had that look that Sam had when he was feeling particularly depressed. There was no light in those beautiful eyes. I wanted to kill myself. I decided right then and there that I was going to fix this if I had to spend the rest of my life trying. I would release a statement on the national news. I would wear an *I Love My Boyfriend* T-shirt in the middle of fucking center field. I would do anything, *anything* to get that agonized expression off his face and to make sure I never had to see it again.

"Oh, Thomas, I'm so sorry..." I whispered.

Thomas sighed heavily and gestured for me to come in. I hadn't seen him in more than a week and I desperately wanted to touch him, to hold him, but I knew better. I hadn't earned that right.

Thomas sat stiffly on the couch and I sat next to him. I didn't even know where to begin.

"There's no reason or excuse I can give you that can ever make what I said okay," I said. Thomas nodded. He wouldn't look at me, but he was listening. "I-I just couldn't come out. Not like that."

"Nobody expects you to come out of the closet, Henry!" Thomas shouted. I had never heard him raise his voice like that before. "Look, I get that you don't want to come out. I understand it could screw your career." He finally turned around to face me. "But did you have to deny that you even knew me?" The hurt in his eyes was almost more than I could bear. "I mean, you stood up in front of the whole world and denied *me*." That was the ultimate sin for Thomas. The most painful, cruel thing anybody could do to him and I had done it. I recalled so clearly the words he bravely said to his father: *You can accept me or reject me, but you will never deny me again.*

"I'm sorry," I said. I could have said it a million more times and it would never be enough.

Thomas looked at me coldly. "How could you use that word, Henry? You know you were talking about me when you said it, right?" I knew. I had barely thought of anything else for the last week.

I swallowed hard. "I know," I said, my voice barely a whisper. "What can I do to make it up to you? Tell me. I'll do anything you want."

"You can't make up for something like that. It can't be done," Thomas said.

"You mean you can't ever forgive me?" I asked. I didn't want to hear the answer. I took his hand in mine. It felt so good to finally be able to touch him. I prayed it wouldn't be for the last time.

"No. I didn't say that," Thomas said, sounding a little more like his usual, gentle self.

"Thomas, I don't give a fuck what happens to me. I don't care what anybody says about me and I don't care if I lose my job. I'll do whatever I can to make you happy again. I'll call a press conference and tell everybody that I'm gay and that I'm with you."

He looked at me curiously. "You would do that for me?"

"Of course I would! Look, I said something incredibly fucking stupid because I wasn't thinking. I was scared. I panicked. But I don't care about those assholes anymore. I'll do it! I'll make a statement and-"

"Henry," Thomas said, squeezing my hand. "I would never, ever ask you to do that."

"You're not asking. I'm offering! I'm gonna do it!"

"I don't *want* you to do it. I've been worried sick enough about you as it is. I'd never let you throw yourself to the wolves like that. I get that you're in a really tough situation here, hon. There's a reason that there's never been an out MLB player. The sport is still too hostile about it. I don't want you to come out. Not now, not as an apology to me. You'll do it when and if you're really ready." Thomas sighed and looked at me wearily. "What you *should* have done was just admit that you were at the parade with friends. You didn't have to say you were gay. Or if that was too risky, if nothing else, you just shouldn't have said-"

"I know." I cut him off. I couldn't bear to have those awful words repeated to me. I took a deep breath. Thomas was speaking softly to me again. He had called me "hon." There was still hope.

I took a risk and reached for him. I put my arms around

him and whispered, "I'm sorry, I'm sorry, I'm sorry, Thomas." I held him and rubbed his back. Not only did he not push me away, but he gently touched the back of my head and ran his fingers through my hair.

"I know you are, Henry. I know."

I let go of him and looked into his eyes.

"You're the last person in the world I would ever, ever want to hurt. I love you, Thomas."

At first, he looked stunned. Then his expression softened and I saw a lot of the pain and sadness in his eyes start to disappear. That was enough for me. All I had really been hoping for was to make him feel better and get that awful, sorrowful look off his face. He tenderly pushed my hair behind my ear. "Oh, Henry. I love you so much."

I could not believe he said it back.

"You *do*?" I said it so loud and I sounded so shocked that Thomas laughed. It was wonderful to hear that laugh again.

"Don't sound so surprised," Thomas said. Surprised didn't cut it. Shocked, stunned, amazed - you name it. I had just wanted Thomas to know how I felt about him. I don't think it ever occurred to me that he might actually say it back.

"You...love me..." I said, trying out the words out loud. Thomas nodded simply. "*Why?*" I asked him, sincerely having absolutely no idea why on earth this wonderful man would possibly love me.

He laughed again and touched my cheek with great affection. "Oh, Henry. Too many reasons to count."

I didn't know how it was humanly possible for anybody to love me right now. I guess this just meant he was already in love with me before I did what I did, and that he had somehow decided he still loved me in spite of it.

"I love you. I love you and I forgive you," Thomas told

me. The warmth had returned to his eyes and he leaned over and kissed me. I couldn't believe that I was able to hold him in my arms again. I kissed him again and again and told him over and over how sorry I was.

"Thomas...I'm sorry. I...don't...deserve....your forgiveness..." I told him between kisses.

"I know you're sorry. I understand how scared you must have been and I know you weren't thinking, but..." Thomas pulled back a bit and looked at me. "I forgive you, but...I mean...this can't ever happen again. I forgive you this time, but I can't....I can't do it again if..."

"I know." I didn't blame him one bit for having a hard time trusting me, but he had nothing to worry about. Nothing like this was ever, ever going to happen again. I couldn't believe I had put my so-called macho image ahead of the man I loved. I would make it up to him. I didn't know how yet, but I would. "I'll never hurt you again, Thomas. Never, never, never." I kissed him and he melted into my arms. I was finally home again. "Mmmm," I said, kissing him all over his mouth and neck. "You know I can't resist you in these scrubs."

"Speaking of which," Thomas said after he broke off one more lengthy kiss.

"Nooo," I whined.

"I gotta go to work. Not all of us have jobs where we can sleep all day." Thomas grinned at me as he got up from the couch. He offered a hand and pulled me up from the couch.

We kissed some more, with him insisting all the while that he had to go. I was rock hard. I don't think I had ever been hornier in my life, and believe me, that's saying something. I hadn't even touched myself in a week, which was a record for me. I had been too depressed. Now my spirits were soaring. Having your boyfriend tell you he loves you will do that for you. I kissed him and pressed my hard cock against his equally solid one.

Thomas moaned in my ear. "I gotta go. Look," he said between kisses. "The O's are off tonight, right?"

"Mmm-hmm," I said, barely coming up for air long enough to respond.

"Why don't you come over tonight..." he murmured seductively, "and we can make up some more..."

"Mmmm....I don't know how I'll be able to make it until then..."

Thomas sighed, sounding as frustrated as I felt. "I know. I love you."

"I love you, too."

I finally let him leave for work. It wasn't easy letting go of him and it would be even harder to wait until that night to be with him again. Though he had hinted that we would have sex when I got back from the road, a hell of a lot had happened since then. On the one hand, I had betrayed him. On the other hand, we had professed our love for each other. It was totally up to him to decide how far he wanted to go with me. I sure as shit wasn't going to pressure him. There were plenty of other things we could do to please each other if he wasn't ready to have sex.

I had to stop thinking about it or I'd never make it until he got off work.

I waited until around 10 a.m. when I knew Thomas would be busy at work and unable to answer his cell phone. I left him a voice mail. I sang a few verses of "Unchained Melody," and then told him I loved him and couldn't wait to see him. I knew my message would make him smile. Then I called Alice.

"We're okay. Everything's okay."

"Oh, I'm so glad," she said, sounding nearly as relieved as

I felt. "Tell me everything." I related to her how things went. How Thomas had actually shouted. Alice said she couldn't even imagine what Thomas yelling would sound like. I had heard him yell before, just not in anger. He cheered for me at the O's games and, you know, sometimes cried out my name when we were fooling around. I left that part out of my conversation with Alice, though. I couldn't wait to tell her the best part. I knew she would flip.

I told her that we said we loved each other.

I had to hold the phone away from my ear on that one.

"Awwwwwwwwwww!" Alice exclaimed. "Who said it first?"

"I did."

"That's wonderful, Peaches."

"Thanks, darling girl. I swear. I had no idea he was gonna say it back. I just wanted, you know, to tell him. He deserved to know after everything that happened," I told her.

"That's so great, Henry. I'm so happy for you!" And she really did sound happy. Good. The last thing I wanted to do was to hurt another person I loved.

I was really grateful I had someone to tell. Alice was the only person in the entire world who I could tell that my boyfriend had told me he loved me. I wondered if Thomas would tell Sam.

It was probably better if he didn't.

Thomas may have loved me, but Sam hated me. With good reason. I knew I had to reach out to him and apologize. I didn't expect him to forgive me, but I owed it to him to at least tell him how sorry I was. I thought about going over to his house to apologize in person.

Then I thought about Jeremy.

I figured maybe I'd better call him instead.

21

I put on a nice pair of pants and a fancy button-down shirt to go over to Thomas' place, though I hoped I wouldn't be wearing either for very long.

I hadn't eaten dinner yet and I doubted Thomas had either, but I had more pressing needs at that moment. If I didn't have an orgasm soon, I thought I would explode. I hoped Thomas felt the same way.

I got my answer when I got to his apartment.

I was barely in the door when he shut it and pushed me, forcefully, against it. I pushed him against this door to kiss him all the time, but he had never done it to me before. And he actually pushed even rougher than I usually did. I loved it.

"I got your message," Thomas said. He pressed against me and was hard already. "Dammit, Henry. You know I'm helpless to resist you when you sing." He grinned at me, then pressed his lips to mine.

"Mmmmm," I said, trying to talk through his kisses. "I thought you would like that."

"I couldn't concentrate at work all day. All I could think about was you." He looked at me mischievously.

"What?" I asked.

Without a word, he dug his fingers underneath the buttons of my fancy shirt and *ripped my shirt right off.* I could hear the pings of the buttons as they bounced around the room. Thomas sighed with satisfaction as he looked at my exposed chest. Then he looked up at me.

"I have wanted to do that to you since the *day...we...met.*" I blinked at him in astonishment. He shrugged and said "You're rich. You can buy another shirt."

"Indeed!" I said, laughing. "I can buy new pants, too, ya know." Thomas chuckled and started kissing my neck.

"Oh, Thomas, I've missed you so much." I moaned loudly as he kept kissing my neck and my now-naked shoulders.

"I've missed you, too, my love. And I have a proposition for you." Thomas said as his kisses traveled further south.

"Is it a *sexual* proposition?" I asked hopefully. He lifted his head up and looked at me.

"Oh, yes," Thomas said seductively. "I will take you into that bedroom and have wild, passionate sex with you..."

"Really?" I said, my eyes lighting up. He put a finger on my lips.

"If, and it's a really big if..." I could tell it was going to be a really big favor, because he seemed to hesitate in telling me what it was. Not only was I desperate to have sex with this man, but I owed him whatever the hell he wanted because of what I had done. Seriously, I couldn't think of a single thing that I wouldn't do for him.

"I'llhavesexwithyouifyouperformatheclub." Thomas said it so fast that I had to rewind it back in my head to realize what he had said.

"No fuckin' way!" I said, laughing and gently pushing him away. Amazing how fast I had forgotten my vow to do whatever he asked.

"Fine," Thomas said, shrugging his shoulders. Then he put his hand down my pants.

"Ohhhh." I rolled my head back so fast I banged it on the door. He quickly pulled his hand out of my pants. He was no idiot. He knew exactly how to get what he wanted. He pressed himself against me again. I had to be careful because at this point I was ready to agree to just about anything.

"Henry. You will never know how you really feel about performing if you don't at least try it." He looked at me more seriously. "I mean it. I've seen your face when you talk about it. I really think it's what you're supposed to be doing with your life. Performing is who you are. It's one of the things I love the most about you."

How was I supposed to say no to that?

"I know, but... you're talking about in *drag*, Thomas."

"And what's wrong with that?" He was teasing me, but he had me right where he wanted me.

"There's nothing wrong with drag queens," I said, running my fingers through his hair. "I happen to be very much in love with one. I just can't see Henry Vaughn, Jr. in a dress."

"Honey, that's the point. It's the only way you could perform without anybody knowing who you are. There's no real risk to it that way. You wouldn't even have to sing! Just lip sync. I just want you to go onstage one time. Just try it one time. That way you'll really know what it feels like." Thomas kissed me softly, then looked into my eyes. "I just think you only have to try performing once and you'll be hooked."

I felt my resolve weakening when I looked into those damn eyes of his. Still, I forced myself to say, "Thomas. I just can't."

"If you say so," Thomas said. "Too bad. I was really looking forward to the two of us in bed together." He was kissing my neck and had me moaning again. "Naked. Doing things you've never done before."

It wasn't fair! My defenses were down due to lack of sex.

But it was fair. At least he was offering sex with him as my reward for agreeing to perform at the club. All he really had to do was look me in the eye and say *you owe me this after what you did.* But he wouldn't do that to me. That just wasn't his way.

"Ohhhh, Thomas..." I moaned as he kept touching me all over. I knew I would live to regret this decision, but right now I would do just about anything to get in bed with this man.

"Come on, Henry," Thomas whispered in my ear as he kept kissing my neck. "Do it."

"Okay, Thomas," I said breathlessly. "Anything you say..."

His eyes lit up. He grabbed my hand and pulled me into the bedroom where we had wild, passionate sex just like he had promised. Then did it again. And again.

It truly was the best sex of my life, and it wasn't just because it was the first time I had been with a man. It was also the first time I had done it with someone I loved. It really was wonderful being with him. Thomas was passionate and sweet and lots of fun in bed. We laughed a lot together, but he never made me feel stupid for my lack of experience. He was a wonderful teacher and I was an eager student. Being in love really does make a difference when you're having sex. It was the little things. The way we wanted to please each other, not just out of male ego and the desire to show off our sexual prowess, but because we really cared about each other's pleasure. The way a kiss on a sweaty forehead was somehow more intimate than a kiss on the mouth.

We were so sex-starved after being apart that the first time was over too quickly. The second time was amazing. I loved taking my time with him and that time, well, I had more of an idea of what to do.

The third time was just gravy.

That time, I think we both thought we were done for now, but then we started kissing and realized we weren't ready to leave the bedroom just yet.

For once, Thomas didn't seem worried that I would regret our sexual activity. I'd been so enthusiastic in bed that I don't think he had any doubts. He was right not to worry. This time, there had been no sense of panic at what I was doing and no fear that we had gone too far. There was only happiness and unbelievable sex. Being with Thomas felt natural and right and wonderful. I hadn't thought it possible, but I was more in love with Thomas than ever before.

So let Kyle call me a cocksucker or anything else he wanted. I didn't care. But if anybody ever spoke to Thomas like that, I'd fucking knock him out.

After our sex marathon, we were both dehydrated and starving, so we downed several beers while waiting for our Chinese food to arrive. It's amazing how fast the alcohol hits you on an empty stomach. To amplify the effect, I had a few shots of Schnapps. Thomas and I sat on the couch with our arms around each other, sexually satisfied and half drunk.

"I can't believe I agreed to do drag. You took advantage of me, young man. You and your sexy wiles," I told Thomas.

He kissed me and said, "I guess that really wasn't playing fair."

"No, it wasn't. How I am supposed to resist this?" I said, squeezing his shoulders and admiring him. I touched his face gently. "Though all you really had to do is look at me and just ask. I can't seem to deny you anything." We looked into each other's eyes, savoring a nice moment. "Alice is right. We are adorable." I took another swig of beer.

"She's such a sweet girl," Thomas said.

"Yeah, she is. Speaking of Alice..." I shot Thomas a guilty look. "I have a confession to make. You know Brady Clayton?"

"Yeah, I know Brady. Daammmn."

"You don't have to say it like *that,"* I said, mock offended.

Thomas patted my cheek. "You're hotter, honey. What about Brady?"

"He's interested in Alice."

"*Really,"* Thomas said, sounding impressed. "Does she kn-" I shook my head before he could even finish his sentence. "Henry, you have to tell her."

"I know," I whined. "That's one of the reasons I'm telling you. I knew you'd make me do the right thing."

"She deserves to be happy. And he could make her happy. I mean, mmmmm," Thomas said.

"Stop that!"

Thomas laughed. "I'm just messing with you."

I sat back and put my feet up on the coffee table. "You're not really gonna make me do this, are you? The club thing, I mean?"

"You better believe I am. You promised me. You had your way with me and now you have to pay up," Thomas answered.

"Sex with me wasn't reward enough for you?"

Thomas kissed my cheek and murmured in my ear. "Henry, you were amazing." Then he sat straight up and said,

"But no. Your astounding sexual performance is not enough. You're doing this." The doorbell rang and he got up to get the Chinese food.

I groaned, but part of me was excited about doing it. I'd never had the guts to get up and perform in front of anybody. Well, I mean, sports aside. That was different. I hadn't ever had the balls to audition for high school plays or anything like that even though I'd desperately wanted to. The first and only time I had done anything creative in front of anybody was that time in the second grade. But that was when Mom was still alive. I guess I kind of lost interest in it for a while after she died.

Grief is exhausting, especially when you're just a kid.

By the time I started realizing I wanted to act and sing and all that, I was already pretty entrenched in sports and all. I didn't know what my dad would say about me just dropping baseball and picking up theater. I didn't want to find out, so I just never tried.

I wasn't happy at all about the idea of performing in a fucking dress. It still kinda weirded me out when Thomas did it, though his talent was a huge turn-on for me. He was incredibly sexy when he was performing; I just preferred watching him rehearse in his living room, lip syncing and wearing guy clothes. Preferably his work scrubs. Oh, baby.

Though I hated the idea of doing drag myself, I confess I'd always felt a little jealous seeing the guys at the club perform. The whole "attention whore" thing I guess. The idea of having everyone watch me acting or singing or whatever instead of playing baseball thrilled me. Thomas knew it. That was why he was forcing me to try it.

Thomas handed me my dinner and sat down on the couch next to me. I had just shoveled in a mouthful of delicious General Tso's chicken when a horrible thought suddenly hit me.

"Oh, shit," I said, but my words were unintelligible because my mouth was full.

"What?" Thomas asked.

I swallowed and looked at him. "Wait a second. How do you know the guys at the club will even let me do this? Doesn't everybody hate me?" I asked.

"They don't hate you, Henry," Thomas told me softly.

"Why the hell not? I would! I wouldn't let me set foot in there after the things I said." I hadn't even thought about Thomas' friends at the club until just now. The friends who had welcomed me with open arms. They knew I was the gay Oriole and any one of them could have sold the story to a national tabloid and made a fortune, but nobody did. They were nothing but sweet and wonderful to me. And I had called them fags in front of the whole world.

"They understand that I've forgiven you and that I want them to forgive you, too. Honestly, they weren't as upset as you might think."

"Really?"

Thomas nodded.

"It's an awful situation you're in with the ballclub and they totally get that. We all saw the news report." I winced and Thomas squeezed my hand. "We saw how those reporters just ambushed you. It's not like you went to them with a well-thought-out quote. If there's one thing the queens at the club understand, it's fear. We've all been there, more or less, but none of us have faced it on the public level that you've had to endure. They know you didn't mean... what you said."

I sighed heavily. I was so relieved to hear that the guys didn't hate my guts. Fear was no excuse for what I'd said, but

I was grateful that they understood that I didn't mean a word of it.

"So you really think they'll let me perform there?"

"Yes."

"You already asked them, didn't you?"

Thomas grinned mischievously. "It's already all set up. Ben's already agreed to give you his spot for a night."

"Ben?" I groaned loudly. "So that means I'm Liza. I have to be fucking Liza Minnelli. Thomas, I don't know if I can do this!" The image of me in drag was becoming so much clearer now. I'd seen Ben do Liza's version of "New York, New York" a bunch of times. I practically already knew all the steps by heart already. I suppose it made sense, but the reality of what I was going to do was starting to sink in.

"I know you can do it, Henry." He said it so matter-of-factly that I started to believe it myself. "You should ask your dad to come."

I almost choked on my beer.

Thomas whacked me on the back to help it go down. "Sorry, love. Just kidding. But you know who you do have to ask? Alice."

"No way! I don't want anybody I know seeing me do this."

"Come on, now. She would *love* it. You know she would."

I couldn't help smiling. Thomas was right. Alice would never forgive me if I performed in drag and she didn't get to see it. I owed her big time for everything she had done for me. Besides, seeing me in a dress would be sure to kill any remaining romantic feelings she might have had for me. I promised Thomas I would call her and let her know about my upcoming debut.

I had to remember to hold the phone away from my ear when I told her because there was sure to be a great deal of laughter and squealing on her part.

I REALIZED it wasn't enough to have Thomas try to explain my horrific behavior to his friends at the Hippo. I wanted to go see the guys for myself and tell them how sorry I was.

I parked my MLB PLYA mobile right in front of Club Hippo. I wasn't trying to hide so much anymore. If somebody saw my car parked outside, so be it. I knew now that I was going to come out. I had to. I'd known all along that the choice would come down to coming out or losing Thomas, and I loved him far, far too much to let him go. It was just a matter of time.

I kept my head down as I walked through the main bar area, but other than that I didn't really do anything to disguise my identity. I walked up the steps to the backstage area and knocked on the door.

Adam answered and smiled at me.

"Hey, Henry. Thomas is off tonight."

"Oh, I know. I wanted to talk to you. And Ben and some of the other guys."

"Oh," Adam said gently. "Okay, sure. Come on in." Adam was always nice, but he seemed to be especially kind to me that night. I think he realized why I was there.

Adam walked over to Ben, who was already in full makeup. He jumped up and gave me a warm hug, his bracelets jangling and heels clicking. I was pretty sure he dressed like that all the time, and not just when he was performing. He was such a character. I really liked him.

"Hey, baby! Long time no see."

I turned to Adam and asked, "Could you get Tony and Jeff?" Adam nodded. I wanted to make sure I had a chance to talk to Thomas' closest friends at the club. I couldn't imagine how humiliating it must have been for Thomas to have the guy he loved to go on television and deny that he even knew him.

Once I had all of Thomas' friends together, Ben put a gentle hand on my back and the others looked at me with supportive faces. They really didn't hate me. *Wow.*

"I just wanted to tell you how sorry I am about what I said on television. I-I was just so scared when the lights and the cameras hit me and I just didn't know what to do. I-I just panicked. I'm just really sorry. You guys have all been so nice to me and...well...there's no excuse for what I said. I'm gonna fix it, though. I-I think I'm gonna come out soon."

"Wow," Adam said. "Really?"

"Yeah, but don't tell Thomas. I haven't told him yet and, he...well, he worries..." They all nodded. They knew how he was.

"So you'd be the first player..." Jeff began and I nodded. The first MLB player to come out of the closet. The idea scared the hell out of me, but when I pictured Thomas' face, I knew I could do it. I wouldn't let him down. Not again.

"Yeah. I just...I really love Thomas, and..." my voice cracked with emotion. "I want to go public for him."

Ben put his hand on his heart and looked like he was about to cry. I hoped he wouldn't, because then I would probably start.

"So...so I-I just hope you all know I'm sorry and I didn't mean what I said."

"I know, baby. Come here." Ben engulfed me in a huge, gay hug. I loved it. "I'm just sorry you had to go through all that. Everybody deserves the chance to come out when and if they're ready. They had no right chasing you down like they did." His soft, warm eyes turned a bit sad. "And doing that to you on television like that. People have killed themselves over less than that. I've *known* people who have-" he stopped, choking up a bit. He shook his head, not wanting to continue on this subject that was clearly too painful.

"Thanks, Ben. Thanks for, you know, understanding."

"So, you're really gonna do this thing, huh?" Adam asked, smiling and looking around at all the other queens getting dressed. I groaned and nodded. All four men grinned at me and I realized that Alice wasn't the only one who was gonna get a huge kick out of seeing Henry Vaughn, Jr. in drag.

"Yeah, I'm gonna do it. I had no choice. Thomas looked at me with those friggin' eyes of his and was like 'Please, will you do this for me?'" I said that last part in a perfect imitation of Thomas and the guys cracked up.

"Oh, man. Those eyes of his. I swear, he uses those things like girls use their tits," Adam said, shaking his head. I burst out laughing as I realized how true that was.

"I guess I better go. Thanks, you know, for everything. See you soon." I looked around at the room. "Sooner than I'm ready for..." Ben smiled and patted me on the back, bracelets still jangling.

I PHONED Jeremy from my car, which was still parked in front of the Hippo. I hoped he would answer my call.

"Hey, Jeremy. It's um, Henry."

"Oh. Hi." He didn't sound exactly thrilled to hear from me, but he didn't sound like he wanted to kill me either.

"I just wanted to call to say how sorry I am about everything. I really didn't mean what I said, you know. I-I just didn't know what to do and I wasn't thinking."

"I took up for you, you know that? I got in fights with my boyfriend over you," Jeremy said angrily. "Sam didn't want to have anything to do with you. I kept telling him that you were going through a rough time. I reminded him that we'd all been there and told him he should give you a break."

"I know you did," I said. It was true. Jeremy was always sticking up for me, even though it made Sam mad.

"You're lucky you were out of town, dude. I wanted to kill you after what you said." Jeremy sounded pretty scary. I'd never heard him talk like that before.

"Yeah. I know..." Alice had warned me. She wasn't kidding.

"You really hurt Thomas. Badly."

"I know," I said quietly. I closed my eyes and drew in a breath, recalling the look on Thomas' face the first time I saw him after I'd said those awful things. "I'm gonna regret that for the rest of my life. Thanks for, you know, being there for him. I know you guys took care of him while I was away." I paused for a moment, not sure of what else to say. "I guess that's all I wanted to say. I'm just really sorry."

"I know you are," he said, his tone finally softening a bit. "Look, it'd be great if we could all be out and proud and all that, but it's hard to know what any of us would do if we were in your shoes. It's hard enough for us, you know, dealing with people, but you've got it worse with the team and the media. I do get that, okay?"

I exhaled slowly and felt a little better. "Thanks. And Jeremy, I'm really sorry that I hurt Sam. Please tell him that. Tell him I've thought a lot about him lately and I'm really sorry to be another person in his life who let him down."

"Yeah. Look, you know, I can forgive you. But Sam..."

"No, no. I know. It's too much to ask of him. I know that. That's why I didn't call him. I didn't want to make things worse. He doesn't have to forgive me if he doesn't want to. But, you know, please tell him I'm sorry."

"I will."

"Thanks," I let out a deep breath, relieved that I had gotten the call to Jeremy over with. I made a mental note to mention both Sam and Jeremy in my coming out speech. I wanted to give them a public apology, too.

I started up the car. As I put the phone in my car dock on the dashboard, I saw there was a text message from Thomas.

"Wow. Word travels fast," I said aloud.

Heard you visited the guys at the club. I love you :)

22

My legs felt rubbery and weak as I walked up the stairs of the Hippo. I had gone into this dressing room a dozen times, but always to visit Thomas while he got ready. I couldn't believe that this time I was the one who had to go on. Thomas held my hand and pulled me along.

"Come on, hon. You're gonna be fine," Thomas seemed more nervous than I was, which really rattled me. He was the calm one. I was the one who was always a mess. He was the one making me do this, so I think he felt responsible for my success.

"Henry, baby! You all ready?" Ben asked.

"No. No, not at all," I said truthfully.

"You're gonna be great, darling. Just great," he said.

"Thanks for giving up your spot, Ben."

"Anything for my favorite guys," Ben said, kissing me on the cheek and then kissing Thomas.

"Come on, honey. Let's get you ready!" Ben exclaimed.

Ben led me over to the mirror. I couldn't look while he put the makeup on. I tried not to think about it. I imagined I was in a trailer somewhere, getting ready to go on a movie set. To play the hero. A guy, for fuck's sake. When he was done, Ben stepped back to admire his handiwork. He clapped his hands in delight.

"Baby, you're gorgeous!" Ben started to spin me around but I stopped him.

"Don't! I just...I'm not ready to see it yet." He nodded, understanding. I was really afraid that if I looked, I wouldn't be able to go through with it. I refused to put the wig on until the very last minute, so Ben just set it on the table.

I walked around, avoiding the mirrors everywhere, to find Thomas. He had to bite his lip to keep from laughing when he saw me.

"Stooooop!" I whined at him. "You do this all the time, you know."

"I know. It's just...you look so different." He kissed me on the cheek.

"Careful, you'll smudge his makeup!" Ben called out.

"Ohhh, that's not something I ever thought I would hear," I groaned. I bent over like I was in pain, but Thomas pulled me up.

"Come on, Henry. We gotta get you in your gown." I swear I heard him chuckle when he said it.

I noticed Jeremy standing over at the door.

"Jeremy's here," I told Thomas as he led me to a private room to help me get dressed.

"He and Sam came to see your show."

"They did? Sam's here, too?"

"I wanted them to come," Thomas said quietly. Well, that explained it. Sam couldn't say no to Thomas any more than I could. Sam didn't have to like it, but he knew Thomas loved me. If Thomas wanted Sam there to support me, he didn't have much of a choice.

I saw the dress I was supposed to wear hanging on the door. It was a flashy, shiny, gold and black number. Ben was a pretty big guy. He was almost the same size as me, so the dress should fit pretty well. I closed my eyes and took a deep breath. I really wasn't at all sure that I could go through with this.

"It's all right, Henry. It's just a dress." I opened my eyes and glared at him. "Come on. I'll help you." He stripped me out of my clothes. My wonderful, manly clothes were now lying in a heap on the floor. I felt dizzy as I stepped into the dress, one leg at a time. Thomas helped me on with it and zipped it up the back.

He stood back and looked at me in all my glory. Makeup and dress in place; all I needed was the wig. He pressed his lips together.

"Go ahead and laugh," I told him wearily.

"I'm not gonna laugh at you, my love," Thomas said tenderly. Of all the sweet names he called me, "my love" was my favorite. He touched my hair gently and tucked it behind my ear. "Besides, I know what you look like underneath those clothes and you're all man." That made me feel better. He always made me feel better.

We walked back into the main dressing room together. At first, nobody paid any attention to me, as they were too busy getting ready themselves. Then Sam spotted me. He was standing near the door with Jeremy.

Sam's jaw dropped when he saw me.

He came walking over to Thomas and me, his eyes wide. Jeremy followed closely, protectively, behind him.

"Henry..." Sam began, covering his mouth. "I never wanted to see you again, but...." He just burst into laughter and could barely speak. "But...this...was totally worth it!" He was quite literally doubled over in laughter. Tears were in his eyes. Sam had waited for a moment like this since the day he'd first met me in the doctor's office.

Whenever you see somebody, anybody, laugh this hard, people just can't help but join in. It's just so damn funny to see somebody lose it so bad that they can't even talk. Jeremy was cracking up almost as bad. Thomas covered his mouth. God love him, he fought it so hard...Everyone in the room looked up to see what all the fuss was about. Other people started laughing, too, when they realized it was me in my girly getup.

In a moment like this, I figured I could run out of the room and succumb to total humiliation, or I could just go with it.

I rolled my eyes, smiling self-consciously. Might as well give the people what they wanted. I held my arms out and turned around a couple of times and let everybody get a good look at me. I saw Adam, Ben, Tony, and Jeff grinning as they checked me out. Somebody started applauding and soon everybody was clapping.

I'd never felt so embarrassed and so loved in my entire life.

Thomas looked so proud of me that I knew, whatever happened, this would all be worthwhile. I'd do it for him.

"Hey, Sam. Do me a favor." Sam looked at me curiously. "Here, take a picture, would you?" I handed him my cell phone and I put my arm around Thomas. Sam took a picture of the two of us together. "Thanks!" I said, taking the phone back. I didn't look at the photo yet. I still didn't want to know what I looked like.

Now that Sam had calmed down enough for me to be able to speak to him, I figured I would take a chance. "I'm really sorry for everything. For everything I ever said to make you feel bad. I'm just...I'm really sorry," I told him.

"Good luck tonight," he said stiffly and walked away.

I exchanged a sorrowful look with Thomas. He knew how bad I felt about hurting Sam. Thomas shrugged and sighed. He gestured at me to follow him and he took me back over to the dressing table and sat me down. He spun me around to face him because he knew I still didn't want to look at myself in the mirror. He expertly affixed the wig to my head.

"You're so brave for doing this, Henry. I can't wait to see you out there."

I suddenly had an idea that was either utterly brilliant or completely stupid. I supposed I would find out later which one it was.

"Hey. Stay here a minute. I'll be right back." I jumped up from the chair and Thomas looked worried.

"Henry, where-"

"Don't worry. I'm not gonna run off or anything. I swear. I'll be right back, okay?" Thomas glanced at the clock, but nodded. He still looked worried, but he trusted me.

I dashed out of the room and went down the stairs. I nearly fell wearing that fucking gown. I had to lift it up so I could walk without killing myself, and I suddenly had new sympathy for what women went through for the sake of beauty. Fuck, I hadn't even put on the heels yet. I was just in my stocking feet. Yes, stockings as in pantyhose. Blechh. I tried not to think about it.

I burst into the downstairs bar room, startling the patrons. I heard a few whistles and I waved as I ran through. I headed to the room where they did karaoke several nights a week.

"Excuse me!" I said, startling the D.J. who was still setting up his equipment. Drag queens were hardly an unusual sight at the bar. They often wandered around down here before a show. They just didn't usually come running in at full speed. "I'm sorry to bother you. I was wondering if I could borrow just one CD from you real quick? Can I have the karaoke version of "New York, New York"? I promise I'll bring it right back."

If I was going to perform in front of all these people, I was going to do it right. No lip syncing for me.

I was going to sing.

"Sure." The karaoke guy nodded and handed it over to me. He squinted curiously at me and I stifled a laugh. I think he was trying to figure out where he knew me from. I was nearly unrecognizable in this getup. If he only had a clue...

As I headed back toward the dressing room, I saw Alice come in.

"Alice!" I called to her. She heard my voice and looked right past me. Alice was used to seeing drag queens all over this place, so my presence didn't surprise her. But she had no idea it was me. When she glanced in my direction, I called her name again. Her eyes grew wide and she covered her mouth. She wasn't laughing yet; she was still in shock at realizing it was me. I just dashed over to her and grabbed her hand. "Come on, let's go upstairs."

I heard her start to giggle as she followed me upstairs.

"Don't tell me what I look like. I really don't want to know."

"You haven't looked in a mirror yet?" she asked.

"No. And I don't plan to until I'm done."

"Well, I think you look fantastic." Alice managed to keep a straight face when she said it, but I heard the laughter in her voice.

"There you are!" Thomas said as I came back in. He looked relieved. I think he really thought I was gonna make a run for it. "Hi, sweetheart," he said to Alice, kissing her on the cheek.

"What have you done to him?" Alice asked, laughing. "Seriously, he looks great."

"Back in a sec," I told him. Thomas looked at me warily. I think he wanted to keep an eye on me until show time. Just in case. But I had to slip away to give the CD to the other D.J. who was in charge of the drag show. I also had to make sure he gave me a microphone, or nobody would be able to hear me sing.

When I got back, Thomas said, "Please stay here. You're making me crazy!"

"Sorry. I'm ready now."

"You okay?" Thomas asked me.

"Yeah. I guess," I told him.

"Look, I'll stay with you right up until it's time for you to go on, then I'm gonna run downstairs so I can watch." He glanced over at Sam, Jeremy, and Alice. "We're all gonna stand somewhere where you can see us, okay?" I nodded. I knew if I could look at his face, I might actually be able to pull this off.

Thomas smiled at me, but he looked really worried. I think he was having second thoughts about making me do this. He hated seeing me go through all this stress and if it didn't go well, he would never forgive himself. I would forgive him, though. He was doing this for me. If he hadn't asked me, I'd never have had the balls to try to perform anywhere. It would all have been just a lifelong, unfulfilled dream.

Just as I was about to go on, I made a huge, huge mistake.

I looked up and caught a glimpse of myself in the mirror.

I looked way more convincing as a woman than I would have liked to have believed. Ben had done an incredible job on the makeup. I mean, I looked like a fucking *girl*. At least my face kinda did, which I found both frightening and annoying. I'd always thought I had a very masculine kind of jaw line, but Ben had done wonders with softening my face. Ugh. There was no way anybody on the planet could have ever truly mistaken me for a woman, though. Not with my huge arms visible in this ridiculous dress with the spaghetti straps. I was never so grateful for my muscles.

Thomas followed my gaze and looked alarmed at the look of sheer panic that crossed my face when I saw myself. I almost started hyperventilating. Good thing I had taken a shot of my inhaler not long ago or I would have fucking passed out.

Panicked and breathless, I grabbed Thomas by the shoulders. "Thomas! I can't do this. I can't do this! I-"

"Yes you can, Henry!" Thomas shouted at me. Alice blinked and stepped back. Now she knew what it was like to hear Thomas actually yell. "You can do this! You're going to do this!"

I heard the announcer say, "And now, making her debut with us tonight, Queen Henry!"

I whipped around and said, "Queen Henry? *Thomas!*"

"It was either that, or Dolly Hard-On. Now get out there!" Thomas said as he practically shoved me out to the stage area. He had held up a brave front for my sake, but I heard him moan, "Oh God, Alice...what have I done to him..." He was terrified for me.

"He's gonna be *great*, Thomas. You'll see!" I was grateful to hear how confident Alice sounded. Out of the corner of my eye, I saw her take charge and grab his hand to lead him downstairs so they could watch me from where Thomas promised they would be standing.

The lights hit me and I froze in terror.

All I had to do was remember to breathe.

Thomas and Alice made it downstairs in record time, with Sam and Jeremy following close on their heels. Thomas looked more scared than I was.

The opening notes of the karaoke version of "New York, New York" began.

I looked straight at Thomas and I began to sing.

Thomas stared at me, bewildered. He and Alice exchanged astonished looks as the two of them, along with everybody else in attendance, slowly started to realize that I was really singing. That sure as fuck wasn't Liza Minnelli's voice. I couldn't help but glare at my god-awful high-heeled pumps as I sang the line about "vagabond shoes," but other than that, I was doing okay.

At first, Thomas just stood there nervously, with his fist over his mouth. I saw him visibly start to relax as he realized I was doing well.

I was actually singing. And my voice sounded pretty damn good, at least so far as I could tell. At first, the audience just kind of sat there, not quite knowing what to think of me. I don't think they'd ever seen a drag queen sing here before, and my bizarre mash-up of Liza Minnelli and Frank Sinatra must have seemed really weird.

At first, Alice had both her hands over her mouth. When she finally dropped them, she shook her head in wonder. I managed to lock eyes with her from the stage and she smiled at me. Sam stood there with his arms crossed, shaking his head. I saw the grudging smile on his face. He was actually impressed.

I watched Thomas' face change from terror to relief to

pride to joy. I don't think I'd ever seen him look happier. The look on his face was worth everything, even wearing an evening gown.

Once the crowd caught on to what I was doing, they started really getting into it. It was incredible.

It was a dream come true.

I heard people cheering and whistling for me.

For me.

And there wasn't a baseball or bat in sight. The more the crowd encouraged me, the more I got into it. I started moving around more and putting all the passion I had in me into that song. And it's such a great, wonderful, classic song. An upbeat, hopeful tune all about making your dreams come true.

I couldn't wait to hit that last, wonderful, glorious note, that last "York" of the song. I knew I could fucking nail it.

And...I...did.

That was one of the most wonderful moments of my life. Thomas was right that this was where I belonged. Well, minus the dress, anyway.

I finished the last note and looked around, stunned, at what happened next.

People stood up.

One by one, they all stood up and applauded.

I had gotten a fucking standing ovation my very first time onstage.

Thomas must have run upstairs because he was out of breath when he got there. As soon as I saw him, I tore the wig off my head and threw it to the ground like I was spiking a football in victory. Thomas opened his arms and I ran into them, nearly knocking him down.

"Henry, you were amazing! You actually sang! What

made you go out there and actually sing?" Thomas asked me in wonder.

"Temporary insanity, I don't know. I just had to try, you know?" Thomas nodded. "And I never would have done it if it weren't for you. Thank you so much," I said. I kissed him and I heard people in the room applauding.

"I get to follow that? Thanks, asshole," muttered Adam, who was on next. Then he punched me playfully in the shoulder.

"Baby, you were amazing," Thomas said. He looked at me and those eyes, those beautiful, soulful, loving eyes were filled with tears.

"Don't. You'll get me started," I told him, gently wiping his eyes with my thumbs.

"I'm so proud of you," Thomas said. "Remember that rookie you told me about? The one that was all choked up about being at the ballpark?"

I nodded, understanding immediately.

"That's what this moment is for you. Right now. This is what you're meant to do."

I wrapped my arms around him and didn't ever want to let go.

Alice looked like she was about to cry, too. She had such a big heart, that girl. I knew she loved seeing us together.

I engulfed her in a huge bear hug. "Thanks for coming, darling girl."

"Henry, I'm so proud of you. You were so wonderful out there." She turned her head toward Thomas. "You're a lucky man, Thomas."

"I know." Thomas smiled. When Alice had her back to him, hugging me again, Thomas mouthed *tell her about Brady*. I nodded. I was fine with telling her about Brady liking her. I didn't need her anymore. Well, as a beard anyway. She was one of my dearest friends and nothing would change that, but she could date Brady all she wanted now.

Because I was definitely coming out of the closet. As soon as humanly possible.

Suddenly, Sam came bursting into the room. He looked very upset. He came running up to me, breathless.

"Henry, you gotta get out of here! Kyle McCracken's downstairs. He must have followed you here," Sam said. Thomas drew in a breath and looked at me, terrified. "He's got his fucking cell phone camera out and he knows you're here. I heard him ask somebody if they saw you." Sam laughed bitterly. "Fucking dumbass. He was skulking around the whole time you were up on stage. He had no idea that was you."

"We'll-we'll-we'll sneak you out the back way," Thomas said frantically.

Alice said in a calm but firm voice, "Listen, Thomas. Let's get him out of this makeup and into his street clothes first. It won't take long. It'll be way too dangerous for him to go out on the street like this. If anybody recognizes it's him in a dress, he's done for." Thomas nodded. He grabbed my hand and started to pull me toward the dressing table.

"No. No!" I said firmly. Thomas looked up at me quizzically. I looked over at Alice. "You know what I have to do now, right?"

Alice winced. "Are you sure? You sure you want to do it like this?"

I nodded and smiled. "I can't think of a better way."

Alice looked worried and sighed, but nodded. She understood. I knew she would. Thomas, on the other hand...

Alice was one step ahead of me. She walked over to

Thomas and put a supportive hand on his back. Once he realized what I was about to do, he was going to completely flip out and Alice would be there to try to calm him.

"Henry, please. We gotta hurry!" His eyes were full of fear. Yeah. Well, I was done with fear. Done with hiding.

"Hey, if Kyle wants a picture of me, let him have it!" I said, spreading my arms and showing off all my drag glory.

"Henry, what the-"

"It's time, Thomas. It's time for me to stop hiding. I'm ready to come out of the closet now, so why wait?"

Thomas' eyes went wide with terror. "No. No, Henry! Not like this!" I started to walk downstairs and he grabbed my hand. "Henry, you're not thinking clearly! Look, just sleep on it tonight and if you're still ready to come out, you can issue a statement or call a press conference or whatever you want to do." He gestured at my outfit. "This-this-this is too much, Henry. It'll be awful for you."

I put my hand on the back of his head and looked into his eyes. "I want to do this. I want to do it for you, Thomas. This is the only way I know to even begin to make up for what I did before."

"You don't have to do this, Henry! I forgive you! We all do!" I looked around and heads were nodding everywhere. The other queens looked worried, too. So did Jeremy and even Sam. Nobody wanted me to come out like this. I was incredibly touched that they were so worried for me. Reason number five million to do this. For their sake. They deserved somebody to speak out in public on their behalf. Somebody famous.

I grabbed Thomas and kissed him and said, "I'm doing this." I had never been so sure of anything in my life. This was the right thing to do. It was time.

"Henry, please! Don't do this! *Please!*" Thomas cried after me as I broke free of his grasp. Poor Thomas. He had his hands on his head and he was almost literally tearing his hair out. I saw him turn to Alice as I headed toward the stairs. "This is my fault! It's all my fault! I made him do this! I made him perform and now-"

"He knows what he's doing, Thomas," I heard Alice tell him gently. "I know it seems like this is totally spur of the moment, but he's been thinking about it for a while now." The last thing I saw before I disappeared down the stairs was Alice taking Thomas into her arms, comforting him. "He loves you, Thomas. He just wants everybody to know."

I went downstairs and looked for Kyle.

"Hey, it's the guy from the show." A couple of people sitting at the bar recognized me from my performance and raised their glasses at me. New fans. *Cool.* I saluted them and kept walking around, looking for Kyle. I finally spotted him standing at the bar, scanning the room. My Corvette was parked just outside the Hippo, so he knew I was still here somewhere.

I sneaked up behind him and grabbed his ass. Kyle jumped a mile high in the air. Heh heh. I remembered when I used to flinch like that when a guy touched me. He turned around and looked at me. He was startled to find a drag queen there, but he didn't know it was me at first. I had dispensed with the wig already, but the rest of my outfit was still intact.

"Hey, sailor. New in town?" I asked. Kyle stared at me for a second, and then his eyes got wider than I'd thought was humanly possible.

"Henry?" he asked, astonished. I nodded and he slowly looked me up and down, not believing what he was seeing. "You mean, that was you?" Kyle asked, gesturing to the club-room where the drag show was still going on. I nodded. "Wow." He seemed actually impressed with my singing.

"Sure was. Aren't I faaaabulous?"

"Henry, what the *fuck*?"

I grabbed the cell phone in his hand, turned on the camera, and handed it back to him. "What are you waiting for? Henry Vaughn, Jr. in drag in a gay bar. It's the scoop of the century."

Kyle stared at me, bewildered, as I posed for him. When he finally realized I was serious, he took a few pictures.

"Happy now?" I asked, then I spun around on my heels and left to go find my boyfriend, who was surely still a wreck over all this.

When I came back upstairs, Thomas looked at me pleadingly, hoping I'd somehow changed my mind about letting Kyle take a picture of me.

"Found him. Done."

Thomas groaned and slumped against Alice. She put her arms around his neck and kissed him on top of his adorable little head. "It's gonna be fine, Thomas. You'll see."

"Come here, baby," I opened my arms and Thomas went into them.

"Henry, I didn't want you to...I never asked you to..."

"I know, hon," I said, stroking his hair. "I know you would never ask me to do this, but I wanted to. I wanted to do it for you. Try not to worry. It's gonna be fine."

I kissed him and I felt him finally start to relax a little as I held him in my arms.

I FELT SO MUCH BETTER after getting back into my guy clothes. Those heels were a fucking killer, man. Props to all the ladies who wore them. I thought about all the women I'd met in bars who wore those high stilettos. Man, they were so sexy in those things. The way they showed off those long legs...wow. Still, I didn't think I'd ever be able to look at them again without thinking how painful they must be.

It felt good to get outside into the fresh air after being in the club all night. I held Thomas' hand as we walked down the street. I'd never done that in public before. Sam, Jeremy, and Alice were with us, too, and we were going to try to find someplace to eat that was open late.

"Hey, Mary," Sam said.

Thomas looked at me and grinned. He had told me that the names "Mary" and "Blanche" were terms of endearment in the gay community and that if Sam ever called me by one of those girl names, it probably meant he was softening toward me.

"What?"

"I gotta admit. You sounded pretty amazing tonight."

"Thanks, Sam. That means a lot coming from you."

Thomas' pace suddenly slowed. I stopped walking.

"You okay?" I asked him.

"I'm not sure," Thomas said. He took a couple of very deep breaths.

"Thomas!" I said, alarmed. "What's the matter?"

"I-I don't feel well." He looked really pale all of sudden. Before I knew what was happening, his eyes rolled back into his head and he collapsed. I barely managed to catch him before he hit the sidewalk.

"Thomas!" I shouted. I sank to my knees next to him. Sam came running over and practically pushed me out of the way. Sam was the one with medical training, so I stood back.

Sam's voice was worried but calm. "I think he's just

fainted. Put his head between his knees and loosen his shirt."

My hands trembling, I fumbled with the buttons on his shirt. "Thomas? Thomas?" He was still unresponsive. Sam counted quietly as he took Thomas' pulse.

"It's just a little bit slow, but he's okay." Sam looked up at me. "It's all right, Henry. He probably just passed out from the heat in the club, but he's got high blood pressure so I'm gonna call an ambulance just on the off chance that it's his heart." Sam started to dial. "It's just a precaution, Henry."

I nodded, numb. I held Thomas' limp body in my arms. I could feel him breathing, thank God.

Alice knelt down and took Thomas' hand in hers. "He's gonna be fine, Henry." She rubbed his hand rapidly as if willing him to wake up. Her words were comforting, but she sounded terrified.

Sam went with Thomas in the ambulance and I followed in my car. My hands shook on the steering wheel as I drove. Alice rubbed my back and kept repeating, "He'll be okay, Henry. He's gonna be just fine."

Then Sam texted me the most beautiful words I had ever seen in my life: *He's awake. Seems okay.*

Alice patted me on the back and leaned back in her seat and smiled. "Thank God," she breathed out, barely a whisper.

Thomas had regained consciousness during the ride over, but I had to see for myself that he was all right. The bitch nurse at the hospital wouldn't let me see him at first.

"Please, can't I just go check on him real quick?" I pleaded with her. We might have had better luck if we'd gone to Johns Hopkins where Sam and Thomas both worked, but the ambulance had taken him to Mercy Hospital instead.

"I'm sorry. Family only. His brother is in there with him now." Sam had been smart enough to say he was family. I hadn't thought that fast. I couldn't believe they wouldn't let me see him. I'd heard horror stories about gays and lesbians not being able to visit their sick partners in the hospital. How horrible that in some places, even in this country, Thomas could be my husband and they still wouldn't let me in to see him.

Alice held my hand and tried to comfort me as we waited. Sam suddenly bounded into the waiting room. He didn't look too worried, so I started to relax.

"There you are! What are you doing out here? He's been asking for you!" Sam said.

"They won't let-"

"It's okay. He's our brother, too," Sam told the nurse.

"But he said he wasn't related!" the nurse said.

"Yeah, well, we're stepbrothers. Dad just got married again for the fourth time and it's hard to keep track." The nurse looked at him dubiously, then shook her head. She was tired of arguing with us.

"Fine. Go on in and see your friend, Mr. Vaughn." It took me a second to realize why the nurse was giving in so easily. Oh. I never told her my name, but she already knew who I was. She'd probably heard the gay rumors and suspected Thomas and I were together. That kind of thing would have upset me before, but not anymore. I was pretty much out, or would be when the photos hit.

"Thanks!" I got up to go see Thomas.

"Is he gonna be okay?" Alice asked Sam.

"He's fine. He just hadn't eaten much all day. He was too nervous about Henry's debut," Sam said, rolling his eyes.

"Good. I'm so glad he's all right. Henry, I'm gonna head out, okay? Give Thomas my love," Alice said.

"Of course." I went over to her and kissed her on the forehead. "Thanks for coming, darling girl."

"You were great tonight, Peaches."

"Thanks."

"We gotta get you back to your car at the Hippo. Sam, can you-" I began.

"No, no. You guys should stay here with Thomas. I'll just take a cab back to the Hippo," Alice said. I nodded. I dug into my wallet and handed her some cash for a cab. I closed my hand firmly over hers, making it clear that there would be no argument over taking the money. I looked up at Jeremy and he was already one step ahead of me.

"I'll make sure she gets a cab safely," Jeremy said.

I nodded and then rushed over to the room where Thomas was resting. He was sitting up in bed and drinking orange juice from a Styrofoam cup when I came in.

"Are you trying to give me a heart attack?" I asked. He grinned sheepishly and put the juice down.

"I know. I'm sorry. I guess my blood sugar dropped too low. No big deal. Didn't have anything to do with my high blood pressure. I just gotta sign some papers and then I'm outta here," Thomas said.

"Thank God," I said. I leaned over and kissed him.

Something was different. Something felt very wrong.

My entire body suddenly felt as heavy as stone as an unthinkable realization tried to sink into my brain. I wouldn't let it. Thomas saw the look of alarm on my face.

"Henry, you okay?"

I shook my head rapidly as if I could shake off the thoughts that were running through my head. "I'm-I'm just worried about you. Just thinking about what might have happened if it was your heart or something," I told him.

Thomas took my hand in his. "Henry, I'm fine."

The nurse came in with the discharge papers. She noticed I was holding Thomas' hand and she smiled. "Here you are, Mr. Palmer," she said, handing him the papers.

On wobbly legs, I walked out to the waiting room. I felt like fainting myself. I must have looked horrible, because Sam jumped up from his chair and came running up to me.

"Something's wrong..." I said slowly.

"What?" He looked terrified and he glanced over at the room where Thomas was. Jeremy got up to see if everything was okay. He put his hand on Sam's back.

"No, no. Thomas is fine. He's getting dressed. It's just..." I slowly looked up at Sam. I didn't want to say the words out loud because then they would be true. "I just think...I think I feel more like I used to...like, you know, when we first met."

It took a moment for Sam to understand what I meant. I think the look on my face told him more than my words did.

The door opened and Thomas came out. It hurt to look at him. My head was spinning.

"Get him home," Sam whispered. "Then we'll talk."

Numbly, I drove Thomas home. I stopped at a McDonald's drive thru on the way to get him something to eat. I ordered a burger, too, just to seem normal. I threw it in the trash after I dropped Thomas off at his apartment.

Still in a daze, I drove over to Sam's house. It was after 2 a.m. already, but Sam and Jeremy were wide awake and waiting for me.

"Hey, Henry," Sam said grimly. He had medical books spread out all over and Jeremy was looking stuff up on the computer. "Now," Sam began carefully. "You're sure you're-" I nodded miserably and he held up a hand, understanding. He knew I was very upset and he didn't want me to have to say any more than I had to.

It had been almost two months since I had taken the

drug. It didn't seem possible that it was the pill, but I guessed it had to be.

My homosexual feelings had just stopped; turned off like a switch. My attraction to men had disappeared as quickly as it began.

But I still loved Thomas. Nothing would ever change that.

Sam pored through his medical books and every once in a while he would call out some kind of medical term to Jeremy, who would see what he could find on the Internet. Jeremy was a photographer and had about as much medical knowledge as I did. I supposed I should have helped them, but I just sat on the couch in a kind of a stupor. The television was on, but I wasn't watching it.

"It's not the Clonazepam, can't be the magnesium stearate," Sam muttered. Jeremy sighed and rubbed his forehead.

"I'm sorry to keep you up so late. You don't have to do this now," I said.

"No, no. It's okay. I don't mind," Jeremy said.

"We'll figure it out, Henry," Sam said, looking up from his medical book. He and Jeremy exchanged a look. I knew they felt horrible about not believing me that it was the pill after all, but I really didn't blame them. I'd said from the beginning that I wouldn't have believed me either. It was just too crazy.

"What about sulfonoxl? Did we look that one up?" Sam asked.

"Not sure. I thought we did. Let me look again," Jeremy said as he went back to the computer. He rubbed his forehead again. "Sam, I got no idea what I'm looking at here."

"I know. I'm sorry. I should let you go to bed," Sam said.

He glanced at me and I nodded wearily. We weren't getting anywhere here and it had been an incredibly long night.

"I will soon. Sulfonoxl, blah, blah, blah..." He kept searching.

Sam flipped open to the index of a medical book and looked up the same term. "Okay, here it is..." He muttered a bunch of medical crap as he read. Wow, sometimes I forgot how smart he was. "Whoa, whoa, whoa... "

Jeremy looked at me and then we both looked at Sam.

"It says here that it's possible for sulfonoxl to affect the hypothalamus," Sam said. Jeremy and I shrugged at each other.

"Okaaay," Jeremy said.

"The hypothalamus is thought to be implicated in sexual orientation."

"Oh," Jeremy said. "So, do you think that's it?"

"Well, I guess that could explain it, but why would it affect just one guy?" Sam asked.

"I don't know. Maybe the other patients were just too scared to speak up?" Jeremy offered.

"I guess so. Maybe," Sam said, shaking his head. He clearly wasn't too convinced. "And how could the effects possibly last so long? If it is sulfonoxl, how was it still in Henry's body this whole time?"

Jeremy turned back to his computer. "Sulfonoxl. Side effects. Yep, says right here has been known to cause people to dress in drag and burst into random show tunes."

I chuckled at that and Sam looked relieved to see me finally crack a smile. I'd been sitting on the couch looking suicidal for the last hour. "It does say here you should avoid intake of drupes because they can extend and enhance the effect of sulfonoxl in the bloodstream." Jeremy swiveled around in his chair and looked at Sam to see if that meant anything to him.

"Drupes? What the hell are drupes?" Sam asked.

"I have no idea." He swiveled back around and typed "drupes" into the search engine. "Drupes, drupes, drupes...okay. Wikipedia says a drupe is a type of fruit in which an outer fleshy part surrounds a shell, or pit, of hardened endocarp with a seed inside."

"I know you're not supposed to eat grapefruit with some medicines. But I've never seen Henry eat a piece of fruit. Ever," Sam said. I shook my head. He was right. I might be an athlete, but a health nut I was not. "Even if he did, he'd have to have a *drupe* every day for it to prolong the effect of sulfonoxl this long."

Jeremy kept reading. "Drupes include cherries, plums, apricots, peaches-"

Jeremy slowly swiveled around and all three of us said it together.

"Peach Schnapps."

"Did you drink any yesterday?" Sam asked.

I shook my head slowly. "I didn't want to drink anything until after I performed. And then we went to the hospital."

"Well, shit," Sam said.

So I guess we had our answer. Freaky asthma pill plus Peach Schnapps equals homosexual.

The three of us just sat there for a moment. Finally, I stood up and so did Sam and Jeremy. Sam walked over to me.

"I'm really sorry, Blanche." *Blanche.* I cracked a rueful smile, oddly comforted that he still called me girl names. "I'm so sorry. I should have believed you."

"It's okay. Really. I mean...even I wasn't sure after a while."

Sam just looked at me sorrowfully. I could see he felt horribly guilty.

"Jesus. No wonder you were so confused. God, this must have been awful for you!" I could see him mentally going through all the events of the last few weeks. Me denying I was gay. The ballclub. The pride parade. The media. Everything suddenly made sense to him.

"It wasn't all awful," I said, picturing Thomas' beautiful face. "Oh God, Sam," I whispered. "How am I gonna tell him?"

Sam wrapped his arms around me and hugged me, something he had never done before. "I'm so, so, sorry." He squeezed me tight and I knew his heart was breaking not only for Thomas' pain, but also for mine.

"It's not your fault, Sam. Really." Sam had been through enough in his life and he didn't need any more burdens to carry. I really didn't want him to feel bad, and I knew Thomas wouldn't either.

Jeremy put his hand over his heart and mouthed, "*Thank you.*" He knew I had every right to be furious with Sam, and he was very grateful that I wasn't. He put a comforting hand on my back and he looked at me with a mixture of sorrow and gratitude. He loved Sam so much, and I figured he must be imagining what it would feel like if he were forced to break up with him.

"I'm sorry, man. This really sucks," Jeremy said, shaking his head.

"Yeah."

That was the biggest understatement I'd ever heard in my life.

∽

THE SUN WAS COMING up when I finally got home. I was exhausted, but I didn't really want to go to sleep. I had to face what I had to do. I had to tell Thomas that I wasn't really gay.

I made some coffee and just leaned against my kitchen counter, lost in thought. When the coffeemaker dinged to tell me the coffee was ready, I opened up my cabinet to grab some sugar.

I saw the bottle of pills.

Sam had given me a supply of the asthma drug when I first met him at Johns Hopkins, but I never took any more of them after that first one.

I shook a few of them into my palm. I stared at the little white pills. For one crazy moment, I realized that all I had to do was keep taking the pills and chasing them with Schnapps and I could stay with Thomas forever.

But I knew that was insane.

I angrily threw the pills in the trash.

I went over to see Thomas.

"WHAT ARE you doing here so early?" Thomas asked when he opened the door. "I thought you'd be exhausted after last night." He still looked nice in his work scrubs, but the effect on me wasn't the same. That depressed me horribly. Those eyes, though. I still loved those eyes. I still loved *him*.

"I am."

"You look awful. What's the matter?" Thomas asked me, his face filled with concern. I couldn't speak. I didn't know how the hell I was going to get through this. "Come here." He led me over to the couch. Thomas knew something was terribly wrong with me and he waited for me to tell him. But how? I couldn't bear for his heart to be broken the way mine was. But it had to be done.

"I-I don't know how to say this."

Thomas looked afraid. He knew whatever it was, it was something terrible.

"Thomas, I-I'm...." I couldn't do it. I couldn't say it. If I never said it out loud, then it wouldn't be true.

Thomas searched my face as if trying to read it. The scary thing was, he always could. He always seemed to know exactly what I was thinking. I knew he would figure it out on his own.

He did.

Thomas gasped softly and put his hand over his heart. "Oh my God...You're not really gay, are you?"

"No," I managed, my voice barely a whisper. "No, I'm not." I couldn't bear to see the look on his face, so I just closed my eyes and reached for him. He put his arms around me and we just held each other. "Thomas, I'm so sorry..."

"Shhh. It's okay, Henry. It's gonna be okay." His voice soothed me like it always did, but I didn't see how anything would ever be okay again.

When he finally let go of me, he glanced guiltily over at the bedroom.

"Dammit. I knew we shouldn't have..."

"Why? Do you regret it?" I asked angrily. I wasn't mad at him. I was pissed at the whole damn world.

"No!" Thomas said, looking horrified that I would even think such a thing.

"Thomas..." He looked into my eyes and nodded, understanding. "I don't regret it either, baby." I took a deep breath and exhaled. I couldn't remember ever feeling so drained. "I love you, Thomas. You know that, right? I still love you."

He nodded sadly. "I love you, too."

"We can still be friends, right? It won't be easy, but we can make it work, right? I don't want to lose you."

"I don't want to lose you either, Henry. Of course, we'll make it work. I'm not going anywhere."

I felt slightly better. I wanted him in my life. Forever. Maybe he couldn't be my lover anymore, but he was still my best friend.

Thomas brightened a little, obviously remembering something.

"Oh, and speaking of doing crazy things you might live to regret..." he said wryly. Thomas reached behind him, picked up a cell phone, and handed it to me.

"What's this?" I asked.

"Kyle McCracken's cell phone. Ben and some of the other guys tackled him to the ground and stole it from him."

"They what?" I asked, laughing.

"They saw me freaking out over what you did and they grabbed Kyle before he could leave with the photos."

"I can't believe they did that!" I said, marveling at the phone in my hand. With so much going on, I had completely forgotten all about the pictures Kyle had taken.

"Queens can be pretty tough when they're protecting one of their own." He said it in a soft tone that told me that I would always be one of them, no matter what happened. I couldn't have been more honored.

Thomas drew in a deep breath and slowly exhaled. "Now nobody will ever have to know." He looked relieved that I was no longer in danger of being outed. "Now your life can go back to normal."

I looked into his eyes, touched his face, and said quietly, "My life may go back to normal, but I'll never be the same." His eyes started to well up. I knew I had to get out of there before I completely fell apart.

I got up and he followed me to the door. I kissed him one last time, but it was a mistake. When our lips parted, I knew he felt it, too. Kissing him felt strange now.

Whatever we had between us was gone.

"I love you. I'm sorry," I whispered as I turned quickly to go. It wasn't quickly enough as I saw his face crumble just before I shut the door.

I managed to make it to the car before I lost it.

23

I calmed down a bit as I drove over to see Alice. I checked my face in the rearview mirror of my car. I was still kind of a mess, but presentable, I supposed.

Alice answered the door and looked surprised to see me. She had her hair pulled back in a simple ponytail and she wore jeans and a blue shirt that brought out her lovely eyes.

"Henry!"

I just looked at her. "You're really beautiful, you know? I'm sorry I never told you that." I'd noticed how pretty she was before, even when I was gay. Of course, I noticed. The more I got to know her, the more beautiful she was to me. I'd just never said anything. I had just told her she was like a mom to me. Ugh. She deserved so much better.

"Thanks," Alice said softly. I knew she had waited a very long time to hear me say something like that, but there was no joy on her face. She was completely focused on the anguish on mine. "Henry, what happened?"

"It was the pill. I'm not gay anymore," I told her.

Alice gasped and put her hand over her mouth. She let the news sink in for a few seconds, and then she engulfed me in a hug and whispered, "Oh honey, I'm so sorry." She just held me close for a little while, not saying a word. I didn't have to tell her how much pain I was in. She knew how much I loved Thomas.

We sat in her living room and talked for a while.

"I hate seeing you like this, Henry," she said, holding my hand as I told her everything that happened. She cried when I told her how I had broken the news to Thomas.

Emotionally drained, Alice wiped her eyes and asked, "Do you want something to drink?"

"Sure. Anything but Peach Schnapps..." I explained to her how the Schnapps had been responsible for this whole thing.

"You've got to be kidding!" Alice said, laughing. I started to laugh, too. I guess that part was pretty funny.

"Yes. The fruit *actually* made me fruity." Alice laughed again and got me a glass of soda instead. She handed it to me and sat back down. "Oh, I nearly forgot. I do have some good news."

"Good, I could use some right about now." Alice had seemed nearly as upset about the breakup as I was. So much for her being desperately in love with me.

"Guess who has a crush on you?"

Alice shrugged. "I don't know. One of the girls from the Hippo?"

I laughed. "That wouldn't surprise me. I mean, look at you! Who could resist?" Alice smiled shyly. It was so easy to make her happy. Why the fuck hadn't I told her how pretty she was before? "One of the guys from the team. A very *special* guy...."

She gasped. "Not..."

I nodded.

Alice was utterly astonished. "Brady?"

"Yep. He's got the hots for you, darling girl."

"No way!"

"Don't sound so surprised."

"I'm not surprised. I'm shocked out of my mind!" She did look stunned, as if it never occurred to her that a hot guy would be interested in her.

"It's true. The hottest guy on the Baltimore Orioles wants you."

She looked utterly delighted, but was kind enough to pat my hand and say, "The second hottest."

"I found out a while ago that he was interested in you. I mean, like, a *while* ago. Alice, I'm so sorry. I should have told you. I let you be my fake girlfriend instead of letting you be his real one."

Alice did look a little irritated as she let that thought sink in a bit. She'd been alone all this time, watching me be happy with somebody else, instead of being with a great guy. As always, she put her feelings aside for my sake. She knew I was already upset and she wasn't about to add to my suffering.

"It's okay, Henry. I know how much you needed to keep your secret," she told me. "Speaking of keeping your secret, why haven't I seen your ass in a dress all over the news?"

I took Kyle's cell phone out of my pocket and told her what had happened.

"Oh, thank God!" Alice said, flipping through the pictures on the cell phone. "What I wouldn't give to have seen Ben take Kyle down!"

I slapped my knee and laughed. "Oh, I know. Kyle got his ass kicked by a bunch of drag queens. Aw, man, that must have been sweet." Adam had gotten a bunch of pictures of Kyle at the club, so there was no way that Kyle would tell people about me. We had evidence that he had been at the

Hippo but he had nothing on me. I sat back in my chair and contemplated everything that happened. Alice watched me quietly, worried.

"I know it's the best thing that nobody will ever know what happened since I'm not really gay. But I'd come out in front of the whole world if it meant that I could stay with Thomas."

"I know you would, Peaches. I know you would."

I suddenly got a wonderful, insane, fucked-up nuts idea. Thomas had said that nobody would ever have to know.

Yeah.

We'd see about that.

24

I sat in front of my computer at home, staring at the screen. I had the picture Sam took of me in drag with my arm around Thomas loaded onto the computer. I had the photo and email message all ready to be sent to the *Baltimore Sun*.

My finger was on the computer mouse. All it would take was one click to send.

I had composed an email saying that I would call a press conference to explain the photograph and make an announcement. Naturally, everyone would assume I was coming out of the closet.

Yeah. I wished.

Thank God I hadn't come out yet. That would have ended up in disaster for the gay community, and that was the last thing I wanted. Eventually, I'd be photographed with some girl and that would just add fuel to the ridiculous argument that being gay was a choice. I knew better than anyone else in the world that it wasn't. It was biological, and you couldn't control it. If I could have chosen my sexual orientation, I would have. I'd have chosen Thomas in a heartbeat. I knew I couldn't announce that I was gay because I wasn't, but I could still try to make up for all the awful things I'd said.

If I clicked "send," this photo would live in infamy. Thanks to the Internet, it wouldn't ever go away.

Click.

Done. Sent.

I waited for the panic to set in once I realized what I had done. It never did. I knew in my heart that this was the right thing to do.

I leaned back in my chair and grinned. And waited for the phone calls to start.

"You crazy motherfucker!" was Sam's way of greeting me. He'd been the first to call me after the news and photo hit. "What did you do?"

I told him how I'd sent the picture and had said I would explain at the press conference. I said I was sure they thought I was gonna announce I was gay, but instead I was going to apologize for everything I'd said before.

"Wow, Henry," Sam said quietly. He was obviously very touched. "That's incredible. I can't believe you're doing this."

"I wonder if Thomas has seen the picture yet."

"Oh, he's seen it. He almost had a fucking stroke."

"Oh, God. He's not upset is he? I thought he'd be –"

"Oh, it's my own damn fault that he flipped out." Sam was laughing, so I relaxed a little. "I come running up to him at work, waving the newspaper. I should have realized he'd take one look at it and think somebody had outed you somehow. Poor Thomas. Henry, I swear to God. He went completely white and he just goes 'Oh, God. Henry...' and I swear I thought he was gonna pass out on me again. I sat him in a chair so I could explain that this was the picture I took of the two of you. On your phone."

"Awwww," I said. My poor Thomas. I was gonna send him to an early grave for all the worrying he did over me.

"But he's okay? He's okay with it now?"

"Yeah! I mean, he's worried sick over what's gonna happen to you because of it, but Henry? He's really proud of you. I wish you could have seen his face when he realized that you sent the picture in yourself. He was always telling me how much it would mean to him if you would just make some kind of public statement in support of gay players. Wow, Henry. This...this means so much to him."

"I love him so much, Sam."

"I know you do, Isabelle. I know."

My cell phone buzzed almost the instant I hung up with Sam. This was the call I'd been waiting for.

I didn't even say hello. "Slow news day, huh?"

"What...did...you...do..." Thomas asked me slowly.

"Whatever do you mean?" I asked innocently.

"Henry!"

"I sent them the picture of the two of us because I want to tell the truth. Well, not the whole truth. Nobody would ever believe it anyway. Thomas, I want to make up for the horrible things I said. I can't come out as the first openly gay player, but I figured I'd do the next best thing. If I've got the balls to do this, then maybe I can make it easier for the guys who really are gay athletes and who are hiding."

I waited for Thomas' response. Silence.

"Thomas?"

"I-I can't believe you did this." His voice sounded soft, sweet, and as always, worried about me.

"Sam always calls you the patron saint of closeted

queens. Well, I wanna be the patron saint of gay athletes," I told him. "And it's all because of you."

"I love you, Henry."

"I love you, too, Thomas. That's not gonna change. Ever. Okay?"

"Yeah," he said quietly.

"So are you gonna make an appearance at the press conference? You're kinda famous now that you're the 'mystery man' in the photo."

"Are you kidding?" Thomas said, sounding delighted. "I wouldn't miss it! And Henry?"

"Yeah?"

"Your father's gonna kill you."

I HAD WARNED my dad before I sent the picture to the *Baltimore Sun*. I wasn't going to let him talk me out of it, but I owed it to him to warn him about the shitstorm that was about to be unleashed. I knew there was a very good chance that he might never speak to me again. Having the whole world see a photo of your son in drag is not a proud moment for most dads. Not only could he disown me, he could very well issue a statement in the media to that effect. I kept thinking of Sam and his family. It was out of my hands. I was going to do what I was going to do and if my dad abandoned me, well, that was his choice. I loved my dad, but I loved Thomas, too. And I knew speaking out on behalf of gay athletes was the right thing to do.

I went to his house and got right to it. "Dad, I have something to tell you."

"Are you gay?" he asked me bluntly.

"What?"

"Henry, what else would you be here to tell me, lookin' all serious? Everybody's saying it. You might as well tell me the truth."

"I'm not gay, Dad." Hank just looked at me. He didn't believe me. "Look, I'm not gay, but I have some very dear friends who are. It was me at the gay pride parade. I was there with a bunch of my friends. When those reporters caught me, I got scared and ended up calling my friends 'fags' in front of the whole world. I'm gonna regret doing that 'til I'm dead, but I want to do something to make up for it. So, I'm going public with my support for my friends and for gay people everywhere, especially gay athletes. I'm a public figure, Dad. I can make a difference."

Hank looked weary, but he was listening.

"The thing is...you gotta know that nobody's ever gonna believe I'm not gay. Not after they see this." I pulled out the picture of me in drag with my arm around Thomas. "See, this is my friend."

Hank squinted at the picture. "Who is she?"

I sucked in a breath. "No, see, that's my friend, Thomas." I said, pointing at the picture. "And that's, well, that's..."

"Oh, dear God..."

"Yeah. Yeah, that...that would be me," I told him.

Hank looked up at me, horrified. "Henry, what the *hell*?"

"Yeah. Kind of a long story? You know?" He looked at me. No, he didn't know. How could he? "That was my friend Thomas' idea."

"Were you drunk?" he asked. Ironic, given that was the first day in weeks I hadn't had a drink at all. I shook my head. "So this guy, here, he's...he's..."

"Gay, Dad. He's gay. And he's my best friend." Hank was not happy to hear this. Not happy at all.

"I see." He tossed the picture roughly aside. I picked it up and put it away so he wouldn't have to look at it anymore. Well, until he saw it on the 5 o'clock news. "Why...why did you do that?" he asked, looking in the general direction of my pocket where I'd stuffed the photo.

"Thomas wanted me to at least try performing. It's something I've always wanted to try, but, you know, never did. He just wanted to encourage me to give it a shot. I was just supposed to get up there and lip sync, you know, pretend, but I sang. I really sang. In front of a bunch of people." It still thrilled me whenever I thought about it. I still can't believe I went through with it.

"You got a nice singing voice," Hank said.

"What?"

"I've heard you, you know, singin' in the car. You used to sing around the house sometimes. You're not bad. So, what, you're saying you wanna go be a singer now?" Hank asked irritably.

"No, no. I'm not gonna leave baseball or anything." I wasn't stupid. I had an incredible job that paid mucho bucks and I wasn't about to be a damn fool and throw it all away. "Just, you know, in the off season I might take some acting and singing lessons and stuff. Take it slow."

Hank shook his head. He even laughed a little. "Your mother was right."

I just stared at him. He almost never mentioned Mom. It hurt too much, even after all these years. We never talked about her.

"About what?" I asked. He pointed a finger at me.

"She always said you would be a performer. When she saw you do Chicken Little in the second grade, she said that it was your calling or whatever. I thought she was crazy."

I was stunned. I couldn't believe my mother knew it so long before even I did.

"She did some plays in high school and college, you know." *Fuck no, I didn't know that.*

"She did?"

Hank nodded, but then shook his head and I knew we were done talking about my mom. For now.

I didn't want to push my luck, but I wanted my dad to be totally clear on what to expect.

"I'm sending this picture in to the newspapers."

"Henry, why? Why, why, why would you do that?" Hank almost yelled.

"Because it's the best way I know how to show how serious I am about this."

"You expect people to take you seriously like that?"

I laughed. I couldn't help it. He had a point.

"I just don't understand all this. This is all completely out of nowhere. I mean, where did this new queer-lovin' attitude come from? You never used to be like this!"

"I just...woke up one day and felt differently, that's all." Hank shook his head. He didn't understand. "Look, it's because I met my friend, Thomas. It's easy to hate people when you don't really know them. I was uncomfortable with gay guys my whole life until I met him and we became really good friends. I just feel differently now. I did a terrible, terrible thing by denying that I knew him and his friends and calling them that awful word. Guys like them suffer enough just for being who they are, and I made it worse by saying all that stuff. Now, I owe it to them to make it right. Look, you don't have to understand it. You don't even have to accept it. I just wanted to warn you what I was going to do."

"Well, I guess you're gonna do what you're gonna do. Sounds like your mind is made up," Hank said, sounding really tired. I just stared at him. He wasn't happy with me, but that was it?

"Wow. You're taking this better than I thought. I was afraid you might disown me or something." I laughed nervously and I think he heard the fear in my voice. He seemed to realize that I had really thought he might abandon me over this.

Hank looked at me like that was the craziest thing I'd ever said. "Henry. You're my *son*."

25

T homas, Sam, Jeremy, and Alice all came to the press conference to support me. I was scared, but I knew that if I could look out into their supportive faces, I could do anything.

I wasn't even 100% sure of what I was gonna say when the time came, but I guessed I'd figure out something. I was really nervous when I walked up to the front of the media room at the Baltimore Convention Center where all the cameras were set up. I saw Thomas in the audience, looking as petrified as he had when I'd gotten up to perform at the club.

I looked out at all the cameras and reporters. It was eerily silent at first as people waited for me to speak. I just looked out at the cameras for a second.

I grinned.

I was still the same old attention whore I'd always been, and all eyes were on me, baby. I whipped out the picture and held it up.

"It's not really my good side, but ..." That broke the ice and I heard laughter in the room.

"So you do confirm that is you in the photograph?" a reporter asked.

"Yep! That's me."

"And the other gentleman in the picture. Is he gay?" he asked.

"Fah-LAMING!" I said enthusiastically. I heard Thomas' laughter ring out above everybody else's. It was music. "He's also my best friend. There he is, Thomas Palmer."

Thomas kind of half stood up and did a bow. Flashbulbs went off like crazy. I could see the headlines now. HENRY VAUGHN JR'S BOY TOY. Yeah. I wished.

"Was that you photographed at the gay pride parade?" someone else asked.

"I'm so glad you asked that, young man. Yes, yes, yes it was." I locked eyes with Thomas and he smiled at me. "I was there with my wonderful friends. I was there, I lied about it, and I'm sorry."

"Why did you lie about it?" the same reporter asked.

"Because I was fuckin' chickenshit, that's why!" Oops. I was pretty sure I wasn't supposed to say words like that on TV. "Sorry," I said to the nearest camera operator. "You got one of those cuss word bleeping things? You might want to, you know, keep it fired up just in case. Look, I was scared because I didn't want anybody to know that I was hanging out with a bunch of gay guys, which was stupid and childish. I was just being a pussy, that's all." I glanced at the camera operator again. "Sorry. And I never, ever, ever should have called them that horrible word. I was only thinking about protecting myself and my so-called reputation. To all my gay friends who have been nothing but wonderful and kind and supportive to me, I say to you..." I looked first at Sam, then Jeremy, then Thomas on each word. "I...am...SORRY."

"Henry, are you, in fact, a gay man?" A reporter finally shouted out the question that everyone was dying to ask. Heh heh. I couldn't resist screwing with them. I drew in a huge breath and I swear I held it for almost a full ten seconds until the room was completely dead quiet. Thomas shook his head, chuckling softly at my dramatic pause.

Finally, I let out my breath and said, "No."

People started shouting out questions and I couldn't hear anybody.

"All right, all right, chill out everybody." Reporters kept talking so I shouted out, "COOL IT! Look, I'm just here to tell you that some of my nearest and dearest friends are gay, okay? I once dressed in drag and performed, just for funsies. I loved going to the gay pride parade, and there's no place in the world that I'd rather hang out than Club Hippo. So you can follow me around and try to get little gay pictures of me or whatever if you like, but all you're gonna find is me hanging out with my buddies. Oh and, by the way, I highly recommend the drag show at the Hippo. Thomas Palmer is a great performer and so are all the other guys. Seriously, dude. Check it out! Oh, and speaking of performing, I'm actually pretty good at singing, if I do say so myself, so you can come see me do karaoke at the Hippo sometimes if you like. The dress was like a one-time deal, as in never-ever-never again, so don't be expecting that. Also, I figure in the off season, I'm gonna to take some singing lessons and see what's what, you know? I looove musicals and stuff like that, so someday I'd love to be in like an off, off, off, off, off, we're talking like fucking Jersey or something, Broadway show or something like that. I'm just telling you now to save you the trouble of following me and finding out I'm singing and acting in the off season. I realize that you'll all assume

I'm gay because of all these things, but, you know, whatever. Don't care."

I saw Thomas shaking his head, laughing, hardly believing how I was just spilling my guts on TV. People were still yelling out questions, but I had already pretty much said what I wanted to say.

"Oh, and while I'm being the poster boy for stuff, I've also got asthma." I pulled out my asthma inhaler and held it up. "Nothing to be ashamed of, folks."

Thomas gasped audibly and covered his mouth. I think that confession shocked him more than me sending in the drag photo. He knew how embarrassed I was about having asthma.

"Oh, and by the way, for all you fuckers out there who will undoubtedly start sending me hate mail, I give you fair warning. For every piece of anti-gay hate mail you send me, I'm sending a $50 donation in *your name* to GLAAD or the Harvey Milk Foundation or something. And if you write me anonymously?" I said, pointing a finger into the nearest camera. "I'm fucking doublin' it."

"Henry, are you sure this isn't just a cover?"

"If you were really gay, would you tell us?"

"Is this guy Thomas actually your lover?"

I sighed heavily. They didn't believe me, but I didn't care. I just wanted to be done and go have a drink with my friends. My real friends. I might even have a Schnapps now that the drug was out of my system.

"Look, I'll say this. There is absolutely nothing wrong with being gay or being a gay athlete. I'm just sorry that people make it so hard on them. If you think there aren't like dozens of gay major league ballplayers and players in the NFL, the NHL, you name it, you are out of your mind. It sucks that they can't come out without being tortured. I just want to say that I fully support gay athletes, and I really hope someday they'll feel safe enough that they can come out. I want gay athletes everywhere to know that, for what it's worth, I got your back."

I'd never seen my beloved Thomas look so proud of me. I looked into his eyes so he would know in no uncertain terms that everything I was doing was for him. He rewarded me with that wonderful look of love, pride, and adoration that he had given me on the day of the gay pride parade. In that moment, I knew that everything I had been through, and would still go through, was well worth it. He was worth it.

"So, in *closing,"* I said, so the reporters would know I was done with questions, "I would like to say that, though I would have been so, so proud to be the first major league baseball player to come out of the closet, I just can't."

"Then I will." someone stood up and said. Hundreds of heads turned around to see who was speaking.

It was Charles Manero.

Tuna.

I just stared at him from the podium.

He shrugged at me. "I'm the gay cousin I told you about. Look, if you're man enough to show everybody a picture of you in a dress, then I can man up and tell the truth. I'm gay." Tuna said.

I found Thomas' gaze again and he looked at me with amazement. I couldn't believe my support of gays was helping already.

The reporters lost interest in me completely.

"Well fine, Tuna! Way to steal my thunder!"

I waved at Tuna to come up to where I was. I mouthed "It's okay." I knew he was scared. I would be, too. He was so brave to do what he was doing. I stepped down from the podium and let him take my place.

Some of the cameras still followed me as I walked away. I marched right up to where my darling Thomas sat in the audience. I grinned at him and offered my arm. He smiled up at me. I swear, that smile of his still made my heart race. Even now. We linked arms, and then I offered my other arm to Sam.

We marched off, but we didn't go far. No way in hell was I leaving Tuna alone. Not at a time like this.

Thomas and Sam and I stood in the back of the room, still arm-in-arm, and watched Tuna deal with the press. I locked eyes with Tuna and nodded at him approvingly. I needed him to know he was not alone. If nothing else, he had me and my friends on his side.

Tuna explained that he had been afraid to be honest about his sexuality, especially after he saw what happened to me when I was suspected of being the gay one. He also explained that Emily Manero was not really his wife, but a close friend. I saw his "scary wife" give him a warm and loving smile from the audience, and I suddenly realized that her bitchiness had all been an act to protect him and to give him an excuse not to have to hang out with the guys.

Sid suddenly got up and walked out in the middle of Tuna's speech. I was sad to see that. I really thought he might be more supportive of Tuna.

Then I realized that he wasn't walking out. He walked right up to Sam, who was still linked on my left arm. Sid smiled at Sam, and then offered his arm. Astonished, it took Sam a second or two to realize what was happening. Sid linked arms with Sam, and then turned to face Tuna. I saw tears form in Sam's eyes. He was so used to people rejecting him and gays in general that Sid couldn't possibly know what his simple but very public gesture of support meant to Sam. To all of us.

Wow.

Then Brady got up. He walked right up to Thomas, who was linked on my right arm. First, Brady offered his hand and Thomas flashed him one of his warmest smiles as he shook it. After they'd been semi-introduced, Brady linked his arm with Thomas'. Thomas turned to me, his eyes wide as if to say *Oh my God, Brady Clayton is touching me!* I chuckled softly. I was happy to see Brady's support. I hoped that meant he would be good to Alice, too.

Speaking of Alice, I sought her out in the crowd. She was watching us standing in the back. As three other players got up to stand with us, I looked into her eyes and saw her tears. I was so glad that she was here to share this amazing experience with me. She just shook her head and looked at me as if to say *Can you believe this is happening?*

Of course, not everybody was supportive. Boomer Wilkens stood off to the side, stone-faced, like he could not believe what was happening to his ballclub. Oh, well. He couldn't very well fire all of us.

Kyle looked positively homicidal. So did Carlos and Jackson.

For the first time, I realized my dad was here. I couldn't believe he came. I nudged Thomas and whispered that my dad had showed up. Thomas looked at me with amazement.

Hank looked back to where I was standing. He didn't smile, but he actually nodded, if a bit grimly. I don't know that he actually approved of what I was doing, but he was there for me anyway.

Wow.

My life was full of surprises lately.

26

About half the team thought it was cool that I had stood up for gay athletes and the other half didn't. Some guys were seriously pissed about our team's image, of course, but they would just have to deal with it. There was definitely a lot of fallout; harsh words and even threats from fans and teammates alike, but Tuna and I weathered the storm together. I was glad that Tuna didn't have to deal with all of this alone. Lots of people still thought I was gay, so I was treated pretty much the same way Tuna was. Boomer never talked to either Tuna or me unless he absolutely had to, which was a major bonus as far as we were concerned. As a team, we started playing better, but it was too late to really salvage the season. I have a good feeling about next year, though.

The guys on my team who did support me still thought I was out of my mind for releasing the picture of myself in a dress. Fair enough. They had a *lot* of questions for me, but they eventually understood that my best friend Thomas was the real drag queen, not me. I told them about how I had gotten up in front of people and sang for real. My friends on the team actually thought that was kind of cool.

As I'd predicted, the photo of me in drag would never die. That was okay. It also meant I had a great picture of me and Thomas together that would be in circulation forever. After hiding him for so long, I was proud to have a picture of us go public.

Speaking of photos, the *Baltimore Sun* snapped an absolutely incredible picture of Thomas and me. It was from when I walked down the aisle to get to him when I was done speaking at the press conference. I was smiling down at him as I offered my arm, and he was looking up at me with those incredible eyes and warm smile. That was my favorite picture of us, and it was splashed all over the news. The way I was looking at him, it was just so obvious that I loved him. It was written all over my face. I was sure lots of people saw that picture and thought it was romantic love. So let them. It was hardly an unfair assessment, but the truth was we were just very close friends because that's all we could be. Alice saw the picture online and emailed us both a copy. In the subject line, she wrote *My Two Favorite Guys...* and in the body of the email, she wrote *Love you both!*

Sometimes fans would bring some of the photos from the *Baltimore Sun* for me to autograph. It always made me smile when somebody handed me my drag photo and asked me to sign it. Of course, lots of people recognized Thomas from the pictures, too, especially when he was at the ballpark. People even asked him for his autograph. He thought that was crazy. He told me he hadn't done anything autograph-worthy. But he never turned anybody down and he always signed the same way: *Thomas Palmer, HVJ's BFF.*

The fan mail I got was just nuts. Sure, I shelled out lots of money to the Harvey Milk Foundation and other support groups every time some idiot wrote something ignorant, but I got lots of other mail, too. Thanking me for what I'd done. The letters from teenagers were the most touching. I got dozens of letters from kids saying that they had considered suicide, but they were starting to understand that maybe things would be okay after all. I was actually asked to do an *It Gets Better* anti-bullying ad with Thomas and Tuna, which was amazing. Thomas was like a kid on Christmas doing that. It meant so much to him.

Alice did start dating Brady. I told Brady a partial truth. I didn't want him to feel weird about dating my ex, so I told him that I had been so worried about the gay rumor that I had used her as my fake girlfriend.

Thomas and I still hung out at the Hippo all the time, where I often performed karaoke. I loved being able to sing without the fucking high heels. We had explained to Ben, Adam, and the others exactly what had happened with me so they would understand when I gave the press conference about being straight. They believed it more readily than I would have thought, but then they had known Sam and Thomas, both medical professionals, for years and had no reason to doubt them. Besides, it was obvious to everybody that Thomas and I still loved each other and hadn't broken up because we wanted to.

Regulars at the Hippo knew who I was, even if they weren't baseball fans. People bought me drinks all the time. The bar even named a drink after me. The drink was a shot of Peach Schnapps, of course.

They called it a Straight-Up Henry.

THOMAS STARTED DATING someone else almost immediately after we broke up.

It was much, much sooner than either of us was ready for, but you can't help when you meet someone. I knew it would hurt like hell to see him with another guy, but his happiness was all that mattered to me.

Ironically, Josh asked Thomas out because of me. He was a pediatric nurse at Johns Hopkins and he'd had a crush on Thomas for a long time. Josh often brought his young patients to Thomas' x-ray department at Hopkins, but he didn't know for sure that Thomas was gay. He found out when our photo was splashed all over the news and I'd announced at the press conference that he was my gay best friend.

Josh used the photo as an excuse to strike up a conversation with Thomas, saying, "It's so cool that you know Henry Vaughn, Jr! I have to admit, I was kinda disappointed to hear he wasn't gay."

"Yeah," Thomas had said ruefully. "Me, too..."

Josh asked Thomas if he wanted to meet for coffee and he didn't have the heart to tell him no. The guy was really cute and sweet and Thomas wouldn't have hesitated to say yes if he hadn't just broken up with me. The two of them hit it off, but Thomas told Josh that he'd had a very painful breakup literally days before and he wasn't ready to jump into a new relationship too fast. Josh told him that he would give him all the time he needed because he knew that Thomas was worth waiting for. True to his word, Josh provided friendship and support and didn't pressure Thomas for so much as a goodnight kiss until he was really ready. I found I was actually grateful that they had met, because Josh served as a great comfort to him as his broken heart healed.

Though it was hard to see Thomas and Josh together, I found I really liked the guy. Josh was fun to be around and treated Thomas like the prince he was, so we got along great. It was obvious to him that Thomas and I had a very close relationship – he had no idea how close – but he didn't seem jealous and never minded me hanging around Thomas.

I was terrified that all that would change when Thomas sat me down one day and told me that he wanted to tell Josh about our relationship. He said he wouldn't tell Josh if I really didn't want him to, but he didn't like keeping secrets from him. Their relationship was getting to the intimate stage and he felt Josh should know about our sexual past, especially since we still spent so much time together.

"But what if Josh says you can't see me anymore?" I asked him.

Thomas gave me that killer smile that still melted my heart. He touched my cheek and said, "Then I'm really going to miss him." He was sweet to say that, but I knew how much Thomas cared about Josh. I wouldn't let them break up over me. It would rip my heart out if I couldn't see Thomas anymore, but I would step aside if that was what Josh wanted. My chest ached whenever I thought about it, but I would not put my happiness over Thomas'. I'd done that once before and it had been the worst mistake of my life.

As it turned out, I had nothing to worry about. Thomas and Sam sat Josh down and explained everything to him. Once Josh fully understood what had happened, he actually felt awful for me. He was such a kind, soft-hearted soul; he was so much like Thomas. He gave me a big hug the next time I saw him and told me how sorry he was to hear about what I went through. He swallowed hard and looked at Thomas.

"It couldn't have been easy, letting him go."

"It was the hardest thing I've ever had to do," I told him. Josh told me what a mess Thomas had been those first weeks after we broke up and that he obviously loved me very much. Rather than being threatened, I think Josh had a deeper respect for my bond with Thomas and I was glad he knew about our past. Josh understood that I was totally straight now and he had nothing to worry about.

While Josh had helped Thomas, Alice had nursed my broken heart as I slowly got over Thomas. She came to watch me sing at the Hippo and she and Brady hung out with Josh, Thomas, Sam, Jeremy, and me on a regular basis. We had so much fun together. I started to really like standup comedy, thanks to the CDs she lent me, and we went to lots of comedy shows together. I saw her perform as often as I could, and she just got better and better. She was incredibly talented. I swear, I never laughed so hard and so often with anyone else in my entire life. We were ridiculous when we got together, Alice and me. Brady would just shake his head when Alice and I were doubled over, laughing, tears in our eyes. We egged each other on so much that we were unstoppable once we got going.

After hanging out with her so much, a very familiar feeling started to wash over me. I recognized the feeling because of what I'd had with Thomas.

I realized I was falling in love with her.

Alice was already my best friend, next to Thomas. I could talk to her about anything. We still sang show tunes in the car and quoted standup comedy lines to each other. I knew I would rather be with her than anybody else. I found myself constantly thinking about her lovely face and her gentle touch. She worried about me, just like Thomas still did, and was always there for me. I loved it when she came to baseball games and cheered me on, wearing a jersey that had VAUGHN 14 on the back. I found myself fantasizing about her more and more. Wearing my baseball jersey...not wearing my baseball jersey...

But she was dating Brady.

It had been so painful to see Thomas with Josh, and now I had to stand back and watch Alice be with Brady. I could hardly stand the thought of Brady making love to her. Still, even I had to laugh when I remembered that there was a time that I had fantasized that Brady was making love to *me*.

I guess it was only fair, though. There had been a time that Alice had a crush on me, and I had totally disregarded her feelings. First, when I had taken all the hot girls home from the bar and then when I had used her as a front so I could be with Thomas. It felt like penance to have to watch the two people I loved most in the world be with other lovers instead of me. Now I knew exactly how it felt.

I finally talked to Thomas about it after feeling this way for months. Josh was sprawled out on the couch reading a magazine, and I was helping Thomas do the dishes since Josh had cooked us a wonderful meal. I wasn't sure how to broach the subject.

"Soooo," I began as I sat down at the kitchen table.

"Soooo," Thomas repeated. He sat down and focused his pretty eyes on me, since I clearly had something on my mind.

I leaned on my elbow and looked at him. "Sooo, I'm in love with Alice."

Thomas face broke out into a wide grin and he cleared his throat loudly, looking over at Josh.

"I heard him," Josh said. He lowered his magazine and smiled wryly at Thomas. "I owe you five bucks."

"It is that obvious?" I asked Thomas.

He put his hand on mine and said, "To me? Yes." He still knew me better than anybody else. I should have known better than to think that I could hide anything from him. "I've been waiting for you to tell me so we could talk about it."

For weeks after that, Thomas patiently listened to my incessant whining about how I'd blown my chance with Alice – not by dating him, but before that when I had completely ignored her in the bar. Brady had recognized right away what took me far too long to realize; that Alice was a funny, confident, beautiful, and sexy woman. She was never more sexy than when she was onstage, performing. I think that's when I knew I was really in love; when I watched her perform and wasn't jealous at all anymore. I would have gladly stayed on the sidelines for the rest of my life, letting her shine. Her dreams were far more important to me than my own ever were.

Then one day the news broke that Brady Clayton had been traded to the Seattle Mariners. Alice cared deeply for Brady, but she told me she didn't love him. They decided not to pursue a long-distance relationship. The day she broke up with Brady was one of the happiest of my life. Thank God I had Thomas to keep me in line.

"You can't be mean about it, Henry. You're happy about the breakup. She may not be. You've got to help her through this before you pounce on her." And of course, he was right. I supported her through her breakup the same way she had taken care of me when I had to break up with Thomas. It didn't take too long for her to start feeling more like herself and, one day, I just blurted out how I felt about her.

We were sitting in my car, talking, and I just told her that I loved her.

"I love you, too, Henry," she said, simply. Casually. She

thought I meant as a friend. Just like I still did with Thomas, I would occasionally say to her, "Love ya, hon." And I did. But in the past, I had meant as a friend.

"No, Alice. I'm *in* love with you."

At first, she just stared at me, taking in my words.

"Since when?" she demanded. She seemed almost mad.

"For a long time," I confessed. "I wanted to tell you, but I didn't want to mess up your relationship with Brady." I looked into her eyes and said, "We were made for each other, you know that?" A line like that should have sounded corny and stupid, but it didn't because it came straight from my heart.

Alice looked down at my mouth and gently traced my lips with her finger. A delicious thrill went through me. Only one other person in the world had ever made me feel that way with just a simple touch. She looked into my eyes and said quietly, "Yes. I know that. But I was starting to think you'd never figure it out."

In her eyes, I saw love, but also a sense of weariness. A sudden realization struck me like a bolt of lightning to my chest. Thomas had been right to worry about Alice's feelings.

She'd been in love with me the entire time I was with Thomas.

Alice loved me and she still did everything in her power to keep Thomas and me together because he was what I had wanted. She knew he made me happy. Seeing her with Brady these last few months had hurt me so much. My stomach felt sick and my heart ached when I knew she was out on a date with him. And yet, Alice had been on dates *with* me and Thomas. How many hours had I spent on the phone with her, talking about how much I loved him? I remembered telling her when Thomas and I had finally had sex and, though I'd had sex countless times before, it was the first time I had actually made love with someone. *How could I not have realized what I was doing to her?* I could only hope the fact that Thomas was a man and not another woman, coupled with how much she loved him, had helped minimize the pain I had caused her.

"I'm an idiot, Alice," I told her, wishing I had the words to express how sorry I was for hurting her. For not realizing sooner how perfect we were for each other. For how grateful I was for her help with Thomas. Thomas had been my first love and I wouldn't trade a moment I'd had with him for anything in the world.

"Yes, you are," Alice said, laughing softly. "But I love you anyway."

I knew I would have to say it a million, trillion times to make up for all the times she'd had to hear me say it to somebody else. I couldn't wait to get started.

"I love you, Alice. I love you, I love you, I love you."

Her eyes filled with tears. She'd probably thought she would never get to hear me say that to her. She better get used to it. I was gonna say it a lot.

I leaned over and eagerly pressed my mouth to hers and we shared our first kiss. It was wonderful. It was exciting and passionate, yet familiar and comforting. She was finally home in my arms where she belonged. It felt so good to be in love again. For so long, I was afraid I would never be as happy with anyone as I'd been with Thomas.

After finally confessing our feelings for each other, we rushed back to my house...and to my bedroom. We'd been lusting after each other for forever and we were already in love, so there was no reason to wait any longer to be together. Being with Alice was absolutely incredible, and not just because I hadn't been with anyone else (male or female...) since Thomas. Though I had wanted so much to rock her world, I didn't last long with her that first time. It had been so long since I'd had sex and she was so beautiful...She didn't make me feel bad about it, though. She wrapped her arms around my neck, told me she loved me, and said we had plenty of time to enjoy each other. I think I made up for it the second time, though, judging by her cries of pleasure and the scratches she left on my back.

Afterwards, I held her in my arms and told her that had been the first time I'd ever actually made love to a woman. She nodded, teared up a bit, and held me closer.

I also told her that I hadn't pegged her as the type of girl who would sleep with a guy on the first date, let alone *before* the first date. She giggled and smacked my face with the pillow.

With all those other girls, I was always afraid they'd still be there in the morning. With Alice, it was more like I was afraid she was going to leave.

She didn't.

I DECIDED to stay with baseball as long as the majors would let me, but I was still serious about my performing career. I worked on it as much as I could during the off season. It was easy for me to get commercial gigs because I was already famous, but I worked hard at getting theater and other roles, too.

I even got to sing the National Anthem at an Orioles game. Tuna talked to the front office about it and set it up as a surprise for me. I was nervous as hell, but it was amazing. The crowd went nuts. All the people I cared about were at that game to support me: Thomas and Josh, Sam and

Jeremy, Alice and my dad. It...was...*awesome*. Even some of the opposing team players came over to shake my hand and tell me I did a great job. It was an incredible feeling to get cheers and applause for doing what I really loved.

I was grateful to have enough money to let Alice fly to Los Angeles or wherever she needed to be to pursue her dream of being a standup comic. I was so proud of her, and I hoped she would become a huge success. I knew she felt the same way about me, and she supported my dreams unconditionally. I was her biggest fan and she was mine.

She was mine.

I found myself reconsidering my vow to never, ever, ever get married. But then, I'd already done an awful lot of things I never, ever thought I would do.

Thomas and Josh are still going strong. I hope they get married someday and I hope they adopt five kids and they all call me Uncle Henry.

Sam still calls me girl names. And I still answer.

Alice still calls me Peaches.

WAIT! BEFORE YOU GO!

If you'd like to have a FREE steamy sports romance, you can get STARTING FROM ZERO, the novella prequel to my Boys of Baltimore Series, simply by following me on ANY of my social networks (listed below) and/or joining my email list!

To get your FREE book, FOLLOW me on ANY of the social networks below and then shoot me an email at lindafausnet@gmail.com and ask for your free book:

Join my Author Reader's Group on Facebook.

Follow my Author Linda Fausnet Facebook Page

Follow me on Bookbub

Following me on Instagram

OR join my email list and you will automatically receive the book in your inbox.

This novella is EXCLUSIVELY available to my readers and is NOT available for purchase anywhere!

Why Leave a Book Review? I'll give you 3 good reasons.

You can do it in <u>less than a minute</u>! Just choose a star rating from 1 to 5 stars and add a sentence or two on how you felt about the book.

1.   Most readers choose the books they read based on the reviews, but <u>only a few readers </u>are kind enough to leave a review.

2.   Most readers are not aware of this, but authors live and die by reviews. We really do.

3.   It only takes a minute to leave a review, but the impact lasts for the lifetime of the book.

Thank you so very much.

ATTENTION ROMANCE NOVEL FANS!

I hope you'll join my romance novel fan club, Romance Novel Addicts Anonymous, on Facebook and Instagram. Join the email list, and you'll receive WHAT'S YOUR PLEASURE? RNAA'S OFFICIAL GUIDE TO FINDING YOUR NEXT GREAT ROMANCE READ.

ACKNOWLEDGMENTS

Heartfelt thanks to everyone who purchased this book. All of the proceeds net of taxes from book sales will go to the Harvey Milk Foundation (milkfoundation.org), an organization founded to carry on the legacy of Harvey Milk, one of the world's first openly gay elected officials. Harvey's famous words that "Hope will never be silent" have certainly proved prophetic, as the voices of equality allies have steadily grown louder to drown out the hate. Love is winning.

Many thanks to all who contributed to my lifelong dream of publishing a book. Thanks to BZ Hercules, editor, and to Evan Lerman for his beautiful cover design. Thanks to Lisa Winders, who not only served as an editor but more importantly, has been my best friend since the third grade. I thank my sister, Zann Wasiljov, who has served as webmistress, tech support, editor, baseball travel companion, and good friend. Heartfelt thanks to my parents, Bernard and Cecelia Wasiljov, who have supported my dreams unconditionally. My mother is always the quickest one to read my books, though she confesses to skipping over some of the steamier parts...

I thank my beautiful children, Celia and Noah, for understanding that Mommy needs time to write or she will go insane. You're still too young to read QUEEN HENRY, but I look forward to the day when I can share it with you. Even at the ages of 10 and 11, you are already equality allies and I couldn't be more proud.

I thank my husband, best friend, and favorite person in the world, Bill Fausnet. Though we are star-crossed lovers – girl who loves to write marries boy who hates to read – we've built a wonderful life together. Everyone, gay or straight, should have the right to live happily ever after as we have.

To all the writers and other dreamers out there - may your hope never be silent.

www.ingramcontent.com/pod-product-compliance
Lightning Source LLC
Chambersburg PA
CBHW020243200626
46816CB00001BA/110